Divine
  Mistress

Divine
Mistress

FRANK G. SLAUGHTER

Doubleday & Company, Inc.

GARDEN CITY, NEW YORK

The characters and the incidents in this book are entirely the product of the author's imagination and have no relation to any person or event in real life.

I went in search of my art, often in danger of my life. I have not been ashamed to learn those things which to me have seemed useful—even from vagabonds, barbers, and executioners. For we know how a lover will go a long way to meet the woman that he loves. How much the more, then, will the lover of wisdom be tempted to go in search of his divine mistress!

—PARACELSUS

Author's Preface

Few periods in world history give more striking proof that truth is often stranger than fiction than the sixteenth century, during which this tale takes place. It is true that Andreas Vesalius, the first great anatomist of history, did live and write his greatest of all anatomical texts in the middle of this century, and many today believe that the history of medicine in its modern period began with him. One version of the later life of Vesalius does correspond with the one used in this story. It is likewise true that Michael Servetus, the great martyr of medicine, did discover the pulmonary circulation well in advance of Harvey, but was so preoccupied even then with the religious beliefs that were to cause his execution at the hands of John Calvin that the only record of one of the great deductive feats of medical knowledge is found as an interpolation in one of his religious works. As to Botticelli's immortal canvas, The Birth of Venus, it is a matter of record that it was lost during part of this century. Furthermore, the story of its model used here is the true one. And if there are those who may scoff and say that hypnosis—labeled magnetism by the incomparable Paracelsus—began with Mesmer, let them be silenced with the information that this strange phenomenon has been practiced by an Egyptian sect for forty centuries, even to its induction with a crystal ball. The truth of the practices of the Inquisition, too, has been set down in many places, especially in regard to the Arch-Inquisitor, Frey Tomás de Torquemada.

But this is a romantic tale and who need know where truth is ended and fancy begun?

FRANK G. SLAUGHTER

Jacksonville, Florida

Contents

Book One

THE SERENISSIMA

Antonio Servetus was not performing the dissection himself today. A slight inflammation of the right index finger, accidentally nicked a few days before with the dissecting scalpel, forced him to keep his hands from contact with the deliquescent flesh of the executed criminal whose body was today's subject for study. Warming weather always caused the cadavers to disintegrate rather rapidly, and besides the increased odor in the anatomy theater, there was the danger of minor wounds to the anatomist and his assistants.

Below the young physician, as he sat on the slightly elevated cathedra with the text before him, the students were gathered around old Guinterius, the prosector. The scalpel in Guinterius's gnarled fingers moved slowly, and the students, accustomed to Antonio's skilled movements, stirred restlessly. Bright spring sunlight poured through the skylight and was reflected from the shining steel of the scalpel in the awkward hands of the old barber surgeon.

A warm breeze came through the open window behind Antonio's chair and caressed his neck, hot and sweating under the collar of his teacher's robe. It riffled the pages of the book before him, turning them and exposing the concise Latin text flanked by the superb drawings of Calcar imprinted upon the parchment by painfully carved woodcuts. In the six years since he had come to Padua in the fall of 1557 to study canon law and medicine, Antonio had learned the text by heart. Now, as he recited the sonorous phrases without bothering to find the place again in the book, his hands moved idly with a crayon between his fingers, reproducing in broad strokes on a white parchment the dissection being carried out on the table below by Guinterius. Muscles were shaded lightly in the sketch, tendons heavier, while the nerves and blood vessels stood out in bold relief.

Antonio frowned at the sketch and for a moment his voice stopped the automatic recital of the text. The silence was loud in the tiny, overcrowded theater. Actually it could hardly be called a theater in its own right, for there was little more than room for the professorial chair upon the cathedra, the dissecting table below it with buckets at each corner to receive waste and scraps, and the vat of sour wine standing in the corner to receive any unusual findings worth preserving for future study.

Startled by the silence, the students lifted their heads to stare at Antonio, their faces white above somber scholars' robes.

There in the anatomy theater that spring morning was written, in the two men concerned with the dissection, the story of medicine in this enlightened latter half of the sixteenth century.

Antonio was twenty-five, tall and strongly built, wearing the long robe affected by teachers, physicians, and apothecaries. His head was well shaped, his hair dark and wavy, and his skin showed both the swarthy tint of his Spanish father and the softer olive hue of his Italian mother. In his cheeks bloomed the high color so often found in natives of the mountainous districts of eastern Spain. But it was his dark eyes that held one's gaze, for in them burned the warmth and zeal of the true scholar, the born man of science whose vision is always in the future. Mobile lips, smiling easily, gave his face the humanity and warm understanding of the true physician. The fingers holding the crayon, too, were well shaped and strong, the sensitive hands of both an artist and a surgeon.

Guinterius belonged to the old guild of the barber surgeons, ignorant for the most part, blindly following the precepts of Galen and the other patriarchs of medicine, still unable to see in the new burgeoning of science, art, and letters the emergence of medicine as a new and important phase of human knowledge. Antonio Servetus, however, stood for the break with the old traditions which had begun with Paracelsus, Cardan, and many others, to find its most ardent voice in Andreas Vesalius, whose text lay upon the lectern before him. Vesalius had dared to dissect the human body, and his findings threatened to blast away the old shaky foundations upon which the medicine of the apothecaries and the barber surgeons was based, allowing it to emerge as a new science and art.

Antonio glanced down at the text before him. The breeze had riffled the parchment sheets entirely through, and he saw only the title page, but his memory did not betray him, however bemused. Without missing a phrase, he took up the recital and, like the enchanted castle in the fairy tale, the normal activities of the theater were instantly resumed: old Guinterius's hand moved again with the scalpel and the students bent over the dissection once more.

The initial pages of the bulky text were sharply black and white where the type had stamped the letters upon parchment sheets:

"*Andreae Vesalii Bruxellensis, Scholae Medicorum Patauinae Professoris, de Humani corporis fabrica, Libri septem.*"

"*De Humani Corporis Fabrica.*" The words flowed smoothly through Antonio's brain. "The structure of the human body," and the first authentic text on human anatomy in the history of mankind. Galen, the authority for more than a thousand years, had dissected pigs, sometimes a monkey from Cathay, and only rarely a human body. It was not surprising, then, that the questing scalpel of Vesalius had shown Galen's findings to be shot through with inaccuracies. But the doctrines of Galen were firmly entrenched in the minds of physicians and the clergy, and the controversy still raged, fully seventeen years after Vesalius published the *Fabrica* and ushered in a new era in the study of anatomy, here at Padua, as well as in most of the world. Schools dominated by Rome still adhered to the outmoded doctrines of Galen, and between them and such centers of scholastic freedom as Padua there was a constant war of words. Sometimes there was more violent action, as when Paduan students fought in the narrow streets with those from the nearby Jesuit University.

Antonio knew well the story of the storm which had burst about the head of Vesalius when the *Fabrica* had been published. The pioneer anatomist had once occupied the very chair in which he now sat, or rather the place occupied by old Guinterius at the table below him, for Vesalius, too, had preferred to carry out the dissections with his own hands. So vitriolic had been the battle of words against the entrenched dogma of the Church that the anatomist, maddened by unjust criticism, had finally burned most of his works in a futile gesture of anger and fled from Padua to become personal physician of Emperor Charles V and lately his son, Philip II of Spain.

"Dr. Servetus." Guinterius looked up from the arm which he was dissecting. "There seems to be an anomalous condition here."

Antonio stepped down to the floor level as the students opened a place for him at the table. The dank odor of rotting flesh, somewhat diffused at the higher level of the cathedra, was a palpable, noxious miasma at the floor level. Antonio did not even notice it, however, for the smell of decaying flesh was as familiar to the anatomist as his scalpels.

"This vein here," Guinterius pointed out, "it should enter the *vena brachialis,* no?"

Antonio made a tentative movement to push aside the dark, semi-liquid muscle tissues with his hand, then drew back as he remembered his inflamed finger. "Professor Fallopius has described such an anomaly," he admitted. "It sometimes enters the *vena capitalis* instead of the *vena brachialis.*" As always, he felt as if he were committing a sacrilege in finding anything in the body not described by Vesalius.

"I thought I remembered it," Guinterius said with satisfaction and took up the scalpel again.

Antonio returned to the dais and, picking up the crayon again, began to sketch the vein in its abnormal position. When the drawing was finished he held it up before him, then shook his head, biting his lip in vexation. The anatomical structures were in their true positions, expertly drawn, but the sketch had none of the sense of dimension, the feeling of life and substance that he wished to impart to it.

Guinterius finished the dissection and Antonio dismissed the students for the noonday recess. His lessons were finished for the day and he could return now to the Dominican priory in the shadow of St. Mark's Cathedral where he lodged, paying his expenses by caring for the library. For five years he had known, among the musty tomes and manuscripts, the quiet, peaceful life of the scholar. In the safe refuge of the priory, surrounded by his books, a life of monkish retirement from the world which he had half decided to embrace had seemed infinitely attractive. He had planned to seek induction into the Holy Orders in the fall, but being a priest would have no effect upon his teaching career, for several of the professors were clerics as well. The search for knowledge here overshadowed everything else, a search approved and encouraged by the patron city of Padua, Venice, *the Serenissima,* Queen of the Adriatic.

Lately, though, the quiet of the library and the crinkle and musty smell of fine parchment had lost some of their charm. Why, he did not know. His training as a physician told him that it must be from an unusual accumulation of noxious humors in his body during the long winter. A good physic should help that, according to both Hippocrates and Aristotle, but he suspected that this time he was suffering from a disorder of the spirit rather than the body.

ii

Antonio came through the low main doorway of the university building, ducking a little from force of habit. His dark teacher's robe flapped about his legs as he walked, the flat velvet cap of the pedagogue sat on the dark waves of his hair, and the precious copy of the *Fabrica* was securely tucked under his arm. Carved into the marble of the keystone, the Lion of Venice towered over his head, proclaiming to all that this institution gave its allegiance only to the Serenissima, lone island of civil and academic freedom in a cleric-dominated Italy and one of the richest cities of the universe.

Illustrious figures by the score had passed through this doorway during the centuries in which the University of Padua had flourished. Vesalius, of course; Leonardo, the Florentine, perhaps, for he had spent some time in Venice, only twenty-five miles away; Michael Servetus, most promising of physicians, who had been burned at the stake by John Calvin; John Caius, the Englishman, who had lived in the same building with Vesalius, in the Casa de' Valli, hard by the Ponte della Poglia.

As Antonio stood for a moment, lost in the memory of those immortals who had preceded him, still another among medicine's great emerged from the building. It was Professor Gabriel Fallopio, affectionately dubbed with the Latin "Fallopius" by the students. As professor of anatomy, he was Antonio's superior, but since he was in poor health from advancing age, much of the teaching had been shifted to the broad and willing shoulders of his assistant.

"*Buon giorno,* Antonio," Fallopius said with a warm smile. "*Dove va?*"

"To the priory, Excellency," Antonio said. "I have a sore finger and Guinterius did the dissection for me this morning."

"A skilled barber, Guinterius," Fallopius agreed, his long beard wagging. Antonio fell into step with the older man, shortening his stride. Overhead the sun was close to the zenith and warm with the promise of summer. A pungent aroma floated to their nostrils as they negotiated the narrow street beside the university building. It was compounded from the stink of the alchemists' furnaces and the putrid stench of the anatomy theater. A mathematician would doubtless have been engrossed by the equation through which the stink became less noticeable as it diffused with the outside air, but Antonio's thoughts were elsewhere, as they often were lately.

Fallopius looked at his young friend keenly. "Is the finger troubling you much?"

"No, Excellency." Antonio recovered his thoughts. "I shall be back at the dissections in a few days."

"I seem to sense that you have not been your usual self lately."

Antonio smiled. "You are overzealous of my health, sir. It is nothing but a slight indisposition of some sort."

"Perhaps only a slight affection of the spleen," Fallopius suggested.

"That might be. They are not infrequent in the spring."

"Undoubtedly an affection of the spleen, then." The professor's beard wagged with satisfaction over the diagnosis. "By all means take peony seeds and honey."

"I shall," Antonio promised.

"And bleeding helps, whatever the disease."

"I drew a little last night."

"Ha! On the same side, I trust."

"Certamente," Antonio said. "You always advise it."

"It is well known," Fallopius stated positively, "that physicians killed the Prince of Piedmont some years ago by lancing the elbow vein on the opposite side to the inflammation."

"In this case I had no choice. I could use only my left hand for the lancet."

"Nevertheless you did right," Fallopius said. "Vesalius gave the same advice in the controversy over venesection." Antonio's predilection for the teachings of the master were no secret to him.

Antonio repressed a smile. He remembered well the very words of Vesalius on this subject: "Don't they seem to you to be having a fine wrangle and to be barking like dogs at each other?" The description of the acrimonious discussions among physicians was very apt.

Thinking of Vesalius, Antonio asked, "Is bloodletting on the same side still forbidden in Spain, Excellency?"

The Spanish physicians were said to be as adamant against bloodletting on the side where the disease occurred as Fallopius was in favor of it.

Fallopius shrugged. "For all I know, they are. They learn slowly. Pierre Brisson was actually expelled from the Faculty of Paris for upholding the principle."

"Anything that so many learned ones object to must be true, I suspect," Antonio suggested slyly.

Fallopius smiled. "Perhaps you have elucidated a new principle there. You should write a book."

"But I am no hand for writing."

"You'd rather draw, I see."

Antonio flushed. "An anatomist should have some capability as an artist, don't you think?" he protested.

"Absolutely. I only wish I had your talent. Nevertheless, it is time you published something. It will help your case when the time comes to appoint my successor."

"I pray that will not be soon, sir. The university needs you."

"No, my son." Fallopius shook his head. "Medicine is a profession for younger minds. There is so much to be learned that young and eager intelligences are needed. Get to work and write your book now, or at least a monograph. I could write the preface myself. *Lo farò*," he said decisively. "It will be on the importance of youth."

While the old professor talked on what was a familiar theme, Antonio was thinking of something else. It hung in his cell at the priory, something to delight the senses of an artist who was also a young man.

"Don't you think that is a good subject?" Fallopius asked, breaking into his thoughts.

"*Senza dubbio*," Antonio stammered. "I am sure that you are right."

"You didn't hear what I said," Fallopius said somewhat testily.

Red with embarrassment, Antonio admitted that his mind had been elsewhere.

"*Una giovane signorina?*" Fallopius hinted slyly.

"Oh no, sir," Antonio protested. "I plan to take the Holy——"

"But you haven't taken them yet," Fallopius said briskly as they turned a corner and left the university behind. "I would not seek to dissuade you, but it seems to me that a physician should know something of the temptations of the flesh, else he cannot rightly treat the ills arising therefrom."

"I have studied the temptations of the saints, sir."

"Hardly what I meant," Fallopius said dryly.

"Isn't that something of a new conception?"

"Yes. And one that is liable to get me into trouble with the Church, even in the enlightened Republic of Venice," Fallopius admitted with a wry smile. "Pay no attention to the babblings of an old man, Antonio, and go the way you have chosen, if you really wish it."

Their way led across one of the ancient wooden footbridges spanning the narrow course of the Bacchiglione, the small river that wound through the city. On the crest of the bridge Fallopius stopped to look down at the slowly coursing stream below. The water was dark and oily, its surface flecked with bits of waste and foam, for it was also a drainage ditch. A little below where they stood a small tributary, fed by a spring behind one of the houses higher up on the bank, burbled over rocks and sand on its way to join the Bacchiglione. The waters of the tiny, spring-fed current were clear and sun-dappled where they poured over the sand.

"Look there!" Fallopius exclaimed, pointing. "See where the small stream enters the larger one." A small half circle of clear water had pushed its way into the side of the dirty flood of the Bacchiglione, as if the fresh, young current were trying to shove the older, fetid one aside and usurp the channel for itself. But the attempt failed, for the zone of clearness marking the joining of the streams was hardly a yard wide before the spring water was gobbled up by the insatiable filth of the Bacchiglione. If anything was added by the gay little visitor, it was not visible ten feet below their juncture.

"There goes the course of human knowledge, my son," Fallopius said a little sadly. "The large stream is the sum of what we know, darkened and poisoned by ignorance, doubt, error, and sometimes by man's refusal to see the truth when it is staring him in the face."

"And the small stream is the sum of new discovery," Antonio cried, catching the analogy, "such as that of Messer Columbus."

"I didn't have the discovery of the New World in mind," Fallopius said dryly, "but rather such things as you and many other active minds will bring to the current of human knowledge."

"Often, Antonio," the old professor continued, "there are those who will not let the clear current from the springs of human genius run freely, but insist on checking them with dams which break their force. Then even if they finally reach the main stream of human knowledge, their effect is almost gone." He indicated the dingy Bacchiglione below the bridge. "Don't let that happen to you, my son. By all means don't let that happen to you." He turned to depart. *"Va bene."*

"Va bene, Excellency," Antonio repeated mechanically as he watched the old man step carefully down from the bridge. His mind was busy with what Fallopius had said.

Could Fallopius have been warning him against entering the Holy Orders? he wondered as he left the bridge and turned toward the priory. It had been the hope of his parents for many years that he would become a priest. They had sacrificed deeply that he might be able to study and graduate in canon law at Padua, but they had not objected when he turned then to medicine. For many of the most successful physicians of the day were clerics, such widely revered figures as Girolamo Cardano and Theophrastus Bombastus von Hohenheim, he who called himself "Paracelsus" because he admitted equality with no one lower than the great Celsus himself.

Here at Padua there were no clerical obstacles to study, even though the insistence by Vesalius that there were but twelve pairs of ribs in the male, and not thirteen, as Galen and the church maintained, had earned him the disapproval of Rome. In other parts of Italy and Europe, Antonio knew, there was little of the traditional freedom of thought that reigned in Venice, and clerical disapproval was a powerful weapon against those who disagreed with the edicts of Rome. There had even been a time in Padua when the Jesuits tried to combat the academic freedom of the university with their own school and their own brand of dogma, but thanks to the courage of the faculty and the support of the *riformatori,* who directed the affairs of the university for the all-powerful Council of Ten in Venice, the attempt had failed.

As a student, Antonio had participated in more than one fracas with the Jesuit students and he remembered well the zest of combat, the solid smash of his fist against yielding flesh, the anguish of a bloodied

nose, and the thrill of eluding the guards hunting a scapegoat. But such
conduct ill befitted his position now or his intention to don monkish
robes, so lately he had traveled only between the priory and his classes,
with occasional side trips to visit professionally the members of the
faculty who required medical attention.

Outside Padua and Venice the professional visits of physicians and
even their methods of prescribing and treatment must conform to a rigid
code set up by papal dogma or be labeled heresy. The rise of the ill-
famed Inquisition in Spain and its gaining strength here in Italy made
departure from accepted lines of conduct extremely dangerous. There
had been talk of arraigning Vesalius before his abrupt departure, and
Michael Servetus, graduate of Padua and one of the most promising
young physicians of the century, had been burned by Calvin and condemned by Rome as well, because he had looked with a critical eye at
the theological concept of the Godhead and had the effrontery, as well,
to claim that there was no opening through the heart walls, as Galen
had maintained, and that blood passed from the right to the left side of
the heart only through the lungs.

iii

Putting the riddles of Fallopius from his mind, Antonio crossed
the Bacchiglione once more and turned down a wider street. And
now his stride quickened, like a lover hastening to his beloved.
Rounding a corner, he reached the great open square dominated by a
huge equestrian statue. He was in the very heart of Padua now, with the
hum of its activities all around him. The crisp, clean smell of fresh vege-
tables rose from the stalls of the market close by. The air was filled with
the cries of hawkers and sellers of wine, whose donkeys, laden with
filled wineskins, resembled mythical beasts of the Apocalypse. Before
him, the glare of the sun from its white walls hurting the eyes, was the
Municipal Palace, site of government in this vassal city. Hard by were
the courts of law where the Podesta held solemn conclave every morning to settle differences and punish those who dared to commit crimes
against the majesty of the Serenissima.

Across the open square Antonio hurried, pausing momentarily to
cross himself before the shadow cast by the towering campanile of St.

Mark's Cathedral, and turned a corner to the priory where he lived. Here the shadows were deep and cool, but he did not stop to rest, although he was hot and sweaty from his rapid walk. Pushing open the massive oak door of the priory, he stepped into another world, a cool, dim-lit place of quiet and meditation, far removed from the bustle of the city. Haste seemed out of place in this house devoted to the quiet contemplation of the divine mercy and glory of God, and he curbed his eager steps and moved more slowly through the corridor. From habit, his feet found the shallow trenches in the stone floor, worn by countless thousands of sandaled feet over the years.

A young priest approached, smiling. *"Pax vobiscum,* Frater Antonio," he said.

"Et tecum, pax," Antonio replied, and pushed on when the other seemed on the point of stopping for further speech, turning through the open door of the library.

There was a musty smell of books in this large room with broad ceiling beams of dark wood. It was compounded of the perfume of old leather and soft, fragrant calfskin, mixed with the fresher ink smell from manuscripts being illuminated by monks in the evenings. Across the room was the door of Antonio's own small cell, and to it he went, glancing over his shoulder to see that no one was near to observe that he had locked his door. He fumbled hurriedly with the key and, when the door opened, stepped quickly through and shut it behind him.

As always, he caught his breath at the arresting loveliness of the central figure in the canvas in the crude easel occupying one entire wall of the cell. Illuminated in all her glorious loveliness by a shaft of sunlight from the single high window of the cell, she seemed on the very point of stepping ashore from the great sea shell which served as a boat. The shell was even tilted a little from her weight, and one foot was lifted, as if tentatively reaching for the dark sands of the shore upon which it had grounded. So real was the illusion of life and movement that the cheeks of the wind-gods who had blown her craft to shore were still puffed. Beside her mistress, the handmaid holding a red flowered robe seemed arrested only momentarily in the act of wrapping it about her body to hide the chaste beauty from profane eyes.

Had an earthly woman ever possessed such unearthly loveliness? Antonio wondered. Did living skin ever shine in such harmony with the pale colors of the morning? Or had a blinding golden cascade of hair been so obviously spun by fairy hands from some enchanted hoard?

His knowledge of the human body, as well as the instincts of the artist, insisted that here was the utmost perfection of line, plane, and curve. The slender column of her neck supporting the small, graceful head. The curve of shoulder and arm and the chaste perfection of the slender fingers of her right hand as it shielded her breast from prying eyes. The pattern of muscles outlined beneath the skin over the smooth roundness of the torso and the flat planes of her loins merging imperceptibly into the delicious curving fullness of the thigh. The graceful symmetry of knee and calf arrested in motion, and the curving arch of a dainty foot. Everything about her was an utter quintessence of beauty such as only a great artist, or the Creator himself, could ever attain.

With a hurried movement he jerked open the drawer of the small table beside his couch and fumbled inside it. Several sheets of paper spilled out on the floor, all covered with half-completed sketches of the thigh, calf, arm, or shoulder. Some were torn across, others stricken out with heavy crossing lines where he had defaced them in angry frustration and despair at his inability to capture the beauty which was so near, yet so completely unattainable.

Taking a crayon from the drawer, he stood with it in his fingers before a blank sheet. His eyes moved to the painting again, although he could have reproduced it from memory, so deeply were its outlines etched in his brain, and a sense of reluctance to begin assailed him, a consciousness of failure before he had even begun. Again and again, since he'd found the painting in a roll of canvases left at the priory by an anonymous person, he had sought to capture that elusive beauty in his sketches, and each time he had given up in baffled despair.

His eyes centered now upon the uncovered left breast. Dare he try to capture the smoothly perfect contour, the sweet fullness, the turgid nipple with its darker-shaded areola? He clenched the crayon in tight fingers, trembling with the intensity of the force inside him, a force which he realized instinctively was something more than the natural urge of the artist to portray beauty wherever he found it. While he sought to imprison that beauty in lines and shadows and curves, some other need within him, a strange, turbulent, demanding need, cried out to touch the painted flesh with his fingers, as if through his touch he might strike the spark of life which seemed always on the point of flaming into being within the painted body.

Forcing himself to curb the urgency of his haste now, Antonio began to sketch, creating the outlines of the breast upon the white paper with broad practiced strokes of the crayon. But when he tried to capture the contours in all their perfection of detail, the delicate shadows of the dark crayon on the white surface which would create the sense of dimension, his strokes slowed and his fingers felt wooden and dull. Grimly forcing himself to continue, he rubbed out, sketched in and rubbed out again, until finally, with a cry of despair and bewilderment, he tore the sketch across and, in a sudden fury of anger at his own ineptness, threw the crayon against the wall where it broke in a black smudge and sprayed the floor with dark powder.

iv

Antonio ate his supper in the great dining hall of the priory. On the dais, slightly elevated above the main floor, rested the table for the prior and his assistants, but Antonio shared a table with the lay brothers at the far end of the hall. Only when he took the Holy Orders would he move farther along the room. If he remained at the priory following his probable accession to the chair of anatomy at Padua, he would someday have a seat on the dais, as befitted the elevated station of a university professor.

The prior's chair was empty tonight, as it had been for more than a week now. Fra Mario Bellarmi, the head of the organization, was Antonio's patient, and by all portents not likely to occupy his chair again. Dropsy, plus a marked weakening of a heart overtaxed for many years by the demands of a gross body freely indulged, was conspiring to remove the prior from a corporeal existence in spite of the best efforts of his physician to avert that end.

Antonio stared with lackluster eyes at the thick bean soup in his bowl. Normally an active trencherman, his appetite had been strangely dulled lately. He dipped a spoon into the soup, tasted it, then shoved the bowl aside. Around him the lay brothers were actively spooning up the thick, nutritious soup, sopping the remainder from their bowls with crusts of dark bread. Wooden trenchers followed, piled high with roast lamb, to be torn apart and eaten with the fingers, for knives and forks were still rarely used except at the nobler tables. Heavy mugs were passed, filled with a thin, sour wine. On the dais the wine would be a fine

Madeira or at least an excellent port. The higher levels of the clergy saw no reason for stinting themselves in the pleasures of the table.

The meal over, the monks and lay brothers filed out for evening prayers, Antonio following with the rest. As he passed the dais, Fra Felipe Santos, the prior's assistant and administrative head of the priory, stepped down from his place at the table, wiping his thin lips with a rich linen napkin.

"*Buona sera,* padre," Antonio said dutifully.

"*Benedicamus,* Frater Antonio," the priest said. "How is your finger?"

"Almost well, God be praised."

"You will be able to attend His Reverence this evening, then?"

"Yes, sir. I had planned to do it immediately after prayers."

"You are excused from prayers," Fra Felipe said. "Fra Mario has a great deal of trouble with his breathing." The tone was properly concerned, but Antonio saw no commiseration in the frosty blue eyes of the subprior for his superior. It was common knowledge that Fra Felipe was waiting only for Fra Mario to draw his last breath before taking over control of the priory himself.

"The plethora must be increasing again," Antonio suggested. In spite of frequent bloodletting, the prior had suffered for months now with a considerable congestion which had so interfered with his breathing as lately to confine him entirely to his bed.

"I am sure that it has," Fra Felipe agreed.

"I will get my lancets," Antonio promised, "and meet you in His Reverence's apartment."

Fra Mario Bellarmi limited himself to no such mean quarters as housed the lesser members of his establishment. Antonio followed the dour-faced servant across a rich carpeted floor, through the lavishly furnished audience room where the prior conducted the affairs of the house, to the no less spacious bedroom beyond. Fra Felipe Santos, straight and spare in the spotless robe of the Dominicans, stood at the foot of the bed.

The prior's enormous bed was itself as large as Antonio's cell, its rich hangings embroidered with scenes of religious pageantry in gold and azure. The bed was piled with bolsters and pillows and the lower frame was entirely hidden by further embroidered drapings. On a taboret carved from priceless Eastern woods stood an array of bottles

and jars, mute evidence that the Reverend Father, like most of his contemporaries, did not trust himself unreservedly into the hands of his
physician, but dosed himself freely with whatever remedies chanced to
catch his fancy or were recommended by others.

Fra Mario Bellarmi was a huge man, whose pendent jowls and
massive forehead gave him somewhat the appearance of a well-fed and
benign mastiff. His pouchy cheeks were crisscrossed by a network of
scarlet blood vessels set against the unhealthy bluish tint of his cheeks.
His lips were puffy and slate gray in color. The veins of his forehead
were markedly distended, as were those of his hands and hairy forearms visible below the fine linen and lace cuffs of his nightgown. Even
in the large room his breathing sounded loud, harsh, and very labored.
The look of apprehension in his eyes was far removed from the benign
acceptance of God's will that he preached so forcefully from the pulpit.
From deep inside his chest came an ominous, wheezing rattle as he sat
almost bolt upright in bed, propped by pillows and cushions.

Antonio knelt by the bedside and the prior's puffy fingers touched
his dark head in a casual blessing. Rising then, he made a quick examination. Dropsy was patent in the swollen belly and the tense, pale skin
of legs twice their normal size. When Antonio pressed with his fingers
over the prior's ankle, the tip sank into the flesh to the first joint, leaving its imprint long after the pressure was removed. His Reverence's
breathing grew daily more labored, the swelling more pronounced.

"What is your opinion, Dr. Servetus?" Fra Mario wheezed.

Tactfully, Antonio said: "The plethora is marked, but I believe the
letting of some blood will make Your Reverence more comfortable."

"Bloodletting," Fra Mario said petulantly. "Can you think of nothing but bloodletting?"

Antonio well knew the Reverend Father's dislike for the lancet. "It
has helped on other occasions," he suggested tactfully.

"Get on with it, then," the prior wheezed. "But gently, my boy.
Gently."

"I have sharpened a lancet especially for Your Reverence." Antonio
opened his case. "There should be little pain."

The prior's eyes brightened. *"Benissimo!"* he rasped. *"Vediamo!"*

Antonio spread a large towel beneath his patient's arm. Then he
drew up the sleeve of the nightgown to expose the entire left arm and
placed a small agate bowl on the towel beside the elbow.

From his instrument case he selected a small, curving blade of the finest Damascus steel honed to a razorlike sharpness. The point was slightly hooked and quite narrow, hardly larger than a needle, and he was sure would be far less painful than the blunter straight blades used by most physicians. With the lancet in his right hand, he reached down to encircle the prior's arm with the fingers of his left, squeezing the already distended veins until they seemed on the point of bursting through the skin. The prior lay with every muscle tense, teeth clenched, his face screwed up in anticipation of pain.

With a single quick stroke, Antonio plunged the point through both skin and blood vessel. Blood, dark and unhealthy in color, spurted upward in a curving stream and fell into the agate bowl. The prior expelled a deep, gusty sigh and relaxed, watching the level in the bowl rise slowly as the small crimson stream spattered into it.

"What am I?" he grumbled. "A blood factory?"

"That is the way with plethora," Antonio explained. "There is so much blood that the circulation is overburdened. Removing a portion of it lessens the load upon the heart."

"*Ella ha ragione,*" the prior agreed. "I am feeling better already."

Ordinarily Antonio would have stopped with half a bowlful, but he judged the prior's condition to be somewhat desperate and allowed the flow to continue until the bowl was filled, a full pint and more. There was no doubting the improvement effected by the bleeding: already Fra Mario's breathing was easier, the distention of the veins in his face and arms was much less marked, while the rattle had almost disappeared in his lungs.

"Surely our Lord has worked a miracle through the hands of our young physician," Fra Felipe Santos said with pious unction. He had moved to the foot of the bed when the bleeding began, well out of range of any spattering drops which might have soiled his spotless robe.

"*Capisco!*" the prior said, crossing himself.

Antonio had his own ideas as to how the miracle had been effected, and how long it would last. He bowed his head for the prior's blessing once more, then gathered up his instruments preparatory to leaving the room. "I think the bloodletting will help you sleep, sir," he said. "But to insure that you get the rest you need, I would suggest a steaming posset at once."

Fra Mario's eyes brightened. He was very fond of wine in any form, but some had advised him against indulging in his present condition. This young physician had sense, he decided, and called the servant to prepare the drink.

Fra Felipe followed Antonio from the apartment. "A good job like that deserves a reward," he said jovially.

Antonio started to protest, for he was anxious to return to his cell and the painting.

"No modesty, now." The priest laughed. "I know your taste for Madeira and I have some questions to ask of you."

Resignedly, Antonio followed him into his quarters, somewhat less magnificent than those of the prior, but still comfortable enough in themselves. Fra Felipe was in a jovial mood as he poured two glasses of the excellent wine he kept for his own use and brought out a silver plate of sweet cakes. Antonio wondered sourly if the jollity did not come from the likelihood that the prior's illness would be fatal, resulting in the elevation of Santos to the head position in the priory. He had no particular love for the lean subprior.

"Too bad about His Reverence," Fra Felipe said, settling comfortably into a cushioned chair. "I wrote his relatives in Florence a month ago that he was ill. How long do you think he will last?"

"It would be impossible to tell. Not very long, I would say."

"Do you expect any permanent benefit from bloodletting?"

Antonio shook his head. "I have never seen a recovery from a plethora of this magnitude."

"Nor have I." Fra Felipe sipped his wine thoughtfully. "I notice that you bled from the left arm tonight. May I ask why?"

"The heart is on the left side," Antonio pointed out.

"Agreed. But most of his trouble seems to be with the lungs, in breathing."

"It is an obscure question," Antonio admitted. He had been struck by the fact that bleeding from the arm seemed to relieve the plethora in the lungs and had wondered at it. Now, as the warmth of the wine in his stomach stimulated his thoughts, he said reflectively, "Perhaps there is some connection between the circulation and the lungs."

"Have you found such in your dissections?"

"No," Antonio admitted. "But I have noticed that the heart is usually very large in cases such as these, particularly the left ventricle."

"An interesting observation," Fra Felipe said. "You suspect a connection, then?"

Antonio's brain was turning the question over and over again, and light suddenly broke through, as if a cloud over his thoughts had shifted. The answer was so simple, so astounding, and came as such a shock, that he cried involuntarily, "But Michael must have been right after all." In the thrill of discovery, he had forgotten that he was not alone.

"Michael?" Fra Felipe said sharply.

Antonio was on guard at once. The slip had been involuntary, torn from him by his sudden, blinding realization of the truth. "I was speaking of Michael Servetus," he explained carefully. "He was an earlier anatomist here in Padua. And," he added as an afterthought, "a distant kinsman of mine."

"Why did you say he must have been right?"

Antonio floundered momentarily under the directness of the question. He had made a bad slip, he realized, for Fra Felipe, once he got an idea, was like a ferret with a mouse. "I was referring to Servetus' theory of the way the vital spirit penetrates the body," he explained.

"Ah! The vital spirit." Fra Felipe's nose quivered like a beagle on the scent. Here was a subject that might be related to theology, his consuming passion. "Tell me more of this," he commanded.

Antonio sought for words and found none suitable to undo the damage caused by his thoughtless utterance. "Perhaps I can remember what Servetus wrote," he said in desperation. "I believe it was: *'The vital spirit is generated by the mixture in the lungs of the inspired air with the subtly elaborated blood, which the right ventricle sends to the left.'*"

The priest frowned and rubbed his pointed chin. "Let me see," he mused. "According to Galen, whose writings are approved by Mother Church, the ventricles of the heart are muscular chambers which contract upon the blood, maintaining a constant to-and-fro motion inside the blood vessels. Galen also states that blood brought to the heart by the great veins escapes through perforations in the partition or septum between the right and left sides of the heart and thus enters the arteries." He was evidently pleased with his own medical knowledge. "I have my facts correct, do I not?"

"That is Galen's doctrine," Antonio admitted. "But Servetus found no such perforations between the right and left sides of the heart."

"Does he seek to refute Galen, then?" Fra Felipe's voice was cold at such heresy.

Antonio cudgeled his memory. "This is what he says about the lung circulation. I think it explains the plethora we found in Fra Mario's case." Before Fra Felipe could object, he repeated the now familiar phrases: *"The communication between the ventricles, however, is not made through the mid-wall of the heart, but in a wonderful way the fluid blood is conducted by a long detour from the right ventricle through the lungs, where it is acted upon by the lungs and becomes red in color, and passes from the arteria venosa into the vena arteriosa, where it is finally drawn by the diastole into the left ventricle."*

"You seem to know this theory very well indeed," Fra Felipe said sharply, "although it disagrees with your master, Galen."

"I am an anatomist," Antonio said. "I study everything which may relate to the human body."

"Nevertheless, the Church can accept no theory which is contrary to Galen."

"But you saw that both the body veins and the lungs were congested by plethora," Antonio argued, "which could only mean that blood arriving in them is not pumped on properly."

"Perhaps," Fra Felipe said stubbornly. "There may be another explanation."

"And since this is true," Antonio continued, "there must not be any communication between the chambers of the heart, else the excess blood *would* escape into the *vena arteriosa*. As it is, the excess blood from the body is also pumped into the lungs, causing a plethora there also. It explains everything logically and completely."

"Galen states differently," Fra Felipe argued mulishly.

"A pox on Galen!" Antonio cried, in exasperation at such stupidity. "Vesalius proved him wrong in many things."

Angry red color surged into Fra Felipe's pallid cheeks. "You would do well to watch your words, Doctor," he snapped. "Mother Church supports Galen. That should be enough for you."

"But Servetus——"

"Servetus be damn——" The priest stopped with the oath uncompleted, and a sudden cunning shone in his cold blue eyes. "Do you mean Miguel, or Michael, Servetus?"

"Yes."

"I believe you said he was a relative of yours."

"Distantly related," Antonio stammered, for he was not accustomed to deviating from the truth. "A cousin or something."

"Could this be the same Michael Servetus who was burned for heresy?"

Antonio was pale now. "Yes. But by John Calvin."

"He was also condemned for heresy by Mother Church, as I remember."

"By the Inquisition," Antonio said bitterly.

Fra Felipe shrugged. "They are the same thing. You knew all this, didn't you?"

Antonio hesitated, but he was trapped already. "Yes," he admitted. "But what has heresy got to do with his discoveries in the field of medicine?"

"What, indeed?" Fra Felipe's eyes burned with a fanatic light and he shook a bony finger in Antonio's face. "It is forbidden even to repeat the words of a condemned heretic or read his writings." With an effort he calmed himself and took a drink of wine. "I am sure you sinned thoughtlessly, my son," he said after a moment. "So many do in their youth. But you must never speak, or even think of, the words of this heretic, Servetus, again."

Antonio started to object, but Fra Felipe raised a prohibiting hand. "Go now to the chapel. Pray to our Lord for forgiveness and ask him to blot out those evil words from your mind and your soul. And remember that the writings of heresy have no place in human knowledge."

"But, Father——" Antonio started to protest.

"Do not try my patience, Messer Antonio. I am being very lenient, for men have been put to death for lesser sins than yours. Go make your penance at once.

v

The chapel was dim-lit, quiet, and peaceful, but there was no peace in Antonio's soul as he knelt before the altar. Above his dark head the Holy Mother smiled down upon him compassionately, with the Child in her arms and the saints flanking her on either side. But he knew that there was no compassion in Fra Felipe's condemnation of him, and he wondered if there had been any compassion in those who had condemned Michael Servetus to the stake. For the first time in his life Antonio found himself doubting his own faith, and the doubt shook him to the very fibers of his being.

Purely from habit, the familiar phrases dropped mechanically from his lips while his thoughts were a maelstrom of churning currents. *"Ave, Maria, gratia plena; Dominus tecum; benedicta tu in mulieribus ..."*

How had he sinned? the logical, scientific part of his mind insisted upon asking. By adhering to the truth? Then Vesalius was a heretic, and Fallopius, as well as the whole galaxy of men whose daring and thought had opened up new vistas of human knowledge. If he accepted Fra Felipe's dictum that utterances contrary to Aristotle and Galen were heresy, how then could he ever learn the thousands of things that his eager mind wanted to understand?

"Sancta Maria, Mater Dei, ora pro nobis peccatoribus ..." Even as he continued his mechanical utterance of the words of the prayer, Antonio's mind was trying to encompass the discovery he had made tonight, the truth of the circulation through the lungs. The evidence in Fra Mario's body had been sufficient, yet how could evidence produced by a body dedicated to the service of God be heresy? Could the edicts of ecclesiastical authority actually change the truth of the organs and the blood vessels, the blood that circulated through them, as revealed by his dissections? As well deny, then, the phases of the moon, the positions of the stars, the immutable truth in the propositions of Euclid, even the very rain that fell from the heavens. Logic told him that truth was truth, no matter from whose lips it came, but dogma stated categorically that it was not. And the Church enforced its doctrine by burning at the stake, if necessary, any who proclaimed truths of which they did not approve. It was this for which they had burned Michael Servetus on that day in October, some ten years before . . . Michael Servetus, his older brother.

"... nunc et in hora mortis——" His voice stopped, but his thoughts went on. "The hour of death!" . . . Once again he was stumbling through the mountain passes with his father on the way to Switzerland that cool October day. Gaunt with weariness and an inner anguish transcending all physical pain, his father had leaned on Antonio's shoulders for support. He had been a stripling then, a sturdy tall lad of fifteen, already overserious and thoughtful, and still unable to understand this great

tragedy of which they had received only the barest warning in their home village in the northern mountains of Italy.

Until yesterday his father had been inordinately proud to be the parent of the famous scholar, Michael Servetus, the popular physician to the great of many cities. On a Saturday night, over his wine in the tavern, he had been known to boast of the scholarly exploits of his oldest son, the brother whom Antonio had seen only a few times and barely remembered. Kings had listened when Michael Servetus spoke, and university halls were crowded when he lectured on medicine, on anatomy, on mathematics, and, lately, on theology.

Only a few months ago the news had filtered into their mountain village that Michael had dared to question the tripersonality of the Godhead, the eternity of the Son, and the Anabaptism. Antonio had not really understood then what these things meant, but he had realized vaguely that such doctrines were a threat to the basic concepts of both Catholic and Protestant religion alike and as such were considered heresy which must not go unanswered.

Only a few days before had come the terrible news of the arrest and trial of Michael Servetus at Geneva, news that was already two months old. Michael himself had not written; it had reached them only by hearsay. But all in a day his father had turned from a strong, healthy man to a broken hulk, and that afternoon the two of them had set out northward on the arduous journey through the mountain passes into Switzerland.

But they had arrived too late to help Michael Servetus; in truth no one could have helped him, for he had stoutly maintained his beliefs, even when he must have known that his fate was settled. The ecclesiastical procession was already winding through the narrow streets of the village of Champel when Antonio and his father had come down from the high mountain paths, their feet stumbling with weariness.

In the crisp October sunshine the white robes and gold embroidery of the gaunt man heading the procession had almost blinded Antonio.

"Calvin," he heard the people mutter as they pushed their way through the crowd toward the procession. There was awe, and respect, and no little fear in their voices, for John Calvin was an avenging angel, striking down all who dared to doubt the truth of the doctrines he preached or the authority of the God whose earthly representative he considered himself to be.

Behind Calvin walked other high Protestant authorities, somber-gowned, for there was none of the bright color and the richness of display here which was so much a part of Catholic ceremonials. The Protestants, particularly the stiff-necked Swiss sect, believed in simplicity and austerity, both in costume and beliefs.

Antonio heard his father cry out beside him, a cry of pain, and thought at first that he had been hurt by the closely packed and jostling crowd. And then he saw the reason.

Behind the priests, behind the grave secular authorities who formed the second phalanx of the procession, a man walked alone. His body was thin to emaciation, and his hair had turned almost white in the two months of his trial, but he walked proudly, head high, his burning eyes fixed on some distant point, perhaps upon the hill where already the dry fagots whose flames would soon consume his body were being piled.

Antonio would not have known his brother, until he saw his eyes. There was no mistaking that burning gaze.

"Miguel! Miguel!" Antonio heard his father's strangling cry. It was the name Michael had borne in childhood, when they had lived in eastern Spain.

The gaunt man did not turn his head, but Antonio saw his burning eyes rest upon them momentarily. He gave no sign of recognition, but Antonio felt, as if by some transmission of thought, a sudden sense of kinship with this brother of his whom he hardly knew. He realized that fear for their own safety in the crowd, if it were known that they were kinsmen of a condemned heretic, prevented any sign of recognition. Then the procession passed them and they were left to struggle with the crowd moving toward the place of execution.

The formalities had been brief. From a vantage point on a cart at the edge of the crowd, Antonio saw his brother shake his head, refusing the last opportunity to recant and admit his guilt. A great sigh went up from the crowd at his action, for by it he had denied himself the relief of death by garroting before the flames could torture his body.

The voice of John Calvin was strained as he thundered out the verdict of death, strained, perhaps, because he himself realized that Swiss law forbade the ultimate torture of death by fire for a religious offense. Only later, when he studied canon law at Padua, had Antonio learned how Calvin's insistence upon reviving the now extinct Code of Justinian had allowed the death penalty in this case. Even the Roman Church which had equally tried and condemned Michael Servetus, though in absence, had not demanded the ultimate penalty, as had John Calvin.

Seeing his brother standing there, proud and unbending in the face of the most horrible of deaths, Antonio had felt a surge of pride in kinship with a man who could adhere to his convictions to the very last.

A groan of pure horror went up from the crowd as the torch was applied to the piled-up fagots. In the silence that followed, the sobs of women in the crowd had formed a muffled overtone. Antonio felt his father turn and bury his head upon his shoulder, but he was unable to turn his own fascinated gaze away from those leaping flames as they consumed the dry wood and reached for the slender body lashed to the stake above them. He could see the curling tendrils of smoke as the condemned man's ragged garments caught fire.

Antonio's throat had filled and he thought that he must cry out and shout his own defiance to the implacable figure of Calvin upon the dais, but his father's tugging hands pulled him away. "Come, Antonio," the old man urged in a hoarse voice. "We must leave now."

Walking down the hill, supporting his father with his strong arms, Antonio could not help but take one last look over his shoulder at the scene they were leaving. The flames were leaping about the tall figure now, the clothing already half burned from his body, but his brother stood there against the stake, defiant to the very end. With a burst of pride and deep-seated elation, Antonio knew that Michael Servetus, even in death, had triumphed over his tormentors.

They had stopped to rest hours later beside a stream, well away from the town. As they munched hard bread and cheese Antonio said fiercely, "I was proud of him, Father, weren't you?"

Slowly his father had shaken his head. "Tonio *mio,* I have brought you up to be a good Catholic. Always remember that your brother was guilty of heresy."

"He may have been right," Antonio argued stubbornly. "Did you see his eyes?"

His father's voice had grown stern then. "Heresy is never right, Tonio. No man has the right to doubt the edicts of Mother Church. From this day on you will forget that you ever had a brother named Michael Servetus."

"But, Father——"

"Put your hand over your heart and swear——"

Slowly, then, Antonio had repeated after his father, "I swear by the Holy Virgin never to repeat the name of Michael Servetus or to acknowledge kinship with him."

"You are a good son, Antonio." His father had clasped him in his arms. "I hope that you will give your life to the Church." Antonio understood that his own life was to be an atonement for the sin of his brother. But as he lay awake on the ground beside the brook that night, it was not of the church, of the sin of his brother, that he remembered; it was his burning eyes and the proud, thin body that refused to slump even when the flames rose about him. . . .

Could it be possible that his brother had been right and the others wrong? Antonio had asked himself, lying there. He had not found the answer then. Could it be possible that he had found it here in Padua tonight, in the gross and diseased body of the prior? . . .

Slowly Antonio got to his feet from the chapel floor and made his way from the quiet room. He had found none of the forgiveness there which Fra Felipe had sent him to seek. Rather his doubts were stronger now than ever, strong enough almost to form a conviction in themselves. Michael had been right about the circulation of the blood; Antonio was convinced of that now. Could it not be that the same mind which had made such an important medical discovery was right about other things as well, about theological as well as medical questions? For certainly, heresy or no heresy, truth was truth.

His thoughts still troubled, Antonio crossed the empty library and unlatched the door to his cell. From the tinderbox beside the door he selected tinder, ignited it with a flint, and watched the tiny glow spread and become flame. Even so, he thought, from one tiny spark of truth might grow a bright flame of knowledge. With the flame he lit candles in brackets on the wall, filling the room with light.

The painting on the easel took life and substance in the light of the candles and the whole room filled with her presence. In the contemplation of that pale, quiet beauty, Antonio's troubled thoughts gradually became calmer. He remembered waking from a dream, as a child, to find his mother standing beside his pallet, her outlines fogged in his sleep-ridden gaze, but the certainty of her presence giving him the sense of safety and assurance he needed. Now the painting was a comforting and reassuring presence in the room.

Kneeling beside the couch, he prayed for help in directing his troubled thoughts.

vi

"Per Bacco!" Gian Savarino exclaimed from the door. "Are you training to be a butcher, Tonio?"

Antonio looked up from the still quivering carcass of the pig stretched out on a small table in the room of the anatomy theater that served for special demonstrations. "Gian!" he cried, his face lighting up. "Come in." He was stripped to the waist and sweat gleamed upon his muscular torso and broad shoulders.

"Lock the door behind you," Antonio advised. "We forgot to do it."

Beside Antonio, old Guinterius was muttering dourly to himself as he worked on a strange apparatus. It was a tall hollow reed to which a sharpened quill was attached by means of melted wax. He was filling the reed with a dark blue fluid, closing off the sharp end of the quill with a gnarled forefinger.

Gian Savarino poked his way fastidiously across the littered floor, avoiding some puddles where blood had dripped from the table. His shoes were of soft Spanish leather, pointed and curled at the tips, with tiny silver bells that tinkled as he walked. Of medium height and a trifle stocky, his blondish hair curled on his shoulders. Light blue eyes twinkled in a round, pleasant face as he leaned over the table to see what Antonio was doing. Although Gian was the son of a rich Venetian importer, he and Antonio had become fast friends several years before, when the Venetian had come to Padua to study anatomy in connection with his avocation of artist.

"What the devil are you doing, anyway?" Gian exclaimed, climbing up on a chair in order to see better, but remaining carefully out of range of the blood spattering from the vessels Antonio was cutting with quick, sure strokes of a heavy dissecting knife. He gathered the skirts of his short tunic of rich velvet about his hips for further protection.

Antonio wiped sweat from his face with his bare upper arm. There was a spray of bright red droplets across his chest and his long fingers were smeared with blood. "I'm opening this pig's chest," he explained, "to get to the heart."

"*Sangue di Dio!* Don't you wait for your subjects to die before you dissect?"

"The pig is dead, but this must be done quickly, before the blood has a chance to clot in the vessels." Antonio turned back to the animal and cut through the soft gristle holding the ribs together and lifted off the front of the pig's chest like a trap door. Beneath, the lungs lay glistening and bluish gray in color. Between them the heart still quivered a little in the final contractions of the death agony.

"We're trying to prove the theory of Michael Servetus in regard to the lung circulation," Antonio explained. He took a sharpened quill from a pile on the table and thrust it through the muscular wall of the left side of the heart, the ventricle which pumped blood out into the great vessels, called the *arteria venosa*. The heart muscle quivered and a fleeting wave of contraction passed over it. Blood dripped red from the end of the quill and flowed over the polished wood of the table.

"The quill is now in the left ventricle," Antonio explained. "Next I will put one into the left auricle where the veins from the lungs empty into the heart. This quill penetrated the thinner-walled auricle without difficulty."

"What about that apparatus there?" Gian asked.

"I am going to use it now. Hold it up please, Guinterius." While the grumbling prosector obeyed, Antonio took the sharpened quill attached to the reed. Carefully he inserted the sharp point through the right side of the heart, penetrating the wall completely. Through the thin wall of the reed, the level of the blue fluid could be seen to descend as it flowed into the heart and mixed with the blood already there.

"We are putting the dye directly into the right side of the heart," Antonio explained. "If now I squeeze the heart muscle, I will be simulating the contraction of the heart itself. You can see why all this must be done quickly, Gian, while the blood is still fluid in the vessels."

"Ingenious!" Gian exclaimed admiringly. "But what does it prove?"

"If none of the dye comes out of the left ventricle immediately, we will know that Galen was wrong and there are no perforations in the septum between the right and left sides of the heart."

"*Dio mio!* You *are* asking for trouble. Remember how hot they made it for Vesalius?"

"Just what I said, Your Magnificence," Guinterius muttered. "But he wouldn't listen."

"He never listens when he gets one of his ideas," Gian said. "He's as stubborn as an abbot's mule."

Antonio paid no attention to their comments. With the quills still in place, he was squeezing the muscular, pear-shaped bulb of the heart in his strong fingers, imitating mechanically the natural beat of the heart itself. The thin-walled arteries leading to the lungs swelled visibly as blood was forced into them by the contraction. Their normally bluish color deepened markedly as the dye mixed with the blood.

"You see," Antonio cried. "Nothing comes from the left side, although I have filled the right side with the dye." It was true. None of the blue color showed there, as it should have done if the tiny perforations existed between the two sides of the heart, as every anatomist had believed for a thousand years.

"*Corpo di Cristo!*" Gian exclaimed. "Vesalius was right."

"And Servetus before him," Antonio said triumphantly.

Guinterius had known Michael Servetus and his fate. He crossed himself now, as if in the presence of evil. "The devil's work," he muttered under his breath.

Antonio relaxed his grip upon the pig's heart and the muscular organ expanded at once to its normal size. The veins entering the heart emptied as blood was drawn from them into the organ itself.

Again Antonio squeezed the heart, distending the arteries to the lungs and sending a surge of blood through them into the breathing organs themselves. "If blood really passes through the lungs," he said, "we should soon see the dye coming from the quill in the left side of the heart."

Hardly breathing, the three of them bent over the table, watching the drip-drip of red from the quill in the left auricle where blood from the lungs would first appear. But only the normal red color showed at the end of the quill.

Then, almost imperceptibly at first, the color of the blood seemed to darken. Antonio snatched up a piece of white parchment from the table and held it beneath the stream, allowing the droplets to fall from the open end of the quill upon the white surface. Seen now against the white background, there was no doubting the bluish tint of the blood spattering upon the paper from the open end of the quill.

Antonio's fingers shook with excitement. "*Eccolo!* The dye!" he cried. "It has come through the lungs from the right side."

Gian swore softly, and even Guinterius grunted in surprise and came closer in order to see this miracle. There was no longer any doubt of the truth, for the blood flowing from the quill in the left side of the heart was definitely tinted a dark blue by the dye. It could have reached there only by being forced through the lungs as Antonio squeezed the heart, repeating the normal course of the blood through the lungs with every heartbeat.

"It had to be this way," Antonio cried, his eyes shining. "Michael was right and Fra Felipe wrong."

"Fra Felipe?" Gian asked. "Who is he?"

Antonio seemed not to have heard him. "You both witnessed this," he said excitedly. "You will swear if necessary to what you have seen."

"*Con piacere!*" said Gian Savarino, but Guinterius shook his head. "I don't know," he muttered. "It is the devil's work to refute Galen."

"We'll refute a lot of others before we're through," Antonio said impatiently. "If Galen could be wrong about this, then he could be wrong about a lot of other things. And so could Aristotle, Ptolemy, and the others."

Gian Savarino's normally cheerful face grew serious at his words. Although Venice was the one place in the world where knowledge was almost unrestrained, everyone knew that the power of the popes extended even here and that there were ways of punishing those who dared to defy a papal edict. The church had espoused the teachings of Galen. Medically, therefore, they were in the same position that Holy Writ was to theology.

"What do you do next, Tonio?"

"Announce my findings to the faculty at once," Antonio said. "They prove that Michael Servetus was right about the pulmonary circulation and that the Church was wrong." He went over to a basin in the corner and began to wash the blood from his hands and chest. "You can clean up, Guinterius. We are through for today."

"*Sì, subito,*" the old man said with alacrity. "The sooner I've seen the last of this devil's work the better I'll like it."

Antonio only laughed and wiped his chest with a rough towel. He felt like breaking out into song. How the members of the faculty would sit up and stare when he made his demonstration. If it worked once, it must work again, and now there would be no doubt about his fitness to fill the chair of Fallopius. And in addition to startling the scientific world, here was unquestionable proof that Michael had told the truth and that those who had persecuted him were wrong.

vii

In the small room at the university where Antonio studied when not dissecting, Gian Savarino lounged in a chair while Antonio moved restlessly about, unable to calm his racing thoughts.

"Start at the beginning," Gian said. "How did you get this idea?"

Antonio recited his experience with Fra Mario Bellarmi and his later talk with Fra Felipe Santos. When he finished, Gian's face was glum.

"*E' semplicissimo,*" Gian said, then added in more sober tones, "I know Santos now. He's a Dominican, and I'm pretty sure he was once connected with the Inquisition."

"But the Inquisition has nothing to do with this."

"The Inquisition pokes its nose into everything. If Santos learns that you disobeyed him, he'll cause trouble for you."

"But I must tell him," Antonio protested. "He must admit the truth when I show him the results of the experiment."

"Don't be a fool, Tonio! There's no one less liable to see the truth than a pigheaded priest when heresy is involved."

"Don't tell me I should keep it a secret!" Antonio exclaimed in exasperation.

"That might be sensible. After all, who was Michael Servetus that you should worry about whether he was right or wrong, even if you do have the same name?"

Antonio turned to face him. "Michael Servetus was my oldest brother," he said proudly.

For a moment Gian was stunned beyond speech. Then he jumped to his feet and began to pace the floor. "*Sangue di Dio!* I am a fool. Why didn't I suspect it?"

"Do you still think I should keep this discovery a secret?" Antonio demanded.

Gian shook his head. "No. Not now." And then his face cleared. "But there's no reason why you have to mention your brother at all."

"I don't understand——"

"Look, Tonio," Gian interrupted. "Publish this as your own discovery and your future is certain. It's important enough in itself to give you the chair of anatomy."

"But it is not my discovery."

Gian threw up his hands. "Do you want to be burned for heresy too? All the writings of a condemned heretic are forbidden documents. If you insist on publishing your findings as a vindication of your brother, you are putting your neck in a noose. Your own writings will be forbidden then, and that means they will be lost to science."

Antonio could see the logic of Gian's suggestion, but he didn't like the idea. It seemed like an act of disloyalty to the slender, emaciated figure who had stood so proud and straight against the stake that afternoon in Champel.

"I have to return to Venice this afternoon," Gian said. "Promise me that you will not do anything about this without consulting me."

"But what can you do?"

"I have some friends among the papacy who are more liberal than the average priest. Let me put this question to them hypothetically, without mentioning your name, and see what they say."

Reluctantly Antonio made the promise, but he was not happy about it. Last night and this morning he had been filled with a sense of exultation in what he had discovered and a great pride in his brother, whatever the church said about him. Even now, in spite of Gian's warning, some questioning voice deep inside him kept insisting that under the same circumstances Michael would not have hesitated at all. Then he remembered the painting; he had wanted to talk to someone about it, and Gian, being an artist and his friend, was the logical person. "Before you go," he said to Gian, "I want some advice on my drawings."

"I thought you'd given that up. What got you interested in art again?"

"If you will come to the priory," Antonio promised, "I'll show you."

"*Benissimo,*" Gian said, sensing something mysterious. "But we will stop at a *trattoria* for bread and cheese. I wouldn't even touch that pig slop they feed the monks at your priory."

Having dined at a sidewalk restaurant between the university and the priory, Gian and Antonio continued on to Antonio's quarters.

"What's this?" Gian exclaimed as Antonio took the heavy key from his pocket. "Locked doors in a priory?"

"Shh!" Antonio flushed.

"*E perchè?*"

"There is something valuable in here."

"You would almost think you were going to an assignation," Gian said.

They entered the cell and Antonio closed the door carefully. Then he went over to the window and drew aside the hanging he had placed over it to shut out prying eyes. Sunlight streamed through the window and fell upon the canvas on the easel, bathing the graceful figure stepping from the shell in a soft radiance.

"*Per Bacco!*" Gian exclaimed in an awed voice. "The Botticelli Venus."

Startled, Antonio asked, "Are you sure?"

Gian moved closer and studied the canvas intently for several minutes. "There is no question about it," he said when he had finished his inspection. "Only a master like Botticelli could have painted that."

"I was sure it was a work of art," Antonio said. "Did you ever see it before?"

"Once. In Florence. But how in the devil did it get here?"

"Someone left a roll of canvases here several months ago," Antonio explained. "It had been thrown into a storeroom and I found it there while looking for some books."

"I heard it was stolen from Florence," Gian said. "Does the prior know about this?"

Antonio shook his head. "He is too sick to be troubled." He pulled several of his half-completed drawings from the table. "I have been trying to copy it in sketches. You can see that I didn't get very far."

Gian studied the sketches, particularly the last, half-completed one of the breast, his shrewd eyes taking in the erasures, the inept strokes which had failed to catch the symmetry and fullness of the breast.

"What did I do wrong?" Antonio asked.

"*Abbastanza!*" Gian snorted in disgust. "How do you expect to draw the breast of a woman when you've never even seen one, Messer Monk?"

Antonio flushed. "I've dissected women."

"As well compare a haunch of venison to a running doe. You'll never know what it is to paint, Tonio mio, until you've really experienced some of the things you try to put on canvas."

"Fallopius said much the same thing about medicine," Antonio admitted.

"A wise old fellow, Fallopius. I hear he was quite a blood once."

"But surely," Antonio protested, "there could be nothing of—of what you say in a painting such as this." To him she was too immaculate, too certain of her beauty and her chaste nudity, ever to be soiled by the human passions which he had always been taught were only base urgings of Satan.

"There speaks the monk." Suddenly Gian began to laugh.

"What are you laughing at?" Antonio demanded, piqued by Gian's raillery.

The Venetian wiped his eyes with a lace-trimmed cambric handkerchief and stuffed it back inside the flaring cuff of his tunic sleeve. "*Eccolo!* You've fallen in love with our seagirt beauty there. It's in your eyes when you look at her."

"Don't be absurd," Antonio snapped. "It is nothing but a picture."

"That's just it, Tonio mio. Being you, with that monkish conscience of yours, you would naturally choose a picture upon which to center your passions rather than a flesh-and-blood woman."

Angrily, Antonio said, "There is no question of passion here."

"No?" Gian drawled. "What are you so angry about?" Then his face sobered. "You've got the wrong idea, Antonio; not that I would expect you to have any other, living in a priory. There's nothing base about a man loving a woman."

"The sins of the flesh, you know they are wrong."

"There's nothing wrong about a man wanting a woman, Tonio." Gian shook his head. "You'll never get closer to heaven than with one in your arms."

"Could *she* look like that," Antonio demanded, "if she were a wanton?"

Gian smiled tolerantly. "You haven't known many women, my boy. The worst of them can act the saint if she wants to."

"I don't believe it," Antonio stated flatly.

Gian started to shrug and then he looked from the softly lighted figure on the canvas back to Antonio's face. For an instant something of what Antonio felt in regard to the woman on the canvas was transmitted to him, and when he spoke his voice was husky.

"Keep that feeling, Antonio mio," he said softly. "You will never find a real-life woman who can give it to you."

Then the spell was broken and Gian stood up. "I must be getting back to Venice," he said briskly. "You promise to say nothing about your experiment until you hear from me?"

"Yes," Antonio agreed, "I promise."

"What about the painting?"

"I want to try some more sketches."

"It won't do any good," Gian smiled. "But have your way. You'll find eventually that mine is better."

"In a few days," Antonio said, "I'll tell Fra Felipe that the painting is here. Florence will be glad to get it back."

"If Venice gives it up. I suspect that your precious Fra Santos will do everything he can to keep it right here in the priory."

"But that wouldn't be honest."

Gian shrugged. "You have a great deal to learn about the world, Tonio. Perhaps it is time I took your education in hand."

viii

It was midafternoon and Antonio was busy in his small cubicle at the university, working out the details for a presentation of his findings on the lung circulation to the faculty, as soon as Gian gave him the word. There was a knock on his door, and when he opened it he saw one of the lay brothers from the priory.

"His Reverence is much worse, Frater Antonio," the messenger said. "Fra Felipe Santos begs that you will attend him at once."

"*Sì, subito.*" Antonio reached for his flat velvet cap and closed the door behind him. "We must hurry."

The prior was indeed worse, Antonio saw as soon as he was ushered into the bedroom. He was in the unmistakable stupor that precedes death, his face almost purple, his breathing stertorous and labored, little more, actually, than harsh, rattling gasps. Fra Felipe Santos stood at one side of the bed. At the other knelt a man with close-cut iron-gray hair and the finely chiseled features of an Italian aristocrat, praying in a low whisper while his fingers moved upon the beads of a rosary.

A girl stood beside the kneeling man, and at the sight of her Antonio experienced an involuntary start of surprise, so familiar did her small, perfect face seem. Everything about her was like something long known and remembered, as if she might have been a member of his family whom he had seen only yesterday—the grayish-blue eyes, the golden hair restrained by a small cap of blue velvet embroidered with seed pearls, the soft red lips, the concerned frown upon her forehead, and even the slender, graceful figure in a simple traveling gown and cloak of darker material. It seemed to Antonio, seeing her for what he was actually certain was the first time, that he must have known her all his life.

Then the man beside the bed rose to his feet and Fra Felipe introduced Antonio. "Messer Girolamo Bellarmi, of Florence, His Reverence's brother. Dr. Antonio Servetus, the physician."

Messer Girolamo acknowledged the introduction graciously. He bore an unmistakable resemblance to Fra Mario, the difference lying mainly between the bloated features of the prior, even in health, and the finely chiseled ones of the brother. His plain robe was edged with fur and there was a gold chain about his neck, the usual attire of a respectable merchant or lesser nobleman.

Antonio knew that he must seem rude from the intensity of his stare, but he was still quite unable to take his eyes from the girl's face. His brain was puzzling with the impression that somewhere he had known her before.

"Madonna Lucia Bellarmi, my niece and ward, Doctor," Messer Girolamo said.

The girl inclined her head in a curt nod. A flush stained her cheek and her lips tightened. She was obviously annoyed by the intensity of his rude stare.

Antonio turned to Fra Mario. He felt the pulse and noted how weak and hurried it was, in keeping with the prior's general appearance. With a napkin he wiped a bloodstained froth from purplish lips. The veins of Fra Mario's bull-like neck were distended with blood until they seemed on the point of bursting.

"His Reverence has been getting worse all day," Fra Felipe said unctuously. "I hated to disturb you at the university, Dr. Servetus, but I felt that you should attend him."

Antonio said in a low voice, "He is dying."

"Is there nothing to be done?" the girl asked.

"I can bleed him," Antonio said. "It may help a little, but it cannot avert the end."

Madonna Lucia turned to Fra Felipe. "Perhaps an older and more experienced physician might be able to help," she suggested.

Antonio flushed, and Messer Girolamo said apologetically, "You will forgive my niece her bluntness, messire? She is very young."

"I am old enough to see that my kinsman is dying, Uncle," Madonna Lucia said hotly, "and nothing is being done for him."

"Silenzio!" the Florentine commanded. "Have we given Dr. Servetus an opportunity to do anything?"

"Dr. Servetus is highly regarded at the university," Fra Felipe said soothingly. "Professor Fallopius himself vouches for his ability as a physician."

"I will draw some blood." Antonio opened his case of lancets upon the bed.

"In Florence the barbers draw blood," Madonna Lucia said sweetly. "Is the physician also a barber, that he bleeds with his own hands?"

Fra Felipe's lips tightened with annoyance at her forwardness. "Dr. Servetus is especially skilled in surgery," he said. "His Reverence has always preferred for him to draw the blood with his own hands."

Skillfully Antonio opened a vein in the prior's arm and let the stream fall into a bowl. When it was flowing well, he looked up at Madonna Lucia. Her face was marble pale, her lips bloodless, and her eyes were fixed upon the crimson stream with the fascinated stare of one watching a poisonous serpent. He saw her sway a little and catch the tall bedpost for support.

"Does Madonna need a stimulating drink?" he inquired. "She looks as if she were going to swoon."

The other men turned to her at once, but his words were all the stimulant she needed. Color surged to her cheeks and she bit her lip in vexation. Antonio turned back to his bleeding with a quiet sense of satisfaction.

Even when a full bowl of blood had been drained from the prior's veins there was little if any improvement. Antonio put his lancets back into his case. The signs of impending death were far too evident for much to be accomplished by this last resort to bloodletting.

The others left the room and Antonio filed out into the hall in their wake. Fra Felipe and Messer Bellarmi were in the lead, after them Madonna Lucia, with Antonio bringing up the rear. He still marveled at the sense of familiarity, even intimacy, that the girl stirred up in his mind. Even from the rear, the set of her shoulders, the slender column of her neck as she tossed her head, momentarily displacing the golden waves of her hair, everything about her seemed as well remembered as if he had known her before. He had to resist an impulse to reach out and touch her, as if to reassure himself that she was real and not a creature from out of his dreams.

"Will you and Madonna Lucia remain here tonight, Messer Bellarmi?" Fra Felipe asked.

Bellarmi said, "Conte Volpi, a distant relative, has offered us shelter in Venice at the Palazzo Pesaro, with a carriage whenever we need it."

"Still, it is twenty-five miles to Venice," Fra Felipe reminded him.

Messer Girolamo turned to Antonio. "Can my brother live through the night, messire?"

"I don't believe so, Your Excellency. I shall attend him constantly."

"Then you and your niece had best remain here," Fra Felipe suggested. "It is most fortunate that you happened to visit Venice at this time."

Antonio had turned back toward the prior's apartment, but he stopped, rigid, his hand on the door, when Girolamo Bellarmi said: "Yes. When I got your letter, I took the opportunity to come to Venice. My niece and I have been searching for a very valuable canvas which belongs to our family, the Botticelli Venus. I had heard rumors that it might be in Venice."

"You would certainly not expect to find it here," Fra Felipe said with a laugh.

Antonio turned to tell Messer Bellarmi that the canvas was indeed in the priory. Then his eyes met those of Madonna Lucia, who had stopped and was staring back at him. At the scorn still present in her gaze, he felt a wave of annoyance at her and the way she had baited him in the prior's apartment, and with it went a perverse determination not to betray his knowledge of the Botticelli canvas, for the moment at least. He turned and opened the door of the apartment but could not resist a final glance in her direction. The two men were some distance away down the corridor, but she was still standing in the same place, a puzzled frown on her face. Then, when she saw him looking at her, she tossed her head and swept imperiously down the corridor toward her uncle and Fra Felipe.

ix

In the early evening Fra Mario dropped into a stuporous sleep, and leaving one of the monks to watch him, Antonio stepped out of the main building of the priory into the enclosed garden, hidden behind the walls. It was a place that he loved, a retreat of quiet and peace, perfumed this late spring evening by the mingled fragrance of the flowers carefully tended by the loving hands of Brother Francis, who was half blind and devoted himself entirely to caring for the garden.

In the center of a small pool fed by a burbling fountain spring stood a bronze statue of the Saviour, smilingly benignly down upon the activities of this house devoted to His service. All paths converged upon this central place, and it was toward it that Antonio turned his steps. His thoughts returned to his experiment that morning, for he was troubled still by questions of what he should really do.

Every tenet of his heritage and training urged that he should make no move counter to the Church, which he had been taught transcended all human desire, all human law. As clearly as on that day by the stream outside Champel, he could remember his father's words and the oath he had sworn. As he walked in this quiet place, another picture kept intruding into his mind, that of an emaciated man standing so proud and defiant against the stake. But now those burning eyes seemed to blaze with a light of disappointment and contempt, filling Antonio with an overwhelming sense of guilt and shame. His foot touched the base of the Christ in the garden, and on a sudden impulse, he dropped to his knees on the rough gravel of the walkway beside the little pool and bowed his head, to pray silently for guidance, for some sign of divine will in his perplexity. But he found no sign there on his knees before the Christ and presently rose to his feet, feeling a deep disappointment that the Deity represented by the bronze figure had given him no help.

Something moved in the shadows, and as a feminine figure began vaguely to take form, Antonio thought for a moment that his prayer had really been answered, that the Holy Mother herself had come to give him the help he needed. Then he saw that it was only Lucia Bellarmi standing in the shadows, muffled in a long cloak that showed only the pale oval of her face in the night.

"Madonna," he stammered, "I did not know you were here."

She came around the base of the statue. "I'm sorry I startled you, Ser Physician," she said, and her voice was soft. "Were you praying for my uncle?"

"N-no," Antonio admitted. "For help in a—a personal matter."

She did not pursue the question. Instead she sat on a bench before the fountain. Antonio moved over to the other end of the bench, marveling at how different she was from that afternoon.

"Why did you stare so at me in my uncle's apartment?" she asked.

"I'm sorry if I was rude," he said in apology.

"But you haven't told me why."

"It is hard to explain," he said awkwardly. "I felt as if I had seen you before, actually as if I had known you for—for a long time."

For a second she did not speak, and when she did her voice was oddly tense. "And you have no explanation?"

"None," he admitted. "I do not think that I have ever seen you before today."

"You have not," she said. And then, changing the subject abruptly, "Fra Felipe says you are taking the Holy Orders. Why would a young man like you want to become a monk?"

Startled by the question, Antonio had no answer.

"If I were a man," she continued, "I would be making a place in the world already."

"Perhaps there are things more important than making a place in the world."

"Certainly not leaving it for the safety of the cloister," she retorted.

"Aren't you too young to understand such things, madonna?" he asked gently.

She stamped her foot on the gravel. "I'm twenty. At your age my grandfather was discovering the New World."

"Your grandfather," Antonio echoed. "Are you related to Messer Columbus?"

"My grandfather was Amerigo Vespucci," she said proudly. "He didn't hide behind walls. He voyaged over unknown seas and risked his life to discover new lands."

"But your name is Bellarmi."

"I am a Vespucci on my mother's side," she explained. "We were bankers to the De' Medici."

"But your uncle chose the cloister."

"Uncle Mario was the black sheep of the family. He chose the church rather than prison. Besides," she added, "it was good business for the House of Bellarmi to have a member in high ecclesiastical circles." It was a truly startling statement from one so young. She had a keen mind as well as a sharp tongue, Antonio decided.

"You are very proud of your family, madonna."

"Why shouldn't I be? The House of Bellarmi is one of the greatest in all Italy."

"Pride goeth before destruction," Antonio started to remind her, but she burst out angrily. "There speaks the monk. Are you a man, Ser Physician, that you must hide from the world and take the safe and easy way?" She stood up and kicked angrily at the path, sending a shower of gravel upon Antonio. "If I were a man you wouldn't find me hiding. Go back to your cell, Ser Monk. I bid you good night."

He watched her slender form as she hurried along the path to a door leading inside. A moment later it slammed decisively, as if she were punctuating the interview with a final period. He remained on the bench after she had gone, for she had summed up in a few words much of the disquiet within him. Here, he realized, was a place of decision, a point from which the current of his life must flow in one direction or another and choose its path before he left this place.

In one direction lay the safe way, the quiet, peaceful, and thoughtful existence which had become so dear to him during these past five years at Padua. With it went the respect of his colleagues, the high position of a Paduan professor, and perhaps an important place in the ecclesiastical world, even the mitered cap of a bishop or the red hat of a cardinal. The other way lay trouble, vituperation, perhaps even torture and death, for those who supported a heretical doctrine through adhering to the teachings of a heretic were themselves condemned by both secular and canon law.

Another, he remembered now, had faced such a choice on a mount called Golgotha. He had not faltered under the burden of truth, even though His way pointed to the Agony of the Cross. A great peace filled Antonio's soul then and he straightened his bowed shoulders with a new surge of pride. He knew now, as he realized he had known all along in his deepest inner self, that there could be no real compromise with truth. It was the one thing upon which man must stand, even though he must fall in the battle and be trampled underfoot.

x

Fra Mario Bellarmi died during the night. Antonio remained with him until the end, but there was no time to speak to either Messer Girolamo or his niece, for Fra Felipe took them from the room as soon as Antonio pronounced the prior dead and he remained behind to help prepare the body for the speedy burial which was necessary at this time of the year.

At the close of the elaborate funeral ceremony the next day, Antonio waited in the cathedral with the rest of the lay brothers while the funeral procession left the church. From his seat on the aisle he saw Madonna Lucia and her uncle moving slowly toward the exit in the wake of the richly garbed churchmen, the cardinal who had come from Venice to perform the ceremony, Fra Felipe, tall and straight in spotless white robes, and a host of lesser prelates. For mourning she had put on the dark cloak she had been wearing that night in the priory garden. It covered her dress and rustled against the floor as she walked. The hood was drawn up and pulled tight about her face to hide the golden hair, giving her a look of innocence and demureness which Antonio knew from bitter experience was not in accord with her temper.

Her eyes met Antonio's as she passed and he bowed politely, but she affected not to see him, and the chill of her glance passed completely over him, as if he were a stranger who had the impertinence to bow. Antonio's features stiffened with annoyance in spite of himself, and in the instant that she passed he saw her eyes light up suddenly with a look of pure mockery. Then she was gone. Messer Girolamo, walking beside his niece, saw Antonio and bowed gravely as he passed.

Antonio was busy with another patient, a professor suffering from erysipelas, until late that night. As he walked back to the priory through the spring-scented night, many people were on the streets, some, obviously lovers, walking hand in hand, others whispering in the shadows. In one dark niche there was the sound of a kiss and a woman's low laugh, as two dark shadows separated quickly, only to merge again as soon as he passed. He felt again the vague disquiet which had bothered

him for several weeks and wondered about its cause. Perhaps a change
of scene would help, he thought. The school year had ended officially
two days before, and he could visit Gian in Venice. And with Fra
Mario dead and his erysipelas patient out of danger, he should consult Gian about the publication of his defense of his brother Michael.

The coolness of the evening was in the air that came through the
small open window of Antonio's cell in the priory as he lay on the
couch. Even with the candles extinguished there was enough moonlight to bathe the goddess of the canvas in a faint glow, and the thought
that he must give her up wrenched at his heart. But he knew that it
would be foolhardy to try to keep the canvas or take it elsewhere. He
could never get it out of the priory unobserved, unless he stole it away
at night, and that his stern conscience forbade him to do.

Tomorrow, Antonio assured his conscience, he would seek out
Messer Girolamo Bellarmi and tell him that his search was at an end.
After all, conscience insisted, he could not keep such a valuable work
of art when he knew to whom it belonged. And even if it were not
the property of the Bellarmi family, he had no right to keep it hidden
here, shut away from the world of artists and art lovers who would find
an enduring pleasure and inspiration in its serene beauty.

Nevertheless, Antonio knew that it would be hard to give her up,
so much had he come to feel that she was a living, breathing presence,
a person whose existence was closely intertwined with his own. He
had never considered marriage, but lying now in the darkness, in the
half state between sleeping and waking, he found himself wondering
if the pleasures of marriage could in any way resemble this serene
satisfaction in companionship, this quiet, reassuring beauty that was
always ready to help troubled human thoughts. Unbidden, the thought
of the physical pleasure said to attend marriage came to his mind, but
he put the idea forcibly from him almost before he was conscious that
the obscene thought had reached his mind.

As he lay now with his eyes closed, the room faded away and he
found himself lying upon a sandy shore in the shade of a leafy green
tree, as he had lain many times as a youth on the shores of the Ligurian
Sea, his hair still damp from swimming in the pellucid waters, mind
and body utterly relaxed and content. Suddenly she was there, stepping
daintily from the shell to the shore, her pink toes hardly setting their
imprint in the sand. so light and graceful was she on slender, arched

feet. Her hair was a golden casque about her small head as she came across the sand to where he lay under the trees and gave him her fingers. With a sensation of floating in the air, he came to his feet, as unashamed of his nakedness as she seemed of her own.

"Tonio. *Mio caro.*" Her voice was like the music of a distantly struck lyre muted almost before its tone was heard.

"Madonna," he stammered, feeling an unfamiliar excitement rising within him.

"Not madonna, Tonio," she whispered, coming into the circle of her arms. "*Caro mio*. My darling."

"My own," he whispered then. "My goddess from the sea." The warmth of her body, so close to his own that one soft breast touched his chest, set fire to his veins and he trembled with the urge to put his arms about her fragile slenderness.

"Kiss me, Tonio," she commanded, lifting herself upon tiptoes and putting her arms around his neck. And when he still held back, fighting against the strength of his own desire, she pulled his head down until his lips met her own. His passion released then by the unrestrained ardor of her kiss, Antonio's arms went about her, all reserve swept away by the promise of her body.

And then thunder cracked and roared about his head and lightning split the tree beneath which they were standing. Momentarily stunned, Antonio was not able to resist when profane hands tore them roughly apart. He heard her cry of anguish, "Tonio! Tonio!" her voice growing more distant even as she spoke. Thrown to his knees by the lightning and the strong hands which had torn his beloved from him, Antonio struggled to his feet. She was yards away now, struggling in the arms of a strange creature, a satyr with the face of Fra Felipe Santos, an apparition straight out of the depths of hell that laughed with demoniac glee even as it ran with her in its arms.

Finding his strength at last, Antonio plunged after the satyr, running and gasping for breath, sweat half blinding him while his own heart threatened to burst from his chest with the force of its beating. Gasping, stumbling, completely spent, he fell to the ground, rose painfully to his knees and crawled a few yards, only to fall face down in the sand again. He lay there panting, and when finally he managed to raise his head he could still see the running satyr faintly in the distance, fading, fading, until finally he could see nothing more and they were gone.

Now his ears became conscious of another sound. "Naked! Naked! Shame! Shame!" The voice was familiar, sharp and acid with disdain and scorn, as it pounded at his ears. He perceived its author now and recognized Lucia Bellarmi, standing under a tree, covered entirely, except for the white oval of her face, by the black cloak she had worn in the garden. She wagged an admonishing finger at him while her lips repeated the words and her eyes seared him with contempt. Even as Antonio, overcome with shame that she should find him thus, scrambled to cover his nakedness and found nothing with which to do so, the cadence of her words increased and the pitch rose until the shrill tones sent a pain searing through his eardrums and into his brain.

Sweating, his body chilled even while he clawed at the bedclothes, his heart pounding furiously, Antonio came wide awake and felt a surge of intense relief that it was only a dream. Swinging his feet to the floor, he sat on the side of the couch, holding his head between his hands until the beat of his pulse slowed, his breathing quieted, and his hands stopped their trembling.

When he could control himself, he drew a robe about his chilled body and, taking some tinder from the box beside the candlestick, struck a spark into it and blew the tiny coal into flame. When it was burning, he lit a candle and inspected the canvas. The figure was unchanged in its divine loveliness. Remembering again how she had lain in his arms in the dream, Antonio felt the familiar excitement stir within him. But he resolutely forced his thoughts into other channels, safely away from such fleshly temptations. Blowing out the candle, he lay down again on the couch and pulled the covers up over his body.

Remembering the dream in all its vivid detail now as he lay, unable to sleep, Antonio began to wonder if there could be a special meaning to it. Could it have been a warning that he must return the canvas to its regular owners? It seemed a logical interpretation. If so, the resemblance of the satyr to Fra Felipe Santos was not accidental and must mean that he should not turn the canvas over to Santos but return it to its original owners. Gian Savarino, he remembered, had said that Santos would probably try to prevent the canvas from being returned to Florence, its rightful home. Antonio made a mental resolve again to seek out Messer Bellarmi in the morning and reveal the whereabouts of the painting.

The same Gian Savarino, wise in experience with the passions that draw men and women together, might well have interpreted the dream quite differently, reading in the scene on the beach the very natural desire of a man to possess a beautiful woman, and in the satyr with the face of the subprior the prohibitions of Antonio's monkish conscience against the pleasures of the flesh, which he had been taught were a constant danger to a man's soul.

But even Gian Savarino would have had trouble explaining the scornful presence of Lucia Bellarmi in the dream, so it is not to be wondered at that Antonio was quite unable to do so.

xl

Fra Felipe Santos was enthroned in the prior's chair on a small dais in the audience room when Antonio sought an audience with him the next day. The cardinal had assured Santos that he would be elevated to the position of prior as soon as a letter could reach Rome and return, and he had lost no time in assuming the prerogatives of the office of which he was for the moment only the acting occupant. His manner was already noticeably more chill and austere, his speech somewhat more clipped.

"What is it you wish, Messer Servetus?" he asked, after Antonio had dutifully kissed the hem of his richly embroidered robe of office.

"I should like to pay my respects to Messer Girolamo Bellarmi," Antonio said.

"You are too late, my son. Messer Girolamo and his niece departed early this morning for Venice." The acting prior smiled benignly. "He spoke highly of you. As for the niece"—his thin lips tightened—"pretty, but a shrew."

Antonio found himself in entire agreement in regard to Lucia Bellarmi, but the early departure of Messer Girolamo had disturbed his plans for disposing of the painting. If he were right in his interpretation of his dream he should not reveal its whereabouts to Fra Felipe. Then he remembered that Messer Girolamo had mentioned staying at the Palazzo Pesaro in Venice, and his thoughts cleared. He wanted to see Gian, anyway, and by going to Venice he could accomplish both aims at once.

"I trust that you have properly atoned for your thoughts in regard to the lung circulation, Doctor," Fra Felipe's voice broke in upon his thoughts.

Antonio bent his head. "I have prayed to be forgiven, as you directed."

"*Benissimo*. You have a promising future. I should hate to see any-thing interfere with it."

Antonio raised his head again, glad to have evaded that pitfall so easily. "I should like to spend a few weeks in Venice, with your permis-sion," he said. If he could persuade Gian to help get his discovery pub-lished, it would take that much time at least to get it into print.

"In Venice? But you are teaching at the university."

"My classes are finished for the summer."

"So they are. But what would you do in Venice?"

Antonio hesitated. To tell the truth would be disastrous, yet he could not lie directly. And then he remembered Gian's suggestion that he study drawing from the living model in order to improve his sense of dimension in his sketching. That would constitute an excellent reason for spending some time in Venice, one which Fra Felipe would proba-bly accept without question, since they had often discussed art and Antonio's interest in drawing.

"I plan to make some special studies in art, Your Reverence," he hastened to say.

Either the statement disarmed Fra Felipe's reservations against let-ting anyone in his establishment escape his authority for long or An-tonio's fortuitous use of the title put him in a warm mood, for he smiled warmly and said, "By all means spend the entire summer in Venice, then. I envy you the cooling breezes of the Lido. Perhaps next year you may be able to paint the frescoes in our new chapel."

"*Dio lo volesse,*" Antonio said dutifully, backing away from the dais.

xii

At the outskirts of Venice travelers from the surrounding country-side left their carriages and took to gondolas, large, slow-moving craft, called *barca* or *batello,* carrying as many as eight passengers.

Antonio joined a group of dusty travelers from the Padua coach early on the afternoon following his audience with Fra Felipe Santos. Down the Grand Canal bisecting the city the large gondola moved, sluggish because of its heavy load, the swarthy man at the oars sweating in the warm June air. In the afternoon sunlight the colored marble façades of the palaces along the waterway shone vividly. In the center of the city, opposite the many-columned and magnificent palace of the

Doge, the *barca* deposited its passengers. Here one had to change to one of the smaller individual gondolas, sleek, colorful craft with swan-shaped prows which darted everywhere like graceful waterfowl on the maze of canals and lagoons which made up this city upon the waters. With the appreciative eye of an artist, Antonio chose a gondola with a blue-fringed canopy supported upon a light arched framework of wood open to the cooling breezes from the Lido near by. The side curtains, rolled up and secured with ties, could be lowered in case of rain, or for the privacy so often desired in this city of romance.

His gondolier was a short, swarthy man with a broad smile revealing toothless gaps in remarkably pink gums. *"Dove va, padre?"* he asked, judging Antonio to be a churchman from his somber garb.

"El Palazzo Pesaro. *È distante di qui?"* Antonio planned to go directly to Messer Bellarmi and reveal the whereabouts of the Botticelli canvas.

"No, non è distante," the gondolier said.

"Vado a il palazzo."

Antonio stepped aboard and settled himself upon a cushioned seat under the canopy. "Do you know the Via delle Galeazze e Vasca?"

"Certamente." The gondolier's eyebrows lifted. "But it is the street of the artists." His manner implied that this was the last place he would expect to be taking a churchman.

"When we leave the Palazzo Pesaro," Antonio instructed him, "you will take me there, to number fourteen."

The gondolier's eyes opened wider. "It is the house of Il Magnifico, Messer Gian Savarino. I have carried him many times in my gondola. With the curtains lowered," he added significantly. *"Eccolo!* What a man!" Knowing Gian, Antonio was not surprised at this revelation of some of his activities, or at the gondolier's knowing him. Gian's father was one of the richest of the merchant bankers of Venice and his son equally prominent among the gay young scions of Venetian families.

"Messer Savarino is my friend," Antonio said with satisfaction.

"A-oel!" The gondolier shouted the high-pitched warning cry of the boatmen. He gave the stern of his light craft a shove and it shot out on the greenish, oily waters of the lagoon.

The traffic in the center of the city was very heavy, and Antonio's gondola was barely able to move, so thickly jammed were the sleek craft, but he was in no hurry. This was a holiday, his first in many months, and a purse filled with the year's pay he had drawn before leaving the university weighed heavily in his belt. He was conscious that his clothing was shabby in comparison with the fur-trimmed robes, gold chains, and velvet hats of the men occupying many of the passing gondolas. In Padua dress had made little difference. Here, he realized customs were different, and he must ask Gian to recommend a tailor.

The slowness of their passage through the great lagoon gave Antonio time to look about him and admire the splendor of the colonnaded palaces, each with its private landing where sumptuous gondolas awaited the pleasure of the owners, the inlays of expensive marbles adorning the buildings and the paved quays before them. Occasionally he could glimpse richly dressed women lounging on the flat-topped roofs which served as sun gardens in the afternoon, cooled by the breezes from the Lido, the nearby shore of the Adriatic. Not for little reason, he thought, was Venice labeled "the Most Serene," for it was the wealthiest and most beautiful city of the world, as well as the center of trade routes from the very ends of the earth.

From the piazza before El Giacommeta and the Rialto, one of the most important trading bourses of the entire world, came the hum of many voices, a deep throbbing note with the clink of gold ducats at the tables of the money-changers around the square sounding a charming obbligato, set to the rhythm tapped out by the small hammers of the goldsmiths at their work. Behind them were the shops, row on row, and towering over these the warehouses in which were stored the rich products of the east.

Beyond the bridge Antonio could see the Fondaco of the German section, their dwellings and warehouses facing the quays where ships that plied the inland seas were tied side by side, disgorging their treasures to eager buyers or loading the exports which made Venice rich. Farther up the canal were docked the vessels that brought food, oil, and wine for the tables of the subjects of the Serenissima, and streams of porters could be seen entering and leaving, like busy ants, the great storehouses of the merchants.

"*Sia stali!*" the gondolier cried, warning an approaching craft that he would turn and that the other should keep right so as not to cross his path. A sweep of the long oar turned the gondola in half its length and they shot into one of the tributary canals. The waterway was narrower here, the houses close to the banks, separated from the water itself only by a narrow, stone-paved quay. Even in the bright afternoon sunlight there were deep shadows against the somewhat less ornate palaces and dwellings that lined the canal. Many of the second-story balconies attached to the houses hung out almost to the edge of the waterway, further shading the narrow quay.

"*Di lungo, il Palazzo Pesaro,*" the gondolier said.

The canal was especially narrow here and the shadows more pronounced. Few people were walking on the quay, but Antonio sighted a slender, graceful figure that seemed very familiar. Two gondola lengths closer and there could be no mistaking the slender, graceful carriage, the small head with its crown of golden hair. It was Lucia Bellarmi, walking toward the Palazzo Pesaro, visible only a few doors away.

Antonio's gondola was almost abreast of her when he saw a man dart from a particularly dark passageway between two of the houses. There was a knife in his right hand, and in the left he carried a short, heavy staff. Before Antonio could shout a warning, the thief had seized the small reticule hanging from Lucia Bellarmi's belt and was slashing at the cord with his knife, with the evident intention of cutting the purse loose and making off with it. There were many such petty thieves in a rich city such as Venice.

"Cutpurse!" Antonio cried in warning and leaped to his feet, rocking the gondola so that the steersman almost fell off his small platform. Seizing the oar from the startled gondolier, he shoved it over hard, driving the boat against the quay, and as it touched the stone wall he leaped ashore.

In the excitement of leaving the gondola, Antonio did not notice that Lucia Bellarmi, warned by his cry, had foiled the cutpurse in his first rush and was now giving an excellent account of herself. She had managed to seize the cudgel from the thief's hand, surprised as he was, too, by the sudden outcry. Swinging it with both hands, she brought it down upon her assailant's head with such force that he was knocked to his knees. All the while she was screaming at the top of her voice, "Thief! Cutpurse! Thief! Cutpurse!"

The thief, stunned momentarily by the blow, struggled to rise while the blows continued to rain down on his head and shoulders. It was into this melee that Antonio precipitated himself, crying, "I am coming, madonna." Whether or not she heard him or whether she thought him another thief, he arrived just in time to receive one of the blows on his own head with the full force of her strength behind it. Knocked completely off his feet, he rolled into a shallow gutter that carried rain water into the canal and he lay there, dazed, while the hubbub over his head went on for a few seconds more, then subsided abruptly.

The cutpurse took the opportunity of the diversion produced by Antonio's arrival to remove himself from this hornets' nest he had unwittingly brought down on his own head when he had expected only to rob an easy prey. Scrambling to his feet, he scuttled into the narrow passage from which he had come.

Still dazed, Antonio arose to face the fury of Lucia Bellarmi. "Stupid donkey" she screamed at him, for the thief had managed to escape with her purse after all, thanks to Antonio's arrival and his bungling intervention.

And then she recognized her would-be savior. "Oh, it's you, Ser Physician," she said with withering scorn. "I might have known it."

"I only tried to help," Antonio stammered in protest.

She stamped a small foot. "I needed no help. The granddaughter of Amerigo Vespucci is more than a match for a low cutpurse."

Antonio swayed a little and put a hand to his throbbing head. "Let me see your head," she ordered in a softer voice.

He bent over, and her fingers moved through his thick, dark hair. He flinched when she touched the spot where the cudgel had landed, but she said, "It is nothing. The skin is not even broken."

The sound of running feet and shouts in the neighborhood indicated that Madonna Lucia's cries had not gone unheard.

"*Dio mio!*" the gondolier cried. "The police! They will arrest us all and take us before the Podesta."

Madonna Lucia again exhibited the ability to think quickly which had enabled her to outwit the thief. "Where are you taking him?" she demanded of the boatman.

"Via delle Galeazze e Vasca."

"Get him in your craft, then, and begone. *Subito!*" She gave Antonio a shove in the direction of the waiting gondola. Still too dazed to protest or to remember his purpose in coming this way, he stumbled aboard the boat, which shot away along the canal as the pilot applied anxious hands to the long oar. His last view of the scene showed Lucia Bellarmi scuttling into the door of the Pesaro Palace.

xiii

Although still aching, Antonio's head had fairly well cleared by
the time the gondolier deposited him on the quay before Gian Savarino's lodgings in the Via delle Galeazze e Vasca, confirming Madonna Lucia's decision that he was not seriously injured. His cap had
been a casualty of the affair, and there was a noticeable and very tender
swelling over his temple.

"*Corpo di Cristo,*" the gondolier said as Antonio bent over his purse
for a coin to pay the fare. "Your Reverence has a fine knob on the side
of your head."

"I'm lucky it isn't broken. It feels as if it were."

"The little lady is strong," the man said admiringly. "*Per Bacco!*
What a beauty!"

"I'll be happy if I never see her again," Antonio said feelingly,
handing him the fare. "*Va bene.*"

"*A rivederci,* Your Reverence."

Throwing his bag over his shoulder, Antonio climbed the stairs
slowly, for Gian's studio occupied the second floor of the building. He
had been here several times before, but the gaiety and abandon of the
artists who were tenants of most of the buildings along this street had
not particularly appealed to his quiet tastes and he had never remained
very long. He was admitted to the anteroom of Gian's apartment by his
servant, a lackey by the name of Dimas, whose mouth was drawn down
perpetually at the corners, as if in disapproval of his master's habits.

"Who is it, Dimas?" Gian called from the studio.

"Dr. Servetus," Dimas replied.

"Tonio!" Gian shouted. "Come back to the studio."

Antonio gave his bag to Dimas, who expressed his contempt for its
meanness with a sniff and went through a bedroom to the studio beyond. It was a large room at the back of the apartment, selected because
of the huge skylight that ran across one side, giving excellent illumina-
tion for Gian's work.

"Tonio mio!" Gian met him at the door, palette in hand, wearing
a paint-smeared smock. They embraced affectionately, the effusive
artist smearing paint on Antonio's robe. "What brings you to Venice?"
Gian demanded.

"I wanted to talk to you, Gian. About my——" Antonio stopped dead still on the threshold of the room, not finishing the sentence. Facing him across the studio was a lovely young woman, tall, and with a wealth of dark red hair. She was standing on a small dais, with one hand uplifted to her hair, as if she were interrupted in the act of arranging it. It was not her presence that startled him, however, but the fact that she was completely nude.

After the shock of the initial glance, Antonio quickly turned his head, feeling the blood surge to his cheeks. Then, in spite of himself, his glance drifted back to the lovely body poised on the model stand. He had known, of course, that Gian often sketched and painted from the undraped model, but this was the first time he had encountered a woman in the studio, as well as one totally naked. She seemed quite unconcerned by her nudity, and in his first quick glance Antonio saw that, although tall, she was quite perfectly proportioned. Then her eyes met his and he saw a fleeting glance of mischief in them, as if she were laughing at him because of his obvious embarrassment while she, although quite nude, was quite unashamed.

Gian noticed Antonio's flaming cheeks and laughed. "Lovely, isn't she, Tonio?" he asked. And when Antonio stood, tongue-tied with embarrassment, Gian was completely overcome and doubled up with laughter. Finally he managed to compose himself enough to introduce Antonio to the lovely model.

"This is Clarice Strozzi, my model," Gian explained. "Clarice, Messer Antonio Servetus, my friend the artist and physician of whom I have spoken."

The girl smiled and Antonio understood now why she was not embarrassed by his presence. He was just another artist to her. "Messer Gian has spoken of you very often, Ser Physician." Her voice was low and throaty in tone.

Antonio bowed, his embarrassment was fading. In the face of the girl's and Gian's casual acceptance of her undress, it seemed foolish for him to be disturbed. And she was exceedingly pleasant to look at, some imp in his brain kept reminding him.

"Signorina Strozzi would be an inspiration to any artist," Antonio found himself saying quite sincerely.

Gian clapped him on the back. "Spoken like a cavalier, Tonio," he cried. "I told you there were the makings of a gallant in you." He turned to the model. "You may rest awhile, Clarice. There is some wine on the sideboard there; pour a glass for the three of us, please."

The girl stepped down from the dais and picked up a light robe lying upon the edge of it and drew it about her body. She moved about the room, gathering glasses and taking the bottle of wine from the sideboard. Antonio and Gian sat on a couch that ran across one side of the room beneath the skylight.

Clarice Strozzi brought them glasses and filled them with wine, taking one for herself. She stretched her body wearily before taking a seat. "Posing for a perfectionist like Ser Gian is hard work, Dr. Servetus," she explained. "But then you are a physician and you know everything about the body."

"Not exactly," Antonio said. "I am a student of anatomy."

Gian laughed. "Now you have a chance to study the subject from the viewpoint of an artist, Tonio. Do you not think that Clarice has a lovely body?"

Antonio felt the color creeping back into his cheeks at the memory of his first view of her. "I have seen only one lovelier," he said honestly.

"*Dio mio!*" Gian exclaimed. "You are not very discreet, Tonio. Never tell a woman that she is anything but the most beautiful in the world."

Clarice Strozzi had been watching Antonio's eyes, and now she said: "I suspect that Dr. Servetus is, above all else, an honest person. Tell us about this loveliest of women, Ser Physician."

"She is not a woman, but a painting."

"The Botticelli!" Gian exclaimed.

"Yes."

"Tonio has fallen in love with the Botticelli Venus," Gian explained.

Clarice Strozzi smiled warmly. "I have seen the Botticelli and I don't blame you. But wasn't it stolen from Florence?"

"Someone left it in the priory at Padua, where I live," Antonio explained.

"Where he keeps it in his room to moon over, like a lovesick gallant," Gian jeered.

Antonio blushed, but Clarice Strozzi said, "As I remember her, she *is* the loveliest woman in the world."

"With that I disagree," Gian said. "Your women in miniature are very well as statues to be worshiped, but give me a real flesh-and-blood woman."

Antonio bent his head to place his glass on the table, and Clarice Strozzi cried out, "You have been hurt, Doctor. There is a lump on your head."

"*Vediamo!*" Gian put his fingers to the puffy place over Antonio's left temple and he flinched from the pain. "Some ruffian must have fetched you a clout, Tonio."

"It was a girl," Antonio admitted.

"A fight with a girl! *Che succede?*"

Antonio gave an account of the fracas. When he finished, the model said, ' What a heartless wench. How did she know that you were not seriously injured?"

"I could walk." Antonio found himself defending Lucia Bellarmi. "And the police were coming."

"But she could at least have taken you into the Palazzo," Clarice Strozzi insisted.

"By the way," Gian said, "the Palazzo Pesaro was out of your way in coming here, Tonio. What were you doing in that locality?"

Antonio explained about his meeting with Girolamo Bellarmi and his niece in Padua and his plan to seek out Bellarmi at the Palazzo Pesaro in Venice, before coming on to the Via delle Galeazze e Vasca.

"But you could have told him in Padua," Gian protested.

"I suppose I didn't because Madonna Bellarmi made me angry," Antonio admitted.

"I would have lured the wench into a dark corner and kissed her soundly," Gian said. "There is nothing like a good buss to turn a woman's heart to water. One minute she's fighting and the next she's putty in your hands."

"You must think me a dolt, Madonna Strozzi," Antonio said, "but my life has been quite different from Gian's."

"There are all kinds of people in the world, Ser Physician," she said softly. "And a place, I suspect, for all of them. I think you are a very important person and that Ser Gian and myself will someday be very small in comparison with you."

"What is this," Gian exclaimed, "a philosophical discussion or a party? Let us drink to Antonio Servetus, artist and physician, but never a monk."

They drank and talked for a while. Then Clarice Strozzi put down her glass and stood up. "I am quite rested now," she told Gian. "The light will not last much longer, if you want to finish the arm today."

"*Ella ha ragione.*" Gian took up his palette and moved to the easel. "We will continue." Antonio saw that he had about half completed an excellent study of Clarice Strozzi's superb body. Antonio got to his feet, feeling a little dizzy from the wine and the throbbing pain in his head. "I think I will lie down awhile," he told them.

"Tell Dimas to show you your room," Gian called from the easel. "I will be finished for the day in a little while."

Antonio bowed to the smiling girl on the model stand. "If the signorina will excuse me?"

"*Buon riposo,* Ser Antonio," she said. "I hope your head is better in the morning."

xiv

At first the dream was the same, the sandy shore, the leafy green tree under which he lay, and the soft lap-lap of water on the sand. And when the goddess stepped ashore from the shell boat, glorious in her beauty, her lips smiled to Antonio in tender welcome. Her fingers were cool and damp from the water when she gave him her hand, and the thrill that poured through his tense body was one of pure rapture.

As before, rough hands tore them apart and he was running, trying to overtake the satyrlike figure whose mocking features were the pale, vulpine countenance of Fra Felipe Santos. Stumbling, Antonio fell in the sand and clawed at it, spent and unable to rise.

Even Lucia Bellarmi was the same in every remembered detail, the scornful tones of her voice as she cried, "Naked! Naked! Shame! Shame!"

But as he scrambled as before to hide his naked body from her gaze, the figure of Lucia Bellarmi drew dim and in its place another, taller woman began to appear. For an instant his heart leaped, for it seemed that the goddess from the sea had somehow escaped from the satyr. Then, as the outlines of the figure took shape, he saw that it was Clarice Strozzi instead who beckoned to him. Eagerly, he struggled to rise from the sand, but a strange paralysis seemed to have claimed his body.

Hardly a yard separated him from her, yet he could not move the leaden weight of his body so much as an inch. A panic gripped him as he saw her outlines begin to dim, as a painting does when viewed in the dying light of the day's end, and he struggled even harder to move the inert lump of clay that was his body.

"Tonio! Tonio!" This was no soft cadence of a woman's voice, but the harsh tones of Gian Savarino. Antonio floated for a moment, suspended in the half-world that lies between sleeping and waking, reluctant to leave the promise of the dream. Then Gian's insistent voice and rough hand on his shoulder brought him awake.

Now he was conscious of the frantic hammering of his heart against his chest, the choking pressure in his throat that made breathing difficult, the rivulets of sweat drenching his body, and the steady pain that seemed to drive through his temples like a sharp metal spike.

"*Che fa lei?*" he mumbled as Gian's face took form hazily before his eyes. "What are you doing?"

"Wake up. You must have been riding the devil's mare."

Antonio sat up and rubbed his eyes. "I was dreaming."

"And what a dream. Who were you fighting?"

"I was trying to get to someone."

"I gathered as much," Gian said dryly. "You kept calling her name."

Antonio's cheeks flamed and Gian laughed at his embarrassment. "I've often wondered what monks dream of. Was she an houri or an angel?"

Antonio chose to change the subject. "I am hungry."

"You missed your dinner, but Dimas probably left something in the pantry."

Gian led him through the deserted studio to the small pantry, where they found a cold joint, some wine, and a hunk of bread.

"You didn't tell me the name of the lady of your dreams," Gian said as he poured the wine. "It sounded as if you were calling Lucretia, Lucia, or something."

"The niece of Girolamo Bellarmi is named Lucia."

"The one who clouted you over the head?"

"Yes."

"*Molto interessante,*" Gian said. "Tell me more about your dream."

Antonio described the two dreams. When he finished, the artist asked: "What do you make of them?"

"I took the dream as a warning that Fra Felipe would want to keep the painting, as you suggested."

"That could be part of it," Gian agreed. "But what about this Lucia?"

"I can't explain her," Antonio admitted.

"And Clarice?'

"Nor her either, can you?"

Gian grinned. "I am no seer, but the answer seems obvious to me."

"I suppose this will be another of your wild flights of fancy."

"No. I am sure this is the logical explanation," the artist protested.

"Let's have it, then."

"Well, it all goes back to what I've told you many times. You're a man, Tonio, and there is no use trying to make a monk out of yourself. Would you dream of lovely women holding you in their arms if you really wanted to be a celibate deep inside yourself?"

"Even the saints were tempted by demons," Antonio objected.

"The same demons that tempt all of us, only some have sense enough not to resist temptation."

"Those are the Devil's teachings," Antonio insisted stubbornly.

"Anyway," Gian said, "the dream is simple. You've fallen in love with the Venus of Botticelli. You have to admit that."

"I feel the very natural admiration of an artist for a beautiful painting," Antonio admitted.

"Now you are quibbling," Gian snorted. "Would an artist moon over a painting the way you do over that Venus?"

"But why the dream?"

"Wait a minute," Gian said suddenly. "You respect the writings of Paracelsus. I think he has something on that subject." He went to a row of bookcases that covered one wall of the studio. "*Vediamo; eccolo qui.*" He plucked a heavy, calf-bound volume from an upper shelf and brought it back to the table. "I think I know the passage," he said as he thumbed the pages. "Yes, here it is. Listen to what Paracelsus says about man:

"One should with diligence take note of the spirit of man, of which there are really two, that are inborn.

"For this is indeed true, that man is in the image of God and thereby has a Godly spirit in him; but on the other hand, man is also an animal, and as such has an animal spirit. These spirits are two antagonists, and yet the one must soften the other."

Gian closed the book with a snap. "There it is. The answer in a nutshell."

"But how does it apply to me?" Antonio asked.

"Simply this, one part of you, the artist or the idealist, loves the painting for itself. The other part wants the woman."

"I still say the dream is a temptation of the flesh, sent by Satan to try my soul."

"And I say the man in you feels a natural desire for a real woman, perhaps this Lucia Bellarmi."

"God forbid," Antonio interjected fervently.

"It could be true, though. Is she beautiful?"

Lucia Bellarmi's image was perfectly clear cut in his memory, even more so than it had been in his dream. Her small head, her golden hair, the proud carriage of her slender body. And yet he had never been particularly conscious of her beauty. Seeing her had been more like meeting again someone whose every feature was perfectly familiar and well remembered. It was this strange feeling which had struck him the first time he had seen her at the bedside of Fra Mario, and it was this now that he remembered most about her. "I don't know whether or not she is beautiful," he admitted.

"You don't know!" Gian cried in disgust. "Were you blind?"

Antonio tried to explain his feeling in regard to Lucia. "She seemed more like a sister or a cousin," he summed up, "and yet I know that I never saw her before."

"Obviously she resembles closely someone you do know quite well," Gian said.

"But who? I don't remember anyone."

"You will have to discover that for yourself. Anyway, I think my interpretation of the dream is correct."

"But you haven't explained Fra Felipe," Antonio objected.

"He is a symbol of that monkish conscience of yours. Remember it was he who took your goddess away just when you had her in your arms."

"And what about Clarice Strozzi?"

"This time I have you, mi Tonio," Gian said with great satisfaction. "Your carnal desire has now turned upon her."

"That is absurd," Antonio snapped angrily, getting up and going to the window. But deep inside him there was a gnawing doubt, for he remembered the wave of feeling which had gripped him that afternoon when he had stepped into the studio and saw her poised there on the model stand. That breathless feeling of anticipation, the excitement diffusing through his entire body, could have been nothing else, he realized now, but the surge of fleshly desire. The thought sent a wave of shame and guilt sweeping through him, for he realized that, had he completely thrown off the temptation when it first presented itself, it should never have persisted in his dream.

"You are right." He turned back to Gian. "Who is your confessor? I must go to him in the morning."

"My confessor would be bored by puny sins such as yours. Wait until you have something to confess. Clarice can teach you things even your monkish temptations never provided."

"But she is your——" He stopped.

Gian shook his head. "Clarice is a wonderful model, but a man can't paint very well a woman he's sleeping with. An artist should be abstract about his subjects. That is why you need a real woman instead of a painting, Tonio." He took the scraps and started scraping them into the waste jar. "I forgot to ask," he said, "why did you come to Venice today?"

"I want you to help me get my monograph published on the pulmonary circulation."

Gian stopped short and stared at him. "As your own work?"

"No. As a vindication of my brother."

"*Maria Sanctissima!* What brought you to that decision?"

"It is the right thing to do," Antonio said simply.

Gian stared at his friend, as if he were seeing him for the first time. Finally he said, a little sadly, "I suppose I should have known this would happen, Tonio, knowing you as I do. You realize fully what this means, don't you?"

"I have thought it all out and will take my chances."

Gian's shoulders drooped a little, as if in resignation. "We will visit Guidobaldo Aldini in the morning, then. He is the best printer in all of Italy."

"Let me go alone," Antonio protested. "There is no need for you to be involved in—in whatever happens."

"You need more help than my own puny efforts, I suspect," Gian said morosely. "But I'm with you to the bitter end." He laughed a little shamefacedly. "It's probably as near as I will ever get to real greatness, anyway."

xv

At Gian's insistence, the first job of the morning was to obtain clothes for Antonio which were more suitable than his old robe, mudstained from rolling in the gutter before the Palazzo Pesaro.

"But I must see Messer Bellarmi and tell him about the painting," Antonio protested.

"And meet the Madonna Lucia in that garb?" Gian raised his eyebrows. "You would offend the sensibilities of any fine young lady."

"All right," Antonio agreed, for he had no desire to appear before Messer Bellarmi in any but a good light. He had conceived a liking for the Florentine merchant, for all that his niece was a shrew.

"That's better. I asked Clarice to accompany us. You will have to become accustomed to the society of women if you are to remain in Venice long."

"But I——" Antonio protested.

"I have everything planned," Gian said. "The best way to avoid trouble, or some of it, when your monograph is printed, is to make friends among the highly placed here. Do as I tell you and you may come through with your skin . . . at least in Venice."

Antonio shrugged. As usual, Gian was right about matters such as this. He was dressed and waiting when Clarice Strozzi appeared, simply dressed, with a silken cloth of bright yellow tied over her dark red hair. Clothed, she was quite as lovely as she had been unclothed. The three of them took a gondola that was waiting on the quay. It was Antonio's pilot of yesterday.

"*Buon giorno, Mattei,*" Gian said as he helped Clarice into the gondola. "The shop of Arnolfo, the tailor, in the Via delle Garmoni."

The gondolier bobbed. "It is a pleasure to serve Your Magnificence . . . and Your Reverence," he added, bowing to Antonio.

Antonio got in beside Clarice, Gian lounging on the cushions at their feet. The sleek craft moved out into the canal, and shortly Antonio was completely lost in the maze of crisscrossing waterways, alive now with the morning traffic of the city. They drew in at the quay before the tailor's shop. Antonio had never seen such a magnificent establishment operated by a tailor. Everywhere there were bolts of rich and varicolored cloth, with apprentices scurrying about carrying partially completed garments. Messer Arnolfo, attired from head to foot in subdued black, approached with a smile and a greeting for Gian, who was evidently a favored customer.

"Your Signore," he caroled, bowing before them. "You have heard of my new cloth from the looms of France?"

"Not today, Ser Arnolfo," Gian said. "My friend, Dr. Servetus, is in need of clothing. You have perhaps something already tailored which would fit him?"

The tailor surveyed Antonio's dingy robe with obvious disdain. Then he snapped his fingers. "I have a short tunic of blue velvet, with hose and doublet to match. It was for a Spanish mercenary who was, unfortunately, slain in a duel."

"But I am of the long robe," Antonio protested. Physicians and apothecaries customarily wore the long robe of their profession, assumed originally to distinguish their guild, but now affected by almost all professional people and teachers. Many physicians had lately taken to the shorter robes worn by the merchants and bankers, however, as more befitting the increasing honor adhering to their profession.

Messer Arnolfo shrugged. "A thousand regrets, Doctor. I have no such in stock." His tone indicated that wearers of the long robe did not customarily buy their clothing in a shop such as his.

"Then you will have to settle for the mercenary's choice, Antonio," Gian said. "You certainly can't wear what you have on."

"Perhaps Messer Arnolfo has a short robe which would fit Dr. Servetus," Clarice suggested. "There are several on the table over there."

"With legs like his, it is a shame not to wear a short garment," Gian shrugged. "All right. Do you have a merchant's robe, Arnolfo?"

The tailor snapped his fingers. "Now that I think of it, we are making just the thing for a silversmith. He is much of a double with you, Doctor. This way."

Gian and Clarice took complete charge of outfitting Antonio, over his protests, and their selection was fitted and altered in the shop. When finally he stepped from the dressing closet, freshly attired from head to toe, Clarice clapped her hands in approval. "Bravo!" she cried. "He is handsome, Ser Gian."

The robe they chose came to Antonio's knees and was of rich dark velvet, edged in fur, and bound about his waist with a tasseled cord. The dark hose clinging to his muscular legs were laced up tightly to his waist. Gian had insisted upon placing a short gold chain about his neck, and a blue feather sat jauntily in the flat velvet cap upon his head.

"*Quanto importa il tutto?*" Antonio asked. Gian had given him no chance as yet to ask about prices, but he was sure that nothing cheap would be sold in an establishment such as this.

"It will go on my account," Gian said before Messer Arnolfo could name the sum. "You can pay me later, Tonio. We must go now."

"Now you look like a man of the world instead of a mangy monk," Gian continued as they were leaving the shop.

Clarice lifted her eyebrows. "A very handsome man, I would say." She took Antonio's arm. "Any woman would be proud to be seen with him."

From a nearby campanile bells pealed the hour of noon. Antonio realized with a start that his fittings at the tailor shop had taken all of two hours. "I must call on Messer Bellarmi," he said.

"Not now," Gian protested. "It is noon and we must dine." He felt the silken purse dangling at his belt. "But first I must pay a call to the banking house of my illustrious parent, or we shall be out of funds." He snapped his fingers to the waiting gondolier and tossed him a coin. "Mattei! You know the *trattoria* across the lagoon from my father's bank?"

"*Certamente, Magnifico.* I have taken you to it many times."

"Take the lady and gentleman there, then cross to the banking house and wait for me."

"*Sì, subito.*" Mattei steadied the gondola for them to step aboard.

"Order some refreshment, Clarice," Gian called as they moved away. "You know what I like. I will join you shortly."

"This is quite different from the university, is it not, Ser Antonio?" Clarice Strozzi asked.

"And even more different from the priory where I lived," Antonio admitted.

"Why did you live in a priory? Do all the professors live there?"

"I am planning to take the Holy Orders," Antonio explained. "They give me my lodging at the priory for looking after the library."

"You are poor, then?"

"I suppose so, although I never worried much about money before."

He had acquired quite a different feeling about material possessions since even so short a time as yesterday, he realized. A natural change, perhaps, engendered by the atmosphere of Venice, with its obvious wealth, commerce, and splendor compared to the quiet scholastic atmosphere at Padua.

"And what will you do, now that you have left the university?"

"But I haven't left. I shall go back at the end of the summer vacation."

"Meanwhile you are enjoying a well-earned holiday."

"I'm enjoying it," he admitted, "but it isn't a holiday. I am writing a thesis, and Gian is arranging for it to be published." He told her of his discovery. When he finished she said, "You're determined to clear your brother's name, then?"

"Would you have me do otherwise?"

Her eyes looked into his for a long moment, candidly, appraisingly, then she smiled. "No," she said. "You wouldn't be you if you were any different. But I don't think you'll be going back to the cloister."

Startled, he asked, "Why?"

"I have a feeling about things sometimes. Intuition, perhaps, but I am sure you were meant for something better than telling beads and saying Mass."

A month ago, Antonio realized, he would have been aghast at the implication that anything the world had to offer could mean more than the service of God through the established Church. And yet he felt no censure now and knew that in her heart she meant only good toward him.

"Gian says the same thing," he admitted. "But I haven't come to any decision."

"Fate makes decisions for us," she said, putting her hand over his on the cushioned seat, "and changes our point of view. I dare say you thought me a naked hussy when you first saw me yesterday."

"You couldn't be that," he protested quickly.

"Some would say so," she insisted, smiling.

"But they would be wrong. A body as beautiful as yours was meant for——" He stopped and blushed beet red with confusion.

Her hand tightened on his and she said softly, "I know what you mean, Ser Antonio." And then she laughed. "But think how far you have come from the cloister already."

The gondola bumped gently against the stone quay in front of a busy restaurant. The tables extended practically to the water's edge, and a throng of fashionably dressed people were taking refreshment in the warm Venetian sunshine. When they entered, the major-domo bowed and greeted Clarice by name. He gave Antonio a quick glance that took in the rich material of his robe, the soft Cordovan leather of his shoes, and the short but heavy gold chain.

"A table for three close to the water, Messer Benedetto," Clarice said. "Ser Gian Savarino is joining us soon."

They were shown to a table in the shade of a potted olive tree, and Clarice gave the order, saving Antonio the embarrassment of showing his ignorance of fashionable menus. She selected a mild cheese, served with wafers, a salad of fresh fruits with the dressing for which Messer Benedetto was famous, tiny sweet onions pickled in brine and vinegar, a pastry, and chilled white wine. "Gian loves these," Clarice explained. "I think you will too."

"It *is* different from the fare of the lay brothers at the priory," Antonio admitted.

"Tell me more about the Botticelli," she commanded while they waited to be served.

Halting and stumbling over words at first, Antonio began to describe the painting. But hardly had he started when his enthusiasm took hold of his tongue. He stopped, minutes later, and Clarice said, "You must love her very much."

"Who?"

"The Venus. You speak of her as if she were a real woman."

"She is real," he admitted. "At least to me. I—I can't explain just how, though."

"I think I know. And someday I hope you find her in real life."

"But that is impossible. The picture was painted sixty years ago, at least."

"That doesn't mean you'll never find another like her," Clarice said earnestly. "If we look, we can always find people so like someone we know that they seem to be identical." She laughed gaily. "Who knows? Someday in your travels you may see a woman and the thought will come to you, 'There goes Clarice Strozzi!' But if you run after her you will find that it was only something about her that reminded you of me."

"She will be very lovely, then. I'm sure of that," Antonio said.

"Why, Antonio," she cried, "what a lovely compliment!"

Antonio blushed and looked about him to see if anyone had heard. Several tables away he saw a man regarding them with a fixed and, he thought, hostile stare. His face was very dark, either from a naturally swarthy complexion or from long exposure to the sun, his features sharp, his eyebrows very bushy, and his eyes dark and extraordinarily intense in their gaze. In spite of the man's somber dress there was something bizarre about him, an inexplicable difference from other men in the restaurant.

Antonio drew his gaze away from the stranger and back to Clarice. He realized that she, too, had seen the man, for some of the color had drained from her cheeks, as though a sudden pall had been drawn over her gaiety. Her teeth were pressed into her lower lip until it blanched white from the pressure, then she bowed and smiled.

"Do you know that man?" Antonio asked.

"He is Lodovici Agnolo, a—a magician," she said. "When I am not modeling, I often work as his assistant."

Antonio turned to look at Agnolo again and, with a start of surprise, found the magician standing beside him, although he had heard no sound of footsteps. He started to rise from the table, but the big man placed a hand on his shoulder, fixing him in his chair.

"Don't get up, Dr. Servetus," the magician's voice boomed out with an amazing resonance.

"Do you know me?" Antonio stammered.

Agnolo smiled, showing strong, even teeth which were so large that Antonio was reminded of the tusks of the boar he had dissected to prove his theory of the pulmonary circulation. "Of course," he said. "I attended several of your anatomy demonstrations in Padua. Someday we must have a long talk, Doctor. I am very much interested in medicine."

"You are not a physician, then?"

Agnolo chuckled, as if at some joke that only he understood. "Not exactly a physician, although I am interested in life . . . and death. My work lies in the study of the stars. They have much to tell us about disease, you know."

"I am sure they do," Antonio agreed politely. "But I am an anatomist and not a practitioner of physic by choice. I know very little of astrology."

"Perhaps we may be mutually helpful to each other," Agnolo sug-

gested. He turned to Clarice, and Antonio saw that she was looking at
the magician with that strange, fixed stare he had surprised in her eyes
a few moments before. "We have work to do this evening, Madonna,"
Agnolo said in a low voice. "You understand?"

She nodded mechanically, with a strange, puppetlike character to
her movements. "Yes, I understand," she said almost in a whisper.

"*A rivederci,* Doctor," Agnolo boomed. "It has been an honor to
meet you."

Antonio bowed, but his eyes were on Clarice Strozzi, fascinated by
that strange quality in her gaze as she followed Agnolo's tall form in
its passage between the tables. Then she seemed suddenly to return to
the present, blinked once or twice and smiled. "What were you saying?"
she asked.

"Nothing. What did Messer Agnolo mean about this evening?"

"I told you that I work sometimes as an assistant to Lodovici. He is
giving a demonstration of magic tonight and will need me to help him."

"What are they like, these demonstrations?" Antonio's scientific
curiosity was aroused by this unfamiliar activity.

"Why, I hardly know. But they are nothing you would be interested
in." She leaned closer, her voice oddly intent. "Believe me, it is nothing
you should be interested in."

A familiar voice hailed them from a gondola just touching the quay
and Gian Savarino joined them. The purse hanging from his belt was
noticeably fatter.

"*Eccolo!* My favorite food." He pulled out a chair and sat down.
"But you two have eaten nothing."

"We were talking," Antonio said, "and didn't notice that the food
had arrived."

Gian's eyes gleamed. "Quite a cavalier already, aren't you, Tonio?"

Antonio blushed. "Besides," he said, "Messer Agnolo stopped for a
chat."

"Lodovici? *Corpo di Cristo!*" Gian swore and shot a quick glance at
Clarice Strozzi. "What did he say?"

"We talked of astrology," Antonio explained. "He is also interested in
anatomy."

"*Per Bacco!*" Clarice shook her head, and Gian immediately changed
the subject. "Well, I replenished my purse at the family coffers. We
should dine well tonight, Tonio."

But in spite of Gian's jovial spirits something seemed to have happened to Clarice Strozzi. There was no obvious change, but an intangible pall seemed to have been thrown upon her spirits and she was no longer the frank and charming companion she had been. Gian chattered like a magpie as usual, and Antonio, finding that he was hungry, attacked his food. When his plate was empty he sat back in his chair and watched the colorful scene on the lagoon as brightly colored gondolas darted here and there upon the dark, greenish-tinted water.

Suddenly Antonio's eyes focused on a gondola in the lagoon. It was a large craft, with bags of goods and luggage piled high. Two people were sitting on the cushioned seat, a man and a girl, and with a start he realized that it was Lucia Bellarmi and her uncle.

At that moment Gian saw them, too, and exclaimed, *"Dio mio!* What a little beauty!"

"Where?" Clarice Strozzi asked.

"There. In the gondola with the older man." Gian's voice was excited and must have carried to the slowly moving craft, for Antonio saw Lucia turn her head. There was an instant of startled recognition in her gaze as she passed, hardly a dozen yards away from them as they sat at the table close to the water's edge. Messer Girolamo recognized Antonio, too, and smiled, but the girl's lips tightened, her cheeks turned pink, and she jerked her head around to stare fixedly in another direction.

"She recognized somebody here," Gian said, looking around him. "I wonder who it is." Then his eyes returned to Antonio and he started. "You," he cried. "You know her, Antonio?"

"Yes. I do."

"Who is she? I never saw such lovely hair."

"That was Lucia Bellarmi," Antonio said. "With her uncle."

Gian's jaw wagged comically with amazement as he tried to speak. "B-but you said she wasn't beautiful, Tonio."

"I said I didn't realize whether she was or not."

"You *couldn't* be that stupid." Gian turned to Clarice. "You saw her. Isn't she the loveliest thing you ever saw?"

"She is very beautiful," Clarice admitted with a smile. "But Antonio doesn't seem to get along very well with her."

Gian threw up his hands. "Of all the stupid oafs." His eyes lit up suddenly. "Didn't you say you were going to see her uncle today, Tonio?"

"Yes. To tell him about the painting before he leaves——But wasn't that a *batello* they were in?"

"Yes!" Gian cried. "And they must be on their way to the post chaises to leave now."

Antonio got to his feet. "We must catch them, then, so I can tell Messer Bellarmi about the painting."

Gian opened his purse and threw several coins on the table. "Come on, Clarice," he said.

She shook her head. "Lodovici wants me to work tonight, so I will go home and rest for a while. You two go on without me."

But it was minutes before they could hail an empty gondola passing the *trattoria*. When they did they leaped aboard. "Palazzo Pesaro," Gian told the gondolier.

"They were probably leaving Venice now," Antonio objected. "Shouldn't we go to the post chaises?"

"There are a dozen places they could have gone to get the chaises," Gian explained. "Our only chance is that they were going by the Palazzo Pesaro."

But their race was in vain. At the Palazzo they learned that Messer Bellarmi and his niece had departed just that afternoon for Florence, leaving by *batello* and post chaise.

"I can write him in Florence and tell him the painting is in Padua," Antonio said as they were on their way back to the studio.

"But I missed meeting a beautiful girl," Gian complained.

"And perhaps getting your head broken."

"You know nothing of women, Tonio," Gian bragged. "In my hands she would be as clay."

After a while Antonio asked, "What is the real relationship between Clarice Strozzi and Lodovici, Gian?"

"She is his assistant. She told you that."

"What else?"

Gian shrugged. "His mistress too, I suspect."

Strangely enough, Antonio felt no shock or censure toward Clarice. When he had noticed Clarice's start of recognition, he had known there was some sort of a deep bond between her and Agnolo. But somehow, as little as he knew about physical passion, he didn't think it was limited to that. "That isn't all there is between them, is it?"

Gian stared at him. "Sometimes you amaze me, Tonio. So you sensed it too?"

"Yes. But what is it?"

"I've often wondered, but I don't know. He seems to have some sort of a power over her. When I ask her she tells me nothing, except to admit that she has been his mistress for several years." Gian looked at Antonio sharply. "You're not falling in love with her, are you?"

"No," Antonio said. "I like her, very much. But I'm not in love with her. I'm quite certain of that."

xvi

The post chaise moved smartly along the road, carrying Messer Bellarmi and his niece on the first lap of their long journey to Florence. "I am glad to be going home," he told her as he settled comfortably against the cushions. "By the way, wasn't that the physician, Messer Servetus, I saw dining with a beautiful lady in that *trattoria* off the lagoon?"

Lucia sniffed. "She was old." But he saw the warm color surge into her cheeks.

"All of twenty-five, I'd say," Messer Bellarmi agreed dryly. "I was very much impressed with that young man, Lucia. If there had been more time, I would have consulted him about myself."

"You have had the best physicians in Florence," she reminded him.

"Yes, but this man seemed to know what he was about."

"He is stupid," Lucia stated flatly.

Messer Bellarmi shrugged. He knew his niece very well and was tremendously fond of her. But sometimes she could be irritatingly positive in her opinions. "I suppose we'll never find the Botticelli Venus now," he said.

Lucia smiled, a secret little smile for herself alone. "I think we will find it."

Her uncle stared at her. "What makes you say that?"

"Because I'm quite certain it is in Padua."

"Padua," he echoed. "Why?"

"Dr. Servetus has seen it."

"Did he tell you that?"

"Not in so many words," Lucia admitted, still with that knowing smile.

"Stop being cryptic, Lucia," her uncle commanded. "Is this another example of what you call intuition?"

She shook her head. "Do you remember how he stared at me when we first met at Uncle Mario's bedside?"

"Yes," Messer Girolamo admitted. "But you are an uncommonly pretty girl, Lucia."

"It wasn't simply that. He explained to me later that he had stared because everything about me seemed so familiar to him, as if he had known me all his life."

"Then he must have known intimately someone very much like you." He stopped and a light of understanding began to dawn in his eyes. "Simonetta?" he asked.

"Of course," Lucia said complacently. "I knew the minute he told me how familiar I seemed to him that he had been studying the Botticelli Venus very closely."

"But how could he know the connection?"

"He doesn't," Lucia said. "He plans to be a monk and doesn't get out into the world very much. He may have heard the story of how the Botticelli Venus was painted from Simonetta Vespucci, the sister of my grandfather, Amerigo, but the connection obviously hasn't come to him."

Her uncle shook his head as if he were unable to believe what he was hearing. "All of Florence knows, Lucia, that you are the living image of Simonetta and that the Botticelli Venus is also her image. It is like a proposition out of Euclid."

"Or a story by a minstrel."

"And now it leads us in Venice and Padua to the lost Botticelli painting." He sat up suddenly. "Driver," he shouted to the coachman, "turn around. We're going back."

"What are you doing, Uncle?" Lucia cried.

"We must go back to Venice and find the physician and the Botticelli."

The coach had stopped. Lucia leaned out the window and called to the coachman sitting almost over her head. "Wait a little, driver. Do not turn yet."

"What is the meaning of this, Lucia?" her uncle said sternly. "You are going too far."

"I don't want to go back to Venice," Lucia explained.

"But the picture——"

"It belongs to me, doesn't it?"

"Yes, of course," he admitted. "Your father willed it to you because of your amazing resemblance to Simonetta Vespucci."

"Then I say let it stay in Padua . . . for a while, at least."

Messer Girolamo threw up his hands. "In the name of God! Are we to lose a valuable painting because of a girlish whim? Lucia, I refuse to let you——"

"Wait, Uncle," Lucia urged. "Let me explain. Dr. Servetus knows the Botticelli belongs to us; he heard you tell that horrible Fra Felipe Santos about it."

"At least we agree about Santos," her uncle said dryly.

"The physician also has a stern conscience," Lucia continued, "for he had planned to become a monk."

"Had?"

"I don't think he will . . . now."

Light was dawning in the merchant's brain. "I think I have it now," he said. "You think that Messer Servetus could get his hands on the painting if he really wanted to."

"I do," Lucia said. "He must have been very familiar with it to be so struck by the resemblance."

"But without actually realizing that you and the Venus are identical."

"He will, in time," she stated. "Men are very stupid about such things."

"Yes, I know. You said he was stupid. Nevertheless, because he has a conscience, you think he will shortly appear in Florence with the painting."

"That is not the whole reason," Lucia said demurely.

"I didn't think that it was." Messer Bellarmi stared at his niece with utter admiration. He leaned over and kissed her cheek. "Lucia, I salute an intelligence far greater than mine."

"Any woman would do the same, Uncle," Lucia said modestly.

"This whole thing is some sort of a test, I take it?" he asked.

"You might call it that," Lucia agreed.

Messer Girolamo leaned out and called to the driver. "We have changed our minds. Drive on, please, we will not be going back."

Leaning back in his seat once more, he began to chuckle. Soon he could not contain himself and began to laugh, slapping himself on the sides, while the tears of mirth ran down his cheeks. Lucia at first sat primly, staring ahead, but soon she too began to chuckle and then to laugh uproariously with her uncle.

On the high seat of the carriage the driver shrugged his shoulders and slapped the horses with the reins. He had heard that Florentines were crazy; now he was certain of it. First they couldn't make up their minds about where they wanted to go. Now they were laughing like mad at nothing . . . nothing at all.

Book Two

THE BLACK MASS

With a crayon held betweeen smudged fingers, Antonio stroked the white surface of the parchment before him, stopping every now and then to glance at the motionless form of Clarice Strozzi, posed on the model stand. He found the curving planes of her body far easier to capture than during those agonizing days at the priory when he had sought vainly for the touch which would reproduce the Botticelli Venus. Now his fingers were surer, more skilled from long hours of practice in sketching. He laid down his crayon, and Clarice smiled from her place on the stand. Across the studio, Gian was absorbed in the delicate shadows of the armpit, shading in the skin tones with meticulous thoroughness. Whatever he might be in other fields, Gian was a passionate craftsman in his artistic productions. He would spend hours, intent upon reproducing every detail of life on the still, flat surface of the canvas, forgetting the model until she reminded him of her weariness.

Looking back upon the past month, Antonio thought that he had come a long way from Padua and the cloister. The manuscript of his study of the pulmonary circulation was finished and had been at the printer's shop for two weeks. Today the first sheets of the final product would be coming from the press of Guidobaldo Aldini, famed printer of Venice. Messer Aldini had been somewhat reluctant to print what was fundamentally a work of heresy, but Gian's well-filled purse had finally overcome his scruples, plus Antonio's guarantee that he would not be held responsible for the content of the printing.

Gian gave a grunt of satisfaction with his efforts and laid down his brush. "You may rest, Clarice," he said. "This part is finished." He wiped his hands on a paint-stained cloth and came to look over Antonio's shoulder. *"Benissimo!"* he said approvingly. "You are getting better every day, Tonio."

"I shall never be an artist, though," Tonio said. "Watching you work has shown me that."

"But you have talent."

"For sketching. Perhaps enough to copy anatomical dissections, but no more."

Clarice Strozzi put on her robe and came over to the easel. "Why should you want anything else?" she asked. "After all, you are a great anatomist and physician, Tonio. When your *consilium* is printed you will be very famous."

"Dimas!" Gian shouted. "Bring food and wine. We have worked enough for the morning."

Antonio got up from the stool before the easel and went to stand before the empty fireplace. "I think I shall return to Padua when the painting is finished," he said.

"Still trying to run away from the world?" Gian asked bluntly.

"I have asked myself that," he admitted, "and I don't know the answer. It is what I have known for so long that nothing else seems more desirable."

"Don't be a fool," Gian snapped. "How do you know that? You haven't really tried anything else."

"I think I understand how he feels," Clarice said. "Antonio lives in a world of the mind while you live in a world of the body."

"What is wrong with the body?" Gian demanded. "You are not ashamed of yours, are you?"

"No. But then we are different from Antonio."

"It isn't good for a man to live wholly in one world," Gian argued. "I read that passage from Paracelsus to you once, Tonio. Look at Avicenna, Vesalius, Cardenas, they were men of the world as well as of the lecture halls. You will never be a great physician until you know people as they really are."

"But I don't want to be a physician, in the sense of treating disease," Antonio protested. "There is still much to be learned from the human body."

"But you could learn while treating the sick at the same time," Gian argued. "After all, Vesalius treated the sick. He became court physician in Madrid."

"I've often wondered if he found satisfaction in such work."

"Of course he did. He's rich, famous, and respected. We know that."

"But he only took it up when publication of his *Fabrica* caused such a storm."

"True." Gian smiled. "And I suspect that you will be much in the same boat, once your theory of pulmonary circulation is printed."

"No one would cause trouble for me in Padua," Antonio protested.

"The clergy hounded Vesalius, didn't they?" Gian pointed out. "And he was professor of anatomy. Do you think they would treat a mere teacher, for all your promise, any better?"

"What would you have me do?" Antonio asked.

"You must be seen in Venice and become acquainted with important people, people who can turn their influence toward propagating your doctrine and defending you when you are criticized."

Antonio had his doubts. The whole idea was foreign to anything he had already done. He turned to Clarice Strozzi. In the few weeks that he had known the tall, calm girl he had come to feel a sort of kinship with her, a sense of confidence and respect for her opinions, as well as real affection for her. "What do you think?" he asked.

"This time I think Gian is right," she said. "After all, if it will help spread the truth of your brother's discovery, that is what you want most."

"See!" Gian cried in triumph. "We are two against one."

Antonio smiled. "I bow to your combined judgments, then."

Dimas came in bringing food and they attacked it with healthy appetites. As they were finishing, Dimas announced, "An apprentice from the print shop with a message."

"Show him in," Gian ordered. "Perhaps your *consilium* is ready, Antonio."

The small apprentice had sharp eyes that darted around the studio, taking in the two men and the casual way that Clarice Strozzi was dressed. Later, in the print shop, the tale of this adventure would be magnified out of all proportion to reality.

"What is it you wish, boy?" Gian asked.

"I have a message for Dr. Antonio Servetus," the boy chirped. "Which of you is he?"

"I am Dr. Servetus," Antonio said.

"Messer Guidobaldo Aldini begs that you join him in his establishment at your convenience, Doctor. The first sheets of your book are ready to be taken from the press."

"*Benissimo.*" Gian tossed the boy a coin. He caught it dexterously, put it between his teeth, and clutched it in an ink-stained fist in one continuous movement while a satisfied smile appeared on his wizened countenance. "Tell Ser Guidobaldo that we will wait upon him at once," Gian instructed the apprentice.

When the boy was gone, Gian seized the wine bottle and filled three glasses. "To truth," he said. "May it always confound its enemies."

ii

The acrid smell of ink greeted their nostrils as Antonio and Gian opened the door of the famous printing shop of Guidobaldo Aldini. The proprietor himself hurried forward to meet them, smiling his satisfaction. Barely sixty-five years old, the Aldini press was already known throughout Europe for its products. Beginning with *Erotemata,* a succession of important works had issued from the low building near the center of Venice. The *De Aetna* of Pietro Bembo, who later became a cardinal, a medical work, *De Epidemia,* the famous medieval tract, *Hypnerotomachia Poliphilli,* and many others were tribute to the skill of Aldini with the new movable type.

"Ah, Doctor," Aldini cried. "The most beautiful work in the history of the Press Aldini."

"You have seen it already?" Gian asked.

"The type I have seen. With such a setting, a beautiful book is a certainty." He clapped his hands. "Come. We will take it from the press now."

Followed by Antonio, Gian, and a queue of printers, pressmen, and apprentices, Messer Aldini led the way to the great press. It stood higher than a man's head, the tall wooden screw with its spiraled threads visible between the four corner supports. At the bottom of the screw was the press itself, with the type face locked in place, screwed tightly against the heavy parchment upon which the page would be printed. Since the thesis was actually very short, little more than twenty-five of the large folio pages, Antonio had chosen to issue it, as Vesalius has his shorter writings, in the form of a *consilium,* an open letter setting forth what he had discovered.

Messer Aldini directed a pressman who inserted a wooden lever in the top of the screw and began to turn it in reverse, releasing the pressure which had transferred the outlines of the inked type to the parchment. When the press was free, he stepped forward and gently separated the sheet of parchment from the type frame, being careful not to smear the freshly inked surface. Antonio's heart pounded as he saw the first page of the publication which would announce his dramatic discovery to the world.

"Bravo!" Messer Aldini cried, in an ecstasy of appreciation of his own work. "It is perfect, Doctor, just as I said it would be."

The dark letters were sharply outlined on the parchment in Latin. Antonio had chosen as a title for the thesis: *De Motu Sanguinem Pulmonale.*

"The motion of the pulmonary blood," or "the circulation of the lungs." His first printed work! Antonio felt a surge of pride as his eyes continued down the title page:

"Anatomia veni et arteriae pulmonale cum descriptio motu sanguinem pulmonale." (Anatomy of the pulmonary veins and arteries with a description of the circulation of the blood through the lungs.)

It was all there on the title page, just as he had written it: "An account of the anatomy of the lungs and the circulation of the blood through them at first discovered by Michael Servetus and now proved through experiments conducted by Antonio Servetus, his brother, teacher of anatomy in the School of Medicine in the University of Padua." The rest contained the date, the fact that it was printed by the House of Aldini, with the permission of the Doge and the Venetian Senate.

"I still think you could have left off that statement about your brother," Gian said.

"It is a vindication of his work."

"But putting it on the title page is asking for trouble."

Messer Aldini looked his alarm. "Remember, you promised to hold me inviolate in connection with the printing, Doctor."

"I shall take the blame," Antonio said quietly. "It is an excellent piece of work, messire. When may I expect the entire printing?"

"Within a few days," Messer Aldini promised.

"Then the trouble begins," Gian said morosely. "I don't know why I ever got mixed up in this."

"You aren't. Your name does not appear on it."

"We said we would be in this together, didn't we?"

"I am still taking any blame there is," Antonio insisted doggedly. "I shall send one of the first copies to Fra Felipe Santos."

"Why put your head in a noose?" Gian demanded. "He will hear of it soon enough."

"Fra Felipe is a servant of God, Gian. He must realize when he reads the *consilium* that it is truth. How could he do otherwise?"

Gian shrugged his shoulders hopelessly. "I should let you go on and become a priest, Tonio. God knows you are pigheaded enough for it."

It was less than a week before repercussions from the appearance of *De Motu Sanguinem Pulmonale* began to be felt. Word went out from the print shop through the pressmen and apprentices about the nature of the document now emerging from the presses. Messer Aldini, too, as was the custom, dispatched unbound sheets to various other printers to impress them with the quality and importance of his products. By the time the actual *consilium* was printed and bound, applications were coming in from all parts of Venice and Padua for copies. For the most part they were from physicians and scientists, interested in such a revolutionary work further refuting the tenets of Galen which church edicts had shaped into an ironbound code, restricting further scientific progress until the outmoded concepts were broken. Others were from churchmen, some enlightened enough to appreciate the importance of such a discovery to medicine, others seeking only evidence of the schism which was rapidly being driven between scientists and the Church.

When the first copy was delivered into Antonio's hands he felt a great resurgence of pride in his accomplishment. Already he was a sought-after person, and scientists of note and noble patrons of the sciences had invited him to visit them. He was careful to send copies of the *consilium* to the quarters where Gian indicated that they would exert the most important influence, to the Doge, of course, and to the greater nobles of the Venetian Republic. The copy to Fra Felipe Santos was duly dispatched by a special messenger with a note recommending it to the prior.

A week afterward Antonio journeyed to Padua personally to place a copy in the hands of Professor Fallopius. As he was waiting for the carriage to Padua, a small, chubby man in the robe of an apothecary or physician bustled into the coach just ahead of him and made a place beside his own plump form. *"Eccolo!"* he said. "We were just in time, Doctor."

"You know me?" Antonio asked politely.

"Capisco. My name is Battista Porzia. I have seen you many times in Padua, and once you attended a friend of mine." He named a professor whom Antonio had treated during a particularly fiery attack of erysipelas.

Antonio acknowledged the introduction graciously. The small man's manner was very pleasant.

"Are you returning to the university now, Doctor?" Messer Porzia asked.

"Just for the day. I am spending the summer in Venice."

"Ah, Venice!" A beatific smile spread over the chubby features. "What a lovely city. It is a city for young men."

"I am making some special studies there," Antonio said a little stiffly, at the implication that Venice was only for those engaged in frivolous pursuits.

"So I have heard," Messer Porzia said. "It is said all over Venice that you have announced a great medical discovery to the world."

Antonio smiled. He still could hardly believe the rapidity with which knowledge of his *consilium* had spread through the city. If even the apothecaries knew of it, the world must share their knowledge before long. "It is just an anatomical finding," he protested. "In fact, it was made earlier by my brother, Michael Servetus."

Messer Porzia wagged his head. "I had the good fortune to read some of your brother's writings, messire. He was a great man."

Antonio could not help warming to the pudgy man's friendly interest and unbending a little from his habitual reserve with strangers. "It is kind of you to say so."

"I was not familiar with his work on the circulation of the lungs," Porzia continued. "But his theological doctrines are sound, very sound." He looked around the coach and lowered his voice. "In fact, I wish you would publish some of those particular writings. Do you have any plans for doing so?"

Antonio frowned. He had never read the theological doctrines which had gotten Michael into trouble because of the prohibitions of his father following the execution. It had been only by accident, while pursuing his medical studies, that he had discovered the passage dealing with the pulmonary circulation. But since he had found his brother correct in one particular, it had occurred to him that he might be correct in others. The little man seemed to have a surprising knowledge of what he might be interested to hear.

"I know little of that side of my brother's life," Antonio admitted. "He was almost never at home."

"*Che peccato!*" Messer Porzia sighed. "I did not know him personally, but a priest in his confidence, Fra Jacques Charmier, was a friend of mine."

"I knew of Father Charmier," Antonio admitted. "I never met him, but I understand that he and my brother were very close."

"As master and disciple. It was he who informed me that the statute under which your brother was executed was not legal."

Antonio stared at the small man. How had he known this?

It intimated that there might have been some truth to Michael's theological doctrines, perhaps as much as Antonio had himself proved there was to his medical ones. "Could you tell me more?" he asked.

"The Code of Justinian was set aside by the Swiss government many years before," Messer Porzia informed him in a whisper. "Of course it is still recognized by Rome, and it was under this statute that he was condemned by the papal courts."

The carriage had filled and begun to move. Antonio saw that several of the passengers were eying them curiously and undoubtedly listening to the conversation. "Perhaps we could continue this conversation at some other time, messire," he suggested.

"*Certamente,*" the plump man agreed. "I could wait upon you at your residence, since I come to Venice often to purchase drugs for my apothecary shop."

"I am at the house of Messer Gian Savarino in the Via delle Galeazze e Vasca."

"I know the region," Messer Porzia said. "I will make it a point to call upon you, perhaps when I have had the opportunity to read your famous *consilium.*"

The conversation turned to a discussion of drugs, of which Messer Porzia, for an apothecary, seemed to have a surprising ignorance. He was much more versed in matters of theology.

iii

Fallopius read the title page and stroked his beard thoughtfully. Then he turned the pages and read through the entire volume without putting the book down. Every now and then he clucked approvingly and wagged his beard. When he had finished, Antonio asked, "What do you think of it, sir?"

"Would that I had the courage to do something like this, my son."

"Then you agree?"

"Everyone must agree. Your demonstration is so clear, your logic and reasoning so balanced, that no other conclusion can be drawn. You have undoubtedly discovered the truth of the pulmonary circulation."

Antonio shook his head. "I merely repeated the work of my brother. The discovery is his."

Fallopius nodded thoughtfully. "I knew your brother Michael. He was very much like you, my son, passionately devoted to the truth and absolutely uncompromising about it."

"Is there any other way to be?"

"Perhaps not, for you and those like you. But had your brother limited his thinking to anatomy and medicine, this discovery might have been made public many years ago. There lies the danger, my son. One can be uncompromising about the sciences, for after all, scientific discovery is only finding out nature's immutable laws. But keep on this track. Don't make the mistake your brother did and turn the light of logic upon things we may not even be supposed to understand."

"Such as a theological dogma."

"Yes. I should hate to see you stumble upon the same obstacle as your brother."

"I have no quarrel with the Church," Antonio assured him.

"One thing worries me," Fallopius said. "Will they have any quarrel with you?"

"Because I found truth in the writings of one they name heretic?"

"Yes."

"But they were wrong," Antonio protested. "It is truth."

"I know," Fallopius agreed. "A scientist can admit his wrong when he makes a mistake, and try another tack. Theology has no such elasticity. Everywhere except here in Venice they are killing men whose sole offense is that of using the minds that God gave them."

"Do you think my position here in the university will be at stake?" Antonio asked.

Fallopius rubbed his chin. "Attempts will undoubtedly be made to unseat you. But you can count on my support, and they will probably fail." He held out his hand. *"Dio lo volesse. Addio."*

As Antonio emerged from the university, ducking from force of habit at the low doorway, he saw a lay brother from the priory waiting beside the entrance.

"Buon giorno, Frater Antonio," the brother said. "His Reverence, Fra Felipe Santos, begs that you will visit him before returning to Venice."

Surprised, Antonio asked: "How did His Reverence know that I was in the city?"

The messenger shrugged. "I don't know, messire. I was only sent to give you the message."

"Very well, then," Antonio said. He might as well meet Santos and get it over with. "I shall join His Reverence within an hour."

The way led across the very bridge spanning the Bacchiglione upon which Antonio and Professor Fallopius had stood not so long ago. He stopped a moment to look down at the dark and dingy stream winding between its grass-grown banks. There was the same small spring of which Fallopius had spoken and, as before, its stream made a small circle of clear water as it vainly strove to influence the main course of the Bacchiglione, only to be swallowed up without a trace.

His own discovery, Antonio thought, was a fresh new stream added to the troubled current of human knowledge. Would it be able to leave its imprint upon the pages of science, or would it, too, be swallowed up by dark currents of intrigue, ignorance, and stupidity?

A cloud crept before the face of the sun, and as the warming rays were shut away there was a slight chill in the air. Antonio repressed a shiver that was not entirely from cold, but rather a deeply sensed warning of something ahead, something which, he understood vaguely, boded him no particular good. Then the sun emerged once more, warming both his body and his spirit, and he turned his steps toward the priory.

iv

Fra Felipe Santos was surprisingly affable. When Antonio had kissed the hem of his robe, he motioned him to a seat beside his own in the audience room.

"I asked you to come to the priory for a certain reason, Doctor," he said.

Antonio waited for a more explicit statement.

"I have read your *consilium* with a great deal of interest," the prior continued. "It follows rather closely the lines of our conversation regarding poor Fra Mario."

"The idea came to me that night," Antonio admitted.

"So I judged. In a way, then, I feel responsible for your doctrine."

"You approve of it, then?" Antonio asked eagerly.

"Approve?" He raised his eyebrows. "Of course not. The laws of the Church regarding heresy are very explicit."

"But this is truth."

"I said the laws are explicit, as well as the punishments prescribed for those who transgress. Remember that, my son. Remember it well."

Antonio's spirits began to fall. But why Fra Felipe's surprising affability in the face of his statement identifying the publication of the *consilium* as heresy?

"Nevertheless," the prior said, "we are inclined to overlook the indiscretions of those whose contributions to the glory of the Church are sufficiently great."

"But I have nothing," Antonio protested, "unless you think my work in anatomy——"

"The Church does not exactly encourage the dissection of the human body," Fra Felipe said dryly.

"What then——" Antonio began, and stopped. The painting! Fra Felipe had discovered it, of course. Suddenly the whole thing was clear, the prior's affability, his summons here today . . . As Gian had predicted, Fra Felipe was not planning to return the painting to its rightful owners. But did Santos realize, Antonio wondered, that he knew Messer Girolamo Bellarmi and his niece were the rightful owners?

"When I found a locked door in the priory," Fra Felipe's voice intruded upon Antonio's thoughts, "I ordered it to be opened. Naturally

I was very much surprised to find that you were hiding something. Where did you find the canvas?"

"In a bundle left here by someone months ago. It was in the store-room."

Fra Felipe looked away, and when he spoke his voice was very casual. "Of course it may not be of much value, a copy, perhaps, of some old master."

"It is the original of the Botticelli Venus," Antonio stated bluntly. "As such, it is invaluable."

"Are you certain of this?" The prior leaned forward, intent upon his answer.

"I showed it to Messer Gian Savarino," Antonio said. "He had seen it before and vouches for the fact that it is the original."

Fra Felipe rubbed his thin hands together, obviously pleased at this confirmation of the worth of the painting. "You have done us a great service, Dr. Servetus," he said, "in finding such a valuable object of art. Its presence in our house will redound to the glory of God."

"But——" Antonio began, and stopped, warned by some inner sense of caution that he had best not reveal his knowledge of the real owners of the painting.

"You were going to say something?"

"I was wondering if you knew who were the real owners?" Antonio said.

"Regrettably, no." The prior's voice never faltered upon the untruth. "We have no choice, then, but to place the painting in safekeeping here."

Fra Felipe did not realize then that he had overheard Messer Bellarmi speak of the Venus. Just how or when this knowledge might be of value to him Antonio did not yet know, but he realized instinctively that he must not reveal it to the prior. "I was only using the painting to make some sketches," he said casually.

"We realized that, since we found some of your drawings," Fra Felipe told him. "I have placed the painting in my apartment for the moment. Later we will arrange a suitable place for it."

Antonio felt a wave of anger sweep through him. His beloved was hidden away in Fra Felipe's apartment, subject to the gaze of those cold, thin-lidded eyes, while he stood here impotent, utterly unable to intervene.

It was the dream brought to life, he realized with a start. He had been warned that this would happen and he had done nothing, although he had himself correctly interpreted the dream. The guilt was his own, then, for he should have realized that eventually someone would find the locked door and open it. And he was even more responsible, because he had let his pique at Lucia Bellarmi keep him from revealing its whereabouts to her uncle. Bitterly now he told himself that he had been a fool, that just as Gian had predicted, he had played directly into the hands of Fra Felipe Santos. But at least he had learned the true nature of the man who sat across from him, studying him with a faintly contemptuous smile.

"As I told you," Fra Felipe said, "the Church is inclined to overlook the transgressions of those of her servants who do her a great service. You have done one in finding this great art treasure and you may do us another, if you will."

"What is that?" Antonio asked.

"Were the presence of the painting here known at this time, we might be troubled by—by false claims of ownership. I feel that for the moment our best interest can be served by remaining silent regarding it."

This was the bribe, Antonio realized. His silence to be bought by letting the charge of heresy against him go unpressed. But somehow, perhaps from the smug complacency with which the prior had put the proposition, Antonio judged that there was something more. "Suppose I should not agree?" he asked.

"I do not think you will be so unwise," Fra Felipe said pleasantly. "But certain precautions have been taken." He struck a tiny silver gong on the table beside him. Instantly a man appeared from the curtained alcove behind the dais, where he must have been hidden during the entire conversation. It was not the man's appearance that startled Antonio, however, but his identity. For it was Messer Battista Porzia, his pleasant companion on the coach that morning.

"I think you have met Messer Porzia," Fra Felipe said pleasantly.

The plump man smiled and bowed. "We meet again, Dr. Servetus, most pleasantly."

Antonio mumbled a response. He felt a sudden sickness inside him, a premonition that all was far from well.

"Messer Porzia has spoken to me of a certain conversation he had with you this morning," Fra Felipe said. "Perhaps he will be so good as to repeat a portion of it for your hearing."

"Certainly," the rolypoly man said happily. "Dr. Servetus and I had a very interesting discussion this morning in regard to certain theological doctrines once voiced by his brother, the condemned heretic, Michael Servetus, and one of his supporters, Fra Jacques Charmier."

"And the nature of this conversation?" the prior asked.

"Dr. Servetus stated his belief that his brother's conviction for heresy had not been legal as far as the Roman Church is concerned and also that he fully subscribed to the heretical doctrines preached by Michael Servetus."

"It is a lie!" Antonio shouted, jumping to his feet. "I said no such thing."

"Careful," Fra Felipe warned coldly. "Messer Porzia's word is not to be doubted."

"Why is his word any better than mine?" Antonio demanded hotly.

"Messer Porzia is a familiar of the Holy Office."

"The Holy Office . . ." Antonio sank into his seat, numbed by the impact of the words upon his brain. "The Inquisition," he whispered, and a rush of memories poured into his thoughts from his childhood in Spain. No one could stand against the powerful arms, the garroting fingers of the Inquisition. No one dared deny the testimony of its familiars. And now this thing of unutterable horror had reached even into the quiet of Padua, undermining the only citadel of freedom remaining in the world. Gian had said Fra Felipe had once been with the Inquisition, Antonio remembered now. That must be why he had been assigned to Padua, to undermine, to bore from within, and destroy the God-given rights of men to search for the truth.

"I, too, am a servant of the Holy Office," Fra Felipe continued. "I see that you fully appreciate the gravity of the situation. Do you not agree that you should keep silent about—shall we say certain matters we were discussing?"

Antonio pushed himself to his feet. "I agree," he said hoarsely. "I agree."

"I thought you would," Fra Felipe said. *"Pax vobiscum, frater."*

"Et tecum, pax," Antonio muttered as he turned and left the audience chamber. But there was no peace in his soul.

But halfway from the cloister to the point of departure for the coaches bound for Venice, Antonio suddenly began to laugh. Fra Felipe had sworn him to secrecy in regard to the painting by threatening him with the Inquisition. What the prior did not know, for he had not told him, was that weeks before he had written to Messer Girolamo Bellarmi in Florence, shortly after he had missed him and his niece in Venice, revealing that the Botticelli Venus was in the priory of the Dominicans at Padua. And the letter must already have reached Florence.

v

Messer Girolamo Bellarmi sat in his comfortable chair in the Florentine warehouses of the House of Bellarmi, successor to the Vespucci, and regarded his niece fondly. Perched upon a stool, Madonna Lucia was reading a letter, wrinkling her pretty nose occasionally over a phrase, but making a lovely picture withal. When she finished, he said: "Well, you were right, Lucia. The physician admits that he had the painting in the priory."

"I was sure of it."

"But he doesn't say anything about getting it to us," her uncle pointed out. "Or about coming to Florence himself."

"He will come," she stated confidently.

Messer Bellarmi smiled. "Has someone been casting your horoscope, that you can be so certain of the future?"

She shook her head. "Intuition."

"But intuition is not always dependable," he reminded her.

"Mine is."

Her uncle raised his eyebrows. "We shall see, my dear. Now run along and let me do some work."

But when she was gone he did not immediately return to the great ledgers piled up on the desk. Instead he chewed the tip of a quill reflectively for several moments. Then, drawing a fresh sheet of parchment from the drawer, he dipped the quill into a massive bronze inkpot and began to write:

To Messer Antonio Servetus, physician dwelling at Number 14, Via delle Galeazze e Vasca, Venice:

HONORED SIR:

Your communication in regard to the painting by Botticelli known as the Birth of Venus has just reached my hand. It gives both myself and my niece, to whom the picture belongs, great pleasure to know that it is safe in the priory of the Dominicans at Padua. As much indebted to your good graces as we are for telling us the whereabouts of the painting, I cannot but feel that you should have notified us of its location while we were yet in Venice or Padua, so that I could have made arrangements for its transportation to Florence. To our misfortune, this privilege is denied us, since we have left the city. I do not feel that I am placing you under too great an obligation, therefore, in requesting that you personally undertake whatever measures may be necessary to secure the painting and insure its safe arrival here . . .

He stopped and chewed the tip of the quill thoughtfully for a moment. Then, with a smile, he resumed writing:

. . . even if such measures should require that you make the journey yourself. You may rest assured that I shall personally undertake to recompense you for all expenditures, both of time and of money, which you may incur in connection with the undertaking.

Please accept my solicitations for your continued good health, in which my niece joins me.

Honored Sir, I remain obediently yours to command,

GIROLAMO BELLARMI,
Fiorenza Anno Domini, 1563.

When the letter was finished, Messer Bellarmi read it through, then, folding it, melted a bit of sealing wax with a burning taper, dropped it upon the fold, and impressed the seal of the House of Bellarmi into the wax with the heavy signet ring on his left hand. Then he sat back and smiled to himself. A woman's intuition—especially Lucia's—was a wonderful thing, he was prepared to admit. But as a businessman, he knew the advisability of taking certain precautions to insure that events would transpire according to his desires.

vi

Antonio's life was a very busy one now. By day he sketched under Gian's direction, and had the satisfaction of seeing his hand become surer and more deft. Gian also introduced him into the society of the artists and art students. While obviously broad-minded about many of the things which his monkly upbringing labeled sinful, he discovered that they were serious in their professions and often better read than he in history and in the new humanistic concepts which were spreading from Italy to the rest of the world. To a man they worshiped the fullness of life which the ancient Greeks had somehow managed to discover for themselves centuries before. Antonio felt stimulated to renew his own studies in Greek, with the vague intention of someday visiting the great cultural centers of Ancient Greece and perhaps reading for himself the great classics in the original mother tongue of science and art.

In the great libraries of San Marco, and in the magnificent collections of Count Quirina-Stampolia, made free for the use of scholars at his palace at Santa Maria Formosa, Antonio renewed his acquaintance with the Aphorisms of Hippocrates, the remarkably lucid writings of Celsus, Avicenna, Galen, Maimonides, the Jewish physician, Rhazes, the Moor, and all of the other illustrious minds who had sought to alleviate human suffering.

In late June he was invited to speak before the Confraternity of Physicians in their famous guildhall, the Scuola di San Marco. He accepted gladly, because approval of his discovery by the Guild would go a long way toward making it generally accepted by the world.

As he stopped before the handsome façade of the Scuola and then walked slowly through the great hall with its remarkable carved ceiling, now almost a century old, Antonio felt a renewed sense of respect for this most honorable of professions. And standing on the dais with his *consilium* open on the lectern before him, he felt something of the exaltation that he knew must have filled Michael, a pride not only in his own work, but a kinship with the divine that transcended petty human laws, the austere ravings of bigoted Calvin, or the more corrupt but equally fatal pronouncements of the Roman Church.

Before him, filling the front seats, were the physicians of Venice, old men for the most part, for medicine was still taught as much by master to apprentice as in the halls of the universities. The apprentices were ranged in the back of the room, earnest young men in worn robes, overserious, and obviously impressed by the deference shown the young physician-anatomist from nearby Padua. Besides Antonio on the dais were the president of the Confraternity of Physicians and Professor Fallopius. With the comforting knowledge of his teacher's support, Antonio began to speak, haltingly at first, then more surely as he launched himself into his great crusade, the proof that Michael had discovered this new truth years before and that he, not the younger Antonio, deserved the credit.

When he finished there was a burst of applause and the physicians crowded around to do him honor. When the tumult had subsided, Antonio walked with Fallopius through the building. "You have a great future, Antonio," the old physician said. "I am announcing my retirement at the end of the coming school year. Your name has already been placed in nomination for the chair of anatomy at Padua."

Antonio started to speak, but his throat was too full for words. He knew that Fallopius had made this move earlier than he had planned as a measure of support for him in any controversy which might arise over his discovery.

"Don't thank me, my son," Fallopius said. "I am doing the university a favor, for I am certain that the world will owe a great deal to your discoveries in the future."

"*Dio lo volesse!*" Antonio said fervently.

"Has there been any trouble yet with the Church?" Fallopius asked.

Antonio shook his head. "The truth is so obvious that none can refute it."

"I wouldn't be too sure," Fallopius warned. "Last week I was visited by a man who, I am sure, is a familiar of the Holy Office."

The very word filled Antonio with a sense of dread. "What did he want?" he asked.

"Nothing very definite. In fact, he professed to be an acquaintance of yours. At least he knew all about your brother and his writings."

"Porzia!" Antonio cried.

"That was his name."

"He *is* a familiar," Antonio assured Fallopius. "And utterly unscrupulous."

"But who is behind him?"

"Fra Felipe Santos," Antonio said bitterly.

"The Dominican prior? *Perchè?*"

Antonio gave Fallopius a rapid account of his controversy with the prior, omitting, however, any reference to the painting.

"That *is* bad," Fallopius agreed gravely. "They cannot attack you in Venice because of a scientific writing, but be sure that your personal life gives them no grounds, my son."

"There is none," Antonio assured him. "I have always been a devout Catholic."

Outside the building Fallopius held out his hand. "Come what may," he said, "I shall expect you to resume your instructions in anatomy when fall comes. Your demonstrations are certain to be more popular than ever before."

Antonio hailed a gondola before the Scuola and lay back on the cushions. What Fallopius had told him about Porzia was disturbing. Why should Fra Felipe set the plump familiar looking into his affairs again, if he had accepted the promise of silence on its face value? Could it be that the prior did not himself intend to keep his side of the bargain and was looking for further evidence which might support a charge of heresy which could not be ignored, even in Venice? A chill sense of foreboding gripped Antonio's already low spirits. All of the elation from his success before the Scuola had now disappeared.

There had been nothing but trouble, he thought, since he had found the Botticelli. And yet he could not blame the goddess; she was too utterly lovely, virtuous, and kind. The thought of her desecration by the lecherous eyes of Fra Felipe Santos set his anger burning again.

"*Sia stali*," the gondolier cried, and the boat turned to pass through the narrow canal that separated the ornate palace of the Doge from the newer state prison. High overhead arched the recently completed bridge joining the two buildings, across which many a condemned man had walked to his death in the courtyard of the prison. Already, although only a few years old, it had been nicknamed "The Bridge of Sighs" by the Venetians.

"Better to pass under than over the Bridge of Sighs," the gondolier observed, crossing himself. Although it was midsummer, Antonio shivered beneath his robe with a dire sense of foreboding.

vii

At the end of July, Antonio received a letter which elevated somewhat his depressed spirits. It was marked "London" and was brought to him by an apprentice from the printing house of Guidobaldo Aldini.

Honored Sir:
Messer Guidobaldo Aldini has kindly forwarded to my printing establishment in London unbound pages of your *consilium* titled *De Motu Sanguinem Pulmonale*. Please, Honored Sir, accept my felicitations upon a most

important anatomical discovery. I have taken the liberty of showing your *consilium* to Dr. John Caius, formerly a student of medicine at the University of Padua and now Master of Gonville and Caius College. Dr. Caius has asked me to extend to you his congratulations until such a time as he can present them in person. He joins me in requesting the favor of being allowed to pub-lish, from my presses in London, your *consilium*, in order that the physicians of England may become acquainted with the most important discovery. Should you see fit to grant this request, please notify Messer Guidobaldo Aldini, who maintains regular communications with me.

I remain, Honored Sir, your most humble and obedient servant,

VALENTINE SIMS, Printer, Dwelling in London, at the signe of the White Swanne on Adling Hill.

Antonio wrote immediately, granting the permission. His spirits were further elevated by the reception given his book in Venice and nearby Italian cities. He was honored by membership in the Scuola of Physicians, and there was even an offer of the chair of anatomy in the University of Bologna.

The arrival of the letter from Messer Girolamo Bellarmi, however, caused still another complication in his already turbulent life. Gian stopped painting when Antonio handed him the letter and read it through. "That Bellarmi is a clever person," he said. "He has devised this scheme to save himself the trouble of sending for the painting by making you feel that you should take it to him."

"I think I should," Antonio said.

"When are you going to stop fighting that silly conscience of yours, Tonio?" Gian picked up his brush. "You have no obligation to take it to him."

"I found the painting."

"*È vero*. That should be enough."

"But if I had told Messer Bellarmi, he could have taken it with him."

"Don't be an ass. I told you before you even saw him and his niece that the painting would never leave Padua. What has happened only proves that I was right." He turned back to his painting. "Stop carrying the load of the world on your shoulders, Tonio. What you need is more relaxa-tion." His face brightened. "*Eccolo!* The Feast of Redentore is on Fri-day. We will join the celebration."

viii

The Feast of Il Redentore, the Redeemer, was one of those religious occasions that the Venetians loved, an excuse, under the guise of a religious celebration, for a general holiday of feasting, dancing, great processions, many theatrical performances, and no little amatory dallying, such as always accompanies such occasions. It began before dawn, when Gian and Antonio joined the great crowd who filled gondolas strung with colored lanterns moving in a procession to the Lido to greet the sunrise that marked the official beginning of the celebration. It was a colorful procession that floated along, with everyone joining in the singing. Many of the crowd were masked already, a custom the Venetians revived at every opportunity, and many gondolas contained bands of musicians to serenade the gallants and ladies.

Antonio found that he was enjoying the crowd, the singing, the color, and the gaiety. When they returned from the Lido there was time only for a hasty breakfast at a *trattoria* before the celebration entered its second stage. This consisted of a procession of gondolas and splendidly outfitted barges through the lagoons and waterways of the city. The boats were festooned with masses of flowers, vying in color with the lavish dresses of the women and the only slightly less colorful garments of the men. Leading the procession was a group of decorated barges and gondolas carrying the young bloods of the city and their companions of the day. Next followed a group of larger barges and converted *batellae,* each bearing an elaborate framework or machine resembling some of the more lavish creations of Leonardo da Vinci. Suspended in the air above the barges floated genii representing the various attributes which raise man above the animals: Humility, Piety, Knowledge, Love, and the like.

Still another train of boats carried King Neptune and his court, tritons, nymphs, and mermaids. In other barges mysteries and other performances were going on continuously while the conveyances floated through the lagoons around the palace of the Doge. Following in the wake of the larger boats were hundreds of gondolas and private vessels, a colorful queue that wound through the city for hours.

Gian, Antonio, and some of the artists watched the procession from Mattei's gondola, which Gian had hired for the day. It was late afternoon when they returned to the artist's studio. "Did you enjoy it, Tonio?" Gian asked while they were waiting for Dimas to prepare food.

"Very much."

"The rest will be even more interesting."

"The rest?"

"This evening you will witness something really unusual. Lodovici Agnolo is presenting an entertainment of magic."

Antonio's eyes brightened. "I have been waiting to see that," he said. "Where will it be?"

"In a place that I know of. It is being kept secret."

"*Perchè?*"

Gian shrugged. "The authorities do not encourage black magic."

"Black magic!" Antonio exclaimed. "Should we go, then?"

"The fact that it is forbidden only makes it more interesting."

Antonio shook his head doubtfully. "I don't know about that."

"As a scientist you should be interested in magic," Gian pointed out.

"But I don't believe in it."

"Come tonight," Gian said with an air of mystery. "Then decide what you believe after you have watched Agnolo."

ix

Although Antonio had learned much about Venice during the summer, he was completely lost long before they had reached their destination that evening. Mattei, swaying gracefully on his perch, plied the long oar and sent his light craft turning now right, now left, through ever-narrower canals, until finally they grounded at what appeared to be the back entrance to a crumbling building. The stone quay was narrow, little more than a ledge between the damp mossy walls and the canal.

Leaving Mattei to wait, Gian led the way through an alley beside the building toward the front. Pushing open a gate hanging crazily on one hinge, they stepped through into a small enclosed courtyard. Antonio saw that they were in the front court of what seemed to be an old ruined chapel, with the remains of a fountain in the center and the crumbling walls of the building rising from a flagstoned pavement. A heavy wooden door led into the chapel itself. Gian knocked and the door was partially opened by a particularly villainous-looking individual with a great deformed hump on his back. He looked them over, his eyes brightening at the sight of the gold coin in Gian's hand, and the door swung wide as the coin was transferred.

The chapel was already half filled when Gian and Antonio found seats at the side near the front. Two large tapers burned in wall brackets on either side of the nave. Otherwise it was lit only by moonlight that came through several broken places in the roof. Half the benches were splintered and broken, and everything about the place spoke of disintegration and decay. The floor was crumbling and had gone through in spots, and in the ghostly moonlight filtering through the roof the rafters showed stark, broken and jagged, like the splintered bones of a skeleton.

"Why would he use a place like this?" Antonio asked. There was something disgusting about this travesty of what had been a holy place.

Gian laughed. "Lodovici used to be a priest. Perhaps he feels at home here."

A glow of light appeared behind a curtain drawn across the nave of the chapel. Someone was going about behind there, lighting two clusters of candles on either side, for their flames showed through the curtain. There was a stir of interest from the crowd at this promise of a beginning to the evening's entertainment. Gian nudged Antonio. "Watch this closely," he said. "You'll never see anything like it."

The curtains before the alcove now began to part, drawn back by two choirboys. There was a virginal quality about their amazingly beautiful features. The starched round collars of their spotless white robes were partially hidden behind the folds of the curtain.

The parting curtains revealed the nave of the chapel illuminated by the lighted candles. Some attempt had been made to hide its decrepit state by hanging white sheets against the wall. At the very back of the nave a narrow door was closed by dark hangings. The nave itself was largely occupied by a long altar, as long as a bier and strangely like one, draped with a white sheet. As Antonio's eyes became accustomed to the light of the candles, the top of the altar began to assume a definite outline, the shape of a prostrate human body beneath the sheet.

"Gian," Antonio whispered. "Someone is lying on the altar."

"*Certamente.* It is the virgin."

"The Virgin?" Antonio echoed. "The Holy Mother?"

Gian laughed. "No. The virgin for the sacrifice. In the Black Mass."

The Black Mass! Antonio's every sense was revolted at the very words. He had heard, of course, of the Black Mass, that travesty of the Catholic ceremony in which the Devil himself was worshiped instead of Christ and the Host polluted with indescribable indecencies. Most horrible of all, so the accounts ran, was the orgy which ended with the sacrifice of a virgin.

Antonio started to rise, but Gian pushed him back. "It isn't really the Mass," he explained. "Agnolo uses this as a setting for a demonstration of magic."

Antonio relaxed a little. After all, if there was no sacrilege, it would be instructive to watch a magician at work. The entire nave was exposed now, and the choirboys stepped from behind the curtains to take their places at either side. With a shock Antonio realized that they were not boys at all, but girls of perhaps sixteen, the budding promise of womanhood already well developed and completely revealed, for their robes were of some gauzy transparency and beneath them they were completely nude.

Gian nudged Antonio and chuckled. "*Eccolo!* I told you it would be interesting."

Somewhere back of the nave a gong sounded a low musical note. The curtains parted and two choirboys appeared. One bore the chalice, the other a silver chafing dish ordinarily used to contain the Host. Like the girls, the striplings were naked beneath their robes. They moved slowly to either end of the altar and placed their burdens upon it, stepping back to stand beside the girls. Antonio was conscious of a powerful stench that rapidly pervaded the hall and recognized the odor of burning tar, suffused with henbane and the dried leaves of the deadly nightshade. He searched for the cause and spied it finally in the brace of black tapers smoldering in holders on either side of the nave and now sending clouds of pungent vapor down upon the crowd.

Again the musical gong sounded, and now a strange figure appeared between the dark curtains. Above the shorter boys and girls, the magician towered to a preternatural height as he stood with arms upraised before him, the light of the candles behind him casting a macabre dancing shadow across the altar. More startling than his height was the chasuble he wore. It was in form the ordinary garment worn by priests for the Mass, covering him from his neck to the toes of his Moorish slippers, but embroidered with a multiplicity of bizarre, cabalistic designs, the signs of the zodiac, astrologer's symbols, and weird oriental figures. His head

was covered by a red cowl, drawn tight so that his countenance had a
Mephistophelean appearance, heightened by the two horns which pro-
jected from the cowl above his temples.

Slowly the magician advanced to the altar. Taking the cloth by the
corner, he whisked it suddenly into the air, from which it instantly
vanished, as if it had never existed. Antonio caught his breath and
gripped the edge of the bench with his fingers. In removing the cloth,
Agnolo had revealed the nature of the altar. Stretched out like a marble
statue, as rigid and as pale as the cold white stone itself, was the nude
body of a beautiful woman. Supported only from the shoulders and just
below the knees, her body was nevertheless as rigid as if it had been
made of stone. Nor was there any mistaking her identity, although her
face was turned away from the audience. Antonio had seen that beautiful body too many times in the past few months not to recognize Clarice
Strozzi.

But it was the strange rigidity that excited Antonio's interest at once.
No human body, he knew, could normally maintain that position for
more than a few minutes at most. Not even the death rigor would be so
marked, and she was not dead, for his keen eyes detected the rise and fall
of her breast with breathing. What strange power was this? What
breaking of nature's immutable laws? Unless, of course, it was an
illusion.

As if to answer his mental question, Lodovici signaled one of the
choirboys, who got down on hands and knees and crawled between the
supports beneath Clarice's body, proving that there was no other means
of support.

Lodovici came around the altar now and descended the steps to the
chancel railing. Facing the body of the girl, he made the genuflections,
first the half length and then the full. In a mocking voice he intoned the
ritual of the Mass while the quartet of youthful voices gave the responses.
The first portion of the ritual completed, he rose to his feet. One of
the youths took up the silver chafing dish and held it high in the air.

"How does he keep her body like that?" Antonio whispered to Gian.
His revulsion at the travesty of the religious performance was driven
away by his scientific curiosity about the strange rigidity of Clarice's
body.

Gian shrugged. "It is a trick of some sort."

Antonio was not satisfied by the explanation. Could it be witchcraft? he wondered. Until now he had possessed little confidence in those who professed to believe in the supernatural. Most things, his scientist's brain assured him, admitted a logical explanation. But this was like nothing with which he was at all familiar.

"*Father of evil, author of sin.*" The voice of Lodovici Agnolo broke into his thoughts. The magician was standing before the altar of Clarice's body, arms uplifted. "*Patron of vice. Satan, God of pleasure, eternal fount of virility and illicit passion, patron of the unchaste.*"

A faint smell of brimstone was in the air. Antonio saw that the black tapers were burning more brightly, with a greenish-blue tint to the flame. Common sense told him that the maker had cleverly placed some sulphur in the center of the tapers and the flame had just reached it, but the spell of the magician's incantations was so strong that he almost believed the brimstone was a warning of the as yet unseen presence of the Evil One himself.

"*Guardian saint of abortionists.*" The magician's voice rose higher, and Antonio felt an almost unbearable sense of anticipation, as if at any moment Satan might appear. "*Patron of murderers and seducers. God of thieves and witches, we bow before you. Bring to us carnal delights beyond all knowledge, pleasures of the flesh unendurable; teach us to abandon ourselves to thy service. . . .*

"*Visit us tonight at this adoration in thy honor, O Antichrist! Rise triumphant from the loins of this virgin dedicated to thy glory; make her the vase in which we shall receive thy gifts. . . .*"

A puff of smoke rolled up from before the altar and poured out across the audience, hiding the nave. The odor of brimstone was almost overpowering, and Antonio felt his senses reeling. Somewhere in the back of the chapel a woman screamed piercingly and a bench was overturned. As in a haze, Antonio saw the diabolical scene in the nave emerge from the smoke. Agnolo had dropped to his knees and the four with him were prostrate upon the floor, as if knocked down by a giant hand, their gauzy clothing ripped from their bodies. Only Clarice, pale and immobile as a statue, was the same. The chafing dish containing the Host had fallen to the floor, and now Lodovici picked it up and, rising from his knees, held it open before him. His voice rang out again, scornful, triumphant with hate:

"*Hated of the Antichrist, proscriber of benevolent demons, destroyer of fleshly delights, Jesus who forbids all pleasure, as priest I command*

*you to incarnate this Host as thy own rotting flesh. Fill it with the musty
foulness of the Sepulcher, sprinkle it with rust from the nails which
pierced thy hands, moisten it with the foul blood which poured from
thy debased body, so that my master, Satan, may defile it as he will someday throw thee down from the high place where thou dost unjustly sit,
to trample thee underfoot, even as we do this Host, and assume the rightful heritage stolen from him by thee."*

Smoke rolled up again from before the altar. With a sudden gesture
of contempt, the magician spat into the chafing dish and flung its contents into the air, scattering the fragments of the defiled Host upon the
floor. A revulsion amounting almost to nausea gripped Antonio at this
foulness, this debasing of all he had been taught was holy, but he was
not able to move from his place or take his eyes from the scene in the
nave. Through the silence that followed the unholy act, Antonio became conscious of a thin wailing, as of an oriental instrument piping a
strange, compelling melody.

"Rise! Servants of the Antichrist," Agnolo boomed. *"Rise! Dance in
homage to our master and shout defiance to the impotent One who
denies us pleasure."*

The four who were lying prostrate leaped to their feet, their bodies
uncovered save for the torn shreds of their gauzy robes. As the wailing,
unseen music rose to a higher pitch their bodies began to move in a
rhythmic cadence of passionate abandon. Stamping upon the scattered
fragments of the defiled Host, they moved about the altar, writhing in a
horrible pantomime of lustful actions, while Lodovici stood, a tall and
satanic figure before the strange altar, arms outstretched.

Gradually the pantomime of lust became no longer a pantomime.
Indecent gestures led to repulsively carnal acts, and youthful bodies,
locked in lustful embrace, rolled upon the floor. Over it all was the high-
pitched wailing sound of the music.

From the front rows of the audience arose a chant, repeated at first
by a few, then sweeping through the room as voice after voice, hoarse
with the spell the magician had cast over them, took up the refrain. "The
Sacrifice! The Sacrifice!"

Antonio heard Gian's voice beside him take up the cry. Then another voice, hoarse and thick with passion, sounded the same refrain.
Overcome with horror, Antonio recognized it as his own, but he could
not control the impulse that drove him to cry out.

With a sweeping gesture the magician plucked a long dagger from the folds of his chasuble. Holding it aloft, he advanced upon the altar, until the knife was held above Clarice's breast.

"No! No!" The words took form in Antonio's heart and brain, but no sound came from his lips, save the words which were sweeping the chapel in rhythmic waves of sound. Every decent urge within him fought for strength to leap from his place and wrest the dagger from the magician's hand, but his muscles seemed no longer to be obeying his brain, yielding to a primitive urge which came from deep within him and which he could no longer control. One part of his mind cried out against this sacrilege, but another, stronger part echoed the cry, "The Sacrifice! The Sacrifice!"

The dagger in Agnolo's hand began its downward plunge, straight toward the lovely uncovered breast. Antonio could not look away, could not even shut his eyes, so compelling, so fascinatingly horrible was the scene. Down, down the dagger plunged, and still her body remained as rigid as stone. Antonio flinched as it touched her breast and felt pain rip through him in sympathy as the dagger plunged to the very hilt into her body.

A geyser of red shot up from the knife, staining the bizarre robe of the magician. With a deft movement, Agnolo caught up the chalice and held it beneath the stream, catching some of it in the silver goblet. And with a shout of triumph, he lifted it to his lips and drank.

Even in the unbearable tension of the moment, Antonio could still wonder that Clarice's body showed no sign of pain, no evidence of the death agony which must surely have resulted from such a mortal wound. How could any rigor, any magician's trick, endure in the face of death itself?

Suddenly, above the sound of the magician's voice, the sobs of women, and the groans and retching of men, there was a thunderous hammering at the door. "Open!" an authoritative voice cried. "Open in the name of the Doge."

"*Dio mio!*" Gian exclaimed. "We have been betrayed."

Pandemonium seized the throng inside the ruined chapel. Antonio saw Lodovici, seemingly not inexperienced in such situations, seize the cluster of candles on either side of the altar and throw them to the floor, trampling out the flames. The entire chapel was plunged into darkness, relieved only by the moonlight filtering through the roof and the smoldering tapers from which sulphurous fumes still arose. "Follow me," Gian shouted over the din. "I think I can get us out through the back."

"What about Clarice?" Antonio asked.

Gian was already moving toward a small door in the side of the building, leaping over benches with little consideration for their occupants. At the front door of the chapel the authoritative hammering was louder and there was the sound of splitting wood.

Antonio hesitated. Common sense told him to follow Gian, but he remembered Clarice, apparently unconscious there on the altar. Perhaps her wound was not fatal after all; in some unbelievable way it still could have been a trick. If so, she might still be alive and in need of help. Hesitating no more, he turned and plunged toward the sulphurous gloom of the nave. He vaulted over the chancel railing and his foot slipped, throwing him with a thud that left him momentarily stunned. Pulling himself up by the supports beneath Clarice's body, his fingers touched her flesh. Quickly he put his hand over her breast and felt the beating of her heart, slow, even, and strong, certainly not the heartbeat of a person dying of a fatal wound.

It *had* been a trick, then! And Lodovici Agnolo, intent as the rest upon saving himself, had left her there, helpless in the strange rigor, to whatever fate befell her at the hands of the guards. Antonio shouted in her ear; her lips moved faintly, but he could not detect any words. Behind him in the darkened chapel people were screaming and the sound of axes and splintering doors was louder than before. His eyes fell upon the dagger lying across Clarice's body, and he seized it and thrust it into his robe, then quickly ripped a sheet from the wall and wrapped her in it. Lifting her in his arms, awkwardly because of the stiffness of her body, he plunged toward the curtained doorway at the back of the nave. As he passed through it, he heard a door crash open at the front of the chapel and the guards pouring through, shouting, "Surrender! Surrender in the name of the Doge!"

Down a flight of steps he staggered with Clarice in his arms, praying that the back entrance to the chapel had been left unguarded. Through a door open at the bottom of the steps the cool, damp air of the canal poured in, and with a surge of hope Antonio inched through it with Clarice in his arms and flattened himself against the wall on the narrow ledge. The dark waters of the canal flowed at his feet, but he knew he had only seconds to spare before the guards would find the door behind the nave. Had he been alone, he would have plunged unhesitatingly into the canal, for he was a strong swimmer, but Clarice made that impossible.

Then the dark shadow of a gondola appeared from the side of the canal where it had been hidden in the shadows. Antonio recognized the squat figure at the long oar. "Mattei!" he shouted. "Mattei!"

The boat darted from the shadows and bumped at the quay near his feet. Antonio leaped for the deck, rocking the frail craft dangerously from his own weight, plus that of the girl. "Get us away," he panted. "The guards."

"*Sì. Subito!*" The gondola shot away into the darkness. Time after time Mattei turned the boat sharply from waterway to waterway. Finally he said with satisfaction, "You are safe, Your Reverence. The devil himself couldn't have followed us."

"Thank God you were there, Mattei," Antonio said. "Take us home."

The gondolier chuckled. "Thank Messer Gian. He told me to wait and see if you got out."

Antonio tossed him a gold coin. Gian was safe too, then. But they had all come close to capture, especially Clarice, who still lay upon the cushions in that strange stupor.

x

Clarice was half awake, however, when Antonio carried her up the stairs and put her on the sofa in the studio. He poured her a glass of wine and she drank it gratefully. "How did I get here?" she asked.

"Don't you remember anything?"

"Lodovici put me into a trance in the chapel. I seem to remember some shouting——"

"A trance!" he cried. "So that is how it was done."

"How what was done?"

He told her in some detail about the performance. When he finished, she said softly, "And you risked your own self to save me."

Antonio blushed. "As a physician," he reminded her, "it was my duty to help you when you were wounded."

She drew apart the folds of the sheet that covered her breast. There was no mark upon the white skin. "See," she said with a smile, "there was no wound."

"But the blood and all, how could that be a trick?"

"Lodovici is clever. And the juice of berries can be made to look like blood."

Antonio fumbled in his robe and brought out the dagger, a long and wicked-looking instrument with a strangely flexible blade. Clarice picked it up and plunged it suddenly at her breast. It seemed to penetrate to the hilt and a small geyser of red spurted across her fingers. "See, Tonio," she said with a smile. "It was a trick." The blade of the weapon was crumpled against her skin, as if it had been made of paper.

"But how?"

She calmly removed the dagger, which immediately resumed its natural shape. "The Spaniards make such a dagger for magicians," she explained. "It comes from the New World, a substance the Indians get from the bark of a tree. Jugglers bounce balls made of it, too."

"And the blood?"

"The handle is hollow. When filled with a red fluid, the opening can be covered with a finger until the handle is squeezed, then the fluid spurts up."

Antonio examined the dagger carefully. "It is a very clever trick," he said admiringly. "There should be many uses for such a substance." But when he asked Clarice about the rigidity, she had no explanation. "I know that is easily done, though," she said. "I have seen him make others as rigid as stone."

"But where did he learn it?"

"In the Orient, I think. I have heard him say that many oriental magicians can produce such a state of trance. Some call it magnetism."

"Of course!" Antonio cried. "Paracelsus speaks of magnetism."

Clarice yawned. "Don't you think I should go home now?"

"The guards were apparently warned of the performance tonight," he said. "They may be looking for you, and the way you are now, they would know you were there."

Clarice laughed. "If I've got to stay here, then, you might be a gentleman and offer me some food."

They ate gaily in the pantry, the horror of the evening already far from their thoughts. Clarice had substituted the robe she kept at the studio while posing for the sheet in which Antonio had wrapped her.

"I'll take the couch in the studio," she said with a yawn when they had finished eating. "Gian must be staying with one of the artists."

"There is a key in the studio door," Antonio told her. "Gian sometimes locks himself in while painting."

Clarice came over to him and put her arms about him. "Don't you think I trust you, Tonio? After all, you saved my life tonight. If they had found us together, I would have been burned as a witch and you with me."

"I didn't even think of that."

"I know. That's why I——" She lifted herself on tiptoe and put her mouth to his. "Good night, Tonio mio," she whispered. "You are very sweet."

The fragrance of her mouth and the soft, yielding pressure of her body sent an exciting current pounding through Antonio's veins. Instinctively his arms went about her, holding her against him. Then she pushed him gently away. "Good night, *caro mio*." Her eyes were warm and bright. "Sleep well."

Preparing for bed in the next room, Antonio was at a loss to understand the tremendous sense of well-being that permeated him. Examining it critically, he decided it must be from relief at escaping from the guards and saving Clarice. The memory of her kiss stirred his pulses again as he heard her moving about the studio and then the creak of the couch as she lay down. Vastly content, he stretched out and was almost instantly asleep.

It was the same dream, the promise of the goddess as he held her in his arms, the mocking face of the satyr, the accusing voice of Lucia Bellarmi, and finally the vision of Clarice and his utter impotence to reach her. As before, he fought to get to her and saw her outlines begin to dim. In a frenzy of fear lest she leave him there, he cried her name.

Then her outlines grew clearer, but they had changed, for now she wore the robe she had worn tonight when she kissed him. And no longer was she a shadow but a kind goddess, whose arms were about him, comforting him and quieting his fears.

"Tonio," he heard her soothing voice. "It is all right, Tonio."

From the depths of sleep he struggled to wakefulness and found that her presence was no dream, but reality. "You were going away." He clung to the reassuring warmth of her body, like a child awakened from a bad dream clings to its mother.

Her hand stroked his forehead and presently his body relaxed on the couch. "It is all right now, Tonio mio." She lay down beside him and took him into her arms. In her soft lips and tender embrace he found the assurance he needed . . . and a promise of pleasures and a fulfillment he had never known. His arms closed hungrily about her. . . .

Sunlight was streaming through the windows when Antonio awakened. For a long moment he lay between sleeping and waking, reveling in a sense of quiet content. Hazily he remembered the events of the night and, turning, saw the print of Clarice's head still in the pillow beside his own. Somehow what had occurred after he had awakened from the dream to find Clarice holding him in her arms seemed only right, a natural consequence of their being together and the warm affection he felt for her and which he knew she returned.

Then, as wakefulness cleared his brain of sleep, his dozing conscience stirred itself. Adultery, it reminded him, was a mortal sin, and carnal knowledge of a woman permitted only in the state of holy wedlock. Antonio sat erect. He could hear Clarice moving about the studio humming a merry tune. He got to his feet and, pulling on his robe, opened the door. She was bending over the table, arranging plates, and raised her head, flashing him a smile. "*Buon giorno,* Tonio," she said. "Are you ready for breakfast, lazy one?"

Antonio went over to her and took her shoulders in his hands. She looked up at him, a smile still on her lips. "I want you to be my wife, Clarice," he told her.

Tears started suddenly in her eyes and she reached up to kiss him. "You are sweet, Tonio," she said. "But I can't marry you."

"But we——" he began and stopped.

"You were going to say that we committed adultery and your conscience tells you that we should be married. Yes, if you want to call it that, I suppose we did." She handed him a plate and sat on the couch, smoothing the cushions for him beside her. "Think of it now and tell me. Was there anything really wrong in what we did?"

"But the Church——"

"Forget the Church for a minute, Tonio, and think of yourself. Last night you needed me and I was glad, even proud, that I could give you what you needed." She lifted shining eyes to him. "I don't think the Creator ever meant to forbid two people who are as fond of each other as we are from finding real happiness in each other's arms, do you?"

Instinctively Antonio realized that Clarice was right and that the happiness and release from tension he had discovered in her arms could not really be sinful. Lorenzo Valla, the first of the great humanists, he remembered, had summed up this question when he said: "Even adultery, which is a natural manifestation of mankind, is only a part of natural law." Now he understood what Valla had meant, and that there might be other things he had not understood before which would have new meanings now.

"I think that for the first time you have made me a complete human being, *cara mia*," he said sincerely. "And I shall always be in your debt."

Clarice laughed. "Then you can repay me by thinking up some way to get my clothes, while we eat."

But that problem was solved by the arrival of Dimas, bleary-eyed from a night of celebration, but still on his feet. He was dispatched to Clarice's dwelling to bring clothes suitable for daytime wear. While they were finishing breakfast Antonio said, "I would still like to know more about how Agnolo put you into that trance."

"Why not ask him?"

"But magicians keep their actions secret, don't they?"

"Not from other magicians, or scientists, perhaps. Lodovici is vain. He might be flattered by your asking about it."

"Then I will ask him," Antonio decided.

"Don't"—Clarice hesitated, then went on—"don't tell him about last night."

"Of course," he agreed. Gian had said Clarice was Lodovici's mistress, but somehow that knowledge did not change his feeling toward her. It was still another part of the change inside him which he could not fully understand, but which he realized now might well alter the course of his whole life.

xi

Antonio was ushered into the apartment of Lodovici Agnolo by a young woman in silken pantaloons and a short jacket covering her breasts. He recognized her as one of the girls who had taken part in the Black Mass. Dark hangings and cushioned ottomans gave the room an oriental flavor, as did the weird designs and astrologer's symbols emblazoned upon the draperies. The floor was heavily carpeted and their feet made no sound.

Antonio sat on one of the cushioned ottomans and glanced nervously around the room. He had not been certain that he should come, but his curiosity to know more about Lodovici's strange power to induce trance had finally overcome his scruples. A small table contained a round crystal on a tiny pedestal, so placed that the sun falling through the window was imprisoned inside it, lighting the center with a deep glowing fire. Antonio's eyes were drawn inevitably to it and, once there, he seemed unable to remove them. He felt his senses begin to swim, as if some force were separating his mind from his body and taking control of it.

"*Buon giorno,* Doctor," a deep voice said beside him.

Antonio jumped nervously. The magician was standing so close to him that the folds of his oriental robe touched Antonio's hand. His dark face was as inscrutable as ever, and the magnetic quality of his gaze as strong.

"*Buon giorno, messire,*" Antonio stammered.

"Forgive me." Agnolo seated himself on an ottoman across from Antonio. "I startled you, did I not?"

Antonio rubbed his eyes. His limbs seemed sluggish, held down by leaden weights. "I was looking at the crystal here," he said, "and must have become bemused."

The magician chuckled. "The crystal of Samarkand has powers over the minds of men." He took a dark cloth from the table and dropped it over the glass ball, shutting away its compelling glow. At once Antonio felt his mind clear and the leaden stupor leave his limbs. "You were in the audience the other night, Doctor," Agnolo said. "How did the demonstration impress you?"

"One part of me was horrified," Antonio admitted. "The other fascinated."

The magician laughed. "As my master, Paracelsus, maintained, there are two selves in all of us."

"But it was also a sacrilege."

"No sacrilege was intended, Doctor. It was merely a feat of magic, an entertainment, and nothing more. By the way, I must thank you for saving Madonna Strozzi. She is a very important member of my troupe."

Antonio controlled a start of surprise. So Agnolo did know something of what had happened that night. But how much? "I am very much interested in the trance in which you placed Madonna Strozzi," he said. "I have never seen such a rigidity produced before."

"There are many things that you physicians do not understand, Messer Servetus. Things which are clear to the seers of the Orient."

"Then this is an oriental trick?"

"A trick? No. Rather a strange power which some possess."

"But the muscular rigidity. How do you explain it?"

"Some think a magnetic force flows from one body to the other," Lodovici admitted.

"Like the magnetism of Paracelsus?"

A gleam of admiration appeared in the magician's eyes. "You are a very learned man, Doctor," he said. "But I am not sure this power is the same."

"Whatever it is," Antonio said, "I think it might be valuable in curing disease."

"I have seen many such cures in the Orient," Lodovici said. "Would you like to learn it?"

"Could you?" Antonio asked excitedly. "Can it be taught?" This offer exceeded his wildest imaginings.

"Some can be taught. If their mental powers are great enough, and I suspect that yours are."

"But can anyone be put into a trance?" Antonio asked. "Whether they wish to or not?"

"The subject must be willing," Lodovici explained. "But many things seem to help in bringing about the trance. For example, a person laboring under a strong emotion, such as fear, is easily magnetized. And it is also true that many persons, even if they do not wish it, can be magnetized before an audience when they might not be susceptible alone."

"What is the nature of this force, then?" Antonio asked. "I do not understand it."

"Neither do I," Lodovici said with an inscrutable smile. "But I respect its powers and do not inquire too much into its cause."

"Could it be witchcraft?" It was a question which had been troubling Antonio.

Agnolo shook his head. "No, Doctor. I am sure that it is a natural occurrence, whatever the actual mechanism may be by which it is produced." He tapped a small gong on the table. *"Vediamo.* We will try an experiment."

The girl who had ushered Antonio into the apartment came through the door hidden by the dark hangings. "Come here, Anya," Lodovici said. "Sit here by the table."

He turned to Antonio. "Now sit across from her, Doctor." Then he whisked the cover from the crystal ball. Once again it took fire from the imprisoned rays of the sun. "Now listen carefully, please, Dr. Servetus. For some reason the state of magnetism can be attained relatively quickly when the subject stares at a concentrated point of light."

"What if such a light is not available?" Antonio asked.

"Then it is sufficient to have the subject stare into the eyes of the master, but that requires more skill. For your tests we will use this crystal, which seems to be better than anything else I have ever used."

"Now, Doctor," Lodovici continued, "look into her eyes. You will note that already they are fixed upon the crystal. It seems almost to have a magnetic power of its own."

Anya was staring at the glowing ball. Antonio had experienced its fascination himself when he had first entered the room, and he could easily believe that it could, of itself, produce a state of trance even in one who did not will it to do so.

"Repeat after me the following phrases," Lodovici said in a low voice. "Think, Anya. Think only of the light. See its warmth and feel it enter your body."

Feeling a little silly, Antonio repeated the words, trying to imitate the deep, throbbing voice of his teacher. "Then say," Lodovici continued, "your spirit is flying away. Your body only remains behind, obedient to my wishes."

Antonio repeated the words, watching the girl closely. He saw her head droop and the lids slowly fall over her eyes. Lower and lower her head drooped, until it lay on her shoulder, as if she had fallen asleep sitting bolt upright in her chair.

"Speak to her," Lodovici commanded. "You will find that she will answer you."

"Are you asleep, Anya?" Antonio asked.

"No, master," the girl replied clearly. "My body is obedient to your wishes."

"Congratulations, Doctor," the magician said. "You have learned quickly."

Still dazed a little by his success, Antonio asked, "But the rigidity?"

"It is simple. Lift her arm and tell her to hold it in place."

Antonio did as instructed. When he tried to push the arm down, it was like a board, resisting all his efforts. "You can do the same with the whole body," Lodovici explained, "merely by instructing her to maintain a rigid state. What is more, you can remove sensation. Tell her that all feeling has left her arm."

Antonio did so, but looked with some alarm at the long pin that Lodovici drew from his turban. Urged by the magician, he jabbed the point into the girl's skin. There was no response, no outcry, not even the involuntary withdrawal which she could not have prevented had she actually experienced any pain. The arm was apparently bereft of all feeling.

"But this could be used for surgical procedures," Antonio cried. "It is astounding."

Lodovici bowed. "I give it to you for what it is worth, Doctor. Now you must learn to terminate the trance state. Tell her she will awaken when you call her name."

At the word "Anya" the girl opened her eyes, raised her head, and smiled.

"You must let me pay you for this knowledge," Antonio insisted.

The magician shook his head. "It will cost you nothing, Doctor. Let us say that it is a favor, a favor which someday I might call upon you to repay."

xii

Under the tutelage of Lodovici Agnolo, Antonio progressed rapidly in the use of the strange, magnetic trance. His teacher was courtesy and helpfulness itself, and yet sometimes Antonio had the feeling that behind the dark face with the hawklike nose and the deep-set eyes Lodovici was playing a game of his own, manipulating him like a puppet on a string and perhaps laughing to himself at some macabre joke which only he understood.

During the period of study the magician allowed Antonio to read books from his own extensive library on magic and necromancy. For the most part, he learned, the magician's trade was pure hocus-pocus, such as the flash of burning gunpowder and the burning tapers of brimstone during the Black Mass ceremony to create in the minds of the onlookers an impression of a satanic visitation. Much of a magician's success, he learned, derived from the fact that once a train of thought was begun in the observer's mind the rest was only a matter of giving free rein and encouragement to the imagination.

Clarice Strozzi, already a frequent subject of Lodovici, was easily magnetized by Antonio. But the crowning evidence of his new-found power came when he was able to put Gian Savarino into a trance. The artist emerged from the magnetic state at his signal and stared at Antonio and Clarice, rubbing his eyes. *"Che ha?"* he asked dazedly. "What happened?"

"You were magnetized," Clarice told him with a smile.

Gian snorted. "Not by Antonio?"

"But you were," Antonio assured him. "Want me to try it again?"

Gian got up hastily. "No. I'll take your word." He poured himself a glass of wine and drank it at a gulp. "If I'd known you were serious about this magnetism, Tonio," he said, "I would have stopped it."

"But why? It will have many uses in medical treatments."

"I don't trust Agnolo. Do you, Clarice?"

The girl's eyes clouded and in them momentarily was the same look Antonio had seen when he first met Lodovici Agnolo. "He is deep," she admitted. "But he respects Antonio."

"He hasn't put you into one of the trances, has he, Tonio?" Gian asked.

"No, but what difference would that make?"

"How do I know?" Gian demanded irritably. "He might get some power over you that way."

"Lodovici and I have talked only of magnetism and medicine," Antonio said, but he realized that something else was troubling Gian. "Why are you worried, Gian?"

"I may be wrong," the artist said, "but I think I have seen Agnolo with Porzia."

"Porzia!" Antonio cried. "Are you sure?"

"Describe him again," Gian said, and when Antonio had finished, he nodded. "I was right. It was Porzia."

"But why should they be talking together?" Antonio asked.

Gian shrugged. "Who knows? One of them could be playing a double game, or perhaps Santos is still trying to get more evidence against you."

Antonio was really alarmed now, for he had no doubts of the prior's venom. The interview in the priory had settled that. "What can we do?" he asked.

"Nothing," Gian said. "Nothing but wait and see."

It was not long before further evidence of an actual plot against Antonio was forthcoming. Clarice Strozzi burst into the studio one afternoon. "Lodovici sent me. To warn Tonio," she told them. "Santos knows that he saved me the night of the demonstration and that he has been experimenting in magnetism."

"Corpo di Cristo!" Gian exclaimed. "How did he learn?"

"I don't know, but Porzia has apparently been asking questions all over Venice."

"But they can't charge me with doing anything wrong," Antonio protested. "It was a scientific experiment."

"The charge is witchcraft," Clarice said, "and the invoking of demons."

"Dio mio!" Gian cried. "Even in Venice you would have trouble defending yourself against that, Tonio. The laws are very strict."

"But I am innocent," Antonio protested.

"That never meant anything to the Inquisition." Gian shrugged. "Besides, there is Clarice to think of."

"Do you mean they would torture her?" Antonio felt suddenly a little sick.

"That is the first thing Santos would think of. If they could make Clarice admit that she was what they call a witch, they would have you too, Tonio."

"But how could anyone be like that?" Antonio asked dumbly.

"It is the Inquisition." There was no more to be said, for the reputation of that dread organization had spread throughout Italy.

"There is only one thing to do, then," Antonio said. "I must leave Venice. Santos is only after me. He will hardly bother Clarice when I am gone."

"But your work at Padua, Tonio," Clarice protested. "You will be giving that up."

"There will not be any work if I am taken," Antonio pointed out. "Still, I don't like the idea of running away. It is cowardly."

"It isn't cowardly to want to live," Gian argued. "Besides, if you are taken now and convicted, they will burn every copy of your *consilium* that has been printed. That is probably what Santos really wants." He rubbed his chin. "No. You must leave Venice. But how?"

"It has to be soon," Clarice said. "Lodovici said that Santos is asking a warrant for your arrest from the civil authorities in the morning."

"We haven't any time to lose, then." Suddenly Gian's face brightened. "I have it. My father is sending a caravan of goods southward tomorrow, to Rome. No one would look for you in a Savarino caravan."

Antonio made immediate protest. "You don't have to be mixed up in this, Gian."

"I got you into it, didn't I?" Gian said heatedly, and then he grinned recklessly. "Besides, I've been wanting a little excitement for a long time. We will join the Rome caravan tomorrow and slip past the border before anyone knows you have left Venice."

A thought struck Antonio. "Do they go by Florence?"

"Florence?" Gian stared at him. "Surely you're not thinking of ___"

"The painting. Yes, I could take it to Messer Bellarmi in Florence."

"But it is in the priory. You would be putting your head right into the garroter's noose."

"Nevertheless, I owe it to Messer Bellarmi to take the painting to him," Antonio argued.

Gian threw up his hands in a gesture of despair. "Of all the stubborn asses, Tonio." He turned to the girl. "Did you ever hear the like, Clarice?"

"I think I understand his reasons," she said.

"You two are always in league against me." Gian shook his head in disgust. "Very well, then. I shall go and make the arrangements to save your precious skin, Tonio. And put that brain of yours to work to figure out how to get the painting from the priory."

When he had gone Clarice said, "You owe it to the world not to let yourself be taken, Tonio."

"But I still don't like it," he protested. "Flight is an admission of guilt."

"Not when you are unjustly accused. And besides, you will be carrying out a mission. That's why you want to take the painting to Florence, isn't it?"

"Yes. But after that, what?"

"I am sure there is some sort of a Providence who watches over people important to the world, Tonio," she said confidently. "This must all be part of a plan."

"Perhaps it is, but I wish I knew more about it." He took her hands. "The worst part is leaving you, madonna mia. I have become very fond of you."

"And I you." Her eyes were bright with unshed tears. "Perhaps it is part of the plan that we shall meet again." She stood on tiptoe and kissed him. "*A rivederci. Caro mio,*" she whispered and was gone.

"*Dio lo volesse.*" He felt suddenly afraid and alone, with the whole world ranged against him.

xiii

On the outskirts of Padua, in the summer dusk, Antonio and Gian waited for night to come, their light carriage hidden behind a hedge. Events had moved fast since Clarice had come to warn them the night before that Antonio's arrest was being ordered. The Savarino caravan bound for Rome now waited south of Venice close to the border of the republic. If their mission were successful they would join the caravan about midnight. Gian had been placed in charge of it by his father, who was no doubt surprised by his son's sudden interest in business matters. According to their plan, Antonio would accompany the caravan, disguised as a priest, a role in which he would hardly be stopped by police searching for an escaped heretic.

In the face of the dangerous mission he was to undertake, Antonio was cool, imbued with a sort of fatalism which had come upon him since he had bidden Clarice good-by the night before. Gian, however, was nervous. "Go over it once more, Tonio," he urged. "There must not be any slip."

"You are to stay with the carriage on the street back of the priory," Antonio repeated patiently. "I will go inside and get the painting. There is a door from the garden opening on the street near where you will wait. It will be the hour of evening prayers and everyone will be in the chapel. You see," he added reassuringly, "nothing can go wrong."

"It is too simple. If only I could go along."

"We have gone over that," Antonio pointed out. "Two would attract attention where one could get through safely. Besides, you wouldn't make a very good priest."

The bell in the campanile of St. Mark's tolled the first hour after sundown. Gian picked up the reins and clucked to the horses. *"Vediamo,"* he said dolefully. It was time to begin the adventure.

The street before the priory was empty, the door lighted by a lamp burning beside it. Antonio left the carriage and flattened himself against the wall in the shadows until Gian and the carriage were around the corner. Then he stepped into the circle of light before the priory door, with no protection save the cowl of his robe, which he had drawn low over his forehead to shadow his face. He tried the door and, finding it, as he had expected, unlocked, stepped inside and closed it behind him. The corridor, with the familiar trenches worn in the stone by countless monkish feet, stretched before him. He concentrated on walking slowly and naturally, for haste in this place of quiet would have attracted attention.

Then he heard footsteps coming along the corridor and, in a rush of panic, looked wildly about for someplace to hide. It was just his misfortune, he told himself bleakly, that some monk or lay brother had been delayed in going to evening prayers. The steps came closer; soon their author must turn the corner and meet him face to face. With a sudden inspiration, Antonio turned and bent over, shuffling along with a limping gait in the direction of the chapel, hoping that whoever it was would think him one of the older monks, many of whom, he well knew, were afflicted with gout.

The steps grew nearer, but Antonio shuffled on without looking up, leaving space for the other to pass. The skirts of a white robe of luxurious material and feet shod in sandals of rich Cordovan leather came within his field of vision, and Antonio felt his muscles go rigid. No one else in the priory wore such a robe or such a pair of sandals except the prior. It could be none other than Fra Felipe Santos himself.

"Do not hurry, my brother," the deep voice said as the other passed. "We are late in beginning our evening prayers." Seconds later he turned into the side corridor leading to the chapel.

Antonio leaned against the wall and pressed his shaking hands upon the stone in a sudden rush of weakness. He still could not believe his good fortune in actually having met the prior without being recognized, and for a long moment he fought against an almost overpowering urge to leave this place where he had come so close to disaster, giving up the dangerous mission. Then he straightened his shoulders and got control of himself. Common sense told him he had twenty minutes now in which there was little chance of detection, for everyone in the priory would be deep in the prayer service, and in that time he should be able to carry out his mission easily. Fortunately Fra Felipe had told him on the day of their interview that the painting was in his quarters. He moved rapidly along the corridors now and let himself into the prior's apartment.

The painting was still on its frame but in the bedroom adjoining the prior's audience chambers. Antonio's heart quickened its beat as his eyes met those of the smiling woman who seemed, as always, on the point of stepping down from the canvas. Almost, he could have sworn, her face assumed a look of tender welcome and pleasure that he had come to take her away with him.

But there was no time for admiring even that chaste beauty, and he set rapidly to work to remove the canvas from the frame. It was much too large to be carried rolled up, and, laying it on the bed, he folded it into a compact package and tied it with cord he had brought for the purpose. He was just lifting the heavy canvas to his shoulders when a familiar voice said from the door, "So it *was* you!"

Antonio whirled, dropping the canvas on the bed. Fra Felipe Santos stood in the door. Antonio realized that he must have entered while he was preoccupied with the heavy canvas. "H-how did you know I was here?" Antonio stammered.

"By the set of your shoulders in the corridor just now. Few gouty monks have such broad shoulders." The prior smiled thinly. "Unfortunately for you, Dr. Servetus, I remembered that during prayers and left the chapel. Why are you stealing my Botticelli?"

Antonio's anger rose at the casual use of the possessive word. "Yours?" he cried indignantly. "You know well that it belongs to Messer Bellarmi in Florence."

"So you knew that all the time," Fra Felipe said. "You are cleverer than I thought, Ser Physician. I was right in making certain that you would not disturb my plans."

"By arresting me on a trumped charge?" Antonio demanded.

A light of cold malice glowed in Fra Felipe's eyes. "I warned you once and you disobeyed me," he said. "Now you will pay for your disobedience at the stake." He turned suddenly toward the dais where Antonio knew he kept a signal to summon his servants. Knowing that his life depended upon stopping Fra Felipe from calling others, Antonio acted automatically. His shoulder struck the spare body in the white robe just as the prior was reaching for the bell on the audience table and spun him away from it. Staggered by the blow, Fra Felipe caught at the table to support himself while the color drained from his cheeks.

"You dared to attack my person," he breathed. "You heretic fool." Antonio saw his hand fumbling on the table behind him, and a second later the thin fingers closed around the razor-sharp stiletto kept there for opening sealed papers. It was a murderous weapon, and Antonio was unarmed, for he had refused to carry a dagger, in spite of Gian's urgings.

His normal cold glance now replaced by a light of murderous rage, Fra Felipe began to move toward Antonio with the stiletto in his hand. Antonio gave ground slowly, searching the room frantically with his eyes for something with which to defend himself. It was obvious now that Fra Felipe did not intend merely to capture him; nothing less than Antonio's death at his own hands would be sufficient. Inching along the wall, Antonio's head struck the base of a silver candlestick in a bracket on the wall. It was a poor weapon against a dagger, but he had no choice. Twisting his body, he seized the bracket and pulled down upon it with all his strength. There was a ripping sound as the supports gave way and the heavy candlestick came loose in his hands.

But, in turning, Antonio had momentarily exposed himself to attack, and Fra Felipe lunged toward him with the stiletto upraised. Twisting desperately, Antonio tried to throw his body away from the weapon. He felt it slash through his robe, and then a flash of almost unbearable pain shot through him as the point cut through skin and muscle to blunt itself against a rib.

It was, after all, the rib that saved him, for the knife halted almost at the beginning of what would have been a fatal wound with the full force of Fra Felipe's wiry body behind the weapon. As it was, the blade glanced from a rib to cut through muscle and skin once more and slit Antonio's robe well below the waist. But Antonio's movement had thrown his attacker off balance. Ignoring the pain, Antonio swung the candlestick as a knight swings a mace in combat, striking again and again at the prior's skull, until the wiry body suddenly went limp and the knife flew from his grasp as he crashed unconscious to the floor.

Panting and reeling from exertion, pain, and loss of blood, Antonio leaned against the wall and gulped air into straining lungs. The warm flood staining his side and the mounting weakness told him that he was losing blood fast. Driven by the strength of desperation, he ripped off his slashed robe and tore strips from it. He could see the wound now by twisting his body: a deep slash, laying open the skin and muscles and exposing the rib beneath. The pain, as he moved the injured muscles, was so sharp that he cried out involuntarily from it, but, working rapidly, he bound the strips of cloth around his chest over the wound. He must depend upon the pressure, he knew, to stop the bleeding and keep the wound closed until he could make good his escape. With trembling fingers he knotted the ends of the improvised bandage and wiped the blood from his body with the remainder of his torn robe.

Now he was stripped to his smallclothes, and he could not escape half naked. Then his eyes fell upon Fra Felipe's body lying on the floor. He forced himself to feel for the pulse and for an instant thought that it was not there, then distinguished its weak beat. He was not a murderer, at least not yet, he knew with a surge of relief, but there was an excellent chance that the prior would not survive such a beating. Not that he would come off any easier if he were caught, Antonio realized. The penalty for attacking a high churchman was just as great as that for murder.

Bending over the prior, Antonio began to strip off the white robe. The robe was tight when he stepped into it, but he could wear it. As for Fra Felipe, he felt no compunction now about leaving him to whatever fate befell him. It had been a fair fight; in fact, more than fair, for Antonio had been forced to defend himself unarmed against a murderous weapon.

Dressed in the white robes of a Dominican of high station, Antonio let himself through the prior's side door into the garden. From the chapel across the priory he heard the voices of the monks and lay brothers lifted in the closing hymn of the evening service. He had been none too soon in making his escape, he realized as he staggered across the garden and opened the door in the wall. His strength was almost spent from the fight, the loss of blood, and the weight of the heavy canvas.

"*Dio mio!*" Gian muttered from the shadows near the gate when he saw a white-robed figure emerge carrying a heavy burden. Could this be some sort of a trick? Was Antonio already taken? Then the man in the white robe dropped his burden and swayed weakly. "Gian! Gian!" a familiar voice called.

Instantly the artist was out of the shadows and supporting Antonio. "Tonio mio!" he cried. "You are hurt."

"A flesh wound," Antonio gasped. "Get the canvas into the carriage. We have no time to lose."

Gian required no urging. As the carriage moved along the back streets toward the roads leading southward from the city, Antonio gave him a quick résumé of what had happened. "I hope you killed him," Gian growled. "That must have been a fine fight."

In the early dawn they found the Savarino caravan waiting beyond the border of the Venetian Republic. The sun was just lifting above the hills, but there was no time to stop, for they must put as much distance as they could behind them before any outcry could be raised or pursuit begun.

Antonio's head was aching and there was a throbbing pain in his side; harbinger, his medical knowledge told him, of serious trouble from the wound. Lying on the cushion of the carriage, half propped up because of the cramped position, every jolt of the vehicle was agony, and more than once he felt his senses leaving him. And yet the wound must be taken care of soon, he realized, and if he were delirious he could not do it properly. He must instruct Gian before delirium claimed him entirely.

When they paused momentarily to water the horses, he gasped out, "When we stop for midday, Gian, you must cauterize the wound."

The artist paled. "I cannot, Tonio," he protested. "I am no physician."

"You must do it," Antonio insisted. "I shall not be able to do so. Listen carefully, now." He clenched his teeth against a spasm of pure agony. It was moments before he could speak again. "Take oil and heat it, or pitch if you can find it," he instructed Gian. "Have it boiling and pour it into the wound. Then bandage it again."

"Lo faro. I will do it," Gian said, sweat beading his brow.

"Apply hot fomentations if I become unconscious," Antonio continued weakly. "No meat or red wine. Draw blood from the left arm. Remember, the left."

His eyes closed then, and when he spoke again an hour later, his voice was thick with the babbling of delirium.

Book Three

PHYSICIAN TO THE QUEEN

At first her face was only a confused and vague blur, seen through recurring waves of pain, like the ripples made by a pebble thrown into a pond. Now it was the Venus of the Botticelli canvas, again it was the face of Lucia Bellarmi which swam before his eyes. But it could be neither, he knew, in his rare moments of lucidity, for the canvas still lay on the floor of the carriage and Lucia was in Florence. The eyes, too, when he managed to distinguish them, were tender and thoughtful, not scornful, as Lucia's had always been in the dream.

He was again on the hill before Champel, watching an erect figure chained to a stake around which flames were leaping. Grasping hands tore at his body and sought to pull him toward another stake, empty but ready. Despite his struggles, they dragged him close enough for him to read the placard tacked to the stake itself:

> Antonio Servetus, heretic, practicer of witchcraft.
> Death to one who dares attack a servant of God!
> Death to the heretic, Antonio Servetus!

Fighting with all his strength, he managed to break away from the hands that seemed always to be reaching out to bring him back. But there would be other battles, he knew, and one of them he must lose . . .

"Dr. Servetus." A soft voice, vaguely familiar, sounded close by. He turned his head and his eyes met the concerned gaze of Lucia Bellarmi.

"Madonna Bellarmi. The painting." A spasm of pain made him gasp.

"It is safe." She changed the moistened cloth on his forehead, and the acrid smell of vinegar reached his nostrils. Her fingers were cool on his skin.

His eyes moved about the room. It was small, but expensively furnished, with draperies of silk and an excellent painting on the wall which he recognized as an early Botticelli head. There was a handsome dressing table in the corner. From the mirror over it a haggard, bearded face, with deep-set eyes and mouth twisted by pain, stared back at him.

"Where am I?" he whispered.

"In Florence. At the Palazzo Bellarmi."

"But we left Padua only yesterday."

"You left Padua a week ago, but you have been very ill from your wound."

He remembered then the fight in the priory, the thud of the candlestick upon the skull of Fra Felipe Santos, the searing pain of his wound, and the agony of the carriage ride through the night until the rising fever from his inflamed wound and shock brought unconsciousness.

"Gian told us about your fight to get the painting," Lucia Bellarmi said. "You were very brave."

He smiled wryly. "I almost didn't succeed."

"I know. Dr. Duval says another inch and your wound would have been fatal."

"Dr. Duval?"

"A French physician. He was with the French armies in Italy and remained to teach in the university here."

Antonio tried to move his shoulder, and a spasm of pain went through him. Madonna Lucia put her hand beneath his shoulder and moved it gently. Her touch was sure and easy. "There," she said. "That should be better."

"It is, thank you," he said. "You are a very good nurse."

"I have had a week of practice on you," she reminded him with a smile. Voices sounded in the corridor outside. "That must be Dr. Duval."

A small man with a pointed beard came into the room. His brown eyes were bright and his face cheerful as he bowed over Lucia's hand before turning to the bed.

"Voilà!" he cried; then beaming, "You have returned to this world, no?"

Antonio managed to smile. "Madonna has been telling me I was close to another."

"Very close. Very close indeed." The doctor began to arrange his dressing material on a table beside the bed. "But for the genius of Dr. Ambroise Paré you might not have returned to this world at all, m'sieu."

"Paré?" Antonio echoed.

"You have not heard of Dr. Paré?"

"Is he the barber surgeon who has described a new method of treating wounds?"

"*Was* a barber surgeon," the Frenchman corrected. "Ambroise Paré is now a Fellow of the College of Surgeons of Paris. But I tire you," he continued briskly. "Let us look at the wound."

Although the French physician was quite gentle in removing the dressings, Antonio was pale and sweating from pain before the wound was exposed. "*Ah! Magnifique!*" Duval exclaimed. "You should see it yourself, Dr. Servetus."

"He can use my hand mirror." Lucia went over to the dressing table and brought back a mirror whose silver back was carved in an intricate design, obviously by a master silversmith. There were other strictly feminine articles upon the table, from which Antonio judged that she had given up her own chamber for him.

When she held the mirror, Antonio could see the wound clearly. It was some four inches long, and the skin around the edges was still swollen from the inflammation. But the depths were clean and healing with fresh pink tissue.

"Is it not beautiful?" Dr. Duval asked.

"Gian did not cauterize!" Antonio exclaimed.

"Fortunately for you, m'sieu."

"But the wound poisons——"

"Dr. Paré has exploded that theory completely!" Duval exclaimed. "When Messer Savarino found himself unable to cauterize the wound as you directed him, he unwittingly gave it the best treatment. See how much better it looks than if treated in the old way?"

There was no questioning the evidence. Had the wound been cauterized with boiling oil, a hot iron, or liquid pitch, as was the custom, there would have been great areas of charred flesh taking months to separate and come away. Now, although only a week old and complicated by a severe inflammation, the wound was clean and healthy. This was something to think about, for if this new treatment always worked so well, all previous methods were not only wrong but dangerous.

Dr. Duval began to prepare a dressing, moistening the linen with a yellowish mixture from a bottle. "A fine healing mixture, Dr. Servetus," he rattled on. "Also the discovery of the so clever Dr. Paré! Egg yolk and attar of rose water, dissolved in turpentine."

The dressing stung the raw surface of the wound, making Antonio gasp, but as the French physician bandaged it skillfully into place, a refreshing coolness replaced the sting. *"Voilà!"* He went to wash his hands at a basin in the corner. "You should get well very quickly, Dr. Servetus. You have youth in your favor . . . and a very pretty nurse."

Lucia blushed, soft color suffusing her cheeks. Once again Antonio experienced the strange feeling that somewhere he had known her so well that her every feature seemed familiar; in fact, more so now than when he had seen her before.

"Do you have any of the writings of Dr. Paré?" he asked Dr. Duval.

"But certainly. A little manual on the treatment of gunshot wounds. But, alas, it is written in French."

"I read French," Antonio said.

"Magnifique! And in return you must let me read this most important work of your own on *le circulation pulmonaire,* about which Messer Savarino and Messer Bellarmi have been telling me."

"I should be honored," Antonio said, pleased.

When Dr. Duval had gone, Lucia bustled about the room, setting things in order and humming a gay tune. Everywhere he went, Antonio reflected, there was something to be learned. And yet he had once been on the point of choosing to remain in the priory and the university, shutting himself away from the outside world. Much of what the world had to offer, he was beginning to understand, was not written in texts. They were things which the simple use of one's powers of observation should make clear, once they were tackled directly, as he had tackled the problem of proving his theory of the pulmonary circulation in the body of the pig.

Vaguely, Antonio realized that the change going on inside himself symbolized a new way of thought in everything, not just in medicine and science, a way which demanded factual proof of truths hitherto taken for granted because spoken by someone in authority. And as he lay there he felt the deep stirrings of a personal sense of pride that he himself had been one of those who showed the way with his experiments, just as he hoped to continue with other studies and other experiments. His contribution, actually, lay not so much in discovering the circulation of the lungs, important as that undoubtedly was, as in the method he had used to prove it, the method of investigation and experiment which had largely been discarded since the time of the ancient Greek philosophers.

He drifted off to sleep, and when he awakened, Gian Savarino had taken Lucia's place. Gian was well scrubbed and pink and his tunic freshly pressed. "So you decided to live after all?" he said with a smile.

"I didn't realize there was so much doubt until this morning," Antonio said.

"For a while I didn't think I would get you here alive," Gian said. "But I couldn't cauterize the wound as you told me."

"Dr. Duval thinks it is well that you did not."

"And you?"

"I am inclined to agree with him after seeing it," Antonio said.

Gian drew a long breath. "I was scared," he admitted. "Driving across the Papal States, I couldn't stop for fear word had gotten ahead of us. The only thing I could think of was to get you to Florence as soon as possible." He grinned. "My esteemed parent will let up an awful howl when he hears how much of his gold I spent in changes of horses."

"I know I owe you my life," Antonio said.

"Well, you did me a favor by getting sick," Gian assured him. "Naturally I had to stay close by, in case I was needed. Meanwhile I have been making progress with the so lovely Madonna Lucia."

Antonio felt a moment of irritation at his friend's words and wondered why. God knew, he assured himself, he couldn't be jealous. Lucia Bellarmi could be very pleasant, as evidenced by her nursing of him, but she could also be a shrew, as he very well remembered.

"Messer Girolamo and his niece were overjoyed to get the painting," Gian went on. "It will be hung in the main gallery of the palazzo as soon as you are up."

"Why wait for me?"

"Messer Bellarmi plans a ceremony in your honor. After all, he should reward you for getting a knife between your ribs."

"I want no reward," Antonio said.

"Don't be an ass, Tonio. After all, you lost a very important position because of the painting. What can you do now?"

"A capable physician can always make a living."

"The arm of Rome is pretty strong in Florence. It would reach you eventually."

"Fra Felipe may be dead," Antonio objected. "No one could suspect me then."

"There is still that fellow Porzia."

"He probably wouldn't do much without Santos," Antonio observed. "Still, I hope Fra Felipe did not die."

"*Dio mio!*" Gian exclaimed. "He tried to kill you, did he not?"

"I still want no man's death on my conscience."

"My conscience wouldn't trouble me on that score," Gian observed. "But the bad ones usually live. Would Santos suspect that you had come to Florence?"

"Yes. I told him I knew who owned the painting."

"In that case, you will *have* to go to Spain."

"To Spain?" Antonio said, startled. "Why?"

"Messer Bellarmi is going to Madrid soon. You know the House of Bellarmi was closely identified with the De' Medici bankers and they have always had heavy interests in Spain."

"But how does that concern me?" Antonio asked.

"His health is none too good, and he tells me he wants to take with him a physician in whom he has confidence," Gian said.

"But what would I do in Spain?" Antonio insisted.

"Do you speak Spanish?"

"Of course. I was born in Spain and my mother was a Spaniard."

"Vesalius is the king's physician in Madrid," Gian reminded him. "He should be glad to have an anatomist of your reputation in Madrid."

Antonio smiled wryly. "My reputation as an anatomist is more of a hindrance than a help now."

"I disagree," Gian insisted. "Your quarrel with Santos is a personal one. In Spain you would be safe. And if not, you could always go to the New World. I have been thinking of going there myself."

"How soon is Messer Bellarmi going?" Antonio asked.

"Within a few weeks."

"But I couldn't travel that soon."

"Take your time about getting well," Gian advised smiling. "I shall have longer to press my suit upon the niece of the house."

ii

When Antonio was ready to walk, Messer Bellarmi sent out invitations to the ceremony of hanging the Botticelli Venus in its rightful place in the main gallery of the Palazzo Bellarmi. His recovery had been speeded by the soothing dressings of Drs. Duval and Paré and the nursing care of Madonna Lucia. He had come to know her much better in the days during which they were together so much of the time, and he had developed a genuine appreciation of her intelligence as well as her beauty. For a woman, he discovered, she was surprisingly well educated. Until the beginning of the sixteenth century and the dawn of the new humanistic concepts of the Renaissance, women had been given very little education and most of them could hardly read and write. But the spread of the new thought included even women, and now many of them in the great wealthy houses of Italy were as well educated as the men. This was true of Lucia.

But there was another reason for her learning, he discovered. Since the death of her own parents in childhood, she had been reared by her uncle very much as a boy would have been brought up. As a result she also had a grasp of business and worldly affairs considerably exceeding that of Antonio himself, shut away as he had been in the cloister and the halls of learning. He found himself stimulated by her mind and in return showed her something of the world of science and medicine in which his own life had been spent. Often their talks developed into spirited arguments. He let her read his *consilium* and was amazed how quickly she grasped its importance as a demonstration of the use of experiment in proving scientific truth.

At these times she was serious, but there were other times when he heard her laughing gaily with Gian and some of the young gallants of Florence who seemed always on the doorstep. And although she chided Antonio on his seriousness, he somehow never felt quite at ease at such gatherings and usually kept to himself, studying instead the writings of Ambroise Paré and his fascinating new approach to disease, or one of the many volumes in Messer Bellarmi's excellent library.

The ceremony of hanging the Botticelli canvas was brief, but impressive. A large number of the more important citizenry of Florence were present, artists, architects, churchmen, physicians, and men of business. Messer Girolamo was unstinting in his praise of Antonio for finding the canvas and returning it to Florence, although he very properly did not go into any details about how its discovery and return had been effected. He referred to Antonio's work at Padua and to his *consilium,* and at the end of the ceremonies a large group of physicians and scientists waited to do him honor. Before they departed, Antonio had promised to lecture on the pulmonary circulation before the physicians of Florence and also before the faculty of the nearby University of Pisa, one of the oldest and most respected educational institutions of that day in all of Italy.

Madonna Lucia was unaccountably absent from the ceremony, which surprised Antonio, since he knew that the painting was actually her property. When the visitors had departed, he asked Messer Bellarmi about her.

A gleam of amusement appeared in the banker's eyes. "Some trifling indisposition kept her away, I believe," he said. "It is nothing serious."

"Perhaps she has tired herself too much attending to me."

"I think not." Messer Bellarmi toyed with the gold chain about his neck. "I believe Gian told you that I am going to Spain."

"Yes, he did." Antonio did not miss the use of Gian's first name. The artist must indeed be making progress in his suit for Madonna Lucia's affections.

"It would be a great comfort to me if you would come as my personal physician," the banker said.

"Are you certain, messire, that it is not gratitude which brings you to make this offer?" Antonio asked.

"By no means," the banker protested. "Lately I have been having a sense of pressure here." He placed his hand over his heart. "And sometimes a pain runs down my arm. Both Dr. Duval and I think that I should be watched closely by a capable physician, and frankly, I don't trust the Spaniards."

"They have a few good physicians," Antonio said. "But not very many, according to all reports." Going to Spain meant cutting all the ties which still bound him to the University of Padua, tenuous though they now were. If Fra Felipe were really dead, it might very well be that no one would suspect his relationship to the death, for suspicion would more likely be directed toward thieves seeking to steal a valuable painting. And without the friar's personal enmity to fan the flames, the charges against him would probably not be pressed. Then, after a decent interval, he might still be able to return to Padua and once more take up his work in anatomy.

But he had no way of knowing what had happened in Padua after his departure, he reminded himself. Nor did he know the extent to which Battista Porzia had been taken into the prior's confidence. So, in seeking to learn these things, he might place himself once more in serious jeopardy. Reason argued, therefore, that it was best to take himself as far from Padua as possible. And where better than Spain?

"You need not decide immediately," Messer Girolamo's voice broke into his thoughts.

"Forgive me, messire. I was thinking what the step might mean. After all, I was offered the professorship of anatomy at Padua."

"And you have lost it because of your devotion to my niece and myself." The banker's face was grave. "We are indeed in your debt, Doctor."

Antonio smiled. "Perhaps everything happens for the best. Already I have learned things which I might well have missed in Padua, and I am sure that I shall learn more in Spain."

"Then you accept?"

"Gladly. But I cannot make the trip yet because of my wound."

"I have considered that," Bellarmi said briskly. "My niece and I must leave within a week, since the Queen of Spain, a distant relative of ours through the house of the De' Medici, has kindly offered to honor Lucia by making her a maid of honor."

"Could I stay behind and take passage later?" Antonio asked.

"Yes. I have thought of that. We have a small villa on the seacoast where you can recuperate more rapidly. Another of our ships will be sailing for Barcelona in a month, and you can take passage on it and join us in Madrid."

When the banker was gone, Antonio stood looking at the great canvas on the wall. Everything changed, he thought, save the serene beauty of the goddess. In the half-light of the room, slowly filling with the shadows of late afternoon, her lips seemed to curve in an approving smile, as though she were thanking him for returning her to her home. As always, a sense of warmth and kinship of spirit with her pervaded him, quieting his doubts and giving him strength. Any service undertaken because of her must be right and even foreordained, he understood now. She had led him from Padua to Florence, and now, still because of her, he would soon be embarking upon a new adventure in Spain. Somehow he was sure that everything would resolve itself into the pattern begun that morning when he had come upon the dusty canvas in the priory storeroom and had unrolled to view for the first time the breath-taking beauty of the divine Venus. To what that pattern led he was not yet sure, but of its purpose he had no doubt.

"Still in love with paint and canvas, Tonio?" Gian's voice intruded upon his thoughts.

Antonio turned to face his friend. "And where are flesh and blood to equal her?" he demanded.

Gian laughed. "There is one somewhere, but I would settle for a little less perfection and more complaisance. I met Messer Bellarmi. He tells me you are going with us to Spain."

"Are you going too?" Antonio asked in surprise.

"Of course."

"But I can't let you do it, Gian," Antonio protested. "You have sacrificed enough already because of me."

"This is not because of you," Gian assured him. "My father was very happy when I wrote suggesting that he make me his representative in Madrid."

"I don't suppose Madonna Lucia's going to Madrid had anything to do with your deciding to become a businessman."

"Nothing at all," Gian assured him blandly. "Besides, I've never been to Spain."

"Why don't you go ahead with them, then?" Antonio suggested.

"I—I came to ask you about that," the artist admitted.

Antonio smiled. "I gathered as much. By all means, go ahead. You will be well rid of me."

When Gian had gone, Antonio, unwilling to return to his bed, sought the enclosed garden at the rear of the Palazzo Bellarmi. The oppressive fall heat was relieved somewhat here by the coolness of the spring which burbled over an elaborate rock garden before disappearing beneath the farther wall of the patio. Looking at the clear pool of water, his thoughts went back to Padua with the Bacchiglione and Professor Fallopius. His own addition to the current of human knowledge, he thought with some bitterness, was already swallowed up by human hate and greed, his future destroyed because Fra Felipe Santos had coveted the beauty of the Botticelli Venus and its value as a work of art.

And then, as if in a dream, although he knew he was awake, her face took form before his eyes, mirrored in the clear surface of the water. Startled, Antonio caught his breath and was leaning over the edge of the pool to see her more clearly when a cool voice said, "Why so intent, Ser Physician?"

He turned quickly. Lucia Bellarmi was standing hardly a yard away along the rock wall that surrounded the spring, smiling. Intent upon his thoughts, he had not heard her approach. Still unable to believe it, Antonio looked at her and then back at her reflection in the water, but it was still the same. "It is impossible," he said in a tone of awe. "But you are the Venus of Botticelli."

"Of course," she said. "Everyone in Florence knows."

"Then that is why you seemed so familiar the first time I saw you," he said. "But I still do not understand it. Such things cannot happen."

She moved over to a bench beside the pool and sat down. "There is an explanation for this resemblance," she said. "My great-aunt, Simonetta Vespucci, was the model for Botticelli when he painted the Venus."

"And you inherited her characteristics." Antonio caught on at once. "It is a miracle, but possible, at that."

"I am surprised that neither you nor Gian has heard the story," Lucia said. Then she changed the subject. "Are you going to Spain with us?"

But Antonio did not hear her. He was pondering on the miracle of the Venus, alive and in the person of Lucia Bellarmi. Now that he knew the connection, he was amazed that he had not discovered it at once in Padua. But without the knowledge of the relationship between Lucia and Simonetta Vespucci, the whole thing would have seemed too fantastic for belief. It must have been that which had kept him from seeing the resemblance, he decided.

"Are you going to Spain with us?" Lucia asked again.

"Excuse me," Antonio said. "I was still thinking of that amazing resemblance."

"Then you haven't decided?"

"Oh yes. I am going," he said, and smiled wryly. "After all, there is a price on my head still, you know."

She put her hand upon his and her fingers were warm and friendly. A current of understanding and warm affection seemed to flow between them. "You risked your life to get the Venus back to me," she said softly, "and I do appreciate it, Tonio."

Suddenly Antonio felt a sense of guilt, almost of sacrilege, that he had allowed even Lucia to take for a single instant the place in his thoughts and feelings reserved for the goddess of the canvas. Without thinking of what he did, he drew his hand away from hers and lay it on the bench.

Lucia's cheeks were suddenly pink with color and points of light glowed in her eyes. "Why did you take your hand away?" she asked, her voice tense.

"I—I don't know," Antonio stammered, surprised by the change in her voice and manner.

"Was it because I mentioned the Venus?"

"Why would that make any difference?" he countered lamely.

"When you were delirious you babbled about her most of the time. What does she mean to you, Tonio?"

"Gian claims that I am in love with her."

"Are you?"

"I don't know," he admitted honestly. "I am . . . strongly attracted to her."

"But she is not human."

"She is to me," Antonio said simply. "To me she seems as real as . . . as you are."

Lucia stood up suddenly. "Then have your Venus, if that is what you want, Ser Moonstruck," she cried. He could have sworn there was a sob in her voice as she whirled in a fury of petticoats and ran from the garden.

Antonio remained staring at the pool with a puzzled frown. Why had Lucia become so disturbed? he wondered. He could think of no reason, and just before their quarrel they had been for a moment closer than ever before. Remembering the warm current of affection and understanding which had flowed between them, he thought that he must see her again tomorrow and ask her what was wrong. He was very fond of her, and now he thought he understood why. It was as if

she were a sister to the divine Venus of the painting, a younger sister
perhaps, but also a twin. It was all very confusing, and he realized
now that the afternoon's activities had left him very tired.

iii

Gian Savarino, crossing the main gallery on his way to look for
Lucia, was startled to hear her voice lifted in angry denunciation of
some unseen person. "I hate you," she cried. "I hate you." There was
the sharp crack of a leather heel upon the tiled floor.

Gian came around one of the columns and saw her standing before
the great canvas which had been hung again just that morning. To
his surprise, she was alone.

"Madonna," he cried, "what is wrong?"

Lucia whirled, her eyes stormy, breathing fast. "What do you want?"

"I was seeking you to suggest a game of patience."

"Patience!" she laughed with a shrill note almost of hysteria in her
voice. "How absurd!"

"Who are you angry at?" Gian asked. "Or are you practicing for a
play?"

"I am angry with her," Lucia cried, indicating the nude goddess on
the wall.

Gian looked up at the painting and then back at Lucia, and his jaw
went slack with amazement. Again he compared them, just to make
sure that his eyes were not deceiving him. But there was no doubting
their identity, now that he saw them together. The slender, fiery girl
before him and the serene goddess of the canvas, feature for feature
they were the same.

"But she is you—you are she," he blurted. "The face is the same. And
in the nude you might be——"

Lucia slapped him hard on the cheek. "How dare you say that?"

Gian rubbed his cheek and began to grin. "Forgive me, madonna,"
he explained. "I am an artist. Naturally I think of the whole figure."

"You shall have no opportunity to verify your suspicions," she told
him acidly, "if that is what you are suggesting."

"Believe me, madonna," he protested, "I was suggesting no such
thing." Just as she stood there, proud and erect and angry, he could
see that there was little about Lucia Bellarmi that was not perfect, as

perfect perhaps as the figure of Venus. The small perfection of her
bosom, the slender waist, and the lovely ankles and feet merely completed the picture, for in figure, as well as in face, she was incredibly
identical with the Venus of the great canvas.

"But how——" he began, and stopped. "*Eccolo!* Simonetta Vespucci, of course. *Vediamo.* Amerigo Vespucci was your grandfather."

"And Simonetta my great-aunt," Lucia said.

"So by a trick of inheritance you could easily be a duplicate of her."
He grinned. "It is like a fairy story."

"About a bad fairy," Lucia said morosely.

"But when you are so proud of your inheritance from the Vespucci,
why do you hate her?"

"Because *he* loves her."

"Who—Tonio?"

"Yes. He just admitted it to me."

"But you couldn't love such a clod as Tonio."

"He is not a clod," she cried in sudden anger. "He is a very brilliant
man."

Gian's face sobered. "You are right, madonna. He is more than that.
But when did he——"

"He doesn't," Lucia said. "That is, he doesn't love me as me."

Gian shook his head. "This is all very confusing. You love Tonio
and Tonio loves the Venus of the painting. But you are identical with
the Venus. If this were a problem in Euclid, since things which equal
the same thing are equal to each other—Tonio would be in love with
you."

"But it isn't a problem in Euclid," she wailed. "And he doesn't love
me."

"In that event, why not try someone else? Here I am eating my heart
out for you, madonna."

"Poor Gian." She smiled in gentle mockery. "How many times have
you eaten your heart?"

"Never so thoroughly as for you," he protested.

"Are you still going to Madrid?"

"Unless you don't want me to go."

"But of course I want you to," she cried. "Haven't we had a world
of fun together these past few weeks?"

He bowed, his hand over his heart. "You have given me new life, madonna. And besides, Antonio may suddenly decide to become a monk again."

"That's what I'm afraid of," she said. "He hasn't found the world outside the cloister a very happy one. He needs us both, Gian."

"To help him solve a problem in Euclid, perhaps?" Gian asked a trifle sarcastically.

"No. I think that will work itself out all right, once I put my mind to it."

"You seem very confident."

"Things usually happen the way I plan them," she said serenely. "Perhaps you don't realize that I knew the Botticelli canvas was in Padua before my uncle and I left Venice."

He stared at her in disbelief. "But surely you didn't leave it there just so Antonio would have to come to Florence to bring it."

"He came, didn't he?"

"*Maria Sanctissima!* You women will do anything for love. But you had just met him. You couldn't have already decided that——"

"I decided the day I met him," she said. "So now you can see why I am sure that everything will turn out as I have planned. And why you must not tell him I love him."

"Meanwhile you and Tonio dangle like puppets on a string?"

"Something like that."

"I will not tell your secret, madonna," he promised, and grinned. "Besides, I'm very fond of puppet shows myself."

iv

After seeing Messer Bellarmi, his niece, and Gian Savarino off for Barcelona and Philip II's new inland capital of Madrid, Antonio returned to the Bellarmi villa beside the warm waters and dark sands of the Ligurian Sea. There was nothing to do but laze in the sun or swim in the warm waters, while he allowed his skin to tan and the hollows between his ribs and in his cheeks to fill out. Dr. Duval had given him a small volume of the writings of Ambroise Paré and, in a burst of generosity, had added a chest of surgical instruments such as the great French surgeon favored. Antonio spent pleasant hours learning the details of Paré's great discoveries in the field of surgery and anticipating the things he might learn from studying with Vesalius in Madrid. Since the anatomist was personal physician to the King of Spain and accompanied him upon all his expeditions, there would be ample opportunity to try out these new ideas of Paré's about the treatment of wounds. The more he thought of it the more Antonio felt a sense of anticipation and a restlessness to begin this new venture in his already turbulent life.

The month of solitude gave him, too, a chance to ponder upon his experiences in the world beyond the university and the cloister, the world in which he had already known so much pain but no little satisfaction as well, since his discovery of the Botticelli canvas had thrust him into the midst of it. As full of imperfections as this world was, he was learning already that it was an interesting and stimulating place to a man who was willing to use his mind. And it was a place, he was beginning to suspect, where a man might learn much and still serve God as well as if he were shut away behind conventual walls.

Fallopius had meant something like this, he realized now, when he had said that a physician could not really treat disease until he had himself experienced some of the ills of the world. Having seen and felt the causes of human tribulations and trials within himself, he would be filled with the compassion for his fellows which distinguishes the true physician.

Antonio was beginning to realize, too, that his original conceptions of the physician's place, molded as they were by the influence of the university, would have to be changed and that it was as important to relieve pain, stem the ravages of disease, and perhaps help the young to be born into the world as it was to discover a new bone in the hand or a new blood vessel in the liver.

Most of all Antonio found that he missed the companionship with Lucia which he had enjoyed so much, at least until that afternoon in the garden after the painting was hung. Try as he might, remembering their conversation, he could not understand the reason for her anger, but she had remained quite cool toward him during the week before she had sailed with her uncle and Gian. Actually he had seen her hardly at all, so busy had she been, or professed to be, with preparations for her new role of maid of honor to the Queen of Spain.

When the ship was ready to sail, he gathered up his belongings, including the small volume of the writings of Ambroise Paré and a case of instruments devised by the French surgeon which Dr. Duval had given him as a parting gift, and journeyed up to Pisa to embark. The

master of the vessel met him at the gangplank, as befitted the personal
physician of the owner, and a cabin boy took his effects to the best cabin
of the ship. Antonio remained on deck to watch the sailing.

Before him as he leaned against the rail were the cluttered buildings
of the water front of Pisa, the tangled gear of the fishing boats with
their varicolored sails and laughing crews, the hustle and bustle on the
wharf as the final preparations for sailing were being carried out. Long
lines of porters, like busy ants, came and went from the great dark
warehouses on the quay, loading the last of the consignment of goods
for Barcelona and the ports of Spain.

Across the tiled roofs of the city's buildings towered the stark leaning
outlines of the tower at which people still laughed because the builders
had been so foolish as not to construct a firm foundation. It would be
fifty years almost to the day before a professor of Pisa named Galileo—
whom many considered mad—would drop cannon balls from its top,
immortalizing the tower and himself, and discovering one of the
great laws of the universe. But now Antonio saw it only as an ungainly,
leaning structure, doubly ugly against the background of the graceful
campaniles dotting the city and the gaily colored tiles of the roofs.

Seamen ran about the decks now, preparing for the sailing, and the
last of the porters left the gangplanks. Others of the crew began to
unfurl the sails and cast off the hawsers which had bound the vessel
to the quay. A crowd of onlookers, always present at a sailing, watched
from the wharf itself, some waving to departing travelers, others merely
idly curious.

Antonio's eyes moved over the scene with casual interest, then suddenly his gaze was rooted to one spot, to one face among the crowd of
onlookers below him as he stood on the higher deck of the ship looking
down. His body grew rigid and a wave almost of nausea went through
him. Stumbling, he turned quickly away from the rail and swayed
dizzily along the deck toward the door of the deckhouse. The captain,
hurrying along the deck, stopped and took his arm.

"*Per Bacco*, Doctor!" he exclaimed. "You are as white as one of my
sails."

Antonio shook his head to clear it. "I shall be all right," he protested.

The captain shouted to a cabin boy, "Here, boy. Take Dr. Servetus
to his cabin."

Guided by the boy, Antonio found his berth and lay down. *"Dio!"* the boy prattled. "Your Magnificence must have seen a ghost."

Antonio tossed him a coin and the boy departed. In a way the cabin boy had been right, but it had not been a ghost that he had seen, although perhaps the next thing to one.

Among the crowd on the quay there had been one distinct and familiar face, the round, close-cropped poll and ingenuous features of Battista Porzia, familiar of the Inquisition and private demon of Fra Felipe Santos.

v

The lights of Madrid twinkled through the early evening as the coach from Guadalajara clattered downhill and rumbled across a bridge over the Manzanares River to enter the city. Already, at this altitude, the cool of early fall was noticeable in the evening air. Turning through the Puerta del Sol, the east gate of the city, the coach rumbled over the cobblestones paving the broad Calle de Alcalá. On the hills overlooking the river, the massive buildings of El Palacio Real, the royal palace, loomed dark and forbidding above the smaller buildings of the city. Not yet a real city by the standards of Toledo, Barcelona, or even Cadiz, Madrid was destined to grow in importance because of its selection by Philip II as his new seat of government.

Antonio's body was sore and weary from days of jolting over rough mountain roads in various public equipages, since he had arrived at Barcelona a full week before. He leaned forward now and spoke to the driver. "Do you know the inn of the Three Brothers?"

"Naturalmente. It is near El Palacio Real."

"I should like to stop there."

"Sí, señor."

The coach drew to a stop in a lighted courtyard, and over the doorway Antonio distinguished the gilt-painted sign swinging in the evening breeze, Los Tres Hermanos. While the driver unloaded his few belongings, Antonio looked curiously about him. The street before the inn was wide and freshly paved with stones. The opposite side was flanked almost to the curbing by high walls surrounding the grounds of the royal palace. At the corner he could see a sentry standing beside a lighted box guarding the gate.

Only with the accession of Philip II to the throne of Spain had Madrid been made the capital. Before that it had been little more than a hunting lodge, favored in summer because of its elevation and the cooling breezes that came with the night. The new king's father, Emperor Charles V, had been wont to spend his few days of residence in Spain each year at Valladolid, but Philip, Spanish by birth and preference, had chosen to locate his site of government near the geographical center of his kingdom, establishing Madrid as his only court, *nos única corte*.

Antonio followed the lackey with his belongings into the inn. His nostrils were greeted with the pleasant aroma of roasting pig and mulled wine and his ears with the clink of mugs and the hum of conversation. The Three Brothers seemed a popular place with gentlemen, he noted as he made his way across the crowded common room to the long bar that lined the farther wall. In the middle of the bar the great fireplace was visible, with coals glowing on the hearth and a pig spitted across the coals. A smutty-faced gnome, back distorted by a massive hump, crouched on the hearth and turned the spit.

The landlord beamed, evidently pleased by the popularity of his establishment with such a well-paying clientele.

"*Servidor de usted?*" he said.

"*Buenas noches.*" The Spanish phrases came somewhat haltingly to Antonio's tongue. "I am Dr. Antonio Servetus, a physician of Florence."

"But of course, *señor médico*. Señor Savarino has been expecting you."

"Is he here?"

"Alas, no! This very morning Señor Savarino departed for the hunt, with some gentlemen of the court."

"I will use his quarters, then, until his return," Antonio said.

"But, Doctor"—the proprietor looked distressed—"that is for the moment impossible."

"Impossible? Why?" Antonio demanded impatiently. "You said he was expecting me."

· "Señor Savarino has given another gentleman the privilege of his room for the evening."

It was like Gian's impulsive generosity, Antonio well knew, to turn his room over to a friend who might need it for romantic purposes. "You can let me have another, then?" he asked.

The innkeeper raised his arms and let them fall in a gesture of impotence. "Tonight every chamber in the inn is filled. Tomorrow it will be different."

"Where do I sleep tonight, then?" Antonio snapped. "In the street?"

The innkeeper's eyes brightened. "Perhaps the other gentleman will not need Señor Savarino's chamber for the entire evening," he suggested. "He is, I understand, meeting a lady, but"—he rolled his eyes expressively—"the gentleman is of some years and the affair may terminate early."

Antonio could not but smile at the droll expression upon the innkeeper's face. Under the circumstances there was nothing he could do but make the best of a bad situation and hope that the landlord's estimate of the amorous gentleman's capabilities was correct. "Can you give me dinner, then?" he inquired.

"But certainly, Doctor. Tonight we have an excellent roast."

At a small table in the corner Antonio finished an excellent meal and relaxed to enjoy his wine. He felt considerably refreshed and took the opportunity to look over the other occupants of the common room. Most of them appeared to be gentlemen; no doubt, he judged, because of the proximity of the royal palace and the court. Two genial-looking priests were eating near the fire, and at a table close by a man, like Antonio, was dining alone. He was quite handsome, somewhat older than Antonio, with a sprinkling of gray already at his temples and deep-set eyes beneath craggy brows. His dress was rich, but of black velvet and so severe in cut as to give him almost the appearance of an ecclesiastic.

To Antonio's surprise, the man stood up, wiped his lips with a napkin, and came across the crowded room, obviously toward Antonio's table. He stopped and bowed courteously. "*Permítame,* Doctor," he said in cultured tones. "I could not help overhearing your conversation with the innkeeper. I am Armand de Quadra and I have the honor of being acquainted with Señor Savarino."

Antonio bowed and asked, "Will you join me, sir?"

De Quadra took the other chair. "If you do not find accommodations for the night, I should be honored to have you rest at my house," he said. "It is quite near by."

"Actually I am not without a place to stay," Antonio explained. "I am employed by Messer Girolamo Bellarmi as his personal physician, but did not wish to disturb him."

"*Bueno!* We shall be neighbors. Señor Bellarmi has taken a house close to my own."

"Perhaps I shall still not have to trouble either of you," Antonio said. "The gentleman using my friend's room may not be very long."

De Quadra shrugged. "The French Ambassador is a man of many amours."

"The French Ambassador?"

"Comte de Quervain. I saw him come in a little while ago and heard him ask for the chamber of Señor Savarino."

"Do you know Dr. Vesalius?" Antonio asked.

"Everyone knows him. Is he a friend of yours?"

"I am an admirer of his teachings, but I have never met him."

"He is away on a military mission with His Majesty," De Quadra said. "May I introduce you upon his return?"

"That would be most kind," Antonio said graciously.

De Quadra's long fingers played idly with the gold chain about his neck. "You have just come from Italy, I believe, Doctor."

Instantly Antonio was on his guard. The question might be perfectly innocent, but he had decided that the less said about his experiences in Italy the better. "I came over from Florence," he explained.

"I judged as much," De Quadra said a trifle dryly. Antonio's instinctive stiffening at the mention of Italy had not gone unnoticed. "Señor Bellarmi, your patron, has so recently arrived from there."

There was a slight commotion at the door, enough to turn every head in the room toward it. A woman entered and hurried across the room to the stairs leading up to the chambers above. She wore a long black cloak, with a hood pulled up about her face so that only her eyes were visible. But at sight of her Antonio half rose from his seat and smothered an exclamation of surprise. Without the additional clue afforded by the tendril of golden hair which escaped from the front of her hood, he still would have recognized that slender figure and graceful walk. Besides, it was the same dark cloak she had worn in Padua.

But was it possible that Lucia Bellarmi had come for an assignation with the French Ambassador, a man noted for his amours? The very idea was incredible, yet he could hardly deny the evidence of his own eyes. But how could she be so misguided as to meet a notorious roué in a common inn?

"Do you know the lady?" De Quadra inquired in a tone of cynical amusement.

"Why, I——" Antonio stopped. For the sake of Girolamo Bellarmi, he must not let the fact of his niece's shameful conduct be bruited abroad. "I thought so at first," he explained lamely, "but no doubt I was mistaken."

"A very lovely young lady, by external signs at least," De Quadra said, rising from his chair. "*Lo siento*. I must go now." He bowed politely. "No doubt we shall have opportunity for further conversations if you remain in Madrid."

Antonio drank the rest of his wine slowly. The more he thought of it, the angrier he became at Lucia for risking the good name of her uncle and the family of which she professed to be so proud. And since Messer Bellarmi was not here to protect her from the consequences of her folly—probably he didn't even know that she would be so foolish— was it not his own duty to interfere?

Antonio got to his feet and started for the stairs. The landlord started to call to him, then thought better of it at the sight of the burning anger in his eyes. At the top of the stairs Antonio stopped. Some dozen chambers opened upon the upper hallway, and Lucia could be in any of them. Then he saw a wench laying a fire in one of the rooms and called to her, "Do you know the chamber of Señor Savarino?"

At the mention of Gian's name the girl's eyes glowed warmly. The artist would have lost none of his ability to charm women, Antonio thought, and must already have made considerable progress with this buxom lass.

"I am a friend of Señor Savarino," he explained.

"It is two doors down the hall, señor." Her eyes roved boldly over Antonio's tall body and dark hair, and he turned quickly to the door she had indicated, lest she see the blush which he had not yet learned to control.

He knocked sharply upon the door of Gian's chamber. There was no answer, but he heard some movement inside and knocked again, more loudly. From inside the room came the sound of a window being raised. Fearful that Lucia might try to escape in a panic and harm herself. Antonio twisted the knob and threw his weight against the door.

To his surprise, it was unlocked, and he catapulted halfway across the room before he could regain his balance, bringing up against the bed with a crash that sent him to his knees. Even in his discomfiture at his ungallant entry he found time to note that the bed was not mussed. Through the open window he spied a pair of elegant shanks in rich velvet scrambling into the branches of a tree that grew close to the window. Then there was the sound of a breaking limb and a thud in the courtyard below, followed by some picturesque oaths in French.

Antonio pushed himself erect and met Lucia's eyes, wide, dark, and fearful, her face devoid of color. She had thrown back her hood but was otherwise fully dressed. She stared at him for a moment in disbelief, and then a warning fire began to glow in her eyes.

"Shame on you, madonna." He tried the tactic of taking the battle to her.

"Shame?" she choked on her own fury.

"Look where I find you! What of your uncle's good name?"

Before he knew what she was going to do, she slapped him so hard that he reeled from the blow, delivered with all the force of her lithe young body. But when she would have struck him again, he seized her wrist, holding it firmly in spite of her struggles.

"Are you angry at having your assignation spoiled?" he snapped. And then, with deliberate contempt, "Perhaps we could arrange another."

She went suddenly limp, all resistance gone and her eyes filled with horror. "You thought that I——"

"What else could I think?" he demanded angrily. "I arrive in Madrid tonight and find you meeting a notorious roué at an inn, alone and at night in his bedroom."

She remembered her vis-à-vis then and went to the window. There were a few shreds of cloth on a broken limb of the tree, but no one was visible in the courtyard below.

"Your lover seems to have escaped," Antonio observed acidly, "though not without losing part of his breeches and perhaps some of his skin."

"Lover?" she cried indignantly, her color rising again. "Oh, you——" She raised her hand as if to slap him again.

"Do that again and I'll put you across my knee," he warned.

Her eyes widened and she dropped her hand, then she reached up

quickly and began to pull at the cords that held her cloak together at
the neck. The folds fell apart and she swept her arms outward, fan-
ning the cloak. She was fully dressed beneath it. "Does this sound as if
I were meeting a lover?" she demanded. "I should be at least half
naked, shouldn't I?"

"Spare me the details, pray," he said. But her manner was convincing and he was beginning to wonder if he could have been wrong.

She drew the cords together at her neck, knotted them quickly, and
pulled the hood over her head again. "Where are you going?" he asked.

"Back to the palace. I live there . . . when I'm not meeting lovers,"
she added scornfully.

"But you can't go alone."

"I came alone," she reminded him proudly.

"Wait. I'll go with you." But her heels were already clicking on the
stairs before he finished speaking. He followed her, tossing the innkeeper a coin for his supper and calling over his shoulder for his effects
to be placed in Gian's chamber. When he came out into the lighted
courtyard he thought for a moment he had lost her, then he saw her
slender figure hurrying along on the opposite side in the shadows of the
high wall guarding the royal palace. Crossing the street, he lengthened
his stride to catch up with her.

Halfway to the corner, Lucia stopped. In the darkness, Antonio
could barely make out a small door set into the massive stones of the
palace wall. She knocked quickly twice, paused, then twice again.
Almost at once the gate opened and he heard a woman cry, "Lucia.
Thank God you are safe." Then she stepped through and the door
closed behind her.

In the shadows Antonio stared at the small gate with a puzzled
frown. Could he have been wrong in his interpretation of the scene at
the inn? Certainly, he remembered, Lucia had not acted like one surprised *flagrante delicto,* although the gentleman had departed in enough
of a hurry. Then with a shrug he turned back toward the courtyard of
the inn across the street.

vi

Antonio was only a few yards away from the small door when he
heard Lucia call him in an urgent voice. The gate was open and she

was standing in the street beside it. When he came closer he saw that her face was bloodless. She swayed and he caught her arm to steady her. "What is it, madonna?" he asked.

"Come inside quickly. Something terrible has happened."

He stepped through the gate and she locked it securely behind them. Another woman, shorter and older than Lucia, stood on the graveled path just inside the gate, wringing her hands and weeping, obviously frightened almost beyond speech.

"Donna Maria de Paredes," Lucia said hurriedly, "this is Dr. Antonio Servetus."

Antonio bowed. The older woman bobbed her head but continued to whimper. "Where is he?" Lucia demanded sharply.

"In the summerhouse." She pointed into the darkness, where the buildings of the royal palace loomed up as dark, angular shadows.

"This way, Tonio." Lucia seized his hand and guided him rapidly along a graveled path that wound through the trees. Señora Paredes trotted along behind them. "He was waiting for you to return, Lucia," she babbled. "They gave the knock and he thought it was you and opened the gate. Then they stabbed him." Her sobs broke out afresh.

Something about the man who lay unconscious on the floor of the small summerhouse struck Antonio more sharply than the obvious evidence of foul play in the spreading dark pool of blood around his body. It was a sound, an ominous whistling-bubbling sort of a noise, as if air were being blown through a straw immersed in a bottle of liquid. He had heard it but once before, when a gentleman run through the chest in a duel had been brought to him in Padua for treatment, only to die a few minutes later.

A sucking wound of the chest! His trained physician's sense made the diagnosis at once, for nothing else made quite that horrible bubbly sound. It had meant death in Padua, just as it had meant death on a thousand battlefields. And it would mean death just as certainly here in the palace grounds of the King of Spain.

Antonio knelt quickly beside the injured man and ripped open the silken fabric of his jerkin and the undershirt beneath. "Bring the light closer," he directed the lackey, who was holding it with trembling fingers, fear written large in his pallid cheeks and sweating brow.

"*Sí, señor,*" the man said, almost in a whisper, but he shied away from the pool of blood, and Lucia herself seized the lantern and held it directly over the stricken man's chest.

Folding a pad of cloth from the ripped shirt, Antonio sponged blood away, searching for the wound. He had no trouble finding it, once the skin was cleared of blood. Although small—unmistakably the work of a poniard or a very light sword—the telltale bubbles and the strange whistling noise in rhythm with the victim's breathing effectively pointed to the wound.

With his pad of cloth, Antonio wiped away the blood that bubbled out of the opening. The sound stopped momentarily, only to begin again as soon as his pad had passed over the wound itself. He wiped away the blood again, every muscle suddenly alert, for he realized now what was happening. The pad of cloth had momentarily stopped the sucking of the wound, as well as the loss of blood. And he had remembered a case from the book of Ambroise Paré, a case just such as this, in which the French surgeon reported saving a nobleman with a sword wound of the chest merely by applying pads and pressure over the wound.

"Quickly, get some long strips of cloth for bandaging," he told Lucia. "There is no time to lose." Even as he spoke he was ripping another piece from the injured man's shirt and folding it skillfully into a compress which he placed over the wound.

At once the sucking noise stopped again, but this time it was not resumed, because he kept the pressure of the cloth pad firmly in place over the wound. If the internal bleeding were not too great, his mind raced with the thought, he might be able to save this man. He was obviously a person of some importance.

He saw Lucia hand the lantern to the lackey and step into the semi-darkness near the summerhouse door. There was a flashing glimpse of swirling silk and white skin before she stepped out of a petticoat and came back inside, tearing it into strips. "Will this do?" she asked, handing him a strip of cloth several yards long and the width of his hand.

"Yes. But we may need more." He turned back to the wound and began to fold another strip of cloth from the shirt into a second pad, reinforcing the first.

"You will have to help me," he told Lucia. "We must turn him to look for another wound."

She had to do most of the lifting herself, but the wounded man was slender and not very heavy. Antonio kept the pad of cloth tightly applied to the skin. Between them they rolled him part way over, and Lucia examined his back. "There is no other wound," she reported.

"It must have been a stiletto or a poniard, then," Antonio said. "A sword would have gone through."

"It was a stiletto," Donna Maria volunteered. "I saw that much."

"Hold the pad for me, Lucia," Antonio directed, "while I apply the bandages."

She put her hand over his and he slipped his fingers out, leaving hers against the cloth. Her shoulder pressed against his, he felt her shiver momentarily as the warm blood soaking the cloth pad seeped up between her fingers. The other woman had ripped up still another petticoat, and now an ample pile of cloth strips for bandages lay beside him.

The lackey was able to put away his fear long enough to help lift the shoulders of the wounded man, and Antonio worked rapidly, circling his chest with the cloth strips, passing them over the pad so that it was held snugly in place over the wound. He overlapped each turn to make a snugly applied swath of bandage which would not allow the vitally important pad to slip and let the wound reopen. The bandage completed, he secured it with jeweled pins provided by his helpers.

The bandaging completed, Antonio lay the patient back on the marble floor and covered him with Lucia's cloak. He felt for the pulse. It was barely perceptible, no stronger that he could tell, but certainly no weaker, which was worth a great deal. "That is all we can do for now," he said. "But he should be moved inside where it is warm."

"Take the lackey and find the queen, Maria," Lucia directed the older woman. "Tell her Don Pedro has been stabbed and we must have help to bring him to the palace."

"You were very fine, madonna," Antonio said while they waited for help to come. "Without your help I could not have saved him."

"Then he isn't going to die?"

"There is a chance. Who is he?"

"Don Pedro y Ruiz, Marquis of Grijalva," she said.

The name meant nothing to Antonio, and he showed it by his blank expression, for she added, "His is one of the oldest names in Spain, and he is a great soldier."

"Why would anyone stab him?"

"Many people hate him because"—she hesitated—"because the queen is very fond of him."

"Is he her lover?"

"What if he is?" she flared. "He is good and kind and honorable. And he loves his country more than the people who would harm him."

"I wasn't censuring him," Antonio protested. "But if he is so fine, why should he have enemies?"

"It is a long story," she said impatiently. "You will learn it in time."

They waited again in silence punctuated only by the hoarse breathing of the marquis. Finally Antonio asked, "Was I wrong about tonight, madonna?"

Color surged into her cheeks. "Were you? You seemed quite certain."

"You must admit——"

"That you have an evil mind?" she said with scorn. "I will admit that freely, Ser Physician."

"But how could I know?" he protested.

"You knew me. We shall say no more about it," she added loftily. "Your opinion matters little to me, Ser Monk-to-be."

Lights approached from the palace, and Donna Maria reappeared, followed by four servants carrying a litter. Under Antonio's direction, they transferred the injured man to it and Antonio walked beside the litter, steadying it lest some unwary foot slip in the darkness and possibly dislodge the bandage.

The little procession entered the palace by a back door and passed through a long corridor, finally reaching a small but sumptuously furnished apartment of two rooms. As Antonio was helping the servants transfer Don Pedro to the bed, a slender young woman with dark hair came in. She was richly dressed, and although she was no older than Lucia, the women curtsied in her presence. Antonio, sensing that this was the queen, dropped to one knee.

"This is Dr. Antonio Servetus, my uncle's personal physician, Your Majesty," Lucia explained. "He arrived only today from Barcelona and fortunately was close by."

The young queen graciously acknowledged the introduction, then went over to the bed to look down at the wounded man. He was older than she by at least a decade, Antonio saw, now that he had a chance to look at his patient as other than a wound, and there was breeding and intelligence written in his high cheekbones and well-modeled head. The queen caught her breath in a sob and lifted dark and imploring eyes to Antonio.

"Is he going to——" She choked over the words and could not go on.

"He is gravely injured, Your Majesty," Antonio said, "but I have controlled the immediate danger."

"Where is the wound?"

"In the chest, through the lung."

"Then it is very serious."

"Very serious. Wounds of this sort rarely recover under ordinary treatment," Antonio admitted. "However, I have applied a new form of dressing, one devised by a physician of France, Dr. Paré——"

"I know Dr. Paré," the queen said eagerly. "He is a very fine physician."

"He has cured some cases by this method."

Some of the anxiety went out of the young queen's face and she held out her hand to Antonio. "Thank God you were here, Dr. Servetus," she said. "I dare say no physician in Spain would have known of this treatment. Will you remain with him?"

Antonio touched her fingers with his lips. "If it is your wish, Your Majesty. But would you not prefer to have one of the regular court physicians examine him also?"

"Dr. Vesalius is our best," the queen said thoughtfully. "He saved the life of the Principe some years ago. But he is away with the king."

"Perhaps another, then?" Common sense urged the wisdom of having some other physician share with him the responsibility for the life of so important a person as the Marquis of Grijalva.

Lucia said, "Dr. Servetus is highly regarded in the University of Padua, Your Majesty. He was once a professor there."

The queen's face cleared. "In that case there is no need for anyone else." She left the apartment, followed by Donna Maria and the servants. Lucia and Antonio were left alone with the wounded marquis.

"Thank you for recommending me," Antonio said.

"Everyone agrees that you are skilled in your *profession*, Dr. Servetus," she said tartly.

"While I am just beginning to realize my ignorance." Antonio smiled wryly. "But for the chance of having been treated by Dr. Duval, I should not have read the works of Ambroise Paré."

"And Don Pedro would not be alive?"

"I'm afraid not."

"When you were treating my uncle Mario in Padua," she said sweetly, "I received the impression that you knew all there was to know about medicine."

"I have come a long way since then, madonna, and so have you," he told her. "Maid of honor and confidante of the Queen of Spain. It is an honor, and a dangerous one."

"Dangerous? Why?"

"Didn't it occur to you that whoever stabbed Don Pedro might have been waiting for you as well?"

Color slowly drained from her cheeks and her eyes grew wide and dark. "I—I never thought of that."

"Then they were?"

"I don't think so," she whispered. "But they might have been." She looked very young and frail and defenseless then. Antonio could understand how, eager and inexperienced, she might have gotten herself embroiled innocently in some dangerous intrigue. Of one thing he was certain now, though: her appearance at the inn had been a part of the plot and not an assignation. The knowledge filled him with a vast sense of relief, whose source he did not try to analyze.

"The queen is very young," Antonio observed. "She is little more than a girl."

Lucia's eyes lit up. "She is wonderful. I would give anything to be able to make her happy." She put her hand on his arm. "That is why you must save Don Pedro. They mean so much to each other."

"In that case, you had better lie down and rest on the couch over there," Antonio said with a smile. "One of us will have to be with him all the time, and we can take turns."

"I am tired," she admitted. "Too much excitement, I suppose." She lay down on the couch. From a closet opening off the bedroom he brought a quilt to cover her. It was embroidered with the royal arms of France, he saw, and realized then that this must be a private apartment of the queen's and the quilt part of her trousseau. Lucia was half asleep when he spread it over her, but she opened her eyes.

"Antonio," she said in a sleepy voice.

"Yes, Lucia."

"About tonight. It was not what you thought."

"I had already decided that. Perhaps you will forgive me for not understanding."

She gave a sigh, like a child whose wish has been gratified. A few minutes later her gentle, even breathing told him that she was asleep.

vii

It was dawn when Lucia stretched herself and opened her eyes. Then she sat up quickly. "Is it my turn to watch?"

"Look outside," he told her. "It is morning."

"And you let me sleep all night?" she cried indignantly.

"You looked too comfortable to disturb. Besides, I slept in my chair."

Lucia rubbed her eyes and pushed her hair away from her forehead. "I must look terrible," she said, in typical feminine concern for her appearance. Actually she looked like a beautiful tousled child. "How is the marquis?"

"A little better, I think. The queen was in several times during the night."

"And found me sleeping! What must she have thought?" A moan from the bed distracted their attention from themselves, and both hurried to the bedside. Don Pedro's eyes were open. He recognized Lucia and his lips moved.

"Doña Lucia. What happened?" His voice was barely a whisper.

"You were attacked and wounded, Your Grace."

A spasm of pain caused him momentarily to set his teeth into his lip. "You gave the signal and I opened the gate," he said.

"Someone else discovered the signal," Lucia explained, "and used it to enter and try to kill you."

"Did you carry out our plan?"

"Partly." Lucia hesitated. "We were interrupted." Antonio realized that she was referring to his interference in the affair at the inn the night before.

Don Pedro's eyes turned to Antonio. "This is Dr. Antonio Servetus, my uncle's personal physician," Lucia explained. "He happened to be close by and took care of you." Then she added, "You may trust Dr. Servetus completely. Her Majesty does."

At the mention of the queen, Don Pedro's expression changed. The look of adoration that shone in his eyes was like sunlight breaking through a clouded sky. It was, Antonio realized, much of the same feeling that came to him when he had first looked at the Venus of the Botticelli canvas. He understood now why he felt no censure toward the queen or Don Pedro, although, by ecclesiastical standards at least, their passion was an illicit one. Untutored as he was in the relationships between men and women, he sensed that there were circumstances when the love of two individuals for each other transcended human laws and must be reckoned a force emanating from the divine.

"Her Majesty will want to know that you are conscious," Lucia said. "I will get her."

When she was gone, Don Pedro asked, "Am I going to die, Doctor?"

"Your wound *is* dangerous," Antonio admitted. "Air was escaping and I closed the opening. If there are no complications——"

"Then you cannot be certain as yet?"

"No, I cannot." There was no point in dissembling, for there was grave danger still. An outpouring of humors forming an empyema, a fresh hemorrhage from the wounded lung, congestion and fever—any one of a dozen complications might swing the balance against the marquis.

When Lucia returned with the queen, she and Antonio retired to the small parlor and shut the door, leaving the two lovers alone. Lucia said wistfully, "It must be wonderful to be loved like that."

"Aren't you rather young to be worrying about such things, madonna?" he asked.

She stamped her foot impatiently. "I am twenty. At that age my grandmother had children."

"I shouldn't think you would have much trouble finding a husband," he said teasingly.

Her expression softened. "And why are you so certain?"

"Well, your family is very rich. You should bring a substantial dowry with you." And when he saw the storm gathering in her eyes, he added, "Of course you are very beautiful, too."

She realized then that he was teasing, but she did not seem displeased. "Fie on you, Ser Monk. What do *you* know about women?"

"I am counted something of an artist, madonna, as well as a physician."

"So you are," she said scoffingly. "I remember now. Your ideal woman is the Venus of Botticelli."

As always, he felt the need to defend his goddess from the sea. "Is there anyone lovelier?"

She shot him a glance in which there was more than a hint of mischief. "It would be hard to tell, wouldn't it? After all, ordinary women are at a disadvantage in such comparisons; we can't go around without any clothes."

Antonio found himself blushing again and momentarily at a loss for words.

"That *is* what men want in a mistress, isn't it?"

"Why ask me?" Antonio said severely. "I have no mistress." But he remembered a night in Venice, the night when he had returned from the ill-starred ceremony of the Black Mass.

"Aren't you a man?" Lucia asked sweetly, too sweetly in truth.

"Cannot one be a man, madonna, without necessarily being a libertine?" he asked stiffly. "And for that matter, I do have a mistress."

It was her turn to be startled, and her eyes went wide.

"Have you read the writings of Paracelsus?" he continued.

She shook her head, but her eyes never left his.

"There is a passage in Paracelsus that goes something like this: 'For we know how a lover will go a long way to meet the woman that he loves. How much the more, then, will the lover of wisdom be tempted to go in search of his divine mistress!' "

" 'Divine mistress,' " Lucia repeated softly, and her eyes began to glow. "What a lovely phrase, Tonio. You are a poet."

"I only quoted Paracelsus," he said, a little embarrassed at her reaction.

"But it could mean your goddess of the painting, too," she said eagerly. "And in your search for wisdom, you may find someone you will love as much as you do her."

The light in her eyes as she stood so near to him, swaying a little toward him in her excitement, kindled an answering warmth within him.

"Lucia," he said, yielding to a sudden impulse, "do you suppose that somewhere or sometime you and I could have known each other before? Perhaps in another life."

"Why do you say that?" she whispered.

"I have the feeling—I can't exactly express it—that somewhere, perhaps centuries ago, we must have meant a great deal to each other. . . ."

The sound of the bedroom door opening brought them suddenly out of themselves. Lucia moved quickly to one side of the room and began to rearrange some books on a side table. The queen came across the room, her hands outstretched, smiling happily.

"What could I do without two such loyal helpers?" she asked, taking them each by the hand. "He *is* doing well, isn't he, Dr. Servetus?"

"Very well, Your Majesty. Of course there may be complications."

"You physicians are all alike," she chided. "Afraid to commit yourselves. I am sure there will be no complications."

"Let us pray that you are right, Your Majesty."

The queen's face sobered. "There are things I fear more than complications. Those who tried to kill the marquis are still free."

"Would not the *polizia*"—Antonio stumbled for the unfamiliar Spanish word—"*el policía* try to find them?"

The queen shook her head. "For the moment we cannot use them."

"But they wouldn't come here," Lucia protested.

"I'm not sure they would not," the queen said. "They might even try to interfere with your treatment of Don Pedro, Doctor."

Antonio voiced a thought which had been disturbing him. "As you know, Your Majesty, I am an Italian and not recognized by your physicians here in Madrid. That was why I suggested a consultation last evening."

"But Dr. Vesalius is the only physician I can trust beside you," the queen protested, "and he is too far away."

"Perhaps Dr. Servetus could have some tangible evidence of your confidence, then, Your Majesty," Lucia suggested.

The queen's face brightened. "Of course. I can appoint him my personal physician. Why didn't I think of it before? I will have a royal commission prepared tomorrow naming you physician to the queen."

"Your Majesty does me too much honor," Antonio stammered.

"It is not entirely an honor, Dr. Servetus." The queen's voice was grave again. "You may need that authority sooner than you think."

"I shall try to be worthy of it, then," Antonio promised.

"I am sure you will. Come with me, please, Lucia."

Antonio went back to the bed and stood looking down at the sleeping marquis. There was much here that he did not understand, talk of danger without identifying its source, of conspiracy with no mention of conspirators. But he had evidence that the danger was real, for it had almost cost Don Pedro his life, and because of it the queen had been willing to place an extraordinary trust in a man whom she had known less than a whole day.

viii

As it turned out, Antonio had almost immediate need of the authority granted him by the queen. Don Pedro was sleeping and he was nodding in the chair when there was a peremptory knock on the outer door.

A tall, swarthy man, elegantly dressed, stood in the doorway when he opened it, surveying him arrogantly with pale blue eyes. Behind him stood a burly fellow, villainous in appearance, carrying a case such as physicians of the day used for their instruments and drugs. The elegant visitor was further identified as a physician by the large ball at the end of his cane, used, as Antonio well knew, by many physicians to carry camphor and other volatile oils said to be a preventive against the Black Death and the more recently epidemic *morbus Gallicus*.

"*Dr.* Servetus?" The newcomer placed undue emphasis upon the title, as if he doubted its authenticity.

"I am he," Antonio admitted.

The visitor stalked into the room, followed by his servant. "I am Dr. Juan Alvarez, Fellow of the Medical Faculty of Madrid and Paris and Honorary Physician to His Most Catholic Majesty, King Philip II. This is my servant, Valdez."

Antonio bowed, but he was not impressed by the array of titles. He well knew that the most arrant quacks often wormed their way into the favor of a prince and obtained all sorts of titles and honors, which they then used to cow other physicians and impress a credulous public.

Without being invited, the swarthy doctor went on into the other room where Don Pedro lay. "Did you obtain your degree from a university, sir?" he asked. It was a studied insult, Antonio sensed, deliberately planned to anger and humiliate him.

"Perhaps Your Magnificence has heard of the University of Padua, from which I received my diploma in medicine, and where I lately taught anatomy and surgery," he suggested, with a tinge of mockery in his voice.

Alvarez looked startled and for a moment lost some of his assurance. *"De veras?"* he said and turned toward the bed. "His Majesty's Minister of State, the Bishop of Toledo, has sent me to attend the wounds of the Marquis of Grijalva."

"How did the bishop learn that the marquis was wounded?" Antonio asked.

The court physician chose to ignore the direct question. Instead he moved closer to the injured man and stood looking down at him. *"Voto a tal!"* he exclaimed. "The breathing is labored. No doubt there is an accumulation of humors."

"Perhaps there is," Antonio admitted, moving up to the bed himself. The servant, Valdez, stayed close to him. As physician in charge, Antonio had every right to eject both Alvarez and his servant, but he knew better than to try it alone and he was not certain that help was in earshot. "Of course it is too early to tell about the effect upon the humors yet," he said.

"Naturalmente. But you are bleeding to prevent such an accumulation?"

"The marquis has lost quite enough blood already," Antonio said shortly.

Before he could interfere, Alvarez flipped open the collar of Don Pedro's sleeping shirt. "A tight bandage!" Alvarez cried in a shocked voice. *"Madre de Dios!* You must know that in wounds of this type the humors must be allowed to escape."

"I don't remember telling you the type of wound, Dr. Alvarez," Antonio said pointedly, "and the bandage covers it completely. Where did you learn the type?"

A dull red color stained Alvarez's swarthy cheeks; guilty knowledge was written in his eyes.

"Perhaps his assailant told you the nature of the wound," Antonio suggested.

The shot told, and Alvarez, unable to hide his guilty knowledge, could only bluster, "Evidently you do not understand me. I have been entrusted with the care of the Marquis of Grijalva by His Majesty's Chief Minister."

And then the whole plot became clear to Antonio. The assassins, having learned that their attempt upon the life of Don Pedro had failed, were adopting another line of attack. With the wounded man no longer in Antonio's care, it would be easy to insure death without it being an obvious murder. A simple matter of bleeding, a procedure about which there was a great deal of controversy among physicians, a loose dressing on the pretext of allowing escape of retained humors, almost anything at all might easily insure death. At all odds, Antonio realized, he must not let himself be drawn into a position where he would lose control of the case.

"Well, Doctor?" Having played his trump card, Alvarez's studied insolence had returned.

"The Marquis of Grijalva is my patient until I am discharged by him," Antonio said stubbornly.

"*Al contrario,*" Alvarez said haughtily, "since the marquis is incapable of making such a decision, His Majesty's representative must make it for him."

"And if I don't accept your order?" Antonio was playing for time now, hoping that Lucia would return and could be sent to find the queen.

"*Lo siento!*" Alvarez shrugged. "Valdez will remove you and arrest you on order of the Bishop of Toledo."

The burly servant was already moving toward Antonio when a clear voice said imperiously, "Stop! In the name of the queen."

It was Lucia. In the heat of the interchange none of them had heard her enter the apartment, but Antonio had never been happier to see her. "Get the queen, Lucia," he said urgently. "This doctor is taking over the case."

"On order of the Bishop of Toledo," Alvarez said importantly.

"Dr. Servetus has a higher order than a mere minister," Lucia said sweetly. "I think this might interest you, Dr. Alvarez." She removed a folded paper from her bosom and handed it to him.

Alvarez lifted the silver-rimmed eyeglasses that hung from his neck by a slender silver chain. With a supercilious gesture he held them before his eyes and scanned the note. Then the eyeglasses dropped from his fingers and, like a torn sawdust-filled doll, the stuffing of arrogance and haughtiness trickled out of him. Finally he collected his wits enough to bow. "With your permission, señorita, we will withdraw."

"You have my permission," Lucia said graciously.

The Spanish doctor turned to Antonio. "My humble apologies for this unfortunate mistake, Doctor," he said smoothly. "Perhaps I may personally have the honor of presenting your name to the Faculty of Medicine later."

Antonio understood nothing of what was going on except that Don Pedro was saved. When the door closed behind Alvarez and his assistant, Lucia began to laugh. "If you could have seen your faces, Antonio," she gasped. "You were like a pair of fighting cocks ready to leap at one another."

"Perhaps you will let me know the secret of your amusement," he said stiffly.

She wiped her eyes and handed him the small paper which had so markedly affected Dr. Alvarez. The paper was embossed with the queen's crest and the message was short and to the point:

To ALL LOYAL SUBJECTS:

With this writing we do appoint Dr. Antonio Servetus our personal physician and charge all our subjects to respect his wishes and his authority as they would our own.

ELIZABETH,
Queen of Spain.

"Where did you get this?" Antonio asked.

"I forged it," she said complacently.

"But how?"

"I came back a few minutes ago, probably right after Dr. Alvarez came, but I waited in the next room. When it looked like they were getting the best of you, I got some of the queen's note paper—this is her private apartment, you know—and forged the commission. After all," she added impishly, "she did appoint you her physician. All I did was put it down in writing."

ix

Lucia took over for Antonio during the early evening to let him sleep. Three hours before midnight she awakened him and handed him a note. The message was brief:

ANTONIO,

I have just returned from the hunt and need you badly. Please come to the inn of the Three Brothers at once. Don't fail me.

GIAN.

"Who brought this to the palace?" Antonio asked.

"A hostler from the inn the lackey said. Do you suppose Gian was injured while hunting?"

"But he doesn't know that I am in Madrid," Antonio protested.

"He could have learned," she pointed out. "Everyone else seems to know."

"And this isn't Gian's writing."

She studied the message again. "It was obviously written in a hurry, perhaps by one of his companions, but you have to go, Tonio, if Gian needs you."

"Yes, I suppose so." But he still had misgivings. Somehow the note didn't sound like Gian.

"I will stay with Don Pedro," she said, "if that is worrying you. Take the key to the small gate near the inn. It is shorter that way."

A number of gentlemen were drinking in the inn of the Three Brothers, but when Antonio came in there was no sign of Gian. He made his way across the room to the bar, where the host was drawing tankards of mulled wine.

"Is Señor Savarino in his chamber?" he asked.

"But no, señor." The man looked up and recognized Antonio. "He has not yet returned from the hunt, Doctor."

"Are you sure?"

"Quite certain. I have been expecting him since sundown. Is anything wrong with Señor Savarino?"

"I don't know. Someone sent me a message, to meet him here. One of your hostlers brought it to the palace."

"*Plegue a Dios,*" the innkeeper protested. "I sent no hostler to the palace."

"You are absolutely certain of that?" Antonio asked.

The landlord shrugged. "*Naturalmente, señor.* I would know. Is anything wrong?"

It was the question Antonio was asking himself. And he could get only one answer. Something must be wrong, badly wrong, and he thought he understood now what it was. Nothing could have drawn him away from the palace quite so effectively as a note from Gian intimating that he had been hurt, and someone had used that knowledge for his own purpose, most probably to remove him from the palace and leave Don Pedro unguarded.

Then Lucia was in danger, Antonio realized suddenly, and cursing his own stupidity at being drawn away by such an obvious decoy, he turned and left the inn.

A party of horsemen, dusty and travel-stained, were entering the courtyard, and for a moment he was not able to push his way through to the street. Then he heard a familiar voice shout, "Tonio! Tonio, is it you?"

It was Gian, dusty from the hunt, his face alight with excitement at finding Antonio. He leaped from his horse and the two embraced quickly.

"Did you send for me, Gian?" Antonio asked quickly.

"Why, no. I have just arriv——"

"Look at this." Antonio handed him the note and Gian read it quickly.

"*Dio mio!* I did not write this."

Antonio explained quickly what had happened since his arrival at the inn the evening before. Before he finished Gian said, "We must get to the marquis at once; it may be too late." He reached up to his saddle and jerked his sword from where it had been strapped. "Are you armed, Tonio?"

"No. I never carry arms."

"You need them now." Gian's voice was grim. He reached into his saddlebag and took out a short, stubby weapon. "Can you shoot the *pistole?*"

"I have fired a wheel-lock musket," Antonio said. "But is it necessary?"

"We may need more than this." Gian snapped the cover off the priming pan and glanced at the charge of powder there. Then he twisted a key set into the side of the stock of the small weapon and wound up the spring mechanism which turned the wheel lock. Antonio was familiar enough with it to recognize that the wheel lock did away with the necessity of a slow match, as in the older firearms. When the trigger was sprung, the wheel spun from the force of the spring against a piece of iron pyrites and sent a shower of sparks into the priming pan, igniting the powder charge inside the barrel.

Gian handed Antonio the cocked *pistole* and slung the baldric of his sword over his shoulder. "Let's go," he said. "We may be too late already."

They opened the small gate and stepped through into the palace grounds. "Don't make any noise," Gian warned in a whisper. "There may be a guard here somewhere."

The sound of metal sliding against metal, as a sword was drawn from its scabbard, ripped the darkness, and Gian whirled in the direction from which the sound had come, just as the man waiting in the shadows leaped to the attack. Antonio saw only a lean form, dressed in black, the face covered entirely by a black mask.

"Get to the marquis, Tonio," Gian shouted, and when his assailant would have turned his attack against Antonio, Gian parried skillfully and drove him back. Antonio plunged into the darkness toward the door of the palace. Finding it, he raced through into the corridor and along it to the apartment where he had left Lucia and the marquis. Thrusting the door open, he went through the outer room and into the bedroom, stopping short on the threshold.

The man bending over the bed was burly and tall, his face, too, covered by a black mask. The light from the candles burning on the wall gleamed from the blade of a poniard in his hand as he looked up to see the cause of the interruption.

Antonio swept a quick glance around the room and saw Lucia, lying tied and gagged on the couch, but very much alive, as her struggles against the bonds indicated. He could give her only a cursory glance, for the intruder was moving across the room to attack, the poniard held high in a huge fist.

Forgetting for a moment the weapon in his hand, Antonio backed away, for the man attacking him loomed up in the small room like a gargantuan figure. He felt a sudden rush of panic as he remembered the searing pain of just such a weapon when he had fought against Fra Felipe Santos in Padua. He had almost sustained a fatal wound then, and the man moving toward him was far larger and stronger than the prior.

Then he remembered the weapon in his hand. It seemed ridiculously small to stop such a threatening figure, but Antonio leveled it and his finger tightened upon the trigger. Even then he found time to think that if the pistol failed to discharge—as these weapons often did—nothing could save him and Lucia, for the assassin would be upon him.

For what seemed an eon the trigger resisted his pressure, then he felt it give as the mechanism of the wheel lock was released with a snap and the spring applied its force to the toothed wheel. The grind of the wheel against the pyrites sounded loud in the room and a shower of sparks crackled into the pan. Then a spurt of flame from the priming charge seared Antonio's nostrils with the smell of burning powder and the small weapon jerked suddenly against his palm. A thunderous noise smote his eardrums, reverberating through the room.

The masked figure halted as if a giant hand had been thrust against it. Arms upflung, the man was suspended for a moment as if nailed to an invisible crucifix. Then a scream of pure agony ripped the room, for where his left breast had been was suddenly a spurting fountain of red. It ended in a gurgling moan as the red flood poured down from beneath the black hood covering his head. For a single instant he hung there, all movement arrested by the force of the ball driven from the pistol by the powder charge, then he crashed to the floor at Antonio's feet.

Antonio ran to Lucia and began to loosen the gag in her mouth. The knots of cord about her wrists refused to come loose and, spying the attacker's poniard on the floor, he picked it up and cut them and lifted her in his arms. She clung to him sobbing, and, still holding her in his arms, he moved over to the bed and looked down at Don Pedro. But the marquis was still asleep, breathing evenly and apparently uninjured, and Antonio realized that he had arrived barely in time to prevent a murder.

"How could I have been such a fool?" Lucia wailed when he set her on her feet.

"You couldn't have stopped him," Antonio assured her.

"Anyway, I kicked and bit until he tied me up," she said with satisfaction.

"Then you probably saved the marquis' life," Antonio said. "If he had not spent so much time taking care of you, the murdering scoundrel would have finished what he came to do before I arrived."

Gian appeared in the door, with excited faces behind him. "What happened?" he cried. Then he saw the prostrate figure on the floor and knelt beside it. "Per Bacco! Tonio, you are a fine shot. Right through the heart."

"He was practically on me before I remembered the pistol," Antonio said. "How about the other one?"

"He fought like the devil himself," Gian said, "but fortunately I devoted some time to the sword in Venice. When your cannon went off in here, he ran like a coward and I lost him in the dark."

Lucia went to the door to quiet the babbling servants and dispatched a footman in search of the queen. Gian slit the mask from the face of the fallen man with the point of his sword. *"Dio mio!"* he exclaimed. "A thorough scoundrel, by the looks of him."

"It's the doctor's servant, Tonio," Lucia cried. Antonio looked at the dead man. It was Valdez without a doubt.

"What doctor?" Gian asked.

"Dr. Alvarez. He was here this morning."

Valdez was beyond need of medical attention, so Antonio moved back to the bed and began to examine Don Pedro more carefully. He found no evidence that Valdez had done him any harm, although there were the signs of fever and congestion which he had discovered that afternoon. As he was finishing the examination, the queen hurried in.

"What is it, Doctor?" she cried. "Is he——"

"Don Pedro is safe, Your Majesty," he assured her.

"Oh, thank God." She leaned against the bed, white as the lace at her throat. "What happened?"

"This man tried to kill him," Antonio explained. "Fortunately Señor Savarino and I arrived in time to stop him."

The queen looked down at the body sprawled out on the floor and shuddered. "Who is he?"

"A man called Valdez. He was here this morning with Dr. Alvarez."

"Dr. Alvarez," she whispered. "He is one of my bitterest enemies."

"I will gladly dispose of him, Your Majesty," Gian offered gallantly.

The queen shook her head. "I will not let any of you endanger your lives any more in my behalf."

"Then may I remain here and help to guard Don Pedro?" Gian asked.

"That would help," she agreed.

"Are you sure he is all right?" she asked Antonio.

"There is some fever and congestion," he explained. "But I would expect that."

When the servants had removed the body of Valdez and the three of them were alone with the sleeping marquis, Antonio said, "Will you two come into the other room? We have something to discuss."

Lucia looked at him with startled eyes, for his tone was curt. "What is wrong, Antonio?" she asked.

He waited until they were in the smaller room and closed the door.

"Two attempts have been made on Don Pedro's life, and tonight all three of us might have been killed," he said then. "I think it is time I knew what we are all getting into."

"Don't you trust the queen?" Lucia demanded a little tartly.

"Why should I? I never saw her before last night."

"You could trust me, then."

"Does your uncle know about your involvement in all this?" Antonio asked.

"Well . . . no."

"Would he approve if he knew that you have been risking your life at the hands of assassins?"

Lucia's color began to rise. "He might," she argued stubbornly.

"And you, Gian. What is your part in all this?"

"If you are afraid," Lucia cut in sarcastically, "why not go back to the inn?"

"Only a fool would not be afraid in a situation like this," Antonio told her angrily. "After all, we could all have been killed."

Gian put his hand upon Lucia's wrist. "Tonio is right, Lucia," he said. "He has every right to know what is happening."

"Nobody asked him to interfere," she argued hotly. "He blundered into this himself."

"Both of you quiet down, now," Gian commanded. "I will try to give you an idea of what we are involved in, Tonio. Then if you want to get out you can."

Antonio took a seat across from Gian and Lucia. Lucia stared stiffly at the door, her color still high, angered by his insinuation that she had gotten into something without thinking.

"You know, don't you, Tonio, that Lucia's family are associated with the De' Medici's in banking and trading?" Gian asked.

"I should," Antonio said tartly. "She has told me often enough."

"It is nothing to be ashamed of," Lucia flared.

Gian ignored the display of temper. "Catherine de' Medici, the Queen of France, is the mother of Elizabeth, Queen of Spain. And Lucia is distantly related to both of them."

"What does France have to do with this?" Antonio asked.

"France is divided politically and religiously into two camps, the Catholic party of the Guises on the one hand and the Huguenots on the other."

"But that is a religious controversy," Antonio protested.

"Political *and* religious," Gian repeated. "In fact, it is more political than religious. Both the Huguenot Bourbons and the Catholic Guises want the throne of France, and the queen mother must keep a balance between them, if she is to keep the throne intact for her own children, the brothers of Queen Elizabeth here."

"But Catherine of France is a devout Catholic," Antonio said. "She would not support heresy."

"She believes in religious freedom, or professes to at the moment," Gian explained. "Unfortunately, Philip of Spain has made himself the champion of Catholicism against Protestantism not only in Spain but in the rest of Europe. And the Catholic bishops here want him to interfere in France and throw the weight of his influence to the Catholic party."

"While Queen Elizabeth is trying to keep him neutral," Lucia interjected.

The whole pattern was beginning to become clear to Antonio now. "But why was Don Pedro singled out for assassination?" he asked.

"First, because he is so friendly with the queen. And second because he is the leader of the Queen's party here in Madrid, which is advocating that Spain stay out of the affairs of France. But the Bishop of Toledo, Philip's minister of state, is very anxious to interfere in France and destroy the Huguenots, which means putting a Guise claimant upon the throne."

"Would the bishop stoop to murder?" Antonio asked.

"Perhaps not with his own hands," Gian said. "But Fra Felipe tried to kill you, didn't he?"

"That was different. He was of the Inquisition."

"Wait until you see Frey Ignacio Molina, Inquisitor of Madrid," Gian said. "Besides, the Inquisition started in Spain and is still stronger here than anywhere else in the world."

Antonio felt a chill sense of dread. Was he never to escape the dark shadow which seemed somehow destined to hang over him all of his life? He had fled from Italy because of Fra Felipe Santos and the threat of the dreaded punitive branch of the Church which he had been taught from childhood was the only true faith. And now, through a series of decisions by fate, over which he had no control, he had been thrust into another controversy involving the Holy Office and the implacable men who served it.

"What are you going to do, Antonio," Lucia asked, "now that you know the facts?"

He turned back to the room where Don Pedro lay. "I shall attend to my patient, madonna. After all, that is the first duty of a physician."

x

Antonio had not expected Don Pedro to recover without some signs of complications, for with a wound of that severity there would always be some accumulation of humors causing fever. But when several days passed and the marquis became steadily worse, he knew that something more than just a normal reaction was taking place. With Lucia's help he examined the wound carefully. It was almost healed over, but he could see a perceptible swelling in the lower right side of the chest pushing the ribs out and obliterating the normal shallow depressions between the ribs themselves. He replaced the dressings carefully, but his concern was written upon his face.

"Is anything wrong?" Lucia asked.

"Yes. Let me draw it for you; it will be easier to understand that way." He took a burnt coal from the fireplace. Quickly he sketched on paper a man's chest, drawing in the outlines of the ribs and the lungs beneath.

"I didn't know you could draw like that," Lucia said.

"Once I thought of being an artist, madonna. Now look here." He marked the location of the original wound. "The blade penetrated the chest here and entered the cavity formed by the pleural membranes around the lungs. The lung itself must have been punctured here in the lower part, which would allow blood and humors to escape and settle in the pleural space around the bottom of the lung."

"That is where you were afraid an internal hemorrhage would occur, isn't it?"

Had he not already known how sharp her mind was, he would have been amazed at her penetration. "Yes, but there was less than I expected. Nevertheless the blood and humors which did settle here seem to be undergoing decomposition, causing fever and delirium. This condition is called empyema."

"But why can't they escape through the knife wound?"

"I had to seal off the wound to prevent the entrance of air. Now the muscles underneath have healed together and there is no opening."

She looked up from the drawing. "Have you had cases like this before?"

"A few. Dr. Vesalius has described several."

"What can you do, then?"

It was a problem which had been occupying Antonio's thoughts during the past few days since he had first suspected an empyema. "There are two alternatives," he told her. "One is to wait and hope that his strength will be sufficient to overcome the effects of such an accumulation of humors."

"But he is getting weaker. I can see that."

Antonio nodded agreement. "The other choice is to make a new opening into the chest and allow the humors to drain out. That means a surgical procedure."

Her eyes widened. "But do patients ever live with such an operation?"

"A few, perhaps half."

"Could Don Pedro stand it?"

"I think so. Without the operation, though, I am sure that he will die."

Lucia shivered. "It's horrible, Tonio. All this because men want power they shouldn't have. Why can't everybody be good and kind . . . like you are?"

"I don't deserve your compliments, madonna. Two days ago I killed a man."

"But he deserved killing. He was a murderer."

"Have we the right to judge? If your and Gian's explanations are true, the murderer was sent by a priest, a servant of God." He turned somber eyes upon her. "Since childhood I have been taught to obey God's law. I even felt that my brother's death was justified because he had broken that law. And yet within the past few months I have killed one man and almost killed another. . . . And worst of all, I wanted to kill both of them."

She shivered. "I wish you had killed that horrible Fra Felipe Santos."

"Now," he said, "I am on the point of taking another man's life in my hands."

"But you would be trying to save it."

"Has any man the right to kill another? . . . I don't know, madonna,

I don't know." Then he threw off the burden of worry and straightened his shoulders. "I suppose we must let fate decide. Will you ask Her Majesty to consult with me when she can?"

But the queen could help Antonio little in his difficult decision, and finally he asked, "Who is his nearest relative?"

"There is Don Raffaele Grijalva, his nephew and heir."

"But, Your Majesty," Lucia protested, "Don Raffaele is——"

The queen smiled and put her arm about Lucia's shoulders. "Don Raffaele is among those who do not wish me well, Dr. Servetus. But you must consult him about a matter as serious as this. I will send a message to him."

When the queen had gone, Lucia said, "Don Raffaele would like nothing better than to see his uncle die. It would be just like him to re- fuse permission if he were sure that Don Pedro would die without the operation."

"Most doctors in Spain would advise against it anyway," Antonio admitted. "Only a few surgeons in the world have performed it success- fully."

"Then he will let his uncle die. You can be sure of that."

"Perhaps Don Raffaele is not quite so black as he is painted," Antonio suggested.

"He is blacker. And I know he will get the best of you. You are so ——" She stopped and bit her lip.

"Are you saying that I am naïve in things of the world, madonna?"

"Well, yes. You know you are, Antonio."

He bowed. "You are paying me a compliment."

She stamped her foot and color rose into her cheeks. "Here we go quarreling again. Why must we do it?"

"The impatience of youth with the slower ways of age, perhaps?" he teased, unable to resist that temptation to stir her up.

"You are not much older than I am, Ser Physician," she said tartly.

Antonio took her chin in his hand and looked down at her lovely, flushed face and soft lips, so close to his own. He felt a sudden impulse to kiss her and bent his head, but she twisted quickly and moved out of reach. "You are liable to get yourself compromised, Ser Monk," she said mockingly. "Remember your divine mistress."

"Do you always have to be such a shrew, Lucia?" Antonio said testily.

She did not answer, but there was an infuriatingly self-satisfied smile upon her face as she took a seat by the fire and picked up her embroidery.

Don Raffaele Grijalva made his appearance with surprising promptness. He minced into the sickroom on heels high in the French fashion. Small in stature and sallow of skin, the dandy was dressed in the height of fashion. His black velvet bonnet was crowned by a gay white plume and the rest of his costume was a skillfully blended mixture of gold and white. Over it he wore a rich cloak, collared with marten's fur and embroidered in gold cord. He wore both sword and dagger, as did most Spanish gallants of the day.

To Antonio's surprise, two older gentlemen were with him. One he recognized as Dr. Juan Alvarez. The other was a smaller, chubbier man with worried eyes, who wore the somber garb affected by most Spanish physicians.

"Dr. Servetus?" Don Raffaele asked.

"I am he." Antonio bowed.

"I am Don Raffaele Grijalva. I believe you know my physician, Dr. Alvarez. And this gentleman is Dr. Ortega."

Antonio bowed politely to the physicians. *"Buenas dias, señores,"* he said. He was surprised that Don Raffaele had brought the physicians with him, but not that one of them was Dr. Alvarez. Still, it might be better to get the whole thing over with at one time.

"I believe you have news of my uncle, the Marquis of Grijalva," Don Raffaele said.

"Your uncle is very ill," Antonio told him. "I feel that an operation is necessary."

Don Raffaele looked startled. *"Cáspita!"* Surgical operations were a novelty almost anywhere, and only rarely were they resorted to in Spain.

"What sort of an operation?" Alvarez inquired.

"For empyema," Antonio explained. "But come closer, gentlemen; you will want to examine the marquis."

The examination by the Spanish physicians was exceedingly cursory. Afterward Antonio took up the drawing he had made for Lucia and retraced the steps which had led him to a diagnosis of empyema. Dr. Alvarez said, "A most admirable presentation, Doctor," and Ortega clucked agreement.

"Is this operation very dangerous?" Don Raffaele asked. He had remained well away from the bed during the consultation, obviously bored by the whole proceeding.

"Very dangerous," Antonio said.

"And if I do not allow you to proceed?"

"I am sure your uncle will die."

"Then there is little choice either way," the nephew stated, as if that ended the discussion once and for all.

"He is certain to die without it," Antonio said. "But he has a chance of living with it."

"That is only your opinion," Don Raffaele said haughtily.

Antonio turned to the other two doctors. "What do you say, gentlemen?"

Alvarez looked at Don Raffaele, and Antonio saw the fop shake his head in warning. When the doctor spoke, his voice was smooth and ingratiating. "As you know, Dr. Servetus, we do not resort to surgery so readily here in Spain as you do in Italy. I am afraid I will have to consider the question more thoroughly."

"Come, gentlemen," Don Raffaele said impatiently. "We will acquaint you with our decision, Dr. Servetus." The three filed out of the apartment, leaving Antonio standing speechless with anger at the obvious discourtesy of the proceedings.

He was still fuming when Lucia entered the apartment. At her insistence he recounted the interview. "I knew he would do it," she said. "He wants Don Pedro to die, so he will refuse to let you try to save him."

"I think you are right," Antonio admitted.

"But it isn't right."

"Is there anything that is right in this world of ours?" he said glumly.

"I am beginning to think not."

But Antonio and Lucia were both wrong in their estimate of Don Raffaele Grijalva, for late that afternoon a note arrived giving Antonio permission to proceed with the operation. Dr. Alvarez and Dr. Ortega also begged that they be allowed to witness so daring a procedure.

Antonio read the note and passed it along to Lucia and Gian, who was on guard. "This is a surprise," he said. "What do you two make of it?"

Gian frowned. "There is something behind it, if I know my scoundrels."

"But what, Tonio?" Lucia asked. "We were sure that he would refuse."

"Don Raffaele may feel that allowing the operation is merely a way of insuring his uncle's death," Antonio suggested. "So little surgery is performed in Spain that it is a natural conclusion for him to reach."

"But he could accomplish the same thing by forbidding it."

"I thought of that too." Antonio shrugged. "Well, we should know soon enough. I want to go ahead with the operation in the morning, as soon as I get my instruments prepared."

The instrument case was with Antonio's belongings at the inn of the Three Brothers, and he sent Gian over in the early evening to bring them. When the artist returned, his expression was grim. "I have found out why Don Raffaele gave you permission to operate, Tonio," he said.

"How did you do it?" Lucia asked.

"He was at the inn, drinking with some friends. I heard him boast that if his uncle dies from the operation, he is going to have you arrested for murder."

"But he couldn't do that," Lucia cried.

"I suspect that he could," Antonio said, "if Alvarez and Ortega swore that I did not present the case to them in its true seriousness."

"They would swear to it, all right," Gian said grimly. "The three of them must have planned this move together after they left here this afternoon."

"But why would anyone want to harm me?" Antonio asked. "I am only doing my duty as a physician."

Gian drew his dagger from his belt and tested its point with his thumb. "You foiled them in two attempts upon Don Pedro's life, Tonio. That in itself would be enough, but I suspect that the physicians of Madrid would just as well not have a doctor of your ability residing here. Your arrest for murder would take care of everything."

"Then you must not do the operation, Tonio," Lucia urged, her eyes dark with concern and fear. "You can't risk your life like that."

He smiled at her and squeezed her shoulders gently with both hands. "You risked your life once, madonna, for a cause you believe in. I happen to believe in saving lives when I can."

Unaccountably she burst into tears and ran from the room. "I'd like to sink this into Don Raffaele," Gian said, shoving the poniard back in its sheath. "But he is only one of them. Have you ever stopped to think when all this began, Tonio?"

"Of course. When I found the painting in the priory."

"And when will it end?" Gian shrugged. "Who can tell?" Then he added. "There is something I want you to know . . . about Lucia and me."

Antonio waited for his friend to continue.

"We"—Gian stumbled—"we have agreed to go separate ways."

Startled, Antonio asked, "Why?"

Gian shrugged. "It suited both of us. . . . You like her, don't you, Tonio?"

"Why, yes. I am very fond of her."

"Then why don't you court her yourself?"

"Don't be absurd, Gian."

"She likes you very much. There's no reason why——"

"But I have nothing," Antonio protested, "and Lucia is an heiress, a member of an important family."

"That has nothing to do with it."

"And besides," Antonio continued, "I never expect to marry. I decided that long ago."

"Because of the painting? Don't be a damn fool, Tonio."

Stiffly Antonio said, "I wouldn't expect you to understand, Gian."

"But of all the stupid——"

"That is enough," Antonio snapped. "We will say no more about it."

Gian's face was red with anger, but he controlled himself, with an effort. "You may be arrested for murder tomorrow, Tonio," he said, "so we must not quarrel." He turned to the door. "But I don't understand how anyone could be so damned blind."

xi

Methodically Antonio prepared for the operation, but his mind was far from composed. Don Pedro was getting worse rapidly. The continued fever, delirium, and the racking chills which were now added to the picture were depleting his strength rapidly. The absorption of the decomposed humors, doubly poisonous now by virtue of their decomposition, was killing him as effectively as did any slow poison devised by torturers. And unless he were able to remove those humors in some way, Don Pedro would soon be dead.

And if he failed, the consequences were still severe, even without Gian's disquieting news of the intentions of Don Raffaele. Spain was not nearly so well advanced medically as Italy. And even there such surgery as this was something of a rarity. In Spain it could easily be labeled, by those who wished to do so, as an unwarranted interference with God's will. For disease, to the Spaniards, was still a punishment for sin, and only the fear of death sent sufferers to physicians as a last resort. The Inquisition, he knew, would certainly push such a charge of interfering in the will of God by one who was giving comfort to those they considered their enemies.

Merely to stand by was a far safer procedure. He could always announce that a change in Don Pedro's condition made surgical treatment inadvisable, and no one, he was sure, would gainsay him. Certainly Dr. Alvarez would not be so ill advised as to attempt surgery himself when he was certain of the outcome his patron desired through simply waiting.

But Antonio's duty was clear in his own eyes. In his hands, skilled as he was with the scalpel, lay the only possible chance of saving Don Pedro. And Don Pedro was his patient and therefore entitled to his greatest skill. Besides, there was the look in the eyes of the young queen when he had told her Don Pedro might live.

Early in the morning Antonio made his way alone to the small chapel inside the palace. Kneeling before the altar, he prayed to the benign figure of the Holy Mother for guidance and strength in the approaching ordeal. And as he prayed he felt a sense of peace and assurance quieting his doubts. Only when he was leaving did he notice a tall figure standing in the shadows beside the altar. It was a man, dressed in the somber robes of the Dominican brothers. He came out of the shadows then, and Antonio saw that he was frail, with the folds of his robe hanging loosely from narrow shoulders. His neck was long and scrawny and his cheekbones prominent above the deep hollows of his cheeks, emphasizing the surprising depth of the twin caverns of his eye sockets. But the most striking thing about the priest was not his emaciation, or his height, but the cold fire that burned in his pale blue eyes, a fire that sent an involuntary shiver of dread down Antonio's spine.

"Why do you pray so early, my son?" The voice was deep for so frail a body, with vibrating organ tones that filled the chapel.

"For strength and guidance, *Padre*. I am undertaking an important and difficult task this morning."

The priest's eyes bored into Antonio's, as if he were dissecting his very soul. "Are you not certain, then, of the rightness of what you plan?"

"I am now," Antonio said firmly.

"Has God given you that assurance?"

"Yes. I am sure that He has."

The priest's eyes continued to bore his soul. "Be sure you mistake not your own desires for the approval of God." His voice throbbed with vibrant overtones. "Our Father never approves of those who seek to interfere in His will." The words were ominous in sound. What could this strange priest know of him and what he was planning to do?

"Life . . . and death . . . are God's to give or withhold," the deep voice continued. "No mere man has a right to interfere in His intentions. Be sure that those who do will be punished for their presumption, Dr. Servetus." He turned and disappeared into the shadows before Antonio had recovered his wits from the shock of hearing his name pronounced. How had this strange figure known who he was? Or what he had been asking divine guidance in carrying out? Unquestionably the priest had threatened him with punishment for interfering in the natural course of disease, but Antonio was certain, too, that it was a specific warning in regard to Don Pedro.

His spirit gripped by the ominous sense of foreboding induced by the strange interview, Antonio left the chapel and made his way back to the apartment where he had left Lucia with Don Pedro. A priest was just completing the last rites. He came out, followed by his acolyte.

"*Buenas dias,* Doctor." He was a pleasant man, well fed. "Your patient is very ill."

"Gravely," Antonio agreed.

"Do you think he will last much longer?"

"We do not know, Father. I am glad Madonna Lucia had the forethought to send for you. I had overlooked it."

The priest's eyes widened slightly. "But it was Fra Ignacio Molina who sent me, Doctor. Good day, my children."

When the priest was gone, Antonio said to Lucia, "Is Fra Ignacio thin and tall, with hollow cheeks and a deep voice?"

She shivered. "And eyes that freeze you in your tracks. Why?"

He told her about his experience in the chapel. "What Gian heard was true, then," she whispered. "They do plan to arrest you, and in the courts of the Inquisition." She swayed, and when he put out his arm to steady her, she threw herself suddenly into his arms, sobbing, "You can't do it, Tonio. You mustn't let them kill you."

He smoothed the golden hair, so soft and fragrant against his neck. "I have no choice, Lucia. Don Pedro is my patient."

"But it is all my fault," she wailed. "If I hadn't been so foolish."

"You were only being loyal to the queen, just as I am being loyal to my oath as a physician."

She looked up, her eyes still wet. "I can stay with you during the operation, can't I?" she begged.

He smiled. "It is not a pretty sight."

"But someone must watch Dr. Alvarez and Dr. Ortega," she insisted. "I don't trust them."

"I don't either," he admitted. "But I will be armed with a scalpel, and I hardly think they would interfere."

"Just the same, I want to stay."

"Then stay if you wish," he agreed. "Now we had better get some breakfast, if I am going to be strong enough for such work."

Suddenly she raised herself on her toes and kissed him. Her lips were soft and fragrant. He thought she whispered something before she broke away. But he knew he could not have heard her aright, for what she had said sounded like, "God keep you, my darling."

And that, of course, was impossible. . . . Unless Gian was right about Lucia's caring for him. And then, blotting out the memory of Lucia's tear-wet eyes and soft lips, there arose the serene picture of the goddess, in her eyes a touch of sadness and reproach that even for an instant he should have considered anyone else before his pledge of eternal devotion to her divine loveliness.

xii

In trunk hose and jerkin, sleeves rolled well above his elbows to expose muscular forearms, Antonio surveyed his preparations for the operation and found them satisfactory. A narrow table had been moved into the apartment from the palace kitchens, and under his direction, Gian and a pair of strong lackeys placed the sick man upon it. Don Pedro, sleeping from a draught of opium, lay on his left side, with the right side uppermost, his shirt cut away to expose the lower part of the chest. Both hands were bound together and lashed to the table leg. His right leg was drawn back and the left forward, both being lashed to table legs. Held thus, he could move but little, not enough to interfere with Antonio's work.

On a table beside the bed the entire contents of the small instrument chest given Antonio by Dr. Duval were arranged. In the classic empyema operation of Vesalius scarcely any of them but the scalpel would be used, but Antonio had found it advantageous always to be prepared for unforeseen eventualities during surgical operations, and it would be as well to have them handy.

On one side of the small table were the trephines, or *trepannes,* used to create an artificial opening in the skull. In use since the times of earliest antiquity, trepanning had lately come more into vogue since Vesalius had successfully opened the skull of Don Carlos, the Principe, first-born and heir of Philip II of Spain, following a serious head injury from falling downstairs. And yet, so backward was Spain in medical matters that even the king had given credit for the recovery, not to the daring and skill of Vesalius, but to a somewhat more startling method of treatment, the placing of a monk's corpse in bed with the injured Principe.

Next to the trephines were instruments for removing and cutting off teeth, small levers called elevators, used to pry out the body of the tooth, and strong-jawed forceps to grip and remove broken roots. To one side were the curved scalpels for amputations and the saw for cutting bones. And beside them, the slender forceps devised by Paré for control of hemorrhage by ligating cut arteries, rather than the usual method of searing them with hot irons or scalding pitch. Nearest to Antonio's hand were the scalpels, honed to a razorlike sharpness.

Dr. Alvarez stood beside the table at Antonio's elbow, well out of the way of any spurting blood when the scalpel cut through the flesh. Beside him stood Lucia, cheeks pale, lips firmly compressed, her hands hidden in the folds of her gown. Strong lackeys stood ready at the foot and head of the table, superintended by Gian, whose forehead was already beaded with sweat.

With his finger, Antonio indicated the lower ribs. "Here is where the collection of humors seems to have occurred," he told Dr. Alvarez. "Notice how the spaces between the ribs are full, almost bulging, in fact, as if there were some accumulation of pressure beneath them."

"*Ay Maria!* It is true, as you say."

"If I can open directly into the empyema," Antonio continued, "our efforts will be successful."

"But what of the pleural membranes?"

"They are separated here by the accumulated humors. The lung in such cases is shrunken and relatively airless."

Dr. Alvarez breathed heavily. *"De veras,"* he said unctuously. "You are an anatomist without peer."

"There is only one anatomist without a peer," Antonio corrected him. "Andreas Vesalius." He began to count downward along the marquis's ribs. At the tenth he stopped and, placing his finger along the upper edge of the rib, reached for a scalpel. "By entering the chest along the upper edge of a rib," he explained, "we avoid danger of hemorrhage. The blood vessels here run along the lower edge of the ribs."

Tightening the skin with his fingers, Antonio drew the scalpel along the upper edge of the rib outline. The skin parted, and Don Pedro groaned and twisted from the pain. But the lashings, plus the strength of the lackeys, kept him still. Blood spurted from small vessels cut through by the scalpel, and Antonio heard Lucia gasp. For a second he wondered if he had been right in letting her stay, then he remembered that on another occasion she had been shocked by the sight of blood—her uncle's—but had recovered immediately.

The operative wound was about three inches long, extending through the skin and the tissues beneath, exposing the reddish-brown fibers of the muscles which ran here from rib to rib. Dr. Alvarez leaned almost upon Antonio's shoulder in his eagerness to see everything. When Antonio took up the scalpel again, the doctor accidentally nudged his elbow, almost plunging the blade deep into the wound.

"Careful, Doctor!" Antonio snapped. "You are crowding me."

"A thousand pardons," Alvarez begged. "It is just that my interest is so great."

Antonio sponged the wound clean with a pad of linen prepared for this use and took up the scalpel again. Separating the edges of the skin with his fingers, he cut deeply, laying open the muscles, their edges pouting, soft and pink. Dr. Alvarez nudged him again in his eagerness. "Is that the *membrana pleura?*" he asked.

"Not yet." Antonio moved his shoulder so as to get clear of the insistent pressure. "There are several layers of muscle before you enter the chest cavity itself."

Don Pedro was fairly quiet now. There was always more pain in traversing the skin than in any other part of the operation. Again Antonio wiped the depths of the wound clear and examined it carefully. "The direction of the muscle fibers has changed," he pointed out. "We have now cut through the outer layer and are into the inner one, the *musculus intercostalis interna.*"

"*Caramba!*" Alvarez cried. "The fibers now run in quite another direction."

"Exactly as described by Dr. Vesalius in his *Fabrica.*" With the scalpel once more in his fingers, Antonio searched the depths of the wound again, separating the muscle fibers gingerly, cutting through only a very small portion at a time. It was not safe to make bold cuts here, for a slip of half an inch with the scalpel could mean cutting the arteries which ran along the undersurface of the rib above, setting up a dangerous hemorrhage which he might not be able to control.

Dr. Alvarez leaned closer. Suddenly Antonio felt a sharp pressure upon his right elbow. Had he not tightened his muscles involuntarily, the blade would have been driven downward, entering the pleural cavity and almost certainly cutting through the arteries he was seeking to avoid.

"Please, Doctor," he snapped. "Will you stay less close?"

"A thousand par——" Alvarez's voice changed suddenly. "*Por Dios!*" he said, but in a hoarse whisper.

Antonio was too busy to pay any attention to Alvarez, so long as he did not jostle his arm, and he was relieved to find that the Spanish physician seemed to have acceded to his request and moved farther away. There was no more pressure on his elbow now and he could work with freedom.

He felt a sudden change in the tension of the tissues against the blade of the scalpel. Quickly he drew the blade away and wiped the depths of the wound carefully dry. Where before had been the pinkish bellies of the muscle tissue, there was now a brownish-looking structure flecked with whitish patches. It was much firmer to touch, and a sense of elation filled Antonio.

"There is the *membrana pleura!*" he exclaimed. "And it is inflamed."

Dr. Alvarez did not speak, but Lucia asked, "Does that mean you are in the right place?"

"Almost certainly. If the pleura is inflamed, it is from the pressure of decomposed humors in the empyema beneath it."

Antonio looked over the instruments on the table and spied what he needed among the tools for toothdrawing. It was a flat metal elevator, and it could serve a good purpose here, even if not devised for such use. Sliding the flat metal blade along beneath the muscles which were as yet uncut, he could sever them easily now, protected from going deeper and perhaps damaging other structures by the metal itself.

With the muscles separated for the entire length of the wound, he could see more of the inflamed pleural membrane. And what he saw increased his feeling of satisfaction. Those patches of white inflammatory exudate, that leathery resistance in what was normally a paperthin lining membrane of the chest, always meant an empyema, a collection of decomposed blood and humors such as Hippocrates had described more than a thousand years before. Many surgeons had tried to drain such collections through the centuries, but only a few had succeeded.

Taking a fresh pledget of linen, he placed it in the depths of the wound and applied pressure over it with a larger pad, so as to control the oozing of blood which so quickly filled the wound. He wanted to see quite clearly when he made the next and very important step in cutting through the pleura itself. For that stroke would determine whether he was indeed entering the pool of decomposed humors or must search farther for it, with the consequent strain upon Don Pedro's already weakened constitution.

With the pad in place, he glanced about the room. Gian, unaccountably, was grinning broadly. Dr. Alvarez, pale and sweating profusely, was standing a good two feet behind Antonio, with Lucia, her face grim and flushed, close beside him.

"Could you see all right, Doctor?" Antonio asked politely.

Alvarez managed a rather ghastly smile. *"Muy bien, Doctor. Es usted muy amable."*

Antonio turned back to the wound to hide a smile at the doctor's discomfiture. He would have expected Lucia or Gian to have been affected by the operation, but instead it was Dr. Alvarez who looked ill.

The wound was relatively dry now, the slow ooze of blood controlled for the time being by pressure. Picking up the scalpel, he gave all his attention to the business at hand. This was the critical point, the step that determined unqualified success or possible failure. With the very point of the instrument he began to nick the pleural membrane. Mentally he gave thanks to Dr. Duval for these new instruments whose steel was far more perfectly tempered than the relatively primitive scalpels commonly used, the blades thinner, the points keener.

Gently he incised the thick layer, pushing aside the exudate and keeping his finger always deep in the wound, protecting the vessels coursing along the undersurface of the rib above. He could feel the pulse in the artery, throbbing against his finger. The pleural membrane was of the consistency of leather, many times its normal thickness, and for a moment he wondered if by any chance he could be wrong about its identity. Could it possibly be the muscular wall of the diaphragm through which he was cutting? But Vesalius had stated clearly in a special *consilium* on this subject that there was no danger of striking the diaphragm at the upper edge of the tenth rib, and that only the pleural cavity would be entered here. And Antonio had always found this to be true in his dissections.

Then there was a sudden release of tension at the point of the scalpel, warning him of a change in the structure through which he was operating. Instantly he withdrew the blade and sponged out the wound. What he saw sent a thrill of elation coursing through him, for the point was stained with a reddish-brown fluid. And as he wiped the wound clean again, a small geyser of the same color welled up from the very depths of the incision.

"*Corpo di Cristo!*" Gian exclaimed. "What is that smell?"

A putrid stench filled the room, an odor familiar to Antonio from contact with such empyema collections in other patients and in cadavers. But to the others it was almost beyond description, a nauseating stench of such foulness that it was hard to believe any human could live with such a mass inside his body. Antonio heard Dr. Alvarez gag and in a thickened voice gasp, "*Madre de Dios!*"

"It is the empyema," Antonio cried. "I have entered the cavity."

"*Dio mio!*" Gian muttered. "You have entered the grave, from the smell of it."

"Look there in the depths of the wound," Antonio said excitedly. "See how it spurts up with each respiration." He seized the scalpel. "Wait, I will open it wider."

A slight cut gave him space into which he could insert a finger to tighten the pleural membrane and cut it more accurately. And now he forced himself to go more slowly, tempted as he was, in the elation of discovering what he sought, to rush on and lay it wide open. The cavity into which his fingers plunged was warm with the heat of fever and filled with a nauseous purulent flood. The stink in the room was so strong that it seemed to weight them all down, making breathing an effort.

"Get it over with, Tonio," Gian begged. "This is almost beyond bearing."

But Antonio was too elated to worry about Gian's sensitive nostrils. With success in his grasp, he could take no chances by hurrying and perhaps still doing irreparable damage. In fact, slowness was more indicated here than at any point so far, for nothing lay between the scalpel in his hand and his own fingers deep in the cavity but his own skill. A cut finger here meant almost certain inflammation, often death. More than one promising anatomist, Antonio knew, had lost his life because of just such an accidental nick of the finger.

The empyema cavity was a large one, holding two cupfuls of the poisonous contents, more than enough to have caused the dangerous condition of the Marquis of Grijalva. When he was satisfied that there was nothing unusual about the cavity and that it was now fully evacuated, Antonio folded several strips of linen into a large wick which he inserted through the opening. It would furnish path for drainage of any further humors which might escape in this way. Then he took a larger compress from the table and applied it loosely over the wound, adding another until there was a thick pad.

"The cloth will hold the edges of the operative wound open and insure free flow of any noxious humors," he assured Dr. Alvarez.

The Spanish physician showed a rather marked uneasiness which Antonio could no longer explain, unless it was from seeing his plans set at nought by the success of the operation. "*Permítame,* Doctor," he said. "I must attend to some other matters."

"Certainly," Antonio said. "Will you inform Don Raffaele Grijalva that I feel certain his uncle will live?"

"I shall do that at once," Alvarez promised, but he was through the door before he finished speaking. Antonio bandaged the dressing snugly over the operative wound and looked up. Gian was still grinning, and Lucia, too, was looking more relaxed. While Antonio cleaned

DIVINE MISTRESS

up in the adjoining room, Gian and the servants put Don Pedro back
in his bed and the men departed with the soiled table and linen. Lucia
and Gian were standing beside the bed when Antonio returned to the
room, now fully dressed.

"Tonio," Lucia cried, her eyes shining. "See. He is better already."
In the excitement of the moment, she ran to him and threw her arms
about his neck, kissing him.

"I think I shall become a surgeon," Gian said mockingly, "if that is
the reward for a successful operation."

Lucia blushed. "You know I was carried away with excitement over
Antonio's success, Gian," she protested.

Antonio looked down at the sleeping marquis, and an immense
feeling of satisfaction welled up within him, tired though he was. He
put his hand on Don Pedro's forehead. It was definitely cooler already,
the skin beaded with the perspiration which would bring surcease from
the raging fires of fever.

"You should feel better, Tonio," Gian said, "knowing that you cannot be charged with murder."

"Will you believe me," Antonio said, "I had forgotten about that
while I was working."

"I was so scared," Lucia admitted, "that I trembled all over."

"By the way," Antonio said, "what was wrong with Dr. Alvarez?
I thought he was going to be sick."

"He *was* sick." Gian laughed. "But not because of the operation.
Tell him why, Lucia."

She reached into the folds of her gown and drew out a small, slender
poniard, in its scabbard. It was a delicate-looking thing, jeweled at the
handle, the kind often used by merchants to open their letters. But it was
also capable of inflicting a fatal wound. "This is what he was sick
about," she smiled.

"Stop talking in riddles," Antonio commanded. "What happened?"

"You remember when Dr. Alvarez was nudging your elbow, don't
you?"

"Yes. I had to push him away several times."

"I told you that he would try to interfere if he could," she said,
"so I came prepared, with this."

Antonio understood then why Dr. Alvarez had suddenly moved
away from him and the reason for his strange behavior afterward. He

had been in very real fear of his own life. "But you wouldn't have stabbed him," he protested.

"I certainly would have," Lucia said grimly.

Antonio reached out and took them both by the hand. "I would be like a lost child without you two to look after me," he said. "What did I ever do to deserve such loyalty?"

"We have done nothing," Gian protested.

"You risked your life in the fight with the guard outside the palace the other night, while I went on ahead."

"And you risked yours in the fight with Valdez," Lucia reminded him.

"But you have incurred the displeasure of Dr. Alvarez, Lucia."

"He is a pompous ass," she said scornfully.

"But he has powerful friends."

"I don't think they will be so quick to bother us any more," she said confidently.

But remembering the cold light in the eyes of the priest in the chapel, Antonio was not certain. Frey Ignacio Molina was not the kind to give up because of one skirmish lost. This was just the beginning. There would be other conflicts.

xiii

With the poisonous material removed from his body by the operation, Don Pedro improved remarkably. The morning following the operation he was rational, although still quite weak. The queen visited him, and when she came out of the room her face was radiant. "You have worked a miracle, Dr. Servetus," she cried. "A true miracle."

"I merely followed the instructions of others, Your Majesty."

"You are much too modest," she insisted. "But I am going to reward you suitably just the same. My chamberlain will deposit five thousand ducats to your credit in any banking house you prefer."

"B-but, Your Majesty," Antonio protested, "I do not deserve it." Five thousand ducats would make him a rich man! He had never even thought of so much money.

"You shall have it nevertheless," the queen insisted. "And I am sure Don Pedro will reward you even more generously."

"That is too much," Antonio protested to Lucia when the queen had gone. "Far too much."

"For saving one of the greatest soldiers in Spain, and risking your life as well? I think not."

"But what would I do with so much money?"

"Deposit it with the House of Bellarmi of course," she said at once. "I don't like leaving sums like that in Spain, though," she added with a frown. "But, of course, France is the place."

"I don't know anyone in France."

"It doesn't matter. My uncle does business with the De' Medici banking house in Paris. I can arrange to have your funds transferred here."

Antonio smiled. "Suppose I make you the manager of my business, then?"

"I intend for you to," Lucia told him calmly. "After all, you are a babe in arms in affairs of this kind, Tonio. And I am a Bellarmi."

When Don Pedro, as the queen had predicted, insisted upon rewarding Antonio with a like amount, he felt really rich. Lucia took complete charge of his finances. Leaving him a modest account at her uncle's Madrid branch, she arranged for a transfer of the remaining funds to Paris, where she felt they would be safe.

The king was expected to return soon from his current expedition against the rebellious Flemings in the Low Countries, and since it was obviously better for Don Pedro to be out of the palace upon his arrival, it was arranged that the marquis return to his own home, with Antonio in attendance. There one evening he met Don Raffaele Grijalva. The foppish nephew was surprisingly affable.

"Dr. Alvarez tells me that you performed a very remarkable operation upon my uncle, Doctor," he said. "I have been wanting to congratulate you."

"I am well pleased with the results," Antonio admitted.

"*Voto a tal!* You may well be." Don Raffaele took a decanter from the taboret and poured two glasses of wine. "To my uncle's health and safety."

Antonio could hardly help smiling at the nephew's rather transparent attempt to cover up his own attempt to interfere in Don Pedro's recovery. And he could not resist the temptation to twist the iron in the wound. "I am sure Don Pedro owes as much to you as to me, though," he told Don Raffaele.

The nephew looked startled. "*Cáspita!* Why do you say that?"

"It must have been a difficult decision for you to make to allow me to proceed with the operation."

"It was," Don Pedro said fervently. *"Ay Maria!* It was."

"But you dared to let me go ahead and thereby insure that your uncle would live. That was a great sacrifice on your part."

"A sacrifice? How?"

"After all, you are your uncle's heir. Had you been guided only by selfish motives, you must certainly have decided to let him die without the operation."

The weak face of the fop was a play of varying emotions. Finally he managed to smile weakly. "But, as you say, no selfish motives guided me."

"Exactly," Antonio agreed. "You were very magnanimous indeed."

Antonio left Don Raffaele with his thoughts, but as he went upstairs he was laughing in secret glee. It was pleasant for once to torture such an obnoxious brat as Don Pedro's scheming heir and watch him squirm.

Several nights later Antonio was playing chess with Don Pedro when visitors were announced. To his surprise, Don Raffaele ushered into the bedchamber two churchmen. One he recognized at once, for there was no mistaking the tall frame and chilling eyes of the Inquisitor of Madrid. The other—a heavy man with pendulous jowls and a red face already marked by the evidence of choler so frequently seen in high ecclesiastics—Don Pedro introduced as Don Diego de Espinosa, Bishop of Toledo and Minister of State. Antonio was surprised at thus finding the enemy in the house, but when he would have remained behind with the idea of protecting his patient, the marquis asked him to wait downstairs.

"I should like the pleasure of talking to you before I leave, Doctor," Don Diego said pleasantly as Antonio was leaving.

Startled, Antonio stammered, "But certainly, Your Reverence. I shall be in the library."

Don Diego was not with Don Pedro very long. When the bishop came into the library, Antonio dropped to one knee and kissed the heavy seal of his ring.

"I have been wanting to talk to you, Doctor," the churchman said. "Don Pedro tells me that you saved his life."

"I merely treated him according to the best authority in such wounds."

"You mean Galen, of course."

Antonio shook his head. "Dr. Ambroise Paré, a French surgeon."

"Paré." The bishop frowned. "I have heard something of him. Is he a Huguenot?"

"I know nothing of his religious beliefs, Your Reverence."

"I am sure he is a follower of Calvin." Don Diego frowned. "That is a coincidence. Did not Calvin execute a man with your name for heresy some years ago?"

Antonio felt the familiar cold terror begin to gnaw at his insides. Here it was again, the shadow of his brother's heresy which he was not sure now had been heresy at all. Should he deny the relationship? It was not probable that anyone would check his story, for it was a long way from Madrid to Champel and Padua, and communication between Spain and the world of Protestantism was very infrequent. But then he remembered the day in the priory garden at Padua when he had resolved no longer to run away from the memory of what had happened to Michael. The die had been cast then, and he could not turn from the path he had chosen.

"That was Michael Servetus, my oldest brother," he said in a firm voice.

"Ah!" Don Diego's stubby fingers played with the tiny gold crucifix on the chain about his neck. "That is most interesting." He turned small but shrewd eyes upon Antonio. "It is also a coincidence that both of you studied medicine."

"My parents wished me to enter the Holy Orders," Antonio explained. "I studied canon law first at Padua, but turned to medicine because of my interest in anatomy."

"Dr. Vesalius has written a book on anatomy."

"The *Fabrica*. Yes, I studied and taught from it in Padua."

"How did you happen to leave the university?" Don Diego asked.

Antonio hesitated. To tell the truth would be disastrous, and yet he must stay as close to it as possible. "Messer Girolamo Bellarmi asked me to come to Spain as his personal physician, Your Reverence," he explained. "He is a very liberal patron, and I thought I should take advantage of the opportunity to study medicine and surgery as it is practiced in your country."

"A laudable decision," the bishop approved. "And a very laudable ambition. But I hope that you have not given up your intention of entering the Holy Orders." He turned to go. *"Pax vobiscum,* my son."

"Et tecum, pax," Antonio murmured automatically.

There was a shrewd gleam in the bishop's eyes as he left, which, if Antonio had seen it, might have caused him worry. For in his simple and ready answer to the blessing of peace, Antonio had unwittingly revealed that he had once been closely identified with the monastic life, the one thing he had been trying to keep from his questioner.

Don Pedro was sitting up in bed while his manservant prepared the room for the night. Antonio was surprised at his appearance, for all animation seemed to have gone out of his face.

"Is it an impertinence to ask what Don Diego wished with you, Doctor?" he asked.

"Not at all," Antonio assured him. "Our conversation was very trivial. He asked about my life before coming to Madrid."

Don Pedro shifted his position against the pillows. "I have been meaning to have a serious talk with you, Doctor," he said, "And perhaps this is a good time. I believe you know something of why I was wounded."

"A little. It was not my right to ask questions."

"Al contrario, you have every right, since we have involved you innocently in an affair which might have cost you your life."

"But only as a physician," Antonio protested.

"That does not change the situation, as far as those who would harm us are concerned. There are a few of us in Spain who believe that Spain is for the Spaniards," Don Pedro continued. "We feel that our duty lies in helping our own people and protecting our own country and that the more we become embroiled in the affairs of other states, the less we are giving to our own."

"I can understand that," Antonio agreed.

"Unfortunately, to keep Spain at peace, we must help preserve peace in adjacent countries. And sometimes this means supporting people whose religious beliefs differ from our own." He sighed. "The heads of the Church in Spain, however, do not agree with that philosophy. They would like for the king to interfere wherever another religious belief seems to be gaining strength."

Antonio nodded his understanding. It was an accepted principle of the Church to use every means to suppress heresy.

"The King of Spain stands for peace," Don Pedro continued, "even at the expense of allowing dissenting faiths to gain some strength in other countries, although not in Spain. But there are many pressures upon him."

"I can understand that from what I have already seen," Antonio admitted.

"I asked Don Diego to come here tonight because the time seems ripe to settle one controversy. And I think he realizes that this time De Quadra has gone too far."

"De Quadra!" Antonio exclaimed.

"Do you know him?"

"I met an Armand de Quadra at the inn, the night you were stabbed."

"When Lucia carried our plans to De Quervain there?"

"Yes." So that was why she had risked scandal, Antonio thought. And he had doubted her for even so much as a minute.

"It is the same," Don Pedro said. "How did you come to meet him?"

"He heard me asking for Gian Savarino and came over to offer me a bed at his house."

"Was he there when Señorita Bellarmi came in?"

"Yes. But he left almost at once."

"That was when he came to the gate, then," Don Pedro said, his face grim.

"And you think it was he who stabbed you?"

"He or one of his henchmen, undoubtedly. They must have been watching for Señorita Bellarmi to come to the inn, so that they would know that I was waiting for her return."

"Then they had no designs upon her?"

"No. I am sure they did not have, nor do now. But the second time they made the attempt it might have cost all four of us our lives. That is why I have decided to stop all of our activities."

Antonio knew now why the tall man who had attacked Gian in the darkness had seemed familiar. It was De Quadra, unquestionably. The memory stirred a deep resentment inside him once more. "Please don't on our account," he begged. "I am sure both Lucia and Gian would want to help in any way they could."

Don Pedro shook his head. "Spain is my country, Doctor, and I would gladly give my life in her service. But she is not yours, or Madonna Lucia's or Señor Savarino's. We must not involve you in our affairs and perhaps endanger your lives. I asked Don Diego and Frey

Ignacio here tonight to see if we could not arrange some sort of a truce."

"Did they accept?" Antonio asked.

"On the face of it, yes, but we shall have to wait and see if they can be trusted." He smiled wryly. "You have probably not had much dealings with the Inquisition, Doctor. They regard lies and all other forms of chicanery as justified in carrying out their purposes. I shall not be at all surprised if they arrest me within the week on some trumped-up charge."

Antonio felt the same ripple of cold fear travel his spine. Did he know of the ways of the servants of the Holy Office? The evidence of that knowledge was written in the red scar that traversed his lower ribs.

"I am releasing you as my physician tomorrow," Don Pedro continued. "The less you are involved with me the better it is for you."

"But no one could object to a physician treating the sick," Antonio protested.

"You don't know the Inquisition, my friend," Don Pedro smiled wearily. "And I pray you never will."

The next morning Antonio moved his few belongings to the house taken by Messer Bellarmi. The banker was well, and Antonio's duties were light, so that he had ample time to think upon what he had learned from Don Pedro. The more he considered it, the more depressed he became. Was there no honor, no human kindness left in the world? But how could there be, logic asked, when the servants of the Church, representatives of God before the people, stooped to bribery, threats, and even murder?

Antonio's spirits took an even greater drop when he learned that Don Pedro Grijalva had been arrested by the Inquisition. Remembering Frey Ignacio's warning in the chapel and his conversation with the Bishop of Toledo, he wondered how long it would be before he shared the same fate.

Book Four

THE INQUISITOR OF MADRID

With the return of King Philip to Madrid, triumphant for the moment over the rebellious Flemings of the Low Countries, the city took on a new pulse of life. Many tournaments and other affairs were announced, celebrating the success of the sovereign and champion of the Catholic faith in all the world. The first was a great auto-da-fé, designed to give the monarch an opportunity to reiterate his support of the Holy Office of the Inquisition in its relentless fight against heresy. Antonio had sent a note to Dr. Andreas Vesalius, immediately upon his return with the king, requesting an audience. He was surprised to be granted it on the day of the great celebration, but the time suited him well, for he had no particular wish to witness the festival, replete as it would be with evidence of the power of the dread Holy Office and the threat it held for everyone who dared to show initiative of his own which might conflict with the arbitrary rulings of the Inquisitors.

The streets were packed and he had to work his way slowly through the crowds, for Vesalius's home was beside the great Plaza Mayor where the auto was to take place. Already the plaza was filled with a solid mass of humanity, but still they struggled toward it, eager to see the procession, the colorful ceremony of the auto, and the burning of the condemned heretics chosen for today.

As Antonio knocked upon the door the hum of conversation from the excited crowd was like the roaring of the ocean heard in the distance, rising and falling in endless rhythm. A servant admitted him and directed him to the cabinet where the physician received patients and others who came to call upon him.

Vesalius was standing beside a window, looking down upon the crowded plaza below, when Antonio entered the room. Of medium height, his hair was black and curly, his face tanned from the suns of many military campaigns, and his beard scrupulously tended, as befitted the most important physician in the kingdom of Spain. He had discarded the somber dress ordinarily worn by physicians and was garbed instead in a suit of expensive velvet with the high Spanish collar, the ruff at his throat open with the strings hanging free. His stocky legs were encased in dark hose and the fine pouch swinging at his belt showed the tip of a cambric handkerchief. When he turned, Antonio was taken aback by the look of cold hostility in his eyes.

Antonio bowed deeply. "I am honored, Dr. Vesalius," he said. "I should have known you anywhere from your portrait in the *Fabrica.*"

Vesalius nodded curtly, but some of the hostility in his manner faded at the mention of his beloved text. "You wished to consult me?" he asked with a strong Flemish accent.

Antonio had been looking forward for months to the moment when he would meet the master at whose feet he had worshiped so long, but this was certainly not the warm welcome that he had envisioned from a brother anatomist. "Could we not speak Italian?" he asked. "I am still awkward with my Spanish."

Vesalius smiled, as if the mention of Italy brought back pleasant memories. "You are newly come from Italy, then?" he asked.

"But yes," Antonio said in surprise. "I thought you knew."

"All I know is that a physician of whom I have never heard appears in Madrid and is immediately appointed physician to the queen, superseding the king's honorary physicians who are entrusted with the task of caring for members of the royal family in my absence," Vesalius said pointedly.

Antonio was beginning to see the light. "Might I ask from what source your information was received?"

"From His Majesty's Minister of State, the Bishop of Toledo."

"I thought as much," Antonio said. "Did he trouble to tell you that I hold the diploma in medicine from your own university, that of Padua, and that I formerly assisted Dr. Fallopius in teaching anatomy and surgery there?"

It was the turn of Vesalius to be surprised. "Is that true?"

"Of course it is true," Antonio said a little testily. "I made no false pretenses in coming here. I am personal physician to Messer Girolamo Bellarmi, a banker of Florence, now residing in Madrid. It happened that I was called upon to treat a serious wound for the Marquis of Grijalva and successfully used the treatment recommended by Dr. Ambroise Paré."

"Paré!" Vesalius cried. "Do you know Paré?"

"Only through his writings. But I was treated by a follower of his, a Dr. Duval of Florence."

"This is astounding," Vesalius said. "Dr. Paré and I had the honor of working together in treating the wound of the King of France." He indicated a chair. "Sit down, Doctor. It begins to appear as though I were misinformed about you."

"I am sure you were," Antonio told him, "if the Bishop of Toledo was your informant."

"Tell me about this wound of Don Pedro's," Vesalius urged.

Antonio recounted the history of the case, including his decision to operate. When he came to the operation itself, Vesalius could no longer contain himself. "Go on," he cried. "When you entered the pleural cavity did you find the empyema?"

"Exactly as described by you."

"And he recovered quickly, once the empyema was drained?"

"Very quickly," Antonio said. "But he has been arrested by the Inquisition."

"Ah yes, the Inquisition." Vesalius shivered. "It is very powerful here." As if to echo his words, there came a deep-throated roar from the crowd gathered in the Plaza Mayor for the auto-da-fé.

"There is something familiar about you, Doctor," Vesalius said.

"Perhaps it is my resemblance to my brother."

"Your brother? ... *Per Bacco!* Your name *is* Servetus, isn't it?"

"I am a younger brother of Michael Servetus," Antonio explained.

"*Maria Sanctissima!* The brother of my dearest friend of long ago. And I was cool toward you because of those lies. Forgive me, forgive me, my friend."

"You are forgiven," Antonio said with a smile. This was what he had expected to find, and it pleased him that he was not disappointed in the man whom he had come to regard almost as his personal deity.

"But this is amazing," Vesalius continued happily. "We must celebrate. A glass of wine at least."

The servant brought them wine, and they settled down facing each other. "Now tell me about yourself, Antonio," Vesalius commanded. "You will let me call you by your given name?"

"Of course," Antonio said. "Where shall I begin?"

"Begin with Padua." The anatomist sighed. "Those were my happiest days, when I was preparing the *Fabrica*. Why did you leave Padua? It is the most wonderful place in the world."

Antonio hesitated. It was a question that he had been expecting yet half fearing. Seeing his concern, the older physician said, "But I intrude into your affairs, my son. Forget that I asked."

"No," Antonio said in sudden decision. "I would like to tell you. . . ."

When he had finished, Vesalius's expression was grave. "It is always the fate of a thinker to stir up such a hornets' nest," he agreed. "It was the same with me."

"But now that I am here in Madrid," Antonio said, " I am counting on our pursuing our studies together."

The anatomist frowned. "I have done little dissection since I came to Madrid. Still, I am anxious to study this new discovery of yours in regard to the pulmonary circulation."

"I will gladly demonstrate it to you," Antonio suggested. "Can you arrange for a cadaver?"

"Dissection is forbidden in Spain," Vesalius said. "But His Majesty is anxious to improve the quality of medicine here, and perhaps he will allow it. We will both think on it and perhaps we can find a way. But will you be safe here in Madrid, Antonio?"

"There has been no trouble since Don Pedro's arrest."

"Perhaps they will leave you alone, then. At least we can only wait and see." Vesalius shrugged. "In Spain one learns to be philosophic. One day you are happy and well, living a good life, the next you are arrested by the Inquisition and it is the end."

Antonio shivered. "I wish I could be that much of a philosopher."

"You will learn," Vesalius assured him. "We all do."

"I learned something else in Venice which I think might interest you," Antonio said. "At least, I am convinced that it has applications in medicine."

"*Dio mio!*" Vesalius exclaimed admiringly. "Is it not enough to be an anatomist? But tell me of it."

Antonio recounted his experience with magnetism and his studies

of it with Lodovici Agnolo. When he had finished, Vesalius said with
a puzzled frown, "But what is this magnetism? I do not understand it."

"I don't know myself," Antonio admitted. "It is said to be something
that flows from one body to another, but I can see no means of trans-
ferring it, since it is not necessary actually to touch the person being
magnetized."

"We must arrange a demonstration," Vesalius suggested. "I am very
anxious to see it."

The shouting of the crowd in the plaza outside took on a deeper
note, and Vesalius went to the window. "The king is approaching," he
said. "If you have never seen one of these ceremonies, you will be interested." He pointed to another window. "That should give you an
excellent view."

From the street outside the broad open space of the Plaza Mayor
the sound of marching men could be heard. The crowd began to fall
back, like earth before a plow, leaving a furrow through a solid wall of
struggling bodies and craning necks as each fought for a glimpse of this
most stimulating of all spectacles to the truly faithful: the condemnation
and execution of heretics.

Into the plaza itself marched a group of familiars of the Confraternity of St. Peter the Martyr, the Soldiers of the Faith, clad in somber
black. At the head of the marching column standard-bearers held aloft
the great banner with the green cross of the Inquisition swathed in
veils of dark crepe. They moved, with sedate tread and grim faces, between the gallery set up on one side for the accommodation of the royal
family and the great scaffold built to support the trembling bodies of
the poor wretches who were to pay for their sins in today's spectacle. A
little to one side was still another platform, elevated to the same level as
the others but even more handsomely decorated than the one for the
royal family. It was covered by a shining canopy of gold and scarlet,
hanging with tassels of brightest yellow and held at the corners by tall
upright supports of burnished steel. Here would sit the Inquisitors
themselves, supreme arbiters of man's faith in God.

Now there was a new murmur of interest from the crowd, and a
sudden movement of heads flowed across the vast multitude like a wave
sweeping toward the shore. All eyes were drawn toward the royal
gallery and a whisper arose from every throat. "The king. The king."

Antonio leaned forward, the better to see the man who controlled the fates of so many people yet was so little known himself. Then he appeared, a single figure, in the center of the gallery. Antonio saw a slender man of medium height, somberly dressed, seeming not a monarch at all, but a simple man, saddened by the weight of his duties, his brow forever wrinkled by worry. In his two hands, as he stood looking over the crowd, he bore a sword, a great ornamental weapon from whose jeweled scabbard the sunlight was reflected in a hundred sparkling points. Turning slowly, he lay the sword on a small table before his own tall chair.

"The Holy Office has lately conceived the idea of having the sovereign swear publicly to support them," Vesalius said dryly. "It makes a good impression upon the people, and adds to the fear which the Inquisitors inspire in those they judge."

"I can understand that," Antonio agreed. The very preliminaries to the ceremony filled him with a dire sense of foreboding.

As the king took his seat, others began to file into the box. First was the queen. Behind her came a strange figure in brilliant gold-and-white costume, the body bloated, the legs so small as to seem hardly able to support the gross body, the head overly large, so that the total effect was that of a frog in man's clothing.

"Who is that?" Antonio asked.

"Don Carlos," Vesalius said. "The Principe, the son of the king."

At the sight of the next person to enter the royal gallery, Antonio gripped the window sill with his hands and let out an involuntary exclamation of surprise. For there was no question about the identity of the slender, proud girl with a crowning casque of golden hair. It was Lucia Bellarmi.

"Who is she?" Vesalius asked, noting what had drawn Antonio's attention.

"Madonna Lucia Bellarmi," Antonio told him. "The niece of my patron."

Vesalius stared at him quizzically. "You are interested in her yourself, I see."

"Only as a dear friend."

"If I had such a dear friend," Vesalius said dryly, "I would advise her not to stir the interest of the Principe."

Antonio remembered now some of the things he had heard about the heir to the Spanish throne. Son of Philip II by his first marriage, and now about eighteen years of age, the Principe Don Carlos had almost died from a fall several years before, to be saved only by the skill of Andreas Vesalius in trepanning the skull. His saving of the Principe was one of the reasons why Philip was so much attached to his physician. In spite of the mounting evidence that he had fathered a monster, the king was said to love his son dearly and to hope still that he might turn out to be a man in his own right. But all Madrid buzzed with the story of the Principe's profligacy, his strange habits of eating and drinking, of swallowing all kinds of strange objects and often forcing his attendants to do likewise, even when they choked to death before his eyes, and his rages when his desires could not be fulfilled. Worst of all were the tales of debauchery, perversion, and the string of women who had been forced to yield to him, only to be left diseased for life with the French pox, the *morbus Gallicus* with which his body was said to be eaten up.

Lucia's striking beauty could not but attract such a man, Antonio realized. He must warn her against Don Carlos when next he saw her.

The Soldiers of the Faith had now entered the Plaza Mayor, and behind them appeared the scarlet canopy shading the priest who was to celebrate the Mass. It was Don Diego Espinosa, the Bishop of Toledo, who wore the crimson chasuble prescribed by orthodox ritual, his mitered cap upon his head, the Host held high before him as he walked with measured tread. As he passed, the crowd dropped to their knees, beating their breasts and wailing to the rhythm of the clanging bell rung by a marching acolyte.

Immediately following the canopy was still another posse of the somber-clad familiars, and after them shambled the ragged band of prisoners, skeletons with distorted limbs, some twisted from their sockets by the tortures of the question. Many were unable to walk, and these were half carried by the Dominican brothers, in black robes and cassocks of purest white, who walked beside them. Even as they supported the victims in the march to their doom, the lips of the brothers moved in constant exhortations to confess, to acknowledge their sins and receive the pardon of the Church for their heinous sins. These poor scarecrows were the terrible criminals for the saving of whose souls this impressive spectacle was being held.

"Haven't they been punished enough already?" Antonio burst out indignantly. "Look. That man has a dislocation of both hips." Despite the support of a friar, one of the prisoners who was passing waddled like a featherless duck, a travesty of even so low a creature as a waterfowl, and the shreds only of what had been a man.

"Careful," Vesalius warned. "In Madrid one does not question the activities of the Holy Office. The very palace walls have ears."

Antonio tore his eyes away from the horrible spectacle. The hideous yellow of the tunics of the condemned, called the sanbenito, the conical cardboard caps upon shaven heads, splotched with crimson demons and distorted animals, the formless laughter of the already mad—all of it was like an unbelievable nightmare.

"Do you see Don Pedro Grijalva among the prisoners?" Antonio asked.

"Didn't you know?" Vesalius asked. "The king has ordered his release."

"I thought no one countermanded the orders of the Holy Office."

"His Majesty can and does, when he feels that they have erred," Vesalius said. "Don Pedro Grijalva comes of one of Spain's noblest families and he is a great military leader. The Crown has need of all of its revenues since the Flemish uprisings, as well as the services of one of its greatest soldiers."

"Then he will be safe?"

Vesalius shrugged. "There are more ways of executing a man than burning him at the stake."

Now the clank of armor was added to the noise of the procession winding through the plaza below. A group of men-at-arms of the regular police marched in precise rhythm, the sun glittering upon polished morions, tall halberds held stiffly vertical. Metal clinked upon metal as they swung in precise cadence and filed into a position flanking the royal gallery. Their flanking movement created a sudden vacuum in the open triangle of the plaza between the three elevated platforms, and into this danced the most horrible spectacle yet, a group of men who held high on swaying poles the caricatures of those who had been condemned in absence. Each of the swaying dummies was made of straw and dressed in rags, the features painted in a travesty of pain and insanity upon round faces of cloth. And each straw victim wore the correct sanbenito and mitered cap, the *coreza*.

A hush fell over the crowd and an aura of fear seemed to arise, so intense that it was like a pall thrown suddenly over the whole vast multitude. Antonio felt it sweep through him, as the chill breeze from the sea grips the bones in the dead of winter.

Borne by a massive man upon a towering black horse, both encased in armor as black as a moonless midnight, came the banner of the Holy Office, held high upon a shimmering lance. Emblazoned upon it was an oval medallion set against the sable background, displaying the green cross of the Inquisition. To one side of the cross itself was an olive branch, symbolizing the readiness of the Inquisitors to deal mercifully with those who confessed their sins and embraced the true faith once more—a mercy which consisted of the privilege of being garroted swiftly before the flames could sear living flesh. On the other side of the cross stood the sword, sweeping before it all those who dared to defy the will of the true Church.

Behind the banner, riding a lowly mule, was Frey Ignacio Molina, Inquisitor of Madrid, with the lesser judges of the Holy Tribunal riding behind him. Even from his lowly position the Inquisitor managed to look sinister and austerely forbidding, and from the second-floor window from which he watched, Antonio could see the deep-set, burning eyes sweeping the crowd, as if even in the act of punishing one group of heretics he was searching for evidence which would lead to the arrest of another. In such an impressive procession the group of mounted gentlemen riding behind the Inquisitors seemed only an afterthought.

"You will note many gentlemen of the court among the last group," Vesalius said. "It is considered an excellent precaution as a matter of self-protection."

"Do they possess absolute power?" Antonio asked.

"Almost. But the king is scrupulously insistent upon justice, even in the proceedings of the Inquisition. Where there is doubt of guilt, an accused person has the right of appeal to the throne."

The last of the procession had now entered the square, and the great banner with its shroud of black was placed before the altar under the bishop's canopy. Two candles burned upon the altar, and between them a thurible sent up a cloud of smoky incense into the cool afternoon air. The eyes of the crowd were fastened upon the altar as the bishop rose, tall in mitered cap and chasuble, and began the Mass. The condemned huddled on the benches of their scaffold as if they, to whose dishonor the whole proceeding was dedicated, were not important enough to have a part in it. Some slumped over asleep, some cackled insanely, but most sat immobile, paralyzed in mind and body by the realization of what awaited them.

The Mass finished, the bishop launched into a Sermon of the Faith, a scathing denunciation of the sins for which the accused had been condemned, and an exhortation to the poor wretches upon the scaffold to make their peace with Holy Mother Church before the same Church insured their physical destruction by abandoning them to the secular arm for punishment.

Notary after notary from the Holy Office followed the sermon, reciting the sins of each of the condemned. As each account was begun, the half-paralyzed victim was dragged from the scaffold and perched upon a stool, supported if necessary by a Dominican brother, to receive the mercy of the Church and the sentence which would insure his eternal salvation, even if his corporeal existence were to terminate within the hour. Some were sentenced to life imprisonment in the dungeons, a fate perhaps worse than the garrote. Most were for the ultimate punishment at the stake. These were hustled off their stools and summarily turned over to the secular authorities, whose justice was as merciless as it was swift. An alguazil held them up, while the *regidor,* standing by, muttered a formula of sentence. Then the poor wretch was hustled off to the waiting stakes.

Christi nomine invocato! Inhumanity in the name of God!

"Maria Sanctissima!" Vesalius said in profound disgust. "The burning is going to take place in the plaza."

"Isn't that the custom?" Antonio asked.

"They usually have the grace to take them to another place. The Holy Office must feel that the king has been too lenient with the Flemish heretics. This could be a warning."

"To the king?"

Vesalius shrugged. "To everybody."

Today none of the condemned had chosen the ultimate torture of the flame; all had confessed their sins and been given absolution by the Church. That, however, did not absolve them from paying for their heresy with their lives. Each was now bound to a stake, around the base of which was heaped a pile of fagots. But just before the wood was ignited, a burly executioner stepped close to each and deftly dropped a loop of the garroter's cord over the shaven poll. For one single instant the executioner's body hid the victim from the crowd, but all could see the muscles stand out in his massive arms as he twisted the cord, and the victim jerking and flapping against the stake, like a wrung-neck chicken. Then the torch was applied to the fagots and the flames leaped up at a body hardly yet rendered senseless by the garroter's art. As the first flames rose to lick at jerking limbs and sear already overtortured flesh, a deep-throated moan, compounded half of anguish and half of pleasure, rose from the crowd.

Antonio's gaze had been rooted upon the pitiful figures at the stakes, but now it was brought back to the royal gallery. Frey Ignacio Molina was standing before the gallery. The other occupants had filed out, leaving only the king in the center of the stage, his hands resting upon the jeweled sword.

The Inquisitor's voice rang out like the chimes of an organ as a hush settled over the crowd:

Since the apostolic decrees and the sacred canons have ordained that sovereigns must swear to favor the Holy Catholic Faith and the Christian religion, does Your Majesty swear by the Holy Cross to give all necessary support to the Holy Office of the Inquisition and its ministers, against heretics and apostates and against those who help and favor them, and against all who directly or indirectly shall hinder the activities of the Holy Office; and to force all Your Majesty's subjects and the inhabitants of Your Majesty's realms to give obedience to the constitutions and decrees which are published for the defense of the Holy Catholic Faith against heretics and against all who believe, receive, or support them?"

Without hesitation, Philip's voice rang out, a little high-pitched, but perfectly audible. "I swear it before God and upon my sword of office." Lifting high the jeweled sword, he touched it with his lips and placed it back upon the table.

"So be it," Frey Ignacio thundered over the heads of the multitude. The auto-da-fé was over, and soon only a few of the curious remained. But it would be days before the stench of burning flesh and bone was completely evaporated.

Vesalius turned to Antonio. *"Per Bacco!"* he said. "After that we must have some more wine."

A slender figure in black moved at the back of the room, and Vesalius exclaimed, "De Onis! I did not hear you come in."

The man who had been standing in the shadows came forward. He was small and slender, his skin dark and his face as devoid of expression as if it had been a mask, his eyes pale blue. "You were absorbed in the ceremony, sir," he said, bowing. "I did not wish to intrude."

"Come join us in a glass, then," Vesalius said and turned to Antonio. "This is Señor Benito de Onis, who studies medicine with me. Dr. Antonio Servetus, lately of the University of Padua."

De Onis bowed again. "I am honored," he said. "Someday I, too, hope to study at the distinguished University of Padua."

They drank the wine, and after a decent interval Antonio excused himself upon the plea that he must superintend Messer Bellarmi's diet for the evening meal. Lately the banker had been suffering a recurrence of discomfort in the chest and the left arm, the complaint which had led him to ask Antonio to journey to Madrid. But it was not worry for his patron that made Antonio shiver and draw his cloak about him more closely as he hurried toward Messer Bellarmi's house. It was the memory of the horrors he had witnessed that afternoon, grim warnings of the power of the Inquisition.

ii

Antonio and Andreas Vesalius were friends from the beginning. Vesalius obtained permission from the king for the two physicians to study the body of an executed criminal, and a new phase of Antonio's existence began. Their minds were very much alike, eager, searching for truth in what they saw and the implications which could be derived from their studies by careful thought. In a way their minds complemented each other, and Antonio was happier than he had been for a long time. De Onis, the apprentice of Vesalius, was an absorbed spectator in their dissections but he did not take part in the dissection. The repugnance of De Onis toward even touching a dead body was shared by most Spaniards, so deeply ingrained were the teachings of the Church against such profanation. Antonio could not overcome an instinctive dislike for the slender apprentice, although he had no actual cause for affront. When he voiced his feelings, Vesalius laughed.

"You are mistaking obtuseness for venom, my dear Antonio," the anatomist said. "De Onis is none too well endowed with intelligence. In fact, I doubt if he will ever make a very good physician."

"Why do you keep him, then?"

Vesalius shrugged. "His father is a confidant of the king, and His

Majesty himself asked me to train him as a physician. Naturally I can do no less than try."

The morning's dissection finished, Vesalius washed his hands and rolled down his sleeves. "I must visit Doña Catherine Sagredo this morning," he said. "Would you like to accompany me?" It was the first time Vesalius had asked him to see one of his private cases.

"I would be happy to do so," Antonio told him eagerly.

"It is a case of paralysis, in a young woman," Vesalius explained as they were leaving the house.

Antonio's interest was caught at once. Paralysis in the young was unusual, except from wounds involving the vertebral column. "What is the cause?" he asked.

"That's why I need you," Vesalius told him. "I have discovered no cause."

As they were riding to the patient's home in Vesalius's carriage, he gave Antonio the story of the patient they were visiting. Doña Catherine Sagredo, the very beautiful daughter of a lesser noble of Spain, had suffered the ill fortune of attracting the attention of Don Carlos, the Principe. The courtship had been violent, and, according to Vesalius, Doña Catherine had apparently yielded to the impetuous advances of her royal suitor. Rumor varied, but it was generally believed that she had been, at least for a while, the mistress of the Principe; but, as with many previous recipients of his favor, her charms for him had waned with time and he had cast her off.

The paralysis in question had developed immediately after Doña Catherine lost favor with the royal heir. Vesalius had treated her for this condition, now present for about a year, but confessed himself still unable to diagnose its cause.

They were ushered into a room where a strikingly beautiful young woman lay passively in bed, her eyes fixed on the ceiling in a faraway stare. A candle burned before a small statue of the Virgin beside the bed, and a small crucifix hung from a slender gold chain about her neck. Further evidence of her preoccupation with spiritual affairs lay in the beads of the rosary which clicked steadily between her fingers while her lips moved in soundless prayer. Her hands were pale, the veins showing blue through the white skin.

"I have brought another physician to examine you, Doña Catherine," Vesalius said.

The girl gave no sign of having heard. Doña Maria, the mother, wrung her hands nervously. "She is much worse today, Doctor," she moaned. "At times, she does not know me, her own dear mother." The words trailed off in a sob, and her immense bosom rose and fell convulsively.

Vesalius and Antonio made an examination. The condition was as the anatomist had described it: a strange paralysis involving all movement below a line drawn just beneath the navel, with loss of all sensation over the same area. Even when the skin in this region was touched with a needle there was no response, no sign of any perception of pain. The loss was as complete as had been that which Lodovici Agnolo had caused in the girl Anya through magnetism, Antonio thought. Suddenly an idea struck him.

"This is strange," he said to Vesalius. "It is almost as if she had been magnetized."

"Why do you say that?"

Antonio explained how Lodovici Agnolo—although he did not refer to him by name—had been able to remove sensation by magnetism and had said that oriental physicians sometimes performed operations under the strange spell.

"But how could she have been magnetized?" Vesalius asked.

"Perhaps it is possible to induce such a state in oneself," Antonio suggested.

The anatomist's eyes glowed. "Then, since you can remove the magnetism that you transmit yourself, you might be able to remove this also."

"Exactly what I was thinking," Antonio agreed.

"*Santa Maria!* It would be a miracle."

"Are you willing for me to try?"

"Try anything," Vesalius urged. "Anything to relieve such a paralysis."

"We had better warn the mother, then," Antonio said. "I don't want her to think I'm practicing witchcraft."

They returned to the room where the girl lay, and Vesalius talked for a few minutes to Doña Maria. She was so distraught that she made no objection to anything which promised to help her daughter.

Antonio went over to the bed then and stood looking down at the girl. Her eyes flicked from the beads up to him and then quickly back to the rosary. "Do you want me to help you, Doña Catherine?" he asked.

She did not answer, and he repeated the question. This time her eyes were raised momentarily, and he was shocked to see a look of fear in them, as if she were actually afraid that he might be able to do something about the strange paralysis.

"If you will trust me, I think I can help you," he told her. "There is nothing you should fear."

A sound came from her lips, and he bent closer to hear. The words were barely a whisper. "I have sinned. Nothing can help me."

"I think I can, if you will allow me," he insisted.

"You can try," she whispered, "but it is no use."

Antonio turned to Vesalius. "I will need a source of light; perhaps a candle will do." He went about the room blowing out the candles until only one was burning in a small candleholder. This he held in his hand slightly above the girl's head, so that she could see it merely by raising her eyes.

"You must watch the candle closely, Doña Catherine," he told her, "and do exactly as I tell you. Nothing will hurt or disturb you."

She nodded faintly to show that she understood. "I will try," she whispered.

"Look!" he commanded. "Look steadily at the candle."

The girl's glance wavered at first, then, as he encouraged her in low tones, became fixed upon the candle flame. If there were any truth to his belief that the source of light somehow mobilized the magnetic forces, Antonio thought, he should be able to control them now. "Now try to move your feet," he instructed her.

Nothing happened; there was no movement of the covers.

"Try," he urged. "Try once more."

Again there was no response, and he urged her again, but with the same result.

"*Ay Maria!*" Vesalius muttered. "It does not work."

Suddenly Antonio realized what was wrong. If, as he suspected, Doña Catherine's condition was of magnetic origin, it must be that the magnetism was fixed somehow in her body, held there for the time being. But if he were to add to it by magnetizing her again, he might be able to control the entire state.

"Wait," he said to Vesalius. "I think I know what is wrong." He bent closer to the recumbent girl. "Keep looking at the candle, Doña Catherine," he instructed her. Her glance had been wavering, but now it fastened on the candle flame once more. "Don't take your eyes from it."

He moved now so that he could look into her eyes. "You must listen to me," he said quietly. "You have been very sick, but I am going to make you well. An evil force has gripped your spirit. I am providing a path by which it can leave you."

To his surprise, her lips moved and he heard her whisper, "I know. I know."

"You are feeling sleepy," he continued in the same insistent tone. "Your mind is being freed from your body and the evil influences are being driven away."

Even Doña Maria had stopped her asthmatic wheezing, raptly following the drama being played out in the room with the beautiful girl on the bed, the tiny point of light, and the monotonous tones of Antonio's voice urging her to relax.

"Do you feel your mind releasing your body?" he asked.

The girl's head moved slowly in an affirmative nod and her eyelids drooped as if she were falling asleep. Her breathing grew regular and even. "Do you hear me, Doña Catherine?" Antonio asked.

"Yes, I hear you." She spoke in a normal voice, instead of the whispers she had used before. The change was so marked that Antonio saw Vesalius jump. *"Madre de Dios!"* her mother gasped.

Antonio felt a surge of excitement. He had released her voice. Would the rest of the treatment be equally successful? He controlled his own voice carefully when he spoke. "You can feel the life returning to your limbs, Doña Catherine," he said. "You need only to let it do so and you will be well."

A strange thing was happening to the girl. Her eyes remained closed but now her lips were smiling as she whispered in a voice heavy with passion, "My darling. My own dearest Carlos." She held out her arms, as if to embrace a shadowy lover, and in vivid pantomime seemed to draw him to her breast. There was no mistaking the significance of the scene she was acting out with herself and the memory of the Principe on the stage.

Whatever he had loosed here, Antonio realized suddenly, it was not for the mother's eyes and ears. He must somehow contrive to send her from the room. "She may go into a decline," he said, turning to Doña Maria. "Please get some wine at once."

Doña Maria gasped, and for a moment Antonio thought she would faint.

"Quickly!" Antonio said. As she scuttled from the room he signaled to Vesalius to come closer to the girl, for now she was beginning to move not only her arms but her whole body, even the part which had been paralyzed. She writhed in an abandonment of motion which could have only one significance: the reliving of a seduction in which she had played an active and, from all appearances, a willing part. Cries of animal passion came from her lips, and the voluptuous movements of her limbs grew so wild that she thrashed about in the bed in an ecstasy of remembered passion, panting with the effort, her mouth slack. It was startling to see all this take place while her eyes remained closed, apparently in sleep.

Antonio watched with amazement the cataclysm of emotion which he had released. What was this power he had unwittingly acquired? Where lay the strange alchemy by which he could lead a presumably innocent and religious girl to relive so dramatically, in open confession, the pattern of her seduction? The implications of it frightened him.

But there was no more paralysis, he saw, at least not during the spasm. Whether it would return when the scene was over, he could not yet know. In a way it seemed indecent to watch such a display of animal emotion, but he was afraid to move away from the bed lest the girl throw herself from it and be injured. Vesalius seemed to suffer no such prohibition. He was staring at the girl in openmouthed amazement.

Neither of them heard the mother return, bearing a bottle of wine. At the sight of her daughter's body, arched and contorted by the final convulsive effort, she screamed. Then suddenly Doña Catherine was quiet. She lay panting, mouth slack, a look of deep and utter contentment on her face.

Antonio bent over the girl. He must not let this strange state subside, he realized, without making her show beyond question that the paralysis had been relieved. "You can walk now, Doña Catherine," he said. "You have been cured."

"I am sleepy," the girl murmured. "Please let me sleep."

"You must walk," Antonio urged. "Then you can sleep." He took one of the pale hands and pulled the girl gently. Obediently she sat up in bed. "I . . . I can walk," she repeated mechanically and, under his urging, swung her legs slowly off the bed. When her feet touched the floor she raised herself slowly with his help until she was standing with only his hand supporting her.

"Try to walk," he urged her gently. She took a hesitant step and then another. Antonio removed his hand, and she swayed in the center of the room but did not fall.

Now, he thought, was the time to terminate the magnetic state, while the girl was upon her feet and the evidence of her cure was incontrovertible. "You will awaken when I call your name, Doña Catherine," he told her. "And you will walk across the room. Do you understand?"

"Yes," she said slowly. "I understand."

He stepped back. "Doña Catherine. Awaken!" he cried sharply.

The girl's eyes flew open. She stared at them, at Vesalius, at Antonio, and at her mother, standing with the bottle of wine still in her hand. Then she took a faltering step, another, and with a glad cry ran to her mother. The wine bottle dropped from Doña Maria's grasp, shattered and spilled the red liquid over the floor, but neither woman paid any attention. Both were sobbing convulsively in each other's arms.

"Come," Antonio said to Vesalius. He felt suddenly completely spent, as if every vestige of power within him had been completely drained away. "We will leave them together."

But as they were leaving the house, Doña Maria came running after them, tears streaming down her face. She clutched Antonio's robe and fell to her knees. "The Blessed Virgin has performed a miracle in your hands, Doctor," she sobbed. "My daughter is well because you interceded for her."

"It is no miracle, señora," Antonio said gently. "I merely gave your daughter a new form of treatment."

"Before God, I swear I saw the Virgin beside her bed smile and nod," Doña Maria cried. "You are a saint, Doctor. The power of healing is in your hands."

Antonio managed to extricate himself from the grasp of the babbling woman. It would do no good to argue with her now; she was too distraught to be convinced of anything save that her daughter had been chosen by the Virgin for a true miracle.

In Vesalius's carriage Antonio lay back against the cushions and wiped his forehead. He was genuinely disturbed about his success, not so much by the relief of the paralysis as by the emotional storm he had released in the young girl in the course of it.

"What is this strange power I seem to have acquired?" he asked Vesalius. "Was this really a miracle?"

Vesalius combed his dark beard with his fingers. "I hardly think so," he said. "Did you note the extent of the paralysis and loss of sensation before your treatment began?"

"Why, yes. The lower half of the body."

"It was more than that," the anatomist said. "I tested her carefully once, and there was a line of demarcation just above the *symphysis pubis*."

"Just above the——" Antonio stopped. "Do you realize what you are saying?"

Vesalius shrugged. "You also recognized the significance of the convulsion, did you not?"

"It was obviously a simulation of the sexual embrace."

"Exactly. And one which the lovely Doña Catherine had evidently experienced with the Principe."

"Then the paralysis——" Antonio stopped. "But that is impossible."

"It is impossible anatomically," Vesalius agreed. "I will grant you that no set of nerves which either you or I have dissected exactly fits such a paralysis and loss of sensation."

"How could it be, then?"

"What did Doña Catherine whisper to you before you started? When you told her you could help her."

"She said, 'I have sinned. Nothing can help me.'"

"I thought those were the words," Vesalius continued. "And with what part of her body had she sinned, according to the evidence of her own actions?"

Antonio remembered the picture presented by both the paralysis and the loss of sensation in Doña Catherine's body. Vesalius's idea seemed logical, it was true, but there was one part of it that his scientific mind could not accept. "But the nerve pattern does not fit the area of paralysis," he objected.

Vesalius shrugged. "There are things we do not understand about the human body, Antonio. And you learn them only when you treat many people. My guess is that in some way her mind decided that the lower half of her body must not be free to sin again."

Antonio sat up straight. "But this is important," he cried. "It might be more important than discovering the pulmonary circulation."

"It could," Vesalius agreed.

"With this knowledge, I may be able to explore many other of the troubles of mankind."

"But should you do it?" Vesalius asked.

Antonio stared at him in surprise. "Why not, pray?"

"People may not want to have their innermost secrets revealed," the anatomist said thoughtfully. "Think about this case for a minute. If you had not thought to send Doña Maria away, she would have realized the significance of what we saw and the cause of her daughter's illness."

For a moment Antonio did not speak, then he said slowly, "You are right. The dangers of such treatment may be greater than the benefits."

Vesalius smiled. "You may have hit upon a great truth there, my boy. As for me, I shall stick to dissection. You have gone too far for me already."

"I think I shall not be using magnetism very much in the future," Antonio agreed. "As you say, it is too powerful."

iii

If Antonio was convinced of the power of the strange magnetism, he was even more convinced the following day of the power of the spoken word. He was superintending the cooking of Messer Girolamo's morning meal when he heard a pounding at the door. A servant went to answer it, but he came rushing back. "Doctor!" he cried. "A great crowd is outside."

"A crowd?" Antonio frowned. "What do they want?"

"They are shouting for you."

Antonio went to the door. He could not imagine why a crowd would want him at this time of the morning, or any time for that matter. But there was no doubting that they were there. The babble of voices was incessant.

A hunchback, dressed in tattered rags, almost fell through into the hallway when he opened the door. Behind him, on the steps and out in the street, a crowd of people pushed and shoved to get closer to the house. Some were shouting, some weeping, some cursing. Antonio had to push the foremost back in order to get out on the lower balcony of the house. He could see the crowd better now as it milled about in front of the house. There were at least a hundred of them, mostly cripples or obviously ill, and, from their clothing, largely beggars. Some were hopping about on crutches; some, obviously blind, were led by others. A few lay on the grass, obviously unable to walk, striking out with sticks at those crowding around, lest they be trampled underfoot.

At the sight of Antonio a babble of voices broke out. He could make nothing out of it all, and in fact could barely stand, for the hunchback was pulling at his legs. Gently he lifted the man to his feet. "What is it you want?" he asked. "What do all these people want?"

"Heal me," the man implored with outstretched hands, falling again to his knees as soon as Antonio released him. "Heal me, Your Holiness. Remove this hump from my back and make me whole."

"I cannot heal you," Antonio protested. "Who told you to come here?"

"Are you not the doctor they call Servetus?"

"Yes. My name is Servetus."

"You are the one who heals all sickness, then."

"I am a doctor," Antonio said a little brusquely. "But I cannot heal all sickness."

From a crowd a voice cried belligerently, "Did you not heal Doña Catherine Sagredo, she who had not walked for more than a year?"

"Yes, I did," Antonio admitted. Suddenly he realized what must have happened. When he and Vesalius had left the Sagredo home yesterday Doña Maria had been babbling of a miracle. But it was almost incredible that the news had spread so rapidly.

"Who says I heal the sick through miracles?" he asked the hunchback.

"The good Doña Maria Sagredo," the man told him. "I had it from her coachman that you interceded with the Blessed Virgin and healed her daughter." An excited babble arose from the crowd again.

Antonio was nonplused. Under the circumstances, it was a perfectly logical mistake for a hysterical woman to have made. And, too, if Doña Catherine had any inkling of the real cause of her paralysis—as he was sure that she did—it was certainly more convenient to credit the cure to a miracle. But what was he to do about this crowd of beggars and cripples who had come to him for help?

"Heal me, Holy One." A pitiful wretch lying on a sack at the foot of the steps held up pipestem arms to him. The man's frame was literally a bag of bones encased in pallid, scabrous hide, an advanced case of phthisis, Antonio diagnosed merely by looking at him, and quite hopeless as far as any treatment was concerned.

"Listen to me, all of you," Antonio said gently. "I am no miracle worker and I possess no influence to intercede with the Blessed Virgin——"

"But you did heal Doña Catherine Sagredo," the same man called belligerently from the crowd. "Don't deny it."

"I do not deny it," Antonio said. "But I used medical treatment. I will be glad to examine each of you, and if I find that I can help you, the medicines will be free."

"Yahhhhh!" the consumptive shouted. "We want no medicine. Ask the Blessed Virgin to make us well." Yells of frustration and shouts of profanity came from the crowd. Those in front began to push forward, some brandishing sticks and crutches menacingly.

"Listen to me, please," Antonio begged. "I am a physician, not a priest. I will treat your sickness, but if you wish someone to intercede with the Blessed Virgin, you must go to your priest."

"Yahhhh!" the consumptive screamed again. "He will heal the rich who pay him. He is like all physicians, he works only for the rich."

Antonio was becoming angry. "I have offered to treat you," he shouted. "What else would you have me do?"

"A miracle! A miracle!" the consumptive screamed, and the crowd took up the cry until it was a rhythmic and somehow barbaric chant.

"A miracle! A miracle!" Howling, those at the back pushed forward, pressing the ones in front against the house. Fights broke out here and there, and a stone, hurled from the back, thudded upon the floor of the balcony. Another crashed through a window. "There is your pay, physician," someone howled.

Antonio held up his hand for silence. "I tell you for the last time, I know nothing of miracles," he pleaded. "Why can you not believe me?"

A bull-like roar of anger came from the crowd, now working themselves up into an insane fury of disappointment. They plucked small stones from the street and showered them against the porch and the windows. The hunchback and those who had climbed the steps stumbled down them again, leaving Antonio alone. One of them stepped upon the consumptive, and his screams of pain and cursings rent the air. Pandemonium gripped the crowd now, and seeking a target for their frustration, they selected Antonio, standing alone on the balcony. Pebbles and small stones rained upon him as the crowd milled around in front of the house, cursing and screaming at him.

A stone, larger than the rest, struck Antonio on the forehead, driving him to his knees and causing blood to run down his face. Some of those at the foot of the steps ran up again to belabor him with sticks as, half stunned by the stone, he knelt with his arms over his head, trying to protect himself against their attack. A new burst of stones splattered against the house, breaking windows and denting the planking.

Suddenly the wooden railing of the front steps crashed down under the weight of the crowd. The hunchback selected a heavy oak post from the wreckage and began to creep up the stairs toward the kneeling figure on the balcony. His murderous intention was written plainly in his distorted face and catlike movements. Dazed and half unconscious from the beating, Antonio was unprotected.

The hunchback was almost upon Antonio when a tall man, sword in hand and followed by half a dozen stout lackeys bearing clubs, charged around the side of the house. "Stop it, you rabble!" he shouted, plunging into the midst of the crowd and beating about him with the flattened blade of his sword. As the lackeys followed his example, howls of rage gave way to screams of pain and the crowd melted away. In a matter of seconds none was left except the consumptive on the pallet. He crouched with his knees drawn up and his hands protecting his head, evidently waiting for the cudgels to rain down upon him.

"Take this vermin to his hole," the leader directed his servants. He bounded up the steps as Antonio raised his head, still dazed and unable to believe that he had been saved from a horrible beating and probably from death at the hands of the crowd.

"Are you hurt, Doctor?" he asked. Antonio saw that it was Armand de Quadra.

Antonio staggered to his feet. Blood was trickling from a cut over his eyes and his clothing was torn. "Señor de Quadra," he gasped, leaning against the railing for support. "You arrived just in time."

"Those dogs would have killed you," De Quadra said. "Fortunately I live quite close and heard the commotion."

"No doubt your prompt arrival saved my life," Antonio agreed.

"*Cáspita!* The crowd was in a bad mood," De Quadra said. "What set the beggars off like that?"

"They came for a miracle," Antonio admitted wryly. "When I couldn't provide it, they became angry."

"A miracle?" De Quadra looked at him sharply. "Are you sure you are not badly hurt, Doctor?"

Antonio's head felt much clearer now. "Yesterday I went with Dr. Vesalius to see Doña Catherine Sagredo," he explained. "I was fortunate enough to cure her."

"Of her paralysis?" De Quadra asked in surprise.

"Yes."

"*Caramba! Es increible!* The girl had not walked for a year."

"She walked yesterday, after my treatment," Antonio said. "Under the circumstances, it is not surprising, I suppose, that the mother believed it was due to a miracle. She told her servants that I had influenced the Blessed Virgin to heal her daughter. They told the beggars and——" He shrugged. "You saw them."

"You do not think that the cure of Doña Catherine was due to the intervention of the Holy Mother, then?" De Quadra asked with an odd sort of intentness in his voice.

Antonio shook his head. "She was suffering from some sort of a mental affliction which caused her to be paralyzed. I merely corrected it."

"By what means?"

"By magnetism," Antonio explained. "But I don't know exactly how it works."

"Magnetism? I do not understand."

"Few do," Antonio said. "It is a new treatment I learned in . . . in Italy." He was getting a little tired of this questioning and his head was beginning to ache.

"Then it was actually you and not the Blessed Virgin who healed Doña Catherine?" De Quadra asked again.

"How do we know who cures and who does not?" Antonio asked wearily. "I used a new treatment and she was cured. Before that she was not cured. Doesn't it seem logical that my treatment cured her?"

There was a sudden outburst of sound within the house, as if people were rushing about. "If you will excuse me, Señor de Quadra," Antonio said. "Perhaps Messer Bellarmi needs me."

"But of course." De Quadra bowed low. "I am happy to have been of service, Doctor."

"And I owe you my life," Antonio said sincerely. "Perhaps someday I can repay the debt."

De Quadra's brows rose. "Perhaps. Who knows?"

The door opened and a servant thrust out his head. "Doctor!" he cried. "The master has fainted."

Girolamo Bellarmi was lying on the floor in the entrance hall, his eyes closed, breathing stertorously. Quickly Antonio felt for his pulse and found it full and bounding, as if by its very force it would burst the vessels in which the blood circulated.

"What happened?" Antonio asked the servant while he loosened the banker's clothing to make breathing easier.

"It was when they started stoning you," the servant said. "He tried to come to your aid." That explained the whole thing, Antonio realized. Girolamo Bellarmi, none too well, with a tendency toward plethora similar to that which had killed his brother, had become excited by the disturbance outside. In trying to get downstairs to help, he had overtaxed his strength and collapsed. Whether or not he had actually suffered a stroke Antonio could not yet tell, but such an accident was not unlikely.

Moving the banker to a couch, Antonio sent a servant to the palace with a message for Lucia. Then he went for his instruments. Bleeding was indicated in this condition, and the quicker the blood was drawn, the better.

He had nicked the vein with a lancet and blood was flowing into the bowl in a steady stream when Lucia came rushing into the house. She wore a long cloak over her nightdress, for the messenger had gotten her out of bed and she had not stopped to dress.

"What is it?" she whispered, dropping to her knees beside the couch.

"He collapsed in the hall," Antonio explained.

"Is he——" She stopped, but he understood the question. Her uncle

Mario had died from a similar condition. Messer Girolamo had feared
for some time that he might be slated for a similar fate.

"We will have to wait and see," Antonio said gently. He finished the
bleeding and put the bowl of blood aside. "It is too early to tell yet just
how sick he is."

Lucia stood up. She swayed a little and put her hand to her forehead. Antonio saw that she was chalky white, and caught her when
she would have fallen and led her to a chair. "I will get you a glass of
wine," he said.

When he returned she had regained control of herself, but she drank
the wine gratefully. "If I had stayed here with him instead of at the
palace," she said contritely, "this might not have happened."

"It could happen any time," Antonio assured her. "Any time that he
becomes excited or disturbed."

"But what disturbed him this morning?"

Antonio explained about the attack of the beggars. "Then he was
coming to help you," she said accusingly.

"Yes," he admitted. "He was."

"It was all your fault," she accused. Distraught as she was by fear
for her uncle, he could understand her putting this distorted interpretation upon what had happened, but it was close enough to the truth to
increase his own feeling of guilt.

"If you want to put it that way," he said, thinking that it was best
to humor her rather than argue with her.

The choice of tone was unfortunate, he realized when her cheeks
flamed. "Is there any other way to put it?" she demanded hotly.

Their attention was distracted from themselves and the impending
quarrel by a moan from her uncle. Slowly the banker's eyes opened and
he even managed to smile weakly. "I'm sorry, Antonio," he whispered.
"I tried to help."

"It is all right, sir," Antonio assured him. "You had best not talk."

A spasm of pain contorted Bellarmi's face and he put his hand to
his chest, as if to press the pain away. "You must be quiet, sir," Antonio
warned. "You have had a severe attack."

"The pain," he gasped. "Is there anything you can do?"

"I will prepare a draught to relieve it." Antonio went to the sideboard where he kept his medical supplies. Selecting a bottle of wine of
opium, he measured out a generous dose, diluting it with a little red

wine. He supported the banker while he drank. "That will help you get to sleep," he promised.

Again the sick man was racked by a spasm of pain which left him sweating and ashen.

"Please try to lie quietly now," Antonio urged. "It will be better for you."

But Messer Girolamo seemed to have something he wished to get off his mind, for he motioned them both to come close to the couch. "If anything happens to me, Antonio," he gasped, "promise that you will take care of Lucia until she gets safely to Florence."

"But, Uncle—— Lucia started to protest.

He held up his hand. "Do you promise, Doctor?"

"I promise," Antonio said.

"And you, Lucia. You will do as he says."

She hesitated, then in a low voice said, "I will do what he says, Uncle, until I get to Florence." And then, with her voice breaking in a sob, she threw herself upon her knees beside the couch. "But nothing is going to happen to you, darling. I shall pray constantly for that."

The banker lay back and closed his eyes. Soon his regular breathing told them that the pain-killing draught was doing its work.

"Have you had your breakfast?" Antonio asked Lucia.

She shook her head. "There was a reception last night and I was up very late."

"Come along, then. He will probably sleep for several hours from the opium."

They were served breakfast by the servants. Lucia ate heartily, but Antonio hardly touched his food. Looking up from her empty plate and noticing his full one, she asked, "What is wrong? Are you sick?"

Antonio smiled. "At heart. Nowhere else."

"What about, pray?"

"I suppose about my fellow men." He rubbed his scalp. There were many swollen places where the stones had struck, and his forehead felt stiff where the small cut over his eye was sealed with clotted blood.

"You have been hurt!" Lucia cried in sudden concern. "Was there a fight with the beggars?"

"Only half a one," Antonio admitted ruefully. "The first stone felled me."

"But you could have been killed."

"I very nearly was," he admitted, "but for the help of Señor de Quadra." He told her about the intervention of de Quadra and his lackeys.

"We heard about the cure of Doña Catherine last night at the palace," Lucia said. "Tell me about it."

"A physician should not tell the secrets of his patients," he reminded her.

"Everyone knows that she was the mistress of the Principe and that he cast her off. She became paralyzed after that, if she was paralyzed at all. At the court some think it was a trick to keep from having to face people and admit her shame."

Antonio was startled by this analysis, it so nearly resembled the one which Vesalius had made yesterday. "They are wrong, though," he told Lucia. "She was really paralyzed and all sensation was gone below her waist."

"Then how do you explain curing her?"

"I can't," he admitted. "But I am sure that magnetism is no miracle. It is just that we do not understand what causes such conditions."

Lucia put down her napkin. "Where did you learn this magnetism?"

"From a magician in Venice." There was no point in giving her any more of the details about his experience with Lodovici Agnolo.

"Can anyone be magnetized?" she asked.

"I don't know that," he admitted. "But I have never failed."

She tossed her head. "I would not let you do it."

"Is that a dare?" he teased.

"Yes," she said firmly. "I dare you."

"I will take you up on that, madonna," he promised. "When the time is right. What shall be the forfeit?"

"Is one necessary?" she asked warily.

"Isn't it customary for young ladies to forfeit at least a kiss if they lose a wager?"

She smiled then. "I'll not lose this one, sir. So it is safe to wager."

iv

Messer Bellarmi improved steadily following his attack and Antonio's prompt treatment by bleeding. The evening after the attack

Antonio asked Vesalius to examine him in consultation. When they came out of the room Antonio introduced the Flemish physician to Lucia.

"What do you think of my uncle, Doctor?" she asked.

"He is much improved, madonna," Vesalius said. "Thanks to the prompt treatment by Dr. Servetus."

"Then you think he will live?"

"Undoubtedly, as far as this attack is concerned. Of course you realize that there may be others."

"I understand that we will have to be very careful," she agreed.

"Fortunately Dr. Servetus will be here most of the time. I would not want your uncle to be alone very much."

"Do you think I should stay here, rather than at the palace?" she asked.

"It might be best," Vesalius agreed. "You could take some of the load of work off your uncle's shoulders. Dr. Servetus tells me that you know a great deal about his business."

Lucia looked at Antonio. "Did you suggest that, Tonio?"

"You yourself suggested that you should stay, Lucia," he reminded her.

"I suppose he has been needing me," she said slowly. "But he wanted me to see something of court life. I will have my things moved here at once," she continued. "Her Majesty will understand."

"I will mention something of your uncle's condition to her," Vesalius promised. To Antonio he said, "Your cure of Doña Catherine has created quite a stir in Madrid."

"I have evidence of it still," Antonio admitted and went on to describe his experience with the beggars. When he had finished, Vesalius's face was grave.

"That explains something else," he said. "I thought I wouldn't speak to you about it, but perhaps I should, in view of all this."

"Have you heard something else about Doña Catherine?" Antonio asked.

"No. But I had a visitor this morning, one of the familiars of Frey Ignacio Molina."

"What did he want?" Antonio felt suddenly as if the cold and clammy hand of death had been laid upon his forehead.

"He asked in detail about your treatment of Doña Catherine Sagredo. And he seemed particularly interested in whether or not you invoked the aid of the Blessed Virgin."

"But it was a medical treatment," Antonio protested. "There was no miracle."

"So I told him," Vesalius said. "But he was particularly insistent about two things. One was that you did not invoke the Holy Mother. The other, curiously enough, concerned the smell of brimstone."

"Brimstone!" Lucia cried. "Why would he want to know that?"

Antonio said slowly, "The odor of brimstone is said to be apparent in the presence of demons, Lucia."

"Demons!" Her eyes widened. "But they couldn't believe that you invoke the powers of Satan, Tonio."

Vesalius said soberly, "The Inquisition can and does believe anything that it wishes, madonna."

"But Antonio does not use magic," she protested. "It is a medical treatment. He told me so."

"You and I and Dr. Vesalius know that, Lucia," Antonio said. "But Frey Ignacio would like to drive me from Madrid. Remember, I went ahead and operated upon Don Pedro after he had warned me against it."

Lucia shivered. "I wish we had never come to Spain."

"Do you think they will arrest me?" Antonio asked Vesalius.

"They may not, or it may come tomorrow. It all depends upon how much of a case Frey Ignacio feels he has against you, and how soon."

"But what can Antonio do?" Lucia asked.

Vesalius shrugged. "There is no way of fighting the Inquisition . . . save through the king." His face brightened. "But why not?"

"What do you mean?" Antonio asked.

"You could appeal to the king, in case you are arrested. The queen is on your side and you have many influential patients. Besides, you are not a Spaniard and therefore have every right to appeal to His Majesty."

"But would I be any better off than before the Tribunal of the Inquisition?"

"You might be considerably better off. He is called 'Philip the Cautious,' but he is also called 'Philip the Just.' And he has never refused to hear an appeal if there was any justice in it."

"Would he go against the Inquisition?" Lucia asked. "After all, at the auto-da-fé"—she could not repress a shudder even now at the memory—"he swore to support the Holy Office in all of its acts."

"He might not go against the Inquisition," Vesalius explained, "but at least the questioning would be different. In the regular trials of the Inquisition, the accused is not allowed to face the accusers, or to know the exact nature of the evidence against him. Before the king, I am sure that Antonio could insist upon his rights and be granted them."

"Given a fair hearing," Antonio maintained stoutly, "I can prove my innocence."

"God grant that you can, my boy," Vesalius said as he was leaving. "Of course you may not even be arrested if Frey Ignacio cannot make out a good enough case against you. And you may rest assured that I will do everything I can to help you. I have no love for him myself, and I know that he is only waiting for an opportunity to manufacture evidence against me."

When Vesalius had gone, Lucia said gently, "Poor Tonio. I have caused you a lot of trouble, haven't I?"

"You are not to blame for this," he protested.

"But if I had never come to Venice, you could have gone on as you were, happy and contented at the priory."

He smiled. "I'm not sure I was happy. Looking back on it, I think I might not have gone through with it."

"But I thought you had definitely planned to take the Holy Orders."

"I did, once. But even then I was beginning to think for myself, in my work as well as in other things. I can see now that such thinking would inevitably have involved me in conflict with people like Fra Felipe Santos and Frey Ignacio." Then he added, "And of course I would never have known you or the companionship I have enjoyed with you and Gian."

She flushed and looked away. "Does knowing me mean so much, Tonio?"

"Of course it does. We are close friends, aren't we?"

She changed the subject then. "But if you had stayed in Padua you would still have had the painting and your divine mistress."

"The divine mistress quoted by Paracelsus was wisdom," he reminded her.

"But you think of the Venus as belonging to you."

"Yes," he admitted. "I did. But somehow she seems far away now."

With a sharp pang of guilt, he realized that he had not thought of the painting for weeks, even months.

As the days passed, Messer Girolamo improved rapidly. Lucia remained in the house to help him with his business, for she had natural talents in the field. Antonio was busy, for his fame in Madrid was now so great that many persons of consequence consulted him, and his wealth increased steadily. When weeks passed and there was no sign of trouble from the Inquisition, he began to wonder if they had not been unduly alarmed about the activities of Frey Ignacio.

Gian, too, was busy, partly with his father's affairs but mostly with his painting. He had taken a small apartment in a house in another part of the city and had fitted out one room as a studio. Here he was besieged by ladies who wished their portraits painted by so handsome an artist. And if the activities in the studio were not limited entirely to painting, no one seemed to care, least of all the young ladies who served as subjects.

Gian came to Antonio one winter evening, his normally smiling face creased by a worried frown. "I have bad news for you, Tonio," he announced.

Antonio had become very fatalistic in the past weeks, with the threat of the Inquisition hanging over him all the time. But he could not help feeling apprehensive in the face of Gian's obvious concern. "What is it?" he asked.

"My father has written from Venice," Gian said. "Among other things, he mentions that the prior of the Dominicans at Padua has now fully recovered from wounds suffered when he was attacked some months ago in the priory."

Antonio felt the muscles of his throat tighten with the familiar sensation of impending evil. Fra Felipe Santos alive! Then Battista Porzia must have told him of Antonio's departure from Pisa for Spain. "Did your father mention whether the prior's assailant was known?" he asked.

"No." Gian eyed him shrewdly. "Knowing Fra Felipe, would you say that he would publish it abroad?"

"You are right," Antonio agreed. "He would want a personal revenge, if at all possible."

"Exactly what I had decided." Gian hesitated, as if reluctant to mention something else that was on his mind, then continued. "I have been painting a portrait for Doña Elena Mendoza."

The name meant nothing to Antonio.

"She is a close friend of Doña Catherine Sagredo, your former patient," Gian explained.

"What are you getting at?"

"Frey Ignacio Molina has visited Doña Catherine several times. She told Doña Elena that the Inquisitor is very much interested in your cure of her."

Antonio was suddenly tense with dread. If the Inquisitor himself was conducting an investigation of his acts, it must mean that the danger of arrest was grave. "What did she tell him?" he asked. "Did your model know?"

"Doña Catherine described your treatment very closely," Gian said. "She even stated that she felt as if some evil thing had been removed from her. Frey Ignacio suggested that you may have induced an evil spirit to leave her."

Antonio frowned. "But I exorcised no evil spirits. Why didn't she tell him that?"

Gian smiled. "It is rumored that Doña Catherine had been—indiscreet, shall we say, with the Principe. Placing the blame upon an evil spirit is one way of evading her own responsibility in the affair."

"And meanwhile she gives Frey Ignacio the very thing he is looking for," Antonio said bitterly. "An excuse to involve me in the exorcism of devils, which is a crime under Inquisition law, unless you are a priest. Is there no such thing as gratitude in the world, Gian?" he cried suddenly.

The artist shrugged. "If there is, I have not found it." He hesitated, then said, "It is even rumored that your arrest has been ordered. What are you going to do?"

"What can I do?"

"You could leave Spain as quickly as possible."

"How do I know they would let me go?" Antonio asked.

"You don't. But I doubt if they would try to hold you, unless Frey Ignacio thinks the evidence against you is strong enough already."

"But flight is an admission of guilt," Antonio protested.

"Not when you aren't guilty," Gian pointed out. "At least, not as far as your own conscience is concerned. And if they arrest you, they will torture you until you confess that you are guilty, whether you are or not."

Antonio knew that what he said was true. There was no way of escaping the Inquisition, once they had you in their power. And yet he was not guilty of the things they would undoubtedly charge him with if he were arrested. But there was his duty to his patron.

"I cannot leave Messer Bellarmi when his life may be in danger," he said. "And I have promised to look after Lucia if anything happens to him."

"Take them with you," Gian suggested.

"And have the Inquisition brand them as my accomplices?"

"What difference does that make," Gian argued, "so long as you are safe? And you would be safe in France. Catherine de' Medici will protect the Bellarmis and you too."

Antonio considered the tempting prospect. He had money in France, enough to live on for a long time. And there was Ambroise Paré, to whom Vesalius would undoubtedly give him a letter, making his introduction into the highest medical circles a certainty.

And then he remembered the auto-da-fé and the dancing caricatures of those who had been condemned of heresy *in absentia*. Would his own image be carried in the next procession of the Inquisitors if he left now? He had left Padua to save himself from being arrested for the attack upon Fra Felipe when he had been entirely in the right, and it had led to a deeper and deeper involvement. Could one ever succeed by fleeing in the face of a threat when not guilty?

He lifted his shoulders in decision. If he were ever to make a fight of it, he might as well begin now. Somewhere right, truth, and honesty must prevail, and he could never find that place by running from every fight. "I will not give them the satisfaction of driving me away," he told Gian. "Let Frey Ignacio do what he will."

"You are a fool, Tonio," Gian said, but his tone was gentle. "But I didn't expect you to act any differently. What will you say in your defense?"

"That I have done nothing wrong and that the treatment I used on Doña Catherine was merely a new discovery in medicine."

"God grant that you can prove it," Gian said fervently. "I will do what I can."

Antonio stood for a long time by the mantel, staring at the flames in the fireplace. In his mind he went over the course of his life since he had left Padua, and he saw no place where he would have acted differently from the way he had. All his training told him that so long as he was in the right, the Blessed Virgin would protect him and would see that he had justice. That belief was implicit in all his faith in God and in the Church in which he had been baptized and grown to manhood.

He blew out the candles and, taking a book from the shelf on the wall, went into the hall preparatory to ascending the stairs to his own room. Lucia was at the palace this evening and Messer Bellarmi was asleep. Then, with his foot on the stairway, he stopped, his attention drawn by the sound of marching feet in the street outside the house, as if a band of soldiers were passing by. What, he wondered, were marching men doing out here at this hour of the night? The palace guard never passed this way in their regular changes. The sound grew louder, rising to a throbbing rhythm which seemed directed at the house. Antonio knew a moment of cold fear that they would stop, and waited, hardly breathing, for the sound to grow less distinct, showing that the men had passed the house.

Then there was a sharp command and the sound of pikestaves striking the cobblestones. Seconds later an authoritative fist rapped upon the wooden panels of the door. For a moment Antonio could not move, his muscles gripped by the leaden weight of conviction that the summons was for him. Then he forced his muscles into action and opened the door.

An officer, clad in the somber black of the Inquisition guards, with the green cross emblazoned upon his tunic, stood before the door. He carried a rolled-up paper in his hand, and half a dozen guards were ranged in front of the house, leaning on their weapons, the cold winter moonlight gleaming from polished morions. The officer unrolled the paper in his hand. "I have a warrant here," he announced, "for the arrest of Dr. Antonio Servetus. *Está el doctor en casa?*"

Now that the blow had fallen, Antonio found that he could speak calmly. "I am he," he said.

"You will come with me," the officer stated matter-of-factly.

"Why am I under arrest?" Antonio asked.

The officer looked surprised, as if nobody ever questioned an order for arrest issued by the Inquisition. He studied the paper for a moment, then shrugged his shoulders. "It is signed by Frey Ignacio Molina, Inquisitor of Madrid. Come along."

"May I not bid my employer good-by?" Antonio asked.

"You are under arrest. You may see or speak to no one."

"Can I leave a note, then?"

The officer's voice grew sharp. "Nothing is allowed. You are under arrest."

There was no point in resisting. Through the streets Antonio marched between two lines of guards, like a common criminal, he thought, marching to the jail. He could only hope that Lucia, returning from the palace in the morning, would realize what had happened when she did not find him in the house. And, too, some of the neighbors must have noticed the arrival of the guards, for a procession of this size could not well escape detection. Lucia would undoubtedly notify Gian and Vesalius, so that the latter could transmit his appeal to the king.

Soon the walls of the Casa Santa, the premises of the Holy Office, loomed up before them, dark and forbidding. Antonio was marched through stone-walled passages deep within the dungeons beneath the building. Then a turnkey unlocked a cell into which he was summarily thrust and the barred door locked behind him. When the turnkey departed with his lantern Antonio was alone in the darkness, locked in the dungeons of the Inquisition, from which grave many a living corpse had emerged to face the stake, while many another had not emerged at all.

v

In the vast prison of the Casa Santa of Madrid, Antonio was as effectively shut away from the world as if he had been placed alive in a tomb. Twice daily the turnkey, a rough fellow whose vacant stare betrayed a moron's mind, shoved a bowl of the slop that passed for food and a jug of water through the small trap door cut for the purpose in the bottom of the barred door of the cell. To all of Antonio's questions he gave a shake of his head. The cell was dirty with the refuse of generations of former occupants, and the damp cold penetrated to one's very bones, whether sitting, lying, or standing. A narrow couch, actually nothing but a shelf of bare planks, ran across the side of the cell, covered with a ragged quilt in which vermin crawled. It was supposed to serve as a bed. In one corner of the cell a slot had been cut in the wall slightly below floor level and to it ran a groove in the stones of the floor. A bucket of dirty water, sluiced through the trap door, served occasionally to flush away the filth and excreta which accumulated in the cell, allowing it to escape from the floor by way of the groove and the slotted opening in the wall which communicated with stone-lined sewers presumably emptying somewhere on the outside. Judging from the stench that arose from every cell, the sewers had long since become pools of filth.

Michael, his brother, had known all this, Antonio thought during the long hours while he waited for the next episode in his life in the Casa Santa, and had come out still willing to give up his life for his beliefs. Silently Antonio prayed for equal strength, but deep in his heart he knew that he did not possess it. Michael had been fired with convictions for which he was willing to die, but Antonio had done nothing to deserve his fate, save to follow the time-honored principles of the physician: to serve his fellows, and to bring surcease from pain and disease wherever possible.

What would become now, Antonio wondered, of his plans to acquaint the world with his discoveries: the truth of the pulmonary circulation and the even greater truth that medicine must progress not by studying the writings of Galen, Aristotle, and Ptolemy—fruitful as such studies admittedly were—but in searching for the truth of disease in the bodies it destroyed, in the anatomy theater, at the post-mortem table, and in the laboratory upon the bodies of animals? Vesalius had dared to voice these truths once, but the anatomist of Madrid was not the same as the one who had published the *Fabrica*. Something had gone out of Vesalius during those early controversies, driven out by the threat of the very thing Antonio was now experiencing. And if Vesalius had given up the fight without the knowledge of imprisonment or torture, how could he, Antonio Servetus, be expected to carry on?

On the second morning a brace of guards came for him. He was jerked from his cell and forced to march, hands bound and ankles chained, through a maze of corridors into a large room, so brightly lit by the morning sunlight that the glare blinded him and he stumbled upon the portal. One of the guards jerked him unceremoniously into the room, so that, stumbling, he fell to his knees and felt the stinging pain as his skin was scraped on the bare floor. Then the guard seized him by the manacles binding his wrists, jerking him to his feet, and to the pain in his knees was added the stinging agony as the cuffs dug into the flesh. Eyes somewhat accustomed to the glare now, he stumbled across the room to the dais which occupied one end of it.

It was a large room, the walls bare, the furniture plain. At one end were arranged the grim instruments of torture used by the Inquisition, constant reminders of the power of the Holy Tribunal to drag confessions from its victims, with no regard to the truth. At the other end was a broad platform upon which stood a long table. Behind it were three chairs, the center taller than the other two. Before the center chair stood a tall silver crucifix between two burning tapers. A volume of the Gospels lay open upon the table.

In the center chair sat Frey Ignacio Molina, his hands folded upon the table before him. To the right was another priest, the diocesan ordinary, representing the bishop of the diocese, and to the left, in secular garb, the fiscal advocate. A notary sat at one end of the table, writing in the book before him. On the table beside him was a small ball of glass, slotted in the center to form a holder for his quills. As the sunlight fell upon it, Antonio saw that it glowed, very much as the crystal in Lodovici Agnolo's apartment had glowed that first day when he had studied magnetism.

Antonio shivered. Was this an omen? he wondered. For it was magnetism that had gotten him into trouble with the Inquisition finally, giving Frey Ignacio the excuse he needed to order his arrest. And his own experience with magnetism had begun with the glowing crystal.

Waiting for the hearing to begin, Antonio saw Frey Ignacio's eyes move toward the crystal and linger there, as if he, too, felt the same lure of the glowing ball which Antonio had noticed first in Lodovici's apartment.

"The crystal of Samarkand," Lodovici had called it, but Antonio realized now that any ball of glass would do the same, so long as it captured the sun's rays to give it a glow of its own. He must get one, he thought, so that the next time he needed to induce the magnetic state he would be much better equipped. And then he remembered that he might never have a chance to use magnetism again, for few ever left the Casa Santa.

Frey Ignacio seemed to tear his glance away from the crystal with an effort and said to the notary, "Administer the oath." He gave no other sign of even having seen Antonio.

"Repeat these words after me," the notary ordered and began to intone mechanically:

"I swear by the living God and by the Holy Virgin, Mother of Christ, that I will give true answer to all questions, that I will withhold nothing pertaining to the matter about which I am to be questioned, the names of those associated with me, or any other matter concerning which I may be accused."

Antonio repeated the oath. The Gospel was then thrust unceremoniously beneath his chin and he bent to kiss the pages. The notary moved back to his chair and took up his pen. "Your name?" he barked.

"Antonio Servetus, Doctor of Medicine and of Canon Law."

The eyes of the fiscal advocate opened wide, but Frey Ignacio gave no sign that he had heard. Antonio saw that his eyes kept moving back to the glowing crystal.

"Your birthplace?"

"I was born at Todela, in Navarre, but I spent most of my life in Italy."

Frey Ignacio spoke, the deep tones of his voice startlingly loud in the large room. "Then you are a Spaniard."

"No," Antonio corrected him. "I taught at the University of Padua, where I sought and was granted citizenship in the Republic of Venice."

The fiscal advocate toyed with his ring, but Antonio could see that he was impressed. No citizenship in the world was more valued than that of Venice. Frey Ignacio's long fingers drummed on the table but he did not continue the question, and after a moment the notary asked: "What members of your family are living?"

"None," Antonio replied. "My father and mother died some years ago, of the plague."

"Do you have a brother?" Frey Ignacio asked.

"My oldest brother, Michael Servetus, is dead."

"Was he not executed?"

"Yes," Antonio admitted. "By John Calvin at Champel in Switzerland."

"For what crime?"

"The charge was heresy," Antonio admitted. He knew that the admission was damaging to his own case, but obviously Frey Ignacio knew of it already, so nothing was to be gained by a denial.

"What is your profession?" the notary asked.

"I am a physician, a doctor of medicine," Antonio said proudly. "Lately I taught anatomy and surgery at the University of Padua."

"Why did you leave Padua?" Frey Ignacio interposed.

Antonio had been expecting the question, and he answered without hesitation, "To become personal physician to Messer Girolamo Bellarmi, a merchant and banker of Florence, who now resides in Madrid."

"Are you a Catholic?"

"I am," Antonio stated firmly.

"Your confessor?"

"Padre August Contarini of this city." Messer Bellarmi and Lucia had chosen the Italian priest, now a resident of Madrid, and Antonio had followed their lead.

"When did you last confess?"

"A week ago," Antonio replied. He had been scrupulous about the practice of his faith, imbued with it as he had been since childhood.

Frey Ignacio ruffled some papers before him. "How do you plead to the crime which is charged against you?"

Antonio was familiar with Inquisition procedure from his studies of canon law before he had turned to medicine. That was, he knew, an accepted mode of procedure for the Inquisitors, although fundamentally dishonest, trying to make the prisoner incriminate himself by betraying knowledge that he had committed a crime.

"What is the nature of the charges against me?" he asked quietly.

"Answer me," Frey Ignacio said sharply. "Are you guilty or not?" His eyes fixed Antonio, as if by their very intentness he would quell him into submission. Antonio met his gaze and gave him look for look. For a moment the air was tense with the clash of their wills, then, to Antonio's surprise, Frey Ignacio lowered his gaze to the clawlike fingers resting upon the table.

Suddenly Antonio felt a surge of triumph. Whatever might happen, of one thing he could be certain: his will was as strong as that of the Inquisitor, perhaps stronger. In spite of the cold gaze, the sepulchral voice, and the overbearing manner, Frey Ignacio had a human weakness, perhaps a doubt of himself and the essential rightness of the power behind him. It was not wise to antagonize the Inquisitor further, Antonio realized, but he stored that knowledge away in his brain, sensing that somewhere it might be valuable.

"Read the charges," Frey Ignacio ordered.

The notary read from his book: "Antonio Servetus, Doctor of Medicine, is charged with the practice of sorcery, the practice of unnatural magic, and with invoking the powers of demons for the treatment of disease, that which is not of the office of the devil . . ."

Antonio recognized at once the distinction which was being cleverly made. In some courts of canon law the invocation of devils was not itself regarded as heresy, so long as the power of Satan which was invoked was used only for functions ordinarily carried out by Satan, such, for example, as the temptation of women to the sin of luxury. But in specifying the use of demons allegedly to treat disease, the distinction was being made that the use was not one ordinarily carried out by demons, disease being, according to the laws of the Church, a punishment sent from God for sin. Any interference with that punishment by the use of demons was therefore a heresy. It was a specious distinction, but one which the Church had long used to hamper progress in medicine, to restrict dissection, and almost to bar experimentation in medical studies.

"These crimes being a part of the crime of heresy," the reading continued, "Antonio Servetus is charged with this crime according to the *Practica Inquisitionis Heretice Pravitatis.*"

"I am not guilty," Antonio stated firmly. "I have invoked no demons, committed no heresy, nor have I done anything which is contrary to the laws of the Holy Catholic Church."

Frey Ignacio raised his eyes. The malice in his gaze was so undisguised now that it came to Antonio almost as a physical shock. This man in the rough friar's robe hated him, he realized, hated him with all the pent-up fervor confined within that frail body.

But why? he wondered. Could it be because he had gone against the Inquisitor's warning that morning in the chapel and had operated upon Don Pedro? Or was it because he had bested Frey Ignacio just now in the contest of wills?

"How can you say you are not guilty," the Inquisitor thundered, "when the sworn evidence of your accusers proves your guilt?"

Antonio felt a momentary shock of surprise. *The sworn evidence of his accusers.* What and who could that be? Could Doña Catherine have really been so ungrateful as to testify against him?

"Who are these accusers?" Antonio asked.

The priest beside Frey Ignacio looked shocked that anyone should even question the words of the Holy Office, and the light in Frey Ignacio's eyes glowed suddenly with malice, his venom evident in every insulting gesture. "That does not matter," he said. "It is sufficient that you have been accused."

"The law of the Church allows me to know my accusers and to examine them," Antonio insisted doggedly.

The eyes of the diocesan ordinary opened wide, and the fiscal advocate leaned forward, intent upon every word. Antonio sensed from their attitude that it was rare indeed for a prisoner to question the proceedings of the Inquisition, but he was resolved now that he would not be browbeaten by the slender friar. Unless he stood up for his legal rights so that his insistence upon the right of cross-examination would be written into the record by the notary, there might never be another opportunity. Many had disappeared into the dungeons of the Inquisition after the first hearing, to lie for years without being brought to trial again, until the dampness, the cold, and the starvation diet, plus the mental torture of waiting, did its work.

"Very well." Frey Ignacio's tone was now indulgent, as if he were humoring a child. "The notary will give you a summary of the accusations against you."

The notary picked up a sheet and read: "Doña Catherine Sagredo states under oath that Dr. Antonio Servetus did treat her by means of sorcery because of an evil spirit which kept her from walking for many months. In the course of this sorcery he induced in her a trance or deep sleep in which he invoked the aid of demons to entice this evil spirit from her, and she further states that following the end of the trance the smell of brimstone was present in the room and that afterwards one of the demons, a fearful monster, became visible to her."

The notary put down the paper, and Frey Ignacio said in a deceptively mild tone, "What is your reply to that accusation?"

"It is not true," Antonio stated in a firm voice. "I cured Doña Catherine of a paralysis through the use of magnetism."

Frey Ignacio leaned forward. "What is this magnetism?"

"Its exact nature is not known," Antonio admitted. "But it has been used for many years in the treatment of disease by physicians and seers of the Orient."

"By evoking demons?"

"I know nothing of demons," Antonio said quietly. "This is a form of medical treatment, nothing more."

Frey Ignacio leaned forward. "Why do you persist in denying that which we know to be true?" he asked gently. "The witnesses have spoken the truth about you, and you cannot deny it when one of the demons invoked by you remained to threaten the unfortunate woman after your sorcery was ended."

"Doña Catherine is a victim of her own imagination," Antonio stated. "There were no demons."

Frey Ignacio's patience seemed to snap. "Enough of this impudence," he said. "We have other ways of getting the truth from heretics without having to listen to their blasphemy." His implication was obvious: he could mean nothing but the torture chamber.

Antonio's pulse was beating fast, but he kept his voice even. "As a citizen of Venice, I have exercised my lawful right of appealing to the king for a hearing before him. My friends have already sent a petition to His Majesty, and I doubt if he would approve your torturing me before I am allowed to defend myself before him."

Frey Ignacio half rose in his chair, like a striking snake. Body rigid, nostrils flared, he was the incarnation of rage. Then, with an obvious effort at control, he sank back in his chair, but Antonio could see that his whole body was trembling.

"Return him to the dungeons," he commanded, his voice now shrill with rage.

The turnkey brought Antonio his evening meal: a thin soup made of rotten cabbage and scraps of decaying meat, with a crust of black bread. Even the water in the flagon tasted musty, as if it had been scooped up from pools in the courtyard. Hours later, it seemed, he saw a faint aura of light moving toward him through the corridors. His pulse quickened. Could they be taking him to the torture chamber? He knew that most of such activities of the Inquisition were carried on at night, when the cries of the victims were less likely to be heard outside the Casa Santa.

The turnkey put down his lantern before Antonio's cell. With a start he recognized Lucia Bellarmi behind the turnkey, her skirts held up to clear the slime on the stone floor. Swinging the door open, the turnkey stood aside for her to enter and set the extra lantern he carried on the floor. Lucia took a gold coin from her reticule and handed it to him.

"*Gracias, señorita,*" the man mumbled. "I will return in half an hour." He went out, closing and locking the door.

"Lucia!" Antonio seized her hands. "I am glad to see you, but you shouldn't have come." He led her to the hard bench that served him as a bed.

"I had to, Tonio," she said, still holding his hands. "When I came home from the palace and found you gone, I was terrified. You could at least have left some word."

"They wouldn't let me," he told her. "But how did you find out what had happened?"

"A neighbor heard the guards. He told me someone had been taken away, so I knew the Inquisition——"

"Shh!" Antonio warned. "Careful what you say." And, in a lower tone, "How did you manage to come here?"

"The queen helped. And money will always clear the way. But what are we going to do, Tonio?"

"Has my petition for a hearing been filed with the king?"

"Yes. The queen has spoken to him about it, and also Dr. Vesalius."

"But there is no reply?"

"Not yet, but the queen thinks he will hear your appeal."

"Then there is hope," Antonio said. "I had my first questioning this morning."

"Did they——" She stopped, but he knew what she meant.

"No," he told her. "Frey Ignacio would have ordered me tortured, but I warned him that an appeal had been filed with the king, on the grounds that I am a citizen of Venice."

"That hateful Frey Ignacio." She shivered.

"Careful," he warned. It was sometimes the practice of the Inquisition to let prisoners talk freely, apparently unobserved, but to place listeners where every damning word could be heard. Such could be the case even in this cell deep within the Casa Santa.

"He is hateful," Lucia insisted spiritedly. "Why should he punish you for saving Don Pedro?"

"It is more than that now," Antonio said grimly. "He will never forgive me for appealing to the king."

"What a fool I was, Tonio." She swayed against him. "I brought all of this upon you."

He squeezed her shoulder gently. "That's water under the bridge now, Lucia. But there is something I want you to do for me."

"I'll do anything, Tonio. Believe me I will."

"I know you will," he said. After all, it had taken courage to come to the prison tonight. "I want you to go to Dr. Vesalius," he told her. "Tell him that Doña Catherine and her mother have sworn that I invoked demons in the cure of Doña Catherine."

"But they couldn't," she said, aghast at such perfidy. "Not after you cured her."

"They did," Antonio said grimly. "And unless they change their evidence, it is likely to go very hard with me. But I think the king will listen, if they really tell the truth."

"How can we make them do it?"

"That is a job for Vesalius. Tell him to threaten them, to bribe them, or whatever he can do, but make them change their statements and swear that there was no sorcery or magic involved in the treatment of Doña Catherine."

"I will do that," Lucia agreed. "Is there anything else?"

"Nothing that I can think of."

"Uncle Girolamo is also appealing to the king, Tonio," she said. "The houses of De' Medici and Bellarmi have made substantial loans to the Spanish throne at various times."

"Everything will help." He heard the turnkey returning. "And God bless you for coming, but you must not chance it again. One of us in here is enough."

The turnkey was at the door. "Thirty minutes have passed, señorita," he said. "You must go."

Lucia clung to Antonio for a moment. "God preserve you, Tonio," she whispered. Suddenly she lifted herself on her toes and kissed him. "My prayers go with you." Then the key turned behind her and the faint radiance of the turnkey's lantern receded down the hall, leaving him once again in darkness. Wrapping himself against the chill in the verminous quilt, he lay down on the narrow bed.

vi

The cell slowly filled with a soft radiance, the walls receded, and the stone floor became a sandy shore upon which the warm Ligurian Sea lapped gently. Antonio was once again lying on the sand, his body warm and damp from the sea, watching eagerly for her coming. And then his heart swelled as the figure of the divine goddess took form in all her beauty, stepping gracefully from the shell boat as it grated upon the sand.

Now she came toward him, her face warm with a tender smile of welcome. Her fingers touched his, and thrill of pure bliss went through him as he was lifted effortlessly to his feet. "Tonio. Tonio, *caro mio,*" she whispered as his arms went about her, holding her close to him.

Then rough hands tore them apart, thrusting him to his knees. But the intruder, the satyr with the mocking face, was not Fra Felipe Santos. It was Frey Ignacio Molina, and the mocking voice was his as the satyr raced off with the goddess in his arms.

Antonio struggled to rise, to pursue them, but the same paralysis of his muscles chained him to the sand. Then suddenly Lucia Bellarmi stood beside him, but her voice was no longer mocking and her face was kind. She knelt and took his head within her arms, soothing him, and erasing the hurt from his body.

"Tonio," she whispered. "Tonio, my——"

Pain seared through Antonio's cheek and tiny claws tore at his shoulder and neck. Screaming with horror, he came awake and lashed out at the thing that clung to him. His hand struck a furry object that squealed with pain, knocking it to the floor, where it scurried for a foothold before disappearing through the grated door. There was a sudden rush of movement throughout the cells as others of the great gray rats which inhabited the dungeons scurried to shelter.

Antonio sank to the hard couch, shaking with horror. He put his hands up to his face and felt the sticky wetness of blood seep between his fingers. The rat had bitten him several times, he realized, besides the damage from sharp claws. And the bite of a rat often meant death from a raging fever. He had seen more than one poor devil from the prison dungeons of Venice and Padua cross the post-mortem tables of the medical school, on his skin the telltale healed scar of the ratbite, and in his body the unmistakable signs of the dread disease which followed it: the massive swellings in groin and armpit, the wasted flesh, the pallid skin, and finally death from a conflagration which literally burned up the body.

For long moments Antonio sat there shuddering, while the blood on his fingers coagulated and grew sticky and the tiny wounds of the rat's teeth and claws were closed by blood clot. Finally he fumbled in the darkness for his water flagon and, finding it, sloshed water upon his hands and wiped at his face and neck to remove the blood. He could not see the wounds, but he knew that they would be small. It was not the size that counted, but the consuming fever which so often followed them.

He was afraid to lie down now, lest from utter weariness he fall asleep to be awakened again by the pain of sharp teeth and dirty claws cutting through his skin and the horror of stinking gray fur moving over his face. He understood now why so few had the strength to defy the Inquisition, and why, rather than undergo the agony of waiting and the horror of the dungeons, they confessed to crimes of which they were not guilty and found release in the merciful twist of the garroter's noose.

To take his mind off the horror of the rats, Antonio considered the changed picture of the dream. It was logical that Frey Ignacio should replace Fra Felipe Santos, for the Inquisitor of Madrid was so much in his mind. But why had Lucia changed from the mocking, taunting figure of his earlier dreams to the comforting and consoling girl who had held his head in her arms.

Thinking over the months since he had met Lucia, he realized now that she had changed. No longer was her temper as sharp with him as it had been in the beginning, although she would always be a girl of spirit. Gradually there had built up between them a strong sense of companionship, and he admitted to himself now that he had come to admire her very much, her integrity and intelligence as much as her beauty. Had he actually fallen in love with her, as Gian had suggested? It was true that just now in the dream he had been content to rest in her arms, feeling no urge to follow the abducted goddess. But it could be, he reminded himself, because of Lucia's close resemblance to the goddess that he felt as though an intangible bond drew them together.

In the morning the turnkey brought another bowl of the nauseous mess which passed for food in the Casa Santa and shoved it through the trap beneath the barred door. He was almost gone, so casual was the service in his dungeon, when Antonio reached the door and shook it to attract his attention.

"What is it you want?" the turnkey asked, peering through the bars.

"I was bitten by a rat during the night," Antonio said. "Who is the physician to this hellhole?"

"Dr. Andreas Vesalius," the turnkey grunted. Then he grinned, showing toothless gums. "Do not worry, señor. When the rat bites you, you either die or you don't."

"I want to see Dr. Vesalius."

A gleam of avarice appeared in the turnkey's eyes. "It might be arranged, señor. For a price."

"I will pay you. Dr. Vesalius will give me the money."

The man shrugged. *"Mas vale pájaro en mano que ciento volando."*

"But I have no money now. Your thieving guards stripped me of every ducat."

"That gold chain about your neck, señor. It could serve as security until you paid me."

Antonio knew that he could never redeem the chain once it had disappeared into the voluminous pockets of the turnkey's patched and faded coat. But he had to see Andreas Vesalius; he could not go through another night in this stinking hell without knowing something of what the future held in store. *"Bueno,"* he agreed, loosening the plain gold chain that he wore habitually as his single piece of jewelry. "But see that you get him, or I will report you to the Inquisitors."

It was late afternoon when Vesalius arrived. "My dear friend," the anatomist cried, embracing him. "What misfortune has undertaken you?" Then he spied the bite on Antonio's cheek. "You are wounded."

"The bite of a rat," Antonio said. "I made the mistake of falling asleep last night."

Vesalius frowned. He knew well the danger of such a wound, as did Antonio.

"I did not call you for the bite," Antonio continued, "although it was a good excuse. There is nothing to do but wait and see if I develop the fever."

"That is true," Vesalius agreed. "It would have made no difference if I had been here."

"What of my hearing before the king?" Antonio asked eagerly. "Has it been arranged?"

"Yes. The king has assured me that he will give you a fair trial."

Antonio sank to the bench, momentarily overcome with relief at knowing that he would at least have a chance to defend himself. Before the Holy Tribunal alone, he knew, there would be no hope. The personal venom of Frey Ignacio was too strong for that.

"Did Lucia give you my message about Doña Catherine and her mother?" he asked.

Vesalius nodded, but his face showed his concern. "I visited them yesterday and again this morning."

"Did they agree to change their testimony?"

"In a way they did," Vesalius said. "But in a way they did not."

"What do you mean?"

"Doña Catherine is very grateful to you for her recovery," Vesalius explained. "But there are other factors involved."

"Is anything more important than justice?" Antonio demanded impatiently.

"To some people, yes. So long as it is a question of justice for someone other than themselves. A great deal of pressure has been brought upon Doña Catherine to testify that you invoked demons in her cure."

Antonio's spirits dropped. "By the Inquisition?"

"By Frey Ignacio himself, supported by the Bishop of Toledo. I think they plan to make an example of you."

"But why?"

Vesalius shrugged. "Probably as a warning to those who are intriguing against the Catholic party."

"But that is absurd," Antonio protested. "I want nothing to do with intrigues."

"Of course," Vesalius agreed. "But you must remember that your opponents attribute to you the same motives that they possess themselves."

Antonio clenched his fists in bitter impotence. "How can Doña Catherine tell anything except the truth—that I gave her a form of medical treatment?"

"Unfortunately the lady in question has not been discreet," Vesalius reminded him. "She was undoubtedly the mistress of the Principe, but considering the high position of those involved, there was no punishment. Now Frey Ignacio has hinted to her that if she does not testify against you, the Holy Office will arrest her for adultery. Naturally her mother will also do anything to protect her daughter, even to the point of perjuring herself."

"Then they refuse to help me," Antonio said dully.

"Not exactly," Vesalius said. "I have arranged something of a compromise. At my request, Doña Catherine and her mother have agreed to seek a private audience with the king before your hearing. Considering that his son is as guilty as the girl is, he may be influenced to rule that her testimony cannot be used against you."

"But it should be in my favor," Antonio protested. "That will carry more weight."

"I could not arrange that," Vesalius said. "But they have also agreed to send away a servant who testified about the smell of brimstone in the room after the treatment."

"Brimstone?" he echoed. "There was no smell of brimstone."

"The servant told Frey Ignacio there was," Vesalius said. "They overlook nothing at the Holy Office."

Antonio bowed his head, his spirit weighed down by this new link in the chain of false evidence against him. "When will the hearing be held?" he asked dully.

"The day after tomorrow."

"Thank God for that. I couldn't endure much more of this waiting."

Vesalius stood up. "You can be certain that your friends are doing everything they can, Antonio. And the king will give you a fair hearing."

With an effort, Antonio got a grip upon himself again. It would gain him nothing, he realized, to give up, no matter how strong the evidence against him. "Thank you for what you have done, Andreas," he said. "I shall always be indebted to you."

"God guard you, my friend," Vesalius said in parting. "And protect you from the fever of the ratbite."

But it was not the ratbite fever that he had to worry about, Antonio knew, for his fate would be decided long before he could develop that dread disease. And perhaps it would be better, then, if he did.

With an effort of will Antonio forced his racing thoughts to be calm, for he knew that he must try to sleep before darkness brought the furry denizens of the dungeon on their nightly visits. Soon the utter weariness of mind and body from the previous night's sleepless vigil brought on the blessed stupor. He awoke only when the turnkey shoved his evening meal beneath the door.

During the long hours of the night, while the scurrying of tiny feet over the stones reminded him that he must not fall asleep, Antonio forced himself to recall what he could from his studies of canon law. He must insist upon every right that was his under the law, he realized, particularly the privilege of cross-examining witnesses as his own advocate, for he had no way of knowing who else the Inquisitor might have threatened into giving false testimony against him. And here his memory served him well, bringing back whole pages of the tedious collections of ecclesiastical authority which he had spent several years studying in Padua. When morning finally came he was spent with effort and his face was pale and haggard from loss of sleep, but he forced down his nausea at the appalling slop which was fed to the prisoners, knowing that he must eat to conserve his strength. The meal completed, he stretched out on the bench and was almost immediately asleep.

It was late afternoon when Antonio was awakened by the turnkey sliding his dinner beneath the door. It was not the regular hour for the meal to be served, but the man departed before Antonio could ask him why his food was being brought so early. Then the aroma from the wooden tray struck his nostrils and he lifted it up and carried it to his bench. For a moment he could believe neither his nose nor his eyes, for the tray contained a whole roast fowl, half a loaf of bread, and a steaming posset of mulled wine. Suspiciously Antonio eyed the appetizing meal. Could Frey Ignacio have decided to poison him? he wondered. Then he saw a folded piece of paper almost covered by the bread. He drew it out and opened it. There was no mistaking Gian's scrawl:

Tonio,
He fights best who dines well before the battle. God be with you on the morrow. We have done what we could.

It was unsigned, but he did not doubt its authorship or the safety of the food any longer, and he fell to with a vigorous appetite. There was another excellent meal in the morning, but as the hours passed without a summons to his hearing before the king, Antonio's fears began to rise again. Could the Inquisitor have used some excuse to seize Lucia, Gian, and Vesalius? he wondered. Had the king called off his hearing for fear of revealing the debauchery of his son through Doña Catherine's testimony? A thousand doubts assailed him.

Then from down the corridor came the sound of booted feet, marching in cadence. Soon he could hear the metallic jingle of military equipment and feel the jarring, rhythmic tread upon the stone floors. There were six of the black-garbed guards of the Inquisition with an officer in charge. Behind them shuffled the turnkey.

The turnkey fumbled at the lock with the huge key at his belt. Then the door swung open and Antonio stood facing the officer.

"Antonio Servetus, prisoner of the Holy Tribunal," the officer intoned. "Through the graciousness of His Most Catholic Majesty, Philip II, His Reverence the Bishop of Toledo, and Frey Ignacio Molina, Inquisitor of Madrid, you have been allowed the favor of a public hearing before the king upon the charges against you."

He turned to the turnkey. "Strike the chains from his feet."

Shuffling forward, the turnkey unlocked the chains and Antonio stepped out of the metal collars that encircled his ankles. There was no move to unlock his wrist chains and he held out his manacled hands to the officer. "What of these?" he asked.

"*Silencio!*" The officer slapped Antonio's hands with a gauntleted fist, driving the metal cuffs into the skin until the pain made him cry out. Staggered by the blow, Antonio caught at the bars for support. Anger flared within him, but he forced himself to be calm. All this was probably a part of Frey Ignacio's plan, he realized, designed to keep him from the full exercise of his wits when he appeared before the king.

One of the guards pushed him with a pikestaff into a position between the lines of men. Then the return march began, back through the corridors of the Casa Santa. The hearing was not to be held in the grim prison itself, though, for the little procession marched out of the door, along the street to the palace grounds, and through a gate leading to the palace itself. Merely leaving the Casa Santa raised Antonio's spirits a little, but he fully realized that the next few hours were the most critical in his whole life.

vii

The doors of the audience chamber were thrust open by uniformed heralds at the knock of the officer of the guard. Coming from the dim-lit corridors into this room, brightly lit by the winter sunlight pouring through tall windows from which the rich draperies had been drawn, Antonio was almost blinded. As he blinked to accustom himself to the light, he heard the officer who accompanied him announce:

"Antonio Servetus, prisoner of the Holy Office, begs the indulgence of His Most Catholic Majesty, that he may be heard concerning the crimes with which he is charged."

A calm voice said, "Let him come forward."

At a nudge from the guard, Antonio walked down the aisle toward the dais from which the voice had come, while his guards took up positions on either side of the door. Before the dais at the end of the aisle, Antonio dropped to his knees.

"Rise, Doctor," the same calm voice said.

Antonio stood erect, facing the long table that occupied the dais. Behind it were the usual three chairs of Inquisition ritual. In the center sat the king, quietly dressed in black velvet and violet satin, the high Spanish collar beneath his chin open to display the spotless white of his ruff. His only ornament was a heavy gold chain supporting the great medallion lying upon his breast emblazoned with the arms of Spain. Above the white ruff, his dark, serious face was calm, but Antonio thought that there was a trace of pity and sympathy in the dark eyes.

On the right hand of the king sat Don Diego Espinosa, Bishop of Toledo. His mitered biretta surmounted a face tinged bluish already by the plethora which would shortly prove his undoing. Beneath the mozzetta, cassock, and lace-edged surplice that covered his upper body, he wheezed gently as he breathed. His eyes were deep-set, small, and bright with interest as he surveyed the manacled figure before him.

In contrast to the other two, Frey Ignacio Molina was a sinister figure in his plain robe of coarse homespun, his natural pallor accentuated by the bright sunlight of the audience chamber until his skin seemed to be transparent. His eyes rested upon the pale, clawlike fingers lying before him on the table.

The notary sat at the end of the table, his quills arranged in the slotted glass ball which served him as a pen stand. The ball itself glowed brightly with the imprisoned rays of the sun. Beside the quills burned a small candle to provide wax for his seals.

"Of what is this prisoner accused?" the king asked, and the notary began to read the list of crimes which Antonio was said to have committed. They were the same as on his previous arraignment before the tribunal, and he took the opportunity of glancing around the room while the reading continued.

To one side sat the queen, with Lucia, pale and anxious, beside her. The queen gave him a smile of encouragement. Nearer to the center aisle sat Vesalius, with Gian Savarino beside him. On the other side of the room was Don Carlos, the Principe. Antonio recognized many of the great names of Spain in the front rows of the chamber, which was packed by spectators, eager to see this most rare of spectacles, a prisoner of the Inquisition arraigned publicly before the king sitting as a member of the tribunal.

The notary finished reading and resumed his seat, and the king leaned forward. "What is your plea to these charges, Doctor?" he asked, not unkindly.

Antonio raised his manacled hands before him. "I swear by the Lord God, by the living Christ, His Son, and by the Blessed Virgin who bore Him, that I am innocent of witchcraft, of sorcery, of unnatural magic, and of heresy, and that these charges are false and trumped up for reasons known only to those who have made them."

An excited buzzing broke out in the room at his words and the strong conviction in his tones. Here was no supine wretch, broken already by the power of the Inquisition. Don Diego's cheeks purpled and he seemed to be choking. Frey Ignacio did not raise his eyes from the table, but Antonio saw his fingers clench upon the polished wood.

The king said sternly, "You will confine yourself to a direct answer to the questions, Doctor."

Antonio bowed his head. "What I say is true in every detail, sire," he said slowly. "I would not be answering truly if I said less."

Antonio saw Vesalius frown. Lucia, as pale as the ruff about her neck, was biting already bloodless lips.

The king leaned over and whispered something to Frey Ignacio, who raised his eyes from the table but did not look at Antonio. Could it be, Antonio wondered with a rising excitement, that the Inquisitor was unwilling to do so? In their first clash of wills during his previous questioning, Antonio was certain that he had bested the Inquisitor. Could it be that the Dominican was now afraid to meet his gaze? If Frey Ignacio were not entirely sure of himself or of his case, then there must be a weakness somewhere, a breach in the walls of false testimony which he had built up to entrap the prisoner. Somehow, Antonio knew, he must find that breach.

"Do you wish an advocate to defend you, Doctor?" Frey Ignacio asked. "It is your right under the law."

"I shall be my own advocate," Antonio stated firmly.

"Are you certain you do not wish legal advice?" the king added. "It is your right."

"I am a graduate in Canon Law of the University of Padua, Your Majesty," Antonio said proudly.

Again the room buzzed with whispers, and the king rapped upon the table for order. He nodded to Frey Ignacio, who asked, "Has any member of your family been convicted of heresy?"

Antonio knew the effect that the answer would have upon the king and the crowd, but he had no choice except to reply, "My brother, Michael Servetus, was executed by John Calvin for heresy."

"And was not this charge also proved against him by Holy Church?"

"He was convicted by a court sitting in Rome," Antonio admitted.

The Inquisitor paused to let this damning fact sink into the minds of the audience and the other members of the tribunal. When he spoke again, his voice was vibrant once more with confidence, the deep organ tones reverberating through the room. "It is charged against you that you have invoked demons in the treatment of disease."

"I have invoked no demons," Antonio broke in firmly. "The charges are false."

The Inquisitor's lips tightened with displeasure. "What is the nature of this treatment you use, then?"

"It is called magnetism," Antonio explained, "although its exact nature is not known. Wise men of Egypt and the Orient have used it for many years."

"Ha!" the Bishop of Toledo said sharply. "But the Orientals are heretics. You stand convicted of heresy by your own words."

Antonio turned quickly to him. "Does Your Reverence accept the writings of Aristotle?"

"*Naturalmente*," snapped Don Diego.

"Aristotle was a pagan," Antonio pointed out. "Therefore Your Reverence stands convicted of heresy by your own statement, if the same logic applies."

Had a thunderclap burst within the chamber it could have had no more startling effect. The bishop purpled until it seemed that he must explode from the force of his own wrath, and Frey Ignacio Molina half rose in his chair. Only the king remained still, and Antonio thought he saw a ghost of a smile upon his lips at the discomfiture of the two ecclesiastics. A titter of amusement ran around the room.

"As my own advocate," Antonio said quietly, "may I ask that both the bishop's charges of heresy and my own be removed from the records of the hearing? I merely wished to show the dangers of such *post hoc, ergo propter hoc* reasoning."

"It will be removed," the king directed. "You may proceed, Frey Ignacio."

"The notary will read the sworn testimony of Doña Catherine Sagredo," the Inquisitor said quietly.

"'I, Catherine Sagredo,'" the notary read, "'swear upon the Four Gospels that I will make a true statement in regard to treatment administered to me by Dr. Antonio Servetus. Having suffered for more than a year from a painful affliction in which all feeling and use were lost in the lower half of my body, and having been treated by many physicians without relief, I welcomed the services of a physician recommended to me by Dr. Andreas Vesalius. On the tenth day of December, at my home, Dr. Antonio Servetus placed me in a state of trance or enchantment, during which time, in some way unknown to me, he was able to relieve the paralysis from which I was suffering. I further state that during the period of this trance I heard voices in strange tongues which I do believe to have been the voices of demons invoked by Dr. Servetus. I do further state that when I recovered from this enchantment or trance, I found myself standing in the center of the room with no knowledge of how or by whom I was carried there and that noises as of wings were perceptible for some time thereafter. There was further the smell of brimstone in the air, and shortly after the termination of the trance I was frightened by an apparition which I believe to be one of the demons invoked by Dr. Servetus through sorcery and witchcraft. Signed and affirmed by me before witnesses, Catherine Sagredo.'"

When the notary had finished, Frey Ignacio asked, "Do you have evidence to refute this statement, Doctor?"

Antonio had been looking around the room, searching for Doña Catherine. Surely, he thought, this was the time when, if Vesalius's plea had exerted any effect, she would come forward and admit her error. Or if she and her mother had appealed to the king, he would rule against the testimony. But there was no word from the king, and no sign of Doña Catherine. He saw only Doña Maria, the mother, sitting tense and pale in one of the back rows.

The girl had betrayed him, he realized then, her fear of the Inquisition greater than any desire to see justice done or any appreciation of what he had done in curing her. Unless he found some way to nullify her damaging testimony, his cause would surely be lost.

"What do you say, Doctor?" Frey Ignacio prodded.

"Where is Doña Catherine Sagredo?" Antonio asked. "I wish her to swear publicly to the truth of this statement."

"Doña Catherine is prevented from being here by illness," Frey Ignacio said.

"Then I demand that the hearing be recessed until she can appear," Antonio insisted.

Frey Ignacio's voice rang through the chamber. "As a Doctor of Canon Law, you must surely know that the rules of the Inquisition do not require a witness to be present in person to confirm his sworn testimony."

The objection was valid, Antonio knew, according to the laws of the Inquisition. And undoubtedly Frey Ignacio had very carefully seen to it that his chief witness could not be subjected to cross-examination. It was a clever and a damaging move.

"What if this statement was made under pressure?" Antonio asked.

"What kind of pressure, Doctor?" the king asked.

"From the officers of the Inquisition. I have private knowledge that Doña Catherine was threatened by them with severe consequences if she did not give the testimony which has been read."

"That is a serious charge," the king said. "Can you support it?"

In desperation, Antonio said, "I see that Doña Maria Sagredo, the mother of Doña Catherine, is present, and I ask that she come forward."

There was a muffled sob from the back of the room, and the woman tried to bolt from the chamber but was stopped by the guards.

"Who is that?" the king asked sharply.

Doña Maria turned then and stumbled down the aisle, sobbing. The notary took her by the arm and helped her to a chair. She appeared on the point of collapse. "I merely want to ask you a few questions," Antonio said kindly. "You need have no fear of the truth."

At that Doña Maria began to sob again and to wring her hands.

"Is this necessary, Doctor?" the king asked. "Doña Maria seems distraught."

"My life is at stake," Antonio reminded him quietly. "Am I to be denied anything which may help my case?"

"Proceed, then."

The notary administered the oath to the woman, and when she resumed her seat, Antonio said: "Señora Sagredo, you have heard the sworn statement of your daughter, and you were present during the period when I treated her for paralysis. Did you at any time see any evidence that I was invoking the aid of demons or practicing unnatural magic in any way?"

Frey Ignacio's voice broke in. "I have been informed that the Señora Sagredo was not in the chamber during the entire treatment. Is that true, señora?"

The woman caught at the question desperately. "Y-yes," she said in a low voice. "I was out of the room during part of the treatment."

"And who asked you to leave?"

She looked at Antonio. "Dr. Servetus, I think. Yes, I am sure."

Frey Ignacio's expression was bland; he was obviously pleased with her co-operation. "How long were you gone?" he asked.

"Five or ten minutes. I don't remember exactly."

"You may proceed, Doctor," Frey Ignacio said with complete satisfaction.

Antonio realized that the Inquisitor had very cleverly nullified any effect which Doña Maria's testimony might have, but he must improve his rapidly disintegrating defense in any possible way.

"It is true, as you say, señora," he admitted, "that I asked you to get some wine for your daughter during the treatment. Did you not, before you left, see your daughter move her paralyzed limbs?"

"Why, I—" Doña Maria hesitated—"I don't know."

"Think, now," he urged.

She wrung plump hands in her lap and looked wildly about her, finally settling her gaze upon the Inquisitor. He made no sign to her, but Antonio saw the cold gleam of his gaze fix the terrified woman. All color drained from her face then and it seemed as if she were going to faint. Almost inaudibly she whispered, "No. She was still paralyzed when I left."

Antonio felt a sudden cold fear grip him. The pressure of the Inquisition, the fear that her daughter would be publicly shamed for adultery with Don Carlos, either one was sufficient to make the woman perjure herself. Not that such perjury meant anything under the circumstances, he realized, for Frey Ignacio would undoubtedly absolve her from any blame afterwards. That, too, was a recognized part of Inquisition procedure.

"Doña Maria," he said gently. "When I completed my treatment of your daughter, you followed me from the house, crying that the Blessed Virgin had performed a miracle through my hands. Do you still believe this?"

The woman's eyes were like those of a hunted animal. "I—I——" she stammered. "I don't know."

"What made you change that belief?" he insisted.

"I—I don't know."

"Doña Maria," he said more sternly, "I ask you to remember that you are under oath when you answer this question. What threats were made by representatives of the Holy Office against you and your daughter so that you would testify against me?"

Doña Maria swayed in her chair. She tried to speak but no sound came. Then suddenly she slid from the chair in a faint. A buzz of excited whisperings filled the room as Antonio knelt beside her and felt for her pulse. It was slow and full.

"She has merely swooned," he said.

"Dr. Vesalius," the king snapped. "Will you attend to this lady?" He rapped sharply on the table for order.

Vesalius, too, made a rapid examination. "It is only a swoon," he reported. "She will recover in a moment." He took a vial of smelling salts from his pocket and held it beneath Doña Maria's nostrils. Almost immediately she coughed and opened her eyes.

"Let her be moved to another room," the king ordered.

"But, sire," Antonio protested, "she did not answer my question."

The king hesitated, but Frey Ignacio's voice boomed through the room. "Is there need to torture this poor woman? The accusation is infamous in itself."

Such was the magnetic quality of the thin friar's voice that Antonio could see the king's doubts being swept away by it. "That is true," he agreed. "Such a suggestion is infamous."

"But what if it is true, sire?" Antonio was still fighting, but he knew now that this battle was useless. The Inquisition had won, just as it always won, by lies, threats, and torture, justifying the means by the pernicious doctrine that anything was acceptable so long as it helped win souls for the Church.

The king's face reddened with anger. "That is enough. I find myself wearied of this play-acting. Have you other witnesses, Doctor?"

There was still Andreas Vesalius. The testimony of the king's favorite physician must have some effect. Then Frey Ignacio's voice broke in: "I feel that in view of the evidence brought forward to support the charges against this man, his guilt is evident. Any further witnesses are warned that they may be prosecuted upon a charge of heresy should they be led to perjure themselves in favor of the accused."

The strategy behind that announcement was obvious. Frey Ignacio well knew the effect that testimony by Vesalius might still have upon the king. This was tantamount to a threat that should Antonio be found guilty—as there seemed every indication now that he would be—charges would be brought against Vesalius. And the anatomist had told Antonio more than once that the Inquisitor would like nothing better than some excuse to arrest him.

Antonio looked at Vesalius. His friend was pale, but his gaze did not waver. He would give evidence in spite of the warning, Antonio knew. But it would not be fair now to needlessly involve the man he had come to regard as a second father.

"I have no more witnesses, messire," Antonio said quietly. Frey Ignacio met his gaze then, and at the look of triumph and hate in the friar's deep-set eyes Antonio felt an answering anger rise within him. Look for look, their eyes locked, the torturer and the man who was as good as condemned. And as the fire of anger and contempt rose in Antonio's brain, he saw Frey Ignacio's eyes waver and the look of triumph that had been in them was replaced by a look almost of fear and indecision, as if the man, for all his viciousness, were not certain of the justice of what he represented. Then the Inquisitor's eyes dropped before Antonio's angry regard and moved to fix themselves upon the glass ball that held the notary's quills, glowing brightly in the noonday sunlight.

Antonio felt a sudden thrill of inspiration. There was a way, he thought now, a wild, improbable, and utterly dangerous way, in which he might save himself. And by virtue of its very improbability, it might actually work. So long as that chance existed, he must take it.

Quickly he turned to face the king. "Sire," he said, "I realize the weight of the evidence against me. Nevertheless I must protest my innocence. And I stand ready to prove it before you."

Philip frowned. "What is this? You have stated that you have no more witnesses."

"But if I show you without question that the power of magnetism which I have learned is a natural force and unrelated to sorcery, will not all charges against me be disproved?"

"That is true," the king admitted.

"On the contrary, sire," Frey Ignacio broke in, "it would prove nothing. Demons have power against all ordinary men."

"But not against men of uncommon holiness," Antonio said. "Think of the temptations of the saints."

"But where is such a man?" the king asked.

"There is the Reverend Inquisitor, Frey Ignacio Molina," Antonio said softly. "Who can doubt his holiness?"

There was a crash as the candlestick beside Frey Ignacio toppled to the floor. He was half out of his chair. "What monstrous heresy is this?" he cried, his voice shaking with anger. Antonio felt his own elation rise, for he was sure now that he recognized a tremor of fear in the Inquisitor's voice.

"Is the Reverend Inquisitor, then, so uncertain of his faith?" Antonio asked. "In spite of the fact that he sits in judgment upon all others."

For a long moment Frey Ignacio's body remained rigid in the involuntary spasm of anger which had caused him to knock the candlestick from the table. Pallid normally, his face was now totally devoid of color. Slowly then he relaxed, but when he spoke again his voice was still hoarse with tension. "What is it you propose?" he inquired.

"A simple demonstration that the magnetism I use has nothing to do with sorcery or demons," Antonio assured him. "If I am able to place the Reverend Inquisitor in a magnetic trance, that should be all the evidence necessary that I use only natural forces."

"And if not?"

Antonio shrugged. His case was lost already; he could lose no more.

The king turned to Frey Ignacio. "What say you?" he asked.

The Inquisitor seemed not to hear him for a moment, then in a voice which could hardly be heard beyond the dais he said, "Very well. Let him be convicted of his heresy by his own actions."

"When will you do this experiment, Doctor?" the king asked.

"Here and now," Antonio answered promptly. If his diagnosis were correct—and all of his experience in magnetism seemed to support the conclusion—the trance was most easily induced when the subject was laboring under a strong emotion. And Lodovici had assured him, too, that the sleeplike state was always easier to achieve before an audience than in private. Certainly he could never have a more suitable set of conditions in those respects as far as Frey Ignacio was concerned, especially if he were right in his assumption that the friar was uncertain of himself.

But Antonio was relying upon something else, something which he felt certain gave him an even better chance to succeed in his audacious scheme to magnetize the Inquisitor publicly. At his first hearing, he remembered, Frey Ignacio's eyes had kept returning to the glowing glass ball of the notary's quill stand, and today the same thing had happened again. Lodovici had warned him that it was very difficult to magnetize anyone who resisted strongly, but if he could trick Frey Ignacio into the magnetic state without his realizing what was happening, that obstacle would be avoided. And he thought he had figured out a way in which this might be accomplished. Frey Ignacio, like almost everyone, was ignorant of the technique by which magnetism was obtained, and Antonio was planning to utilize that ignorance to his own advantage.

"If you will order these chains removed, sire," he said, "I can proceed immediately."

"Remove them," the king ordered. While the officer was unlocking the manacles, Antonio looked around the room. Everywhere he saw tension written upon the faces of the spectators. Some were avidly eager for the downfall of one who dared defy the Inquisition. Others registered shocked disapproval at such heresy. Lucia was pale, her eyes wide with fear and concern. Gian, trying to smile encouragingly, managed only a grimace.

The metallic cuffs dropped from Antonio's wrists and he turned to the notary. "I shall need to borrow your quill stand," he said.

The notary removed the quills and handed him the ball. It was flattened on one side so that it would stand upright, and still warm with the imprisoned heat of the sunlight. Antonio remembered how he had almost been magnetized himself in Lodovici's apartment, when he had first seen a similar crystal. And in one of the books he had read on magnetism he had found that an Egyptian sect had used such a crystal to obtain a trance state for nearly four thousand years.

With the glass in his hand, Antonio moved to a position in front of Frey Ignacio and placed the ball upon the dark wood of the table. At once it caught the sun's rays from an adjacent window and glowed with a living fire. A murmur of interest went up from the crowd.

But still Antonio was not satisfied; there was too much light other than in the crystal ball itself. "Draw the curtains," he directed the guards. "But leave this window uncovered." He indicated the one through which light fell upon the crystal.

Frey Ignacio's eyes had been resting upon his hands on the table, but now Antonio saw them move to the glowing ball, as if drawn there by loadstone. "Some time it is necessary in order to bring on the magnetic state," Antonio told him. "I will warn you when I am ready. Meanwhile you may put your mind at rest." He waited a moment and, when the friar's gaze remained upon the glowing ball, continued, "Within the glass upon the table are concentrated the beneficent powers of the sun, from which comes all energy, all force. Here is light, glowing as it is gathered by the crystal. Here is warmth, its brightness apparent deep within the center of the globe, just as there is warmth at the center of the earth from which comes the fires of the volcano. As the sun brings warmth and light to the crystal ball, so does it bring warmth and light to men's minds."

All the while he was speaking in a low, intent voice, Antonio's eyes were fixed upon the friar, every force of his will poured into the effort to dominate the resistant will before Frey Ignacio realized what was happening.

"When I begin to apply the magnetism," he continued in the same monotonous voice, "you need have no fear of it nor resist it. You will then free your mind of all thought of self and let it be controlled by the magnetic forces of the sun."

The Inquisitor's gaze was fixed upon the ball, unblinking, unwavering, and Antonio thought he could see the glaze of the magnetic trance beginning to film his pupils. He must control himself now, Antonio realized, and go very carefully. A slight change in his voice, warning Frey Ignacio that he was being tricked, a sudden cloud over the face of the sun, shutting away the light that fired the crystal, any one of a thousand things might intervene now and destroy all the progress he had made.

"In a moment I will begin to induce the magnetic trance," he intoned. "Then you will feel relaxed, and you will sleep . . . sleep . . . sleep."

As he talked, still in the same monotonous tone, he saw the Inquisitor's long fingers begin to relax upon the table, until finally they dropped, palm down, upon the surface of the wood. As if borne on a wave of some strange power traveling through his spare frame, the relaxation of the muscles gradually crept up his arms, into his shoulders, and then down into his body. Before Antonio's eyes, the taut, slender form began to relax, like a bowstring when the bow itself is bent, and a hot fire of triumph began to burn within him. As he had hoped, Frey Ignacio was actually magnetizing himself under the influence of the glowing crystal, while he waited for Antonio to begin what he had obviously planned to make a test of wills. The trick was working, if only nothing happened now to break the spell.

Behind him Antonio could sense rather than see the tense expectancy of the crowd. In the whole large room there was hardly the sound of a single person's breathing, and even the wheezing of the Bishop of Toledo had quieted in the almost unbearable tension of this strange experiment.

Slowly, as a wax statue softens in the summer sun, the tension went out of Frey Ignacio's neck, the rigid lines of his mouth relaxed, and his eyelids dropped across his pupils. Once, twice, they were raised, as if he were fighting now in a final effort of will against the insidious power which was depriving him of control of self.

Then the pale lids dropped and remained closed, the narrow head settled slowly upon a bony shoulder, and Antonio allowed himself the luxury of a deep breath, the first really full one he had taken since the test had begun. Like the rustle of dry leaves in the wind, a sigh went up from the crowd, a sigh of both amazement and fear. Each person recognized the immensity of a power which could triumph over the iron will of the Inquisitor. What they did not know was that Frey Ignacio's resistance had been circumvented by a trick and that actually the Inquisitor had magnetized himself, drawn irresistibly by the lure of the shining glass ball.

"Can you hear me, Frey Ignacio?" Antonio asked, leaning close to him.

"Yes, I hear you." The friar's voice was loud enough to be heard throughout the room. Antonio saw the king start with surprise and lean forward, his fingers pressing into his chin.

"Are you asleep?" Antonio asked.

"No," the friar said distinctly, "I am not asleep."

"Has sorcery, witchcraft, or the invocation of demons been used upon you?" Antonio was quite sure of success now, but he found himself waiting tensely for the answer.

"No," Frey Ignacio answered clearly.

"Are you quite certain?" the king asked, but there was no reply.

Antonio turned to him. "During the magnetic state, sire," he explained, "he is unable to hear you. Only the person inducing the state can communicate with him."

"Ask him if there is anything unnatural about the state he is in," the king insisted.

Antonio leaned close to Frey Ignacio. "Is there anything of unnatural magic about your present state?" he asked.

"No," the Inquisitor replied promptly. "There is nothing unnatural."

"Cáspita!" the king said in an awed voice. "Es increíble!"

"Not incredible, Your Majesty," Antonio corrected quietly. "Merely a use of natural forces. I will give another demonstration, if the notary will loan me his candle."

Taking the small candle used to provide the notary with wax for seals, Antonio said to Frey Ignacio, "You have lost all feeling in your right hand. You can feel no pain, and when I hold this candle close to it you will not feel the heat."

Slowly he moved the burning candle close to the Inquisitor's lean hand. The bishop, the king, and those in front could easily see the red spot that developed where the flame almost touched the skin. "Do you feel the heat?" he asked.

"No," Frey Ignacio answered. "There is no heat."

An awed murmur passed through the audience, and Antonio handed the candle back to the notary. He was almost certain that were he to terminate the trance now, the king would release him, but there was one more thing he wanted to do. Lodovici had told him that in the magnetic trance a person would speak the truth under all circumstances. He had had no chance to verify this fact for himself, but he was willing to take a chance that the magician had been right, for what he had to gain.

"Tell me, Frey Ignacio," he said again, "were any threats used to make Doña Catherine Sagredo testify that I used sorcery in treating her?"

The friar answered unhesitatingly, "Had she not sworn it, she would have been accused of——"

"*Válgame Dios!*" A hoarse shout from the Principe, Don Carlos, drowned out the nature of the charge which would have been pressed against the girl, but Antonio heard the word and he was sure that the king and the bishop of Toledo did as well. Eyes bulging, face congested, the Principe leaped to his feet, overturning his chair with a crash, and lurched from the room.

"Is Your Majesty convinced of my innocence?" Antonio asked quietly.

The king nodded. "Yes, Doctor. I was about to allow a grave injustice to be done you."

"And Your Reverence?" Antonio asked the bishop.

Don Diego seemed to be having trouble with his voice, but finally managed to blurt out, "I agree."

"Then I will release Frey Ignacio from the magnetic state," Antonio said. He turned to the friar. "I will count slowly, Frey Ignacio," he said. "At the count of three, you will awaken. Do you understand?"

"I understand," the friar said clearly.

"One . . ." Antonio began the count. "Two . . . THREE!"

Instantly the Inquisitor raised his head and opened his eyes. He stared dazedly around him for a moment, then his eyes cleared and his body became suddenly taut. "You have failed," he snapped at Antonio, evidently remembering nothing of the trance. "Your guilt is therefore patent."

"On the contrary," the king said evenly, "Dr. Servetus has succeeded in convincing us that he is innocent."

"I refuse to accept——" Frey Ignacio leaped to his feet, fists clenched. As he did so his right hand struck the intricate carving on the back of his chair. All present saw the bright red stain of blood against the pallid skin of his hand, but no one, not even Antonio, was prepared for what happened then.

Rigid, the friar stared at his hand, while his eyes dilated with fear. "My hand," he screamed in a voice suddenly hoarse with terror. "It is dead. There is no feeling."

The king stood up. "There is the proof for all to see," he said quietly. "You are free, Dr. Servetus."

"Thank you, sire." Antonio dropped to his knees and bowed his head. But he was thanking as well his good fortune in forgetting to return the sensation to Frey Ignacio's hand before he removed him from the trance.

Book Five

THE CASA SANTA

Antonio bent over the body of the child on the table, dissecting scalpel in hand, his sleeves rolled up to his elbows. The room was a small one on the ground floor of Vesalius's home which had been transformed into an anatomy theater. As a favor to his physician, and influenced no little by the standing achieved by Antonio following his dramatic hearing before the Inquisition, King Philip had graciously allowed the dissection of several bodies a year for the increase of medical knowledge in Madrid and its environs. Of the dozen men watching Antonio this morning, eight were physicians, the others philosophers and students, with Vesalius's apprentice, De Onis, among them. From the close attention they paid to Antonio's words and the respect they showed him, it was obvious that his situation had changed a great deal since that day when he had entered the king's audience chamber in chains.

Antonio took up the scalpel and made a rapid incision down the length of the dead child's abdomen. Through the windows the soft breeze of spring flowed, still a little crisp, for at this elevation spring came later than on the coast and in the more southerly portions of Spain. "You will note here," he pointed out, "a swelling which does not seem to lie within the abdominal wall, but comes from inside the cavity itself."

"A tumor, perhaps?" one of the doctors asked.

"A tumor of a particular kind," Antonio agreed, "if the diagnosis of Dr. Vesalius and myself is correct. Before the injury which caused its death, this child lived for many years in the swampy regions near the seacoast, where the intermittent fevers are more common than they are here."

"Both Dr. Vesalius and myself have noticed," he continued, "in Italy as well as in Spain, that where there are many attacks of intermittent fever, swelling of the abdomen is common, particularly in the region of the *lien,* or spleen."

He was working rapidly while he talked, absorbed in the dissection, and did not see Vesalius enter the back of the room with another man. The visitor was tall and sturdy, with graying hair and intelligent eyes. He wore the simple dark robe of an academician without ornament and a flat velvet cap.

"Note the muscles of the abdominal wall," Antonio continued. "How they run in different directions, like the bars of a gridiron. These have been described by Dr. Vesalius in the *Fabrica.*"

He cut through the muscles, and now the lining membrane of the abdomen, the peritoneum, appeared deep in the wound.

"Is the tumor caused by the intermittent fever?" one of the watching physicians asked.

"In a way, yes," Antonio said with a smile. "But death did not come directly from the tumor itself."

"From the fever, then?"

"Still indirectly. The child was struck on the side of its body by another while at play, a blow not ordinarily sufficient to cause death. Yet it died within a few hours." He put down the scalpel and surveyed the members of his audience. "Does anyone wish to hazard a guess as to the cause?"

"From an accumulation of humors, perhaps?" one physician hazarded.

"A sudden rise of the intermittent fever?"

Antonio was enjoying the suspense. If he and Vesalius were right in their diagnosis, this was a case to startle even the most blasé of physicians. For it would prove something of which all his medical studies and experience served to convince him more fully as time went on: that in all disease there is a direct relationship between cause and effect.

"This child," he said, "died of hemorrhage."

"*Madre de Dios!*" one of the onlookers muttered. "There is no wound, no blood."

"Both the wound and the bleeding are internal," Antonio explained. "Just as a man can die from a concealed hemorrhage following a stab wound of the lung, so we believe this child died from a hemorrhage following a fracture of the *lien,* or spleen, enlarged from frequent attacks of intermittent fever."

"But the *lien* is very rarely injured," one physician objected, "due to its protected position beneath the ribs. It is shown thus in the *Fabrica.*"

"True," Antonio agreed. "But the enlarged spleen descends below the lowest rib and no longer has such protection. It is therefore more easily injured."

There was a murmur of approval from the audience at the logic of his reasoning, and he reached once more for the scalpel. It was almost like being back in the anatomy theater in Padua, he thought, with an eager crowd of students gathered about the table while he gave the demonstrations. Could it be less than a year since he had left Padua, and hardly five months since his triumph over Frey Ignacio Molina? It hardly seemed possible, for in those five months his rise had been meteoric. Hardly less well known than Vesalius, the physician to the queen was in demand everywhere, whenever he could spare the time from the care of Messer Girolamo Bellarmi, his patron, now a semi-invalid from a gradually weakening heart. Golden ducats and maravedis had poured into his pockets and gifts of rare value had been showered upon him, but none of them had turned his head. He well knew, as did Vesalius, how capricious was the favor of princes and nobles. Every ducat, every gift, except the small amounts needed for his personal use, found their way to Lucia and thence to the vaults of the De' Medici bankers in Paris. He was a rich man, Antonio realized, thanks partly to his good fortune in having bested Frey Ignacio and no little to the friendship and help of Vesalius.

But somehow there was little satisfaction in any of it. Since the king had allowed them to dissect, his flagging interest had revived somewhat, particularly when a problem and a chance for proof of his theories presented itself, as it had today. But the rest of the time he knew that he was merely stagnating here, and the thought was not pleasant.

"We will now open the cavity of the abdomen itself," his own voice brought him back to the present.

The spectators moved closer as he nicked the peritoneal membrane with the scalpel and inserted a finger. Vesalius and the visitor also moved up beside the table where they could see better.

"There is blood in the peritoneal cavity," Antonio announced with quiet satisfaction as he widened the opening he had made. A dark fluid, partly clotted in death, poured out of the open cavity. With the scalpel he extended the incision and cleared out the blood so that the organs could be seen. Then, pushing away the remainder of the abdominal contents with one hand, he lifted the muscular wall with the other, exposing the spleen. "*Aquí está!*" he said triumphantly. "A fracture of the enlarged *lien.*"

"*Diantre!*" one of the onlookers exclaimed. "It is as he said it would be."

Half filling the left side of the child's abdomen, the organ lay, reddish blue in color, its surface rent by a star-shaped rupture of the outer layers through which pouted the inner soft pulp. Part of the surface was covered by a blood clot, as if the body had tried to close the torn and bleeding vessels of its own accord, as indeed it had. But the attempt had failed, and blood had poured from the torn spleen into the body itself, a hemorrhage as effectively fatal as if the heart itself had been penetrated by a bullet or a sword thrust.

Antonio removed the spleen quickly and put it on the table for closer study. "In almost every case, señores," he said, "one is able to find the cause and effect of disease. And if not the cause, always the effect, so that in looking back we may surmise the cause. The true study of medicine will always be at the anatomy table." He lay down his scalpels and went to wash his hands in a basin of water in the corner of the room, but the onlookers crowded around to ask questions and to praise his diagnostic acumen. It was perhaps a quarter of an hour before the room was empty except for himself, Vesalius, and the visitor.

"Dr. Vesalius," Antonio said with a smile, "I did not know you were here. You should have conducted this dissection; after all, the diagnosis was your own."

Vesalius shook his head. "Without the stimulus of a younger mind, I should never have thought of it. This is Dr. John Caius, of London. Dr. Antonio Servetus."

Antonio bowed. "I am honored, sir. The world knows of the work of Dr. John Caius."

"And before long, unless I miss my guess," the Englishman said in fluent Italian, "the world will soon know of the work of Dr. Antonio Servetus. Allow me to congratulate the author of *De Motu Sanguinem Pulmonale*."

Antonio flushed with pleasure at the compliment. Remembering the letter he had received last summer from Valentine Sims, the London printer, he asked, "Has it been printed yet in your language?"

"Four months ago," Caius assured him. "And very well received, too."

"Let us adjourn to my cabinet," Vesalius suggested. "There are many things we can discuss."

The arrival of Dr. John Caius of London was an event in Antonio's life. A student at Padua with Vesalius, having lived in the same house, Caius was now the foremost physician in England and Master of Gonville and Caius College at Cambridge. He was to English medicine what Vesalius had been to Italian.

Over cakes and wine in the secluded room Vesalius asked, "What did you think of our demonstration this morning, John?"

Caius smiled. "I think Dr. Servetus is just such another one as you were at his age, Andreas."

Vesalius twirled his wineglass and stared into the ruby depths. "It is good that you happened to come to Madrid now to remind me of what I might have been," he said slowly. "Had I possessed the courage to fight back against those who tried to stop me, I might have gone on to other discoveries."

"I wonder, Andreas," Dr. Caius said. "Perhaps the time was not ripe. Only this year, for example, have I finally gotten permission from Her Majesty, Queen Elizabeth, to carry on dissection at Gonville and Caius College." He turned to Antonio. "What has been the reception of your *consilium*, Dr. Servetus?"

Antonio smiled wryly. "I am in much the same position as Dr. Vesalius was."

"How so? There is nothing in the pulmonary circulation to bring on an attack from the clerics."

"But I am the brother of Michael Servetus."

"Of Michael——" Caius stared at him incredulously, and then a smile broke over his face. "Of course, I see the resemblance now, for I knew your brother well. But what effect could that have?"

Antonio gave him a brief account of his troubles, leaving out the attack by Fra Felipe Santos. When he had finished, Caius said fervently, "Thank God in England we are almost rid of the ecclesiastical influence in the study of science. Her Majesty has kindly given freedom of thought and action to our students."

Freedom of thought and action! Antonio turned the words over in his mind. How precious such a freedom must be! And what a wonderful land where a man could think and talk, yes, even write, as he pleased.

"What say you, Antonio?" Vesalius asked. "Would you like to study and teach in such a place?"

"It would be wonderful," Antonio's eyes shone. "There are experiments I want to make, studies to carry out, none of which can be done here."

Dr. Caius smiled. "Why not do it, then? The chair of surgery and anatomy at Gonville and Caius is empty. You need only to say the word."

Antonio caught his breath, hardly able to believe the evidence of his own ears. To live without fear, to think without restraint, to dissect and teach with no thought of how his words would be interpreted and distorted by a suspicious clergy. Here were all his dreams come true at once. And then he remembered Girolamo Bellarmi. The banker was growing steadily worse; he could not leave him now.

"You honor me by the offer, Dr. Caius," he said regretfully, "but I cannot desert my patron, Messer Bellarmi."

"Surely anyone would understand," Caius protested.

"He is in a very serious condition," Antonio explained. "Once before I caused him to have a severe attack; another one might be fatal. And I have promised him and his niece that I will watch over him."

"I had not thought of that," Vesalius admitted. "I was anxious for you to continue your work in a safe place, Antonio, so I wrote Dr. Caius several months ago, telling him about you."

"Besides," Antonio said, "I am under constant suspicion by the Inquisition, Dr. Caius. That might make a difference with you."

"I would be more inclined to accept you," Caius said. "But what is their hold upon you?"

Antonio gave him an account of his clash with Frey Ignacio. "I have read of this magnetism in the writings of Paracelsus," the English doctor said. "I had no idea that it was so powerful."

"It is too powerful," Antonio said soberly. "I do not think that I shall ever use it again."

"But if you are having trouble with the Inquisition," Caius argued, "that is all the more reason why you need to come to England where you can work without fear of them."

Antonio shook his head sadly. "Messer Bellarmi has talked of going to Paris," he said. "I thought perhaps Dr. Paré might be able to help, but it is a long journey."

"At least you would be safer there."

"I know," Antonio admitted. "And I could continue my studies."

"Always he thinks of continuing his studies," Vesalius said with a smile, "when already he knows more than most doctors learn in a lifetime." Then his face sobered, "But Dr. Caius is right, Antonio. I am beyond redemption, a fashionable doctor to the nobility but you have your life before you. Why not talk to Messer Bellarmi about it?"

Antonio shook his head. "He was kind enough to help me when my life was in danger. I can do no less than remain with him when he is so ill."

"I respect your loyalty, Antonio," Dr. Caius said. "It may be another six months before I fill the chair, and many things can happen in that time. Until I do, it is yours for the asking."

ii

Messer Girolamo Bellarmi was propped up on pillows when Antonio made his evening visit, carrying his small case of instruments and medicines. The banker's lips showed the bluish tint of plethora and he wheezed with the congested breathing of those whose circulation is slowly failing. The change had been gradual over the past few months, beginning with the severe heart attack on the morning of Antonio's brush with the beggars.

Carefully Antonio made his examination, noting the full and bounding pulse, the swollen ankles. It was his habit to draw a small amount of blood twice weekly, which seemed to decrease the plethora over the ensuing few days. As he was arranging his lancets and bowl, Lucia came in. "You are just in time to assist me," he told her with a smile.

"Unless I remember incorrectly," Messer Bellarmi said, "we three first met on just such an occasion as this."

"I have no taste for bloodletting," Lucia said soberly. "There is liable to be more than we think."

"Is the king really off to the Netherlands again, then?" Antonio asked, continuing his work.

"Soon, they say. And the queen has had another letter from her mother, begging her to keep His Majesty from being so severe with the heretics in the Low Countries."

Antonio thrust the lancet through the skin and vein with a quick, skillful stroke and moved the bowl to allow the blood to flow into it. Catherine de' Medici, Queen Mother of France, he knew, had consolidated her position with both the Catholic and Huguenot parties of her kingdom when she sent an army composed of both faiths against Le Havre to deliver it from the English. The Anglo-French Treaty, signed only a month before, had freed France from the menace of England's occupancy of the channel ports, leaving Catherine free to concern herself with internal affairs. But with the Netherlands in strife against Spain, there was always the grave danger that Catherine might be drawn into it on one side or the other. And since she desired nothing so much as to avoid any conflict, or even a decision, between the Catholics and the Huguenots of her realm, anything which decreased the strife in the Low Countries was to her advantage. For that reason, as well as the opportunity for personal benefit, intrigues were already seething afresh at the Spanish court.

And wherever such intrigues were at work there would be the evil genius of the Bishop of Toledo and his sinister arm, the Inquisitor of Madrid. Now, more than ever, Antonio knew, he must walk carefully, but with Lucia close in the confidence of the queen, it was difficult not to become involved, at least partially, in some of the scheming.

Antonio finished the bleeding and put up his instruments. "I have been thinking again today," Messer Bellarmi said, "about trying to go to Paris."

"But are you able to undertake the journey, Uncle?" Lucia asked.

"As able as I shall ever be, I suspect. And I like not your being involved in these intrigues, Lucia."

"I am wearied of them too," she admitted. "But the queen needs someone to confide in." She sighed. "Life was much happier in Florence."

Her uncle nodded. "Had I the gift of seeing into the future, how much better off we might all be. Certainly I would never have come to Spain."

"At least Spain has made me a rich man," Antonio said with a smile. "Thanks to Lucia's management."

"And my own affairs have prospered greatly here," the banker admitted. "Still I think we had best move on to Paris."

Antonio's heart quickened. Could this be the answer to his prayers? But the strain of travel would be great, he knew, and he must keep foremost in his mind the welfare of his patron, no matter how much he wished to leave Madrid himself. "We could travel very slowly, I suppose," he said. "And rest when you became tired."

"What about you?" the banker asked.

"I am eager to travel to Paris," Antonio told him. "Whenever it is safe for you."

"*Benissimo,*" Messer Bellarmi said. "I will make arrangements to close our business here within the coming month. As soon as that is completed we will leave."

Lucia and Antonio went downstairs for the evening meal. Even the prospect of leaving Spain for Paris, the gayest capital of Europe, seemed not to have elevated her depressed spirits. They began the meal in silence, but halfway through it she asked suddenly, "He is taking a chance with his own life, isn't he? In order to get me safely out of Spain."

"I think he has that in mind."

"Then how could you agree to let him do it?"

"Do you think decisions like this are easy? I have been weighing just this problem since early morning."

"Why since then?"

He told her about Dr. John Caius and his offer of the chair of anatomy and surgery at Cambridge. "That is what you really want, isn't it, Tonio?" she asked.

"More than anything else."

"But with your knowledge and ability you could become far richer in Madrid or Paris."

"There are things other than riches," he said soberly. "In fact, I am sure that gold is the least valuable thing in the world."

For a long moment she did not speak. Then he saw her shudder, as if in fear of her own thoughts. "I can't let him sacrifice himself to get me safely out of Spain," she said finally.

"You must remember," Antonio said gently, "that he knows perfectly well how short a time he has to live."

"Why don't you help him?" she burst out. "You are a physician."

"There are many things we do not understand about disease, Lucia," he said gently. "That is why I would like to work in England, where I would be free to study."

"I'm sorry, Tonio." She put her hand on his. "I have felt so alone in the past few months when Uncle has been so ill. And you——"

"I have been neglecting you, I know that," he admitted. "But I have been so busy."

"Treating the ladies of the court, I suppose." She summoned a smile. "I have heard some of them say how attentive you are."

"Never more than is necessary to treat their illness," he protested.

"Are you sure?" she teased, herself again. "I know at least two who are in love with you."

Antonio blushed. "Nonsense. They become enamored of any man that appears."

"Are you still so devoted to your divine mistress?" she asked softly.

"More than ever," he admitted. It was strange how easily he could talk to Lucia about the goddess; perhaps, he thought, because she was so nearly the divine Venus herself in the flesh.

"Why now?" Lucia asked.

He told her of his experience in the dungeon and the dream. "You never told me before that I was in your dream, Tonio," she said.

"Perhaps because you were always a shrew at first," he teased.

"And I am not any more?"

"At least not in the dream," he teased her again, but when he saw her flush he added, squeezing her hand, "You know that I am very fond of you, Lucia. You are like a sister to me. I can talk to you of things I wouldn't mention to others, even to Gian."

"Such as?" she asked, not meeting his eyes.

"The painting, my hopes for the future, many things. And I have not forgotten," he added, "that you risked everything to come to me when I was in the Casa Santa."

"Of course I would come," she said. "You needed me."

"God grant that you will never need me, Lucia," he said. "But if you do, I will come from the very ends of the earth."

"Why, Tonio," she said, her lips trembling in a smile, "that is the very nicest thing anyone ever said to me." She stood up and, leaning over, kissed him on the lips and was gone.

Antonio remained at the table, a puzzled frown on his face. Lucia had kissed him before, but never like this. The effect was pleasant and somehow familiar, like—the memory set his heart to pounding—the kisses of Clarice Strozzi that night in Gian's apartment after the ill-fated ceremony of the Black Mass.

iii

"Señor Savarino is expecting you, Doctor." Gian's servant took Antonio's cloak. "Please go into the studio." Antonio wondered why Gian had sent for him; the artist was almost never ill. At the door of the studio he stopped. Gian was talking to a tall woman whose back was turned to him, but there was something very familiar about her shoulders, neck, and head. Then she turned and smiled. "Clarice!" he cried. "This is incredible."

"Not incredible, but real, Tonio," she said. With her hands in his, looking into the familiar dark eyes that seemed, as always, to have the wisdom of the ages mirrored in their depths, he could still scarcely believe that it was Clarice. And yet there was no doubting the flesh and blood of her real self.

"We planned this as a surprise for you, Tonio," Gian said, and shouted to his servant, "Bring wine! This is an occasion for celebration."

"But how did you get to Madrid, Clarice?" Antonio asked.

"Lodovici and the troupe have been visiting the capitals of Europe," she told him. "We have been at Barcelona and Toledo and came to Madrid a few days ago."

"Then you didn't know that we were here?"

"No. But we have visited many places—Milan, Florence, Genoa, Marseilles, and now Spain. I told you once that we should meet again, Tonio."

"Then we should thank the fates," he said, but he was wondering if anything besides the fates could have engineered the appearance of Lodovici Agnolo here. They had stopped in Florence, Clarice had said, and the magician could easily have learned there that Antonio and Gian had gone on to Madrid. And there was always the possibility, of course, that Battista Porzia had told him. Still, he could see no reason why Lodovici should have followed him; his relationship with the magician had always been pleasant.

"Another month and you would have missed me, Clarice," Antonio said. "I am going to Paris."

"*Dio mio!*" Gian cried. "What is this?"

Antonio explained about Girolamo Bellarmi's desire to move on and his conversation with Dr. Caius. "I can see that it would be safer for you in Paris," Gian agreed. "But you are getting rich here."

"*Honra y provecho no caben en un lecho* [Honor and riches are seldom united]," Antonio quoted a favorite proverb of the Spaniards.

"I will make a proverb myself," Gian grinned. "It is better to have a whole skin than a filled purse. Besides, you will be teaching in England, and there is certainly no future here in Madrid."

"What is the trouble here, Tonio?" Clarice asked.

"The Inquisition."

"But do they know of your experiences in Italy?"

"So far, no." His face sobered. "Will Lodovici betray me?"

"Oh no," she protested. "He sent word to you in Venice that the order for your arrest was being issued."

Could Clarice possibly be wrong about the magician? Antonio wondered. But Gian was sure he had seen him with Battista Porzia in Venice, and he did not believe Lodovici did anything without some motive, however deep and obscure it might be.

"Tell us about Venice, Clarice," he said, changing the subject.

"We left many months ago," she said. Then she smiled. "Perhaps you knew that the prior of the Dominican monastery in Padua had been attacked by thieves who stole a valuable painting."

"How sad," Gian said, grinning. "Were the thieves identified?"

"I didn't hear, but the prior was grievously wounded and for a while there was doubt of his recovery."

"I knew you should have killed him, Tonio," Gian said.

Antonio shook his head. "I want no man's blood on my hands. Did you hear any more about Fra Felipe, Clarice?"

"Only that he is recovering. But he couldn't find you here, Tonio."

Antonio shrugged. "He was once of the Inquisition, I think. Anything is possible to them. But in a few weeks I shall be safe in France."

"I!" Gian exclaimed in high dudgeon. "You should say *we*."

"But you are doing very well here," Antonio protested.

Gian shrugged. "I am spending my father's money, and that I can do just as well in Paris. Besides, I am tired of painting women with dark skins. That is one reason I was so glad to see Clarice."

"How did you two find each other?" Antonio asked.

Clarice explained, "I usually look up the artists in any city where we are going to stay a few weeks to see if they need a model. The first one I learned about in Madrid was Gian."

"And how glad I was to see her. I am tired of painting women with their clothes on."

"From all I understand," Antonio said dryly, "some of our Spanish beauties have not been so discreet in that regard."

"Why, Tonio!" Clarice exclaimed. "You would never have said that a year ago."

"A lot has happened in a year, madonna," he said soberly. "Perhaps I should have stayed in Padua and become a monk."

"But think of what the world would have lost."

"I haven't done much for the world," he reminded her. "At least not in the past year."

"But there is Paris. And England," she protested. "This is only the intermission between the main acts of the play, Tonio."

Gian said, "Lodovici is giving an entertainment of magic at the palace tomorrow night. Are you going?"

"Not the Black——" Antonio stopped. It was just as well not to mention such things in Madrid.

"Oh no," Clarice said. "This is mainly conjuring. We have given it in many places."

"In that case," Antonio promised, "I shall be there. I always wanted to be a conjurer when I was a boy."

The attraction of that famous astrologer, conjurer, and practitioner of oriental magic, Lodovici Agnolo, was considerable, Antonio saw when he entered the palace. Crowds of richly dressed gentlemen and their ladies were moving toward the great drawing room where the entertainment would be held, and Antonio joined them, stopping to bow over the hand of a lady here, to acknowledge the greetings of a gentleman there. He was well known among the great of the court, many of whom were his patients and all of whom were anxious to do homage to one so favored by the queen.

The room was already darkened for the performance, but he saw Lucia sitting near the front and moved up to her. She was laughing as she chatted with the young Marquis of Portalerta, a handsome young man whose mahogany-colored skin betrayed his recent residence in the New World.

"Tonio," Lucia greeted him with a smile. "Don't tell me that this has taken you from your mortars and pestles."

He touched her fingers to his lips. "What better lure than your beauty, madonna?" he said and exchanged greetings with the marquis.

"I am looking forward to the opportunity of conversing with you, Doctor," the nobleman said. "I think you will be interested in some of the medical practices among the Indians."

Antonio's eyes lit up. "Name the occasion, sir," he said. "I had been hoping to find someone who was familiar with their drugs."

"It will be soon, I can promise you." The marquis excused himself and moved on to greet other friends.

"May I sit beside you, Lucia?" Antonio asked.

"It is shameless of me to say so," she whispered, "but I was holding this seat in the hope that you would come."

At one end of the room a stage had been erected. Slightly elevated above the main floor, it was closed off by fluted draperies, but as Antonio took the seat beside Lucia, they parted a little, revealing a small section of empty stage before a black velvet curtain. A hush fell over the room at this evidence of a beginning to the evening's entertainment.

"Have you ever seen such a demonstration as this?" Lucia asked.

"Not entirely. But the astrologer, Lodovici Agnolo, taught me the use of magnetism."

She looked at him in surprise. "Why didn't you tell me?"

"I only found out yesterday that he and his troupe were in Madrid."

There was a loud popping sound, as of a firecracker exploding. A puff of smoke billowed upward, hiding the open portion of the stage. From it stepped a tall man in oriental costume.

Lodovici Agnolo was an impressive figure, whether in this flamboyant oriental robe embroidered with astrologer's symbols and the conical cap affected by astrologers and magicians or in the chasuble of a priest for the horrible travesty of the Black Mass. As he stood there, his dark face and hawklike profile set off by the white background of his robe while his compelling gaze was turned upon the audience, a deep murmur of interest and astonishment rose from the crowd.

"Your Majesties." He bowed low to the small dais where the king and queen were sitting. "Grandees of Spain, señores and señoras." His deep voice carried to the corners of the room. "It is my privilege to bring to you tonight, for your education, mystification, and entertainment, some feats of conjuring, sometimes called natural magic, which my assistants and I will demonstrate for your pleasure. Strange and incredible though these feats may seem, they are completely explainable by natural means." He smiled knowingly. "If you possess the quickness of eye to see that which it is not intended you shall see, you will immediately realize the means by which they are performed."

The audience laughed. It was plain that many of them did not believe him, and the others wanted not to see the mechanism but to be mystified by the tricks.

"Enough of talk," Lodovici cried. "Let us begin. In Italy, conjuring is called the *giuoco di bussolotti*, the 'game with the measures.' In Germany the conjurer is called *Taschenspieler*. Whatever the country, the trick is the same." He reached behind the curtain and brought out a small wooden table, perfectly bare, which he then covered with a black cloth.

"Behold!" He lifted the cloth and held it some twelve inches above the table, then whisked it away. "The measures!" he cried triumphantly.

Lucia gasped and Antonio leaned forward, incredulous for the moment. Upon the small table now stood three of the tall boxwood cylinders, or measures, which had replaced the cups formerly used in this trick, the "cups and balls" from which it and conjuring got its name.

"And not only do we have the measures," Lodovici continued, "but the balls as well." He lifted each of the wooden cylinders to show the polished ball beneath it. The audience applauded vigorously.

"There is an old Spanish proverb," Lodovici continued, *"Quien mucho abarco poco aprieta.* Alas, how true!" Rapidly he lifted each of the three measures to show that they were now empty, the balls having disappeared. " 'Grasp all, lose all.' It is well said."

"How did he do it?" Lucia whispered.

Antonio remembered the books on magic that he had read in Lodovici's library in Venice. "The balls are in voluminous pockets in his robe," he explained. "Old-time conjurers used to wear an apron for that purpose, and *Taschenspieler* means 'pocket player' in German."

Lodovici was now working the oriental rope trick, a favorite of conjurers, cutting a piece of rope and apparently putting the two ends back together, just as if it had never been cut. From that he went on to more difficult feats, making small animals appear and disappear, drawing several different fluids from the same cask, appearing to cut off the head of one of his assistants, then putting it on again before the startled eyes of the crowd.

Where was Clarice? Antonio wondered. So far she had taken no part in the performance. Could it be that she was merely traveling with Lodovici as his mistress? He had gotten the impression in Gian's studio that she was an active part of the troupe.

"*Señores y señoras.*" Lodovici's voice took on a new tone of importance. "My next demonstration is so amazing that I wish you to watch it very closely. Nowhere in the world today is this feat being performed; not more than a dozen living men know the secret of the strange power which I will use to create before your very eyes a living statue."

There was a buzz of interest from the audience as Lodovici moved back to the black curtain against which he had worked during the earlier tricks. This curtain, too, parted, to reveal a beautiful woman standing in the triangular space thus created.

"Madonna Clarice!" Lodovici cried. "Beauty incarnate."

A murmur of appreciation rose from the audience, particularly from the male members. Clarice stood there, the soft folds of the Grecian draperies she wore clinging to every beautiful line of her body. Lifting her hand, so that the slit sleeves of her gown fell away to expose a perfectly proportioned arm and shoulder, she took Lodovici's outstretched hand and moved gracefully to the front of the stage.

"Tonio," Lucia whispered, "I have seen that girl somewhere before."

"Shh," he said. "Listen to what he is saying."

"As you can see," the magician announced, "Madonna Clarice is living, breathing, and very much alive."

"I know I've seen her before," Lucia said, frowning.

"Watch closely now," Lodovici was saying. "Through that strangest of all forces, magnetism, I shall turn her into marble before your very eyes." He passed his hands over Clarice's face, murmuring words which could not be heard by the audience. As if she were really being turned into marble, Clarice's features seemed to settle into a mask. Not by the slightest change of expression did she betray the fact that she was alive. Slowly his hands moved down over her body, and in their wake every muscle seemed to freeze into immobility.

"*Aquí está!*" Lodovici cried. "A statue of Ancient Greece."

There was only a patter of applause, and for a moment the magician looked displeased. Suddenly Antonio realized why the crowd had not been startled by the feat of apparently changing a woman into stone. Lodovici had stated in the beginning of the trick that he was using magnetism, which was an old story in Madrid, since Antonio's own demonstration of it upon Frey Ignacio Molina, a demonstration which, for sheer drama, no conjurer could ever hope to equal.

Lodovici, a finished performer, recovered his composure quickly. "Observe," he said. "She is truly marble." Assistants pushed two chairs forward, holding them steady by kneeling upon the seats. He lifted Clarice's rigid body now and placed her between the chairs, with her neck resting upon the back of one, the other beneath her knees. Then, using another chair as a step, he placed his full weight upon the rigid, immobile body of the girl, stretched out between the two chairs. Everyone realized that no ordinary human body could maintain such a state of rigidity voluntarily, and Lodovici once more had the undivided attention of his audience.

"Tonio," Lucia whispered while the crowd was applauding, "I am sure I saw that girl in Venice. But where was it?"

Before Antonio could answer, Lodovici's voice rang out. "But humans turned to statues are still alive. Blood still fills her veins and her heart. Look." He drew a long dagger from his robe and held it aloft. "I will show you the proof."

There was a deep, shuddering intake of breath from the audience and a collective gasp of horror as the dagger struck viciously downward toward the unprotected girl. A woman screamed as, his face contorted in a grimace, Lodovici Agnolo drove the blade apparently deep into Clarice's breast. A gory stream spouted upward, and pandemonium broke out among the crowd as the curtains swept shut, hiding the macabre scene.

Lucia was pale with horror, but Antonio said quickly, "It is a trick. Watch now." Almost before the curtains met, Lodovici reappeared. "Do not be alarmed," he said. "I have not killed her." Smiling, Clarice stepped through the curtains to stand beside him, obviously uninjured, and thunderous applause rocketed through the room as they bowed again and again.

"Thank you, señores and señoras," Lodovici shouted. "The demonstration has ended."

"Tonio," Lucia said sharply, "I remember now where I saw her.

She was with you, in a *trattoria* beside the lagoon in Venice, the day Uncle and I left."

"Yes. That was it."

"Then why didn't you tell me you knew her?"

He looked quickly about to see if anyone were listening. "I did not know until yesterday that she was in Madrid," he explained. "She has been posing for Gian."

"Oh." Lucia's eyes opened wide. "Is she a model?"

"Yes."

"Have you ever painted her in the nude?"

Antonio blushed, for no good reason, and the fact that he could not control it irritated him. After all, he told himself, he was not ashamed of having studied art, and nude studies were a part of the preparation of an artist. Still, he wasn't sure that Lucia would understand.

"Have you?" she insisted.

"Well, yes," he admitted. "I have."

Lucia's eyes widened again. There seemed even to be a new look of respect in them. "Is she very lovely?"

Antonio smiled. "You saw her. What would you say?"

"She *is* lovely. I want to meet her, Tonio."

"But she is a performer," he protested. "The queen might not approve."

Lucia stood up. "Messer Agnolo has been invited to the reception, so there is no reason why I should not meet your model. Unless," she added suspiciously, "you don't want me to."

"Why, no," he stammered. "I have no objection."

"Come on, then," she insisted.

Behind the curtain the troupe was packing its apparatus. Antonio recognized the girl, Anya, upon whom he had first exercised the power of magnetism. The magician was not to be seen, but as they stood watching the bustle of activity around them, Clarice came from a small dressing room set away from the stage itself. She was fully dressed, and when she saw Lucia and Antonio she came over to them, smiling in welcome.

"Madonna Lucia Bellarmi, Madonna Clarice Strozzi," Antonio said a little stiffly. Clarice shot him a glance tinged with mischief, but she acknowledged the introduction graciously.

"I wanted to meet you, Madonna Strozzi," Lucia said, "to tell you how lovely I think you are."

"And you, madonna, are lovelier than I expected."

"Expected?" Lucia asked.

"Why, yes. I have heard both Dr. Servetus and Messer Gian Savarino speak of you." It was a sparring match between two skilled contestants, both of whom respected the other's ability, while each waited an opening to deliver a telling blow. Watching it, Antonio felt acutely uncomfortable, but there was nothing he could do.

"I must ask Gian to show me some of his paintings of you," Lucia continued with deceptive sweetness.

A gleam appeared in Clarice's eyes. "I am afraid you would not approve of them, madonna," she said. "You see, they are all in the nude."

"It must be nice," Lucia observed, "to be so much in demand for that type of posing." She turned to Antonio. "You are very fond of such pictures, aren't you, Antonio? . . . He has even sworn fealty to such an image," she explained to Clarice.

"I know," the model said. "The Botticelli Venus. And none is lovelier."

Color surged into Lucia's cheeks, and Antonio saw that she was getting angry but didn't understand why. "I am sure Madonna Clarice must be tired, Lucia," he suggested.

"Of course," Lucia said. "Posing is such hard work, they say. I am sure you will be very popular here in Madrid, madonna. May we bid you good night?"

"Good night, Madonna Bellarmi," Clarice said quietly. "And you, Doctor."

"I hate her," Lucia said between clenched teeth, when they were out of earshot. "The strumpet."

"Now, Lucia," he protested, "Clarice isn't——"

"And you, you—worm. What right did you have to tell her about the Botticelli? The painting is mine, remember."

"But of course it is yours. I just——"

"Is nothing sacred to you, you stupid donkey?" Her voice broke and she turned suddenly and ran toward a retiring room. He watched her go with a perplexed expression on his face, completely unable to understand what had happened.

"Has your lovely madonna deserted you already, Tonio?" He had not heard Clarice come up behind him as he stood just outside the stage.

"She gave me a tongue-lashing and ran away," Antonio admitted ruefully. "And I have not the least idea why."

Clarice smiled. "Perhaps because she is in love with you."   •

"In love with me?" He began to laugh. "You are joking."

"She is a very lovely girl, with a great deal of spirit. You and she would make a fine marriage, Tonio."

"I am not thinking of marriage, Clarice," he said. "I have too much to do."

"With the right woman beside him, a man just begins to realize his capabilities," Clarice told him. "Or am I putting too much emphasis on the part a woman plays in a man's life?"

"No." He shook his head. "No, Clarice. You know I shall be eternally grateful to you for——"

"Thank you, my dear," she said a little huskily. "I shall always treasure that thought. Good night, Tonio."

"But you are coming to the reception," he protested.

"No. It would only make matters worse. Go and find your Lucia, Tonio. And make up with her."

"Make up for what?"

She smiled. "Never worry about what you have to make up with a woman for, Tonio. Just make up with her; she will understand." She disappeared behind the draperies.

As Antonio was crossing the room to the refreshment tables he heard his name called. The Marquis of Portalerta, who was talking to Lodovici Agnolo, beckoned to him, and Antonio joined the two men. "Señor Agnolo has just been telling me that he knew you in Venice, Doctor," the marquis said.

"It is a pleasure to meet you again, Dr. Servetus," Lodovici Agnolo said. "The marquis has been telling me of your success here with magnetism."

"It must have been very exciting," the marquis said. "Would that I had been here for it."

"I can see now that magnetism is an old story in Madrid," Lodovici said pleasantly. "Naturally my use of it would not create the stir that I confess I expected."

"I am a mere novice," Antonio protested. "You are a master, Señor Agnolo."

"Anyone who gets the better of Frey Ignacio Molina is more than a novice," the nobleman said. "By the way, Doctor, I am having a small supper for Señor Agnolo and his troupe tomorrow night. Would you join us?"

Antonio did not want to be discourteous, but he certainly did not want to attend the dinner if it meant spending the evening in the proximity of Lodovici Agnolo, with the magician's penchant for causing trouble. Then he remembered an engagement. "How unfortunate," he said. "Dr. Vesalius and I are addressing the Faculty of Medicine tomorrow evening upon some phases of anatomy."

"*Lo siento.*" The marquis winked and raised his eyebrows significantly. "Señor Agnolo has promised to perform some feats of magic which he does not ordinarily show the public." He spied one of his cronies beckoning to him. "Will you excuse me, gentlemen? Until tomorrow night, Señor Agnolo."

Lodovici said pleasantly, "I have been waiting an opportunity to to talk to you, Doctor, ever since Clarice told me you were in Madrid."

There was no one close to them, but Antonio knew that there were entirely too many ears in Madrid waiting to carry any bit of information they could obtain about him directly to the ears of Frey Ignacio. "Shall we go over there?" he suggested, indicating a small alcove. "We will be less liable to be interrupted."

Agnolo smiled. "The whole of Madrid is talking of your brush with Frey Ignacio Molina. Having had some experience with the Inquisition, I can understand your being careful." In the alcove he went directly to the point. "Since there are things neither of us would like to have revealed, Doctor," he said, "shall we agree to a mutual pact of silence in regard to our former affairs?"

As much as Antonio hated the thought of a bargain with the magician, there was little he could do but accept, in spite of Gian's belief that Lodovici had first betrayed him to Fra Felipe Santos and Battista Porzia and then had warned him for some obscure reason of his own.

"Perhaps you are wondering if I played any part in your troubles in Venice." The magician's voice interrupted his thoughts. "I can assure you, Doctor, that your suspicions are unjustified. Although I might well have some reasons to dislike you," he added with sardonic emphasis.

"I had no such thoughts, sir," Antonio stammered, "I assure you." But there had been a threat in that last statement, he was sure.

"Then you agree that we should remain mutually silent?"

"Yes. I agree."

"*Bueno*. Now you must tell me something of your use of magnetism."

Antonio gave an account of the cases he had treated. Lodovici was particularly interested in his cure of Doña Catherine Sagredo, and although Antonio had not planned to tell the details, he found that they were skillfully brought out through the magician's shrewd questioning.

"An extremely interesting case," Lodovici said. "I shall certainly investigate this phenomenon more thoroughly in the future. But it grows late and I weary you." They bowed politely, and Lodovici moved across the room toward the crowd around the refreshment tables.

Antonio was putting on his cloak when Gian Savarino came out. "Wait, Tonio," he said. "I will walk home with you."

"What were you and Lodovici talking about?" Gian asked as they left the palace.

Antonio told him of their pact. "You don't believe him, do you?" Gian asked.

"I don't know," Antonio admitted. "But it would be to the advantage of both of us to say nothing."

Gian shook his hand. "It would be like that devil to delude you with such a promise while he plans to betray you to the Inquisition for his own profit."

"But he could not testify against me without revealing his own guilt."

"Trust him to figure out a way," Gian said. "Are you attending the supper of the Marquis of Portalerta tomorrow evening?"

"No. Andreas and I are lecturing to the Faculty."

"I think I shall go," Gian said. "They are interesting affairs, and I would like to know more about what is going on behind the scenes these days. And besides," he added, "someone should keep an eye upon the so smart Lodovici Agnolo."

iv

Antonio was grinding a sleeping potion for his patron in a small mortar when Lucia came into the room where he was working. She was dressed in the brighter fashion introduced by Elizabeth of Valois as a welcome variant of the traditionally somber Spanish styles. Her dress was of white and gold, the ruff spotless but very narrow, the inner sleeves embroidered in lines of tiny pearls. The enormous leg-of-mutton outer sleeves, just now becoming popular with the women of Madrid, were gathered to display the rich fabric beneath. Upon her golden hair she wore a gauzy cap embellished with touches of red, and her face was powdered dead white, in the French fashion, save for patches of rouge on either cheek and upon her lips. The rich fullness of her skirt was gathered up on the sides to display the delicate lace of the underskirt.

Antonio put down the pestle and gazed at her in frank admiration. "What a beauty you are, Lucia!" he exclaimed.

"You are not the only one who thinks so," she said tartly, but he knew that she was pleased.

"I am sure of that," he agreed. "Is that a new dress?"

"Just arrived from Paris," she said proudly and turned, swirling the skirt about her like the petals of a gorgeous flower. "The Queen Mother of France sent it to me."

Antonio began to grind again. She seemed to have forgotten their little rift of the night before, for which he was grateful. "Is there another reception tonight?" he asked. Many social functions were being held prior to the departure of the king on his newest expedition to the Netherlands.

"A supper," she told him. "At the home of the Marquis of Portalerta. Gossip has it that your friend the astrologer is to present some very daring feats of magic."

Antonio frowned. Was it possible that Lodovici would have the effrontery to present the Black Mass ceremony here? Surely he must know that the attitude of the Inquisition was quite different here from pleasure-loving Venice. But Lodovici might not realize that, and the Marquis of Portalerta, having just returned from the Indies, could well have a different attitude toward such things. It was rumored that among the natives of the New World pagan ceremonies and orgies were very common.

"Who is taking you?" he asked.

"The marquis is sending his carriage. Besides, it is quite near."

Antonio dropped the pestle into the mortar. "I wish you would not go, Lucia," he begged.

"Not go!" She regarded him with astonishment. "And why not, pray?"

He fumbled for words. "It is the astrologer. I am not sure you should see some of his feats of magic."

"Have you seen them?"

"Yes. In Venice."

"Then why can't I?" she demanded. "After all, your Clarice will be there," she added sarcastically. "Surely such a fine lady would not attend if there was anything wrong."

Antonio knew that he was beaten. He could hardly pursue the subject any further without revealing his own presence at the Black Mass ceremony in Venice, and he wanted that to remain a closed page. "Promise me this," he urged her. "If Lodovici presents anything which you know you should not see, you will return here at once."

"I will promise no such thing," she said indignantly. "After all, Antonio, I am not a child."

"Then come back here when it is over," he begged. "I will wait for you downstairs."

She looked at him with annoyance. "I can't understand you, Tonio," she said. "But I was coming back here tonight anyway."

"I shall wait up for you," he promised.

The meeting of the Faculty was over quite early, and Antonio was nodding as he waited in the front parlor of the Bellarmi house for Lucia to return. The windows were open, for it was warm, and he sat up quickly when he heard rapid footsteps in the street outside. He opened the door and ran down the outer steps just as Lucia stumbled on the lower one and fell into his arms. He saw that she was completely spent from running and her gown was torn and dirty where she had evidently tripped and fallen. As he carried her up the steps and into the room, she sobbed unrestrainedly and clung to him like a scared child.

"It is all right, Lucia," he soothed. "You are safe with me now."

Presently her sobbing stopped and she said, "Tonio. Thank God you told me to come home. I was terribly afraid."

"Of what?" he asked. "Did anyone trouble you?"

"N-no. I don't think they even saw me go." She sat up. "They were all too intent upon—— Tonio, it was horrible. Why didn't you tell me?"

So Lodovici had performed one of his more ugly travesties upon religious ceremony, then. "I did warn you," he reminded her gently.

"But not that it would be so bad."

"What really happened?"

"He had a stage prepared, like the altar of a church. And he wore a chasuble . . . I thought it was a joke at first," she whispered, "until those horrible boys and girls——"

"Don't talk about it any more," he begged.

"What scared me was that I wanted to stay, Tonio. I wanted to see those things." She buried her face against his chest. "Am I depraved, like them," she asked in a whisper, "because I wanted to stay?"

"Of course not," he reassured her. "Horrible things have a way of holding your attention, like a snake."

"Somehow I feel as if I were not clean any more," she wailed.

"You are good and very sweet," he told her. "You didn't know what you were going to find, that is all."

"I kept remembering my promise to you," she said. "And then I knew I had to leave, or I would stay through the whole thing."

"I am glad you came home," he told her. "And you are safe now, so you had better go upstairs to bed." He raised his head suddenly, for his ears had detected a new sound, borne on the summer breeze through the open windows. It was the noise of shouting and running feet in the distance, and it came from the direction of the Marquis of Porta-lerta's house.

"Tonio," Lucia whispered. "What was that?"

"I don't know. Come over to the couch by the window, and be very quiet."

They crouched before the open window, so close that their bodies touched. Lucia's hand crept into his and he squeezed it encouragingly. The sounds they had heard were growing louder now. Occasionally they could see shadows darting through the trees along the street, and once there was the boom of firearms in the distance.

"Tonio," Lucia whispered, "that could be the Inquisition guards."

"Yes. I think it is."

"Then they discovered what was happening."

"Thank God you hurried," he said fervently. "A few minutes more and it would have been too late."

She crept closer to him. "I—I'm afraid."

Antonio was afraid himself. Suppose it were revealed that Lucia was at the ill-fated supper? Would the Inquisition arrest her? And Gian had been there too. "Listen," he said. "If anyone asks you where you were tonight, you went to the supper but came home at once. You have been here with me for the past several hours."

She giggled nervously. "In a house alone downstairs with a handsome young man. I would be compromised."

"Better to be compromised than tortured," he reminded her. "Now remember that story."

They huddled close together on the couch in the darkness, instinctively seeking comfort from their fears in each other. Lucia's head was upon Antonio's shoulder, and he did not realize that she was asleep until her deep, even breathing warned him. Then he shifted quietly and put his arm about her. She sighed, without waking, and settled comfortably against his shoulder. Presently he, too, drifted off to sleep.

It was hours later when Antonio came awake with the distinct feeling that he had heard his name called. Lucia was lying in the curve of his arm, sleeping peacefully. Gently he shook her into wakefulness.

"Tonio! Tonio!" The sibilant whisper sounded again, but this time, he recognized Gian's voice, calling from the stairs.

"Gian," Antonio called. "Down here."

They heard footsteps on the stairs, then the rectangle of the door was shadowed by the artist's body. At the sight of Lucia's white dress he stopped and chuckled. "Did I interrupt anything?"

Lucia sat up. "No, silly. I—I guess I went to sleep. Let me get a tinderbox and make a light."

"*Dio mio!* No light, please," Gian warned. "The Inquisition guards are everywhere."

"Then they did raid the Marquis of Portalerta's house," Antonio said.

"In force," Gian said. "But Lucia was there. How did you get away, little one? I have been running through the backyards of Madrid for two hours."

"I left early," Lucia explained, "before the guards came."

Gian chuckled. "Fortunately Portalerta had the good sense to blow out the lights and pretend he thought the guards were thieves. I even managed to break a head or two myself."

"What about Lodovici and the troupe?" Antonio asked.

"Trust him to get them out. I imagine they all escaped."

"Lucia was here with me tonight, Gian," Antonio said. "She came home very early, remember that."

"I remember it very well," Gian said, chuckling. "In fact, I was here too. And I am going to stay here. The streets are not safe tonight."

But it was a long time before Antonio could get to sleep. Lucia had narrowly escaped disaster tonight, more narrowly than she realized. Whoever had betrayed the Marquis of Portalerta's affair to the Inquisition might well have been among those attending the ceremony —it was not an unusual procedure for the Inquisition—and would have a list of those present. The thought of the slender body he had held in his arms tonight being hoisted on the rack or stretched out on the fiendish ladder of the *potro,* the "water torture," made him shudder. He remembered vividly the waddling gait of those victims at the auto-da-fé whose joints had been torn apart, the cackling laughter of the broken minds, and the stolid indifference of those to whom the torturers could bring no more pain because they were beyond all feeling. Before he would see her tortured, he vowed, he would take her life with his own hands.

v

The morning was bright, birds were singing, and the fears of the night seemed groundless in view of the beauty of the day. Antonio was busy until late afternoon, attending his patients. It was almost time for the evening meal when he returned to his patron's home. Gian and Lucia met him at the door, and he knew from their faces that there was grave trouble.

"Clarice was taken by the Inquisition last night," Gian told him.

For the moment Antonio was speechless with shock. "But I thought you said the troupe escaped," he said finally.

"They did. But Clarice was in a magnetic trance."

"I don't understand," Lucia said. "Why would that keep her from escaping?"

"She knows nothing of what happens while she is magnetized," Antonio explained. "Unless Lodovici released her, she would remain for hours without waking."

"The marquis sent word to me this afternoon that she had been captured," Gian said. "He had seen her in my studio and knew that I would want to know."

"Where is she now?"

Gian shrugged. "In the Casa Santa. Where else?"

Antonio could imagine the pleasure that Frey Ignacio and his assistants would get from torturing that lovely body. And since the Inquisitor must realize by now that Clarice had known him before coming to Madrid, he would not stop until he had extracted as much information as he could from her about the former life of the man he hated. "We must help her, Gian," he said. "But how?"

"Why must you risk yourself to help her?" Lucia demanded. "The magician is her employer. Let him do it."

"She is a friend," Antonio explained.

"Perhaps she is more than that." Lucia's cheeks were bright.

"What if she is?" Antonio said sharply. "That has nothing to do with it."

The color drained from Lucia's cheeks. "So she *was* your mistress," she said slowly.

"Don't be absurd, Lucia," he snapped. "I would help anyone taken unjustly by the Inquisition."

"She may betray you to save herself," Lucia protested.

"She would not do that," Antonio said. "I am sure of it."

"No. Clarice would never betray anyone," Gian agreed.

"Then what are you going to do?" Lucia's voice broke, and suddenly she put her head between her hands. She was distraught, and had every right to be, Antonio realized. He had been wrong to snap at her in his concern for Clarice. "Don't cry," he said, putting his hand upon her shoulder in a gesture of comfort. "I am sorry I was short with you."

She recoiled from his hand. "Don't touch me, you—you adulterer," she cried. "Oh! I hate you!" She jumped to her feet and ran up the stairs.

Antonio stared after her, perplexed. "What caused that? I was only apologizing."

"You are a good physician, Tonio." Gian shrugged. "But you certainly haven't learned anything about women."

"Don't be cryptic," Antonio said testily. "Do you have any idea where Lodovici might be hiding?"

"No. Why?"

"He could save Clarice by swearing to the Inquisition that she knew nothing of what she did while in the magnetic trance."

"Would they accept that explanation?" Gian asked doubtfully.

"It is a part of canon law on heresy," Antonio explained. "Anyone who performs a heretical act while under a spell cast by another person is not guilty of the crime."

"But he might involve you too," Gian protested. "If you got him to do it, which I don't think he will."

"I would be willing to take the chance," Antonio said, "if it would help her. But how can we find him?"

That particular question was answered sooner than Antonio expected. Sometime during the night a note was slipped beneath the door of Messer Bellarmi's house. A servant brought it to Antonio as he was going in to his breakfast. Lucia was already at the table. She returned his greeting coolly as he sat down and began to read the note.

Dr. Servetus,
If you would help one who lies in the Casa Santa, meet the writer at midnight tonight at the north corner of the Prado. Bring a filled purse; it will be needed.
Taschenspieler

"What is that?" Lucia asked, her curiosity getting the better of her pique.

He passed the note to her and she read it through. "Who is this Taschenspieler?"

"That is the name of a conjurer in German."

Her eyes widened. "Then this is from the magician?"

"I am sure of it."

"But you are not going, Tonio," she said quickly.

"Yes," he said. "I am."

"But it could be a trick. He might kill you."

"Why would he want to kill me?" he asked.

"And why not?" she demanded. "You will bring him money, which he needs if he is going to escape. And he may be afraid you would betray him to the Inquisition, to save—to save her."

It was a line of reasoning that a thoroughgoing scoundrel like Lodovici might take, Antonio realized. But if there were some way in which the magician could help Clarice and he failed to meet him, her blood would be on his conscience when she was executed. Besides, there was another alternative. If Lodovici made any threats, he could capture the magician and bargain with Frey Ignacio for the greater prize.

"Promise me you will not go, Tonio," Lucia begged. "It is a trap. He knows how trusting you are and is taking advantage of that."

"But I must see him, Lucia," Antonio said. "He might actually want to help."

"Then go on and get killed," she cried angrily, jumping up so precipitately that she overturned her chair. "It is no more than you deserve for being so stupid."

Antonio finished his breakfast and left the house. If it became necessary to try to capture Lodovici, he thought, he would need a weapon. But he possessed none, and besides, he was not adept in their use. Then he remembered Gian's small *pistole* with which he had killed Valdez. It had served him in good stead once and it might do so again.

The artist was not in his studio, but the servant let Antonio in without question and gave him the *pistole*. Antonio charged the small weapon with powder and ball, as he had seen Gian do, filled the priming pan, and placed a fresh bit of pyrites where it would strike properly when the powerful spring turned the wheel lock. Then, putting the *pistole* into his pocket along with a second charge of ammunition, he left the house.

It was still a half hour before midnight when he reached the Prado. A wooded glen on the outskirts of the city, it was a favored trysting place for lovers as well as for the early morning duels of the hot-blooded nobles of the court. But near midnight the Prado was a place of menacing shadows, of whispering voices that threatened, and dark recesses where a murderer might lie in wait for his victim, stab him dead, and melt into the shadows unseen. Antonio shivered, although the night was not cold, and wondered if he were not, as Lucia had said, a fool for coming here to meet Lodovici. The note had said the north corner of the Prado, and he was early, so instead of cutting through the woods he traversed the path along the edge, staying in the open spaces where the pallid face of the moon cast a little light.

As he walked he loosened the weapon in his belt and tested the tension upon the spring with his thumb. Tensely he stared into the shadows, walking more slowly as he approached the appointed corner. The woods were between him and the city now as he moved along the outer side of the wooded space, and he felt alone and apprehensive.

Then a familiar voice said, almost in his ear, *"Buenas noches,* Doctor. I see that you got my note."

Antonio jumped. He had neither seen nor heard the magician, yet Lodovici was standing almost at his elbow. Had he wished to do so, Antonio realized, Lodovici could have planted a dagger between his shoulder blades without his ever knowing what had happened.

"W-why, yes," Antonio stammered, moving away from the magician's tall form. "What is it you wanted to tell me?"

"You brought the gold I mentioned?"

"Yes." Antonio felt for the *pistole* with a furtive movement. He did not like Lodovici's being so obviously concerned with his purse. Then his hand stopped and his body went suddenly stiff with fear.

"If you are looking for the little *pistole,*" Lodovici said sarcastically, "I relieved you of it just now. It occurred to me that you might think of taking me to the Inquisition."

"N-no," Antonio protested feebly. "I had no such thought." Lucia was right, he thought. Lodovici had made a fool of him and he would be lucky to escape with his life.

"I am sure you did not," the magician said briskly. "And now to business. We are both rather fond of Madonna Clarice. Unless I am mistaken, you have been, shall we say, rather intimate with her upon occasion?"

Antonio wondered if Lodovici could see the rush of blood to his face in the darkness, betraying his guilt.

"Madonna Clarice has been my mistress for many years," Lodovici continued, "so you can understand, I am sure, that I had every reason to kill you, especially when I found you armed. In fact," he added with cool impudence, "you owe me your life, Dr. Servetus."

"What about Clarice?" Antonio asked hoarsely. "You could have prevented her being captured by stopping to terminate the trance."

"There was not time. And unfortunately no one was there to attend to her, as on a former occasion."

"You could at least swear that you forced her to take part in the Black Mass ceremony while in a state of magnetism," Antonio said. "That would be the truth."

"And put myself on the *garrucha?*" Lodovici inquired. "I am sure you understand my reluctance to do that." The *garrucha* was the hoist, a popular torture engine with the Inquisitors. "But there is another way," he continued. "It would mean some sacrifice on your part, however."

"I will do anything I can," Antonio promised.

"You are a rich man, I understand, Doctor. It is often possible to arrange an escape if funds are applied in the right places."

"But the agents of the Inquisition are everywhere."

"True. But to a master of deception such as myself it should be possible to make one's way to France, where the Inquisition is not in power. Some gold would be needed, naturally."

"Most of my funds are in France," Antonio said. "I have only about three hundred ducats with me."

"So?" Lodovici's disappointment showed in his voice. "That is little enough. I will take it and see what I can do."

Antonio reached for the bag at his belt and began to untie the strings. Then a new thought occurred to him. "What guarantee do I have that you will not use this to leave the country yourself?" he asked. "Without Clarice?"

The magician's laugh was not pleasant. "No more guarantee than you had that I was not luring you here to slit your throat."

Antonio untied the bag of coins and handed it to Lodovici. "Will you keep me informed of the progress you make?"

"Naturally." Lodovici secured the bag at his own belt. "After all, are we not countrymen?" His tone was mocking. *"Buenas noches,* Doctor." The tall form melted into the shrubbery, like one of his own illusions.

Antonio turned away to the path leading around the wooded Prado toward the sleeping city. It was as Lodovici had said: he had to trust him. But the more he thought about the magician's manner, the less confident he became.

Whether it was the rustle of a sleeve as the dagger arm was uplifted or the strange sixth sense that sometimes warns of danger, something made Antonio turn before he was three steps away from the spot where Lodovici had disappeared. In any event, the movement saved his life. The magician stood almost over him, the moonlight gleaming upon a naked blade in his hand. In his youth Antonio had been accounted a good wrestler, in the catch-as-catch-can style favored by the tall mountain people of northern Italy. Long forgotten as it was, the instinctive memory of this lore served him well now, and as the black-robed figure struck viciously with the dagger, he threw himself sideways and reached for the dagger arm. His fingers closed about a wrist that seemed made of steel bands, but the movement was sufficient to divert the blow, and Antonio thrust out his right hip to catch the magician's body in a pivoting wrestling throw.

Unbalanced by the sudden movement of what had seemed an easy prey, Lodovici Agnolo was tossed end for end to crash against a tree. Antonio saw the dagger fly from his hand and bury itself to the hilt in the soft earth. Automatically he stooped to pluck it from the dirt, but Lodovici kicked upward and sank his foot into Antonio's groin. Retching, almost blinded by the pain from the foul blow, Antonio sagged to the ground, but rolled instinctively to put himself out of reach of those powerful legs. His arm struck the dagger and his fingers closed upon the handle even as Lodovici, having gotten to his feet, leaped upon him with the evident intention of finishing him off. Setting his back against the earth, Antonio pulled the dagger from the ground and at the same time kicked upward to deflect the magician's body away from him. Tripped by the movement, Lodovici fell heavily just as the dagger came free.

There was a gurgling cry and the metal blade was wrested from Antonio's grasp. A sickening warm flood poured over his face and neck, and a heavy weight sagged upon him, suddenly limp. With a surge of triumph, and horror, too, Antonio realized what had happened. Lodovici had impaled himself upon the dagger, and it was blood which was pouring over his face and neck. Slowly, trembling and weak, Antonio pushed aside the limp body of the conjurer and got to his feet. Panting with the effort of the fight, swaying wildly on unsteady feet, he looked down at the dark lump which had so nearly been himself, then, quelling his revulsion at touching the now inert body, he stooped and untied the bag of money from the dead man's belt. As he straightened up he heard someone shouting his name.

"Tonio! Tonio!" It was Gian's voice.

"Over here," Antonio called. "The north corner."

A crashing in the bushes near the center of the Prado marked Gian's progress toward him. Seconds later the artist appeared, panting heavily and carrying a naked sword in his hand. "Have you seen Lodovici yet?" he gasped.

Antonio pointed to the dark figure on the ground.

"Sangre di Cristo!" Gian recoiled in horror. Then he saw that Antonio was covered with blood. "You look like a butcher. Tell me what happened."

When Antonio came to Lodovici's cowardly attack, the artist cursed savagely. "You have rid the world of a scavenger," he said. "Did you get the money back?"

"Yes." Antonio held up the small pouch.

"Then we must go. Someone may have heard me shouting."

"What about him?" Antonio asked.

"Leave him for the vultures," Gian said callously. "He was one himself."

Halfway across the Prado, Antonio asked, "How did you know to come here tonight?"

"Through no help from you," his friend growled. "Lucia got worried about you and came to tell me about the note. When my servant told me that you had taken the *pistole,* I knew you had been fool enough to fall into Lodovici's trap." Then he chuckled. "Not that you needed me. You have learned to take care of yourself very well, what with killing two scoundrels in half a year."

vi

It was Antonio's custom to stop at the home of Vesalius shortly after the morning meal. But when he entered the anatomist's cabinet two mornings after his encounter with Lodovici Agnolo, he stopped short in the door. Sitting in one of the comfortable leather chairs across from Vesalius was a tall, spare man in the habit of the Dominican Friars. It was Frey Ignacio Molina.

Vesalius rose to greet his young associate. "We were just waiting for you, Antonio," he said.

"Buenas dias, my son," Frey Ignacio said blandly. "God be with you on this lovely day."

"It is indeed a fine day." Antonio found his voice.

"For the righteous, yes," Frey Ignacio said. "But not for a poor heretic conjurer named Lodovici Agnolo, I am afraid."

Antonio forced himself to be calm. He must be careful not to display too much interest.

"The city guards found him in the woods of the Prado yesterday," the Inquisitor continued, "foully murdered. Knowing that a warrant for his arrest had been issued by the Holy Office, they brought him to us." He clucked sadly. "Stabbed to death, he went to his fate unshriven and forever damned. Had we been able to take him sooner, we might have been able to convince him of the error of his ways and thus insure the salvation of his soul."

"What of the murderer?" Vesalius saved Antonio the trouble of asking.

"For the moment, he is at large. But we suspect his identity and no doubt he will be captured." The Inquisitor's eyes were upon Antonio's face, watching every change of expression. "Fortunately we were able to save one of the conjurer's assistants."

"Save?" Antonio echoed. "I don't understand you."

"The poor woman was so misguided as to practice witchcraft," Frey Ignacio explained. "I still have hopes of saving her soul from eternal torment."

"At the price of the garroter's noose," Antonio thought to himself.

"Frey Ignacio has just been telling me about this woman," Vesalius said. "It seems that she was taken during a magnetic trance, and the stupor lasted for some hours."

"It would terminate itself in natural sleep," Antonio said, "unless ended sooner."

"I am very much interested in this strange power of magnetism," the Inquisitor said. "Perhaps we can discuss it sometime."

Antonio bowed. "It would be a privilege, Your Reverence." Frey Ignacio was driving at something, he was sure, but he could not yet tell what it was.

"The Holy Office," the friar continued, "does not often have the unpleasant task of putting a woman to the question, and there are some who have unkind things to say about us. In the case of this poor victim, it has occurred to me that we should have a physician in attendance during the questioning."

Antonio stiffened. What more diabolical scheme could the lean figure opposite him have planned than this? Suspecting that Antonio had known Clarice before, he would have him witness the horror of her being put to the question. From one or the other of them, he undoubtedly expected to obtain evidence which might place Antonio, too, in his power.

"Dr. Vesalius agrees with me," Frey Ignacio said, "that it would be best if you assisted us in this matter."

"But Dr. Vesalius is a physician of far more experience than I," Antonio protested hoarsely.

"Not in cases involving magnetism," Vesalius pointed out. "And since this woman was taken in a trance, I felt that you would understand her condition better than I."

Antonio felt a cold fear settling deep within his body, clamping a band of steel about his heart. How diabolically clever the lean friar was! He had tricked Vesalius himself into suggesting that Antonio be present at the questioning, putting him in a position where he could hardly refuse.

Frey Ignacio got to his feet. "Can we count upon you, Dr. Servetus?" he asked. "I would like to hold the next hearing this evening."

"I will endeavor to be there," Antonio agreed. Actually, he realized, there was no choice. If he failed to appear, the wily Inquisitor would have still another reason for suspecting his guilt of heretical practices and ordering his arrest. But of one thing he was certain: Frey Ignacio would not arrest him again until the evidence was strong enough to insure his execution at the stake.

When Frey Ignacio was gone, Vesalius said, "It is curious, but I don't remember a physician being asked to attend a questioning before."

"This is merely for my benefit," Antonio told him. He explained about his previous acquaintance with Clarice Strozzi and Lodovici Agnolo.

Vesalius combed his beard with his fingers. "This is all beginning to fall into a pattern," he said thoughtfully. "Your favor with the queen, your saving Don Pedro's life, your first experience before the Inquisition, and now their second attempt to involve you."

"What pattern do you mean?" Antonio asked.

"The affair with the Netherland heretics," Vesalius said. "It seems quite evident that the king is about to change his tactics against them. Did you know that he is planning to replace the Duke of Alba with Don Pedro Grijalva?"

"But that would mean the abandonment of the policy of persecuting the Flemish heretics!" Antonio cried in astonishment.

"And a signal victory for the Queen's party and Catherine de'

Medici," Vesalius agreed. "It is about time. Alba's policies were a disgrace to our civilization."

"But the Bishop of Toledo would not take such a decision without a fight, would he?" Antonio asked.

Vesalius shrugged. "Maybe he is resigned to the inevitable. He is giving a dinner tonight, and I hear that Don Pedro Grijalva has been invited."

Frey Ignacio Molina raised his eyes from their habitual contemplation of his fingers as Antonio entered the audience chamber. "It was kind of you to come, Doctor," he said. "Please sit at the end of the table."

Antonio knelt before the crucifix for a moment, then moved to the place assigned him. The make-up of the tribunal was as he had seen it before.

"The poor sinner we are going to question has already had one hearing," Frey Ignacio explained. "Unfortunately she still refuses to divulge the names of her associates."

"But if she were taken in a magnetic trance," Antonio protested, "she would have no knowledge of what she did."

"True," the Inquisitor admitted. "But undoubtedly she had participated in such ceremonies before. She must have known for what reasons the trance was induced." He turned to the guards. "Bring in the accused heretic," he ordered.

At the sight of Antonio, Clarice paused for a second, then, without any further sign of recognition, she walked, straight and lovely, to stand before the table and her judges. Her cheeks were marble pale, and Antonio saw, from the rapid flutter of the pulse at her throat, that her heart was pounding rapidly.

"Clarice Strozzi," the notary read. "Prisoner of the Holy Tribunal, accused of the heresy of witchcraft and sorcery, and of associating in these practices with the necromancer, Lodovici Agnolo."

"Yesterday, my daughter," Frey Ignacio said, "you confessed to the sin of participating in the heresy of the invocation of Satan through the ceremony known as the Black Mass. Be sure that your confession to this grievous sin has removed a great load from your soul. But sin is not expiated by confession only. You must identify those who have been associated with you in such practices, so that they, too, may be saved from eternal damnation."

Clarice lifted her head. "I take the burden of sin upon myself, Holy Friar."

Frey Ignacio's voice changed; it grew kind and soft, and Antonio looked at him in surprise. "Now it is very foolish of you, my daughter, to persist in this denial when the details of this matter are well known to me. Already others have named some of them."

Was he lying? Antonio wondered. Had any others of the troupe been captured? It was an accepted practice of the Inquisition, he knew, to make such statements, even though not true, on the grounds that any amount of dissembling was justified if it were intended to save souls from the eternal torment demanded for heretics.

"My daughter," Frey Ignacio persisted, "do you still refuse to identify those guilty of heresy with you?"

"I have nothing to say," Clarice murmured.

"Look there at the end of the room, then," he commanded. "These are the instruments which must be used, according to Holy Law, to teach those who refuse stubbornly to admit their sins the folly of their stand. It is not my desire that you should suffer the pain of these instruments, but if you insist upon defying us, we have no choice under the law but to proceed. Look at them now and tell me if you persist in your stubborn refusal."

Seen close at hand, the machines of the Inquisition were diabolically simple, for all their power to break human wills. Simplest of all was the hoist, nothing more than a rope running through a pulley attached to one of the crossbeams of the ceiling, a simple application of the principle of the pulley to be found everywhere. But its use here was peculiarly suited to the needs of the Inquisitors. Nearer was the rack, that devilishly ingenious Procrustean bed designed to separate limb from limb by rupturing the joints themselves. And to one side, by itself, the instrument favored most by the Spanish Inquisitors since the time of Torquemada, the *escalera,* ladder, or "water torture." Nothing ever designed by the evil genius of the Holy Office equaled in horror this combination of garrotement and strangulation.

Other methods of torture, less spectacular but effective, such as rubbing the soles of the victim's feet with fat and toasting them before a naked flame, tearing out the fingernails with pincers, and hanging from the ceiling by the neck, only to be cut down just before strangulation was complete, were favored by some Inquisitors.

"There is nothing else to confess," Clarice said. "I have told you everything."

Frey Ignacio's fingers clenched and the light in his eyes burned brighter. "The *potro*," he said softly.

A squat man who had been waiting beside the machines came up to her. "Raise your arms," he commanded.

Clarice tried to obey but could hardly move them, and the man reached out and jerked them up. She screamed with pain, and Antonio gripped the edge of his chair as the reason became clear to him. This was not her first experience with the torture instruments; she must already have experienced the hoist. Nothing else crippled the shoulder joints quite so effectively as that simple machine. With the wrists lashed together behind the back and a rope attached to them and carried up over the pulley, the victim's arms could be lifted backward merely by pulling on the other end of the rope. As the pressure was gradually increased, the heels of the victim could be cleared of the floor, leaving the whole weight of the body to be borne by the overextended arms and shoulder joints. Should this preliminary agony not suffice to bring the desired confession, the body was then hoisted upward and let drop, to be arrested suddenly, a maneuver which frequently dislocated the shoulder joints.

"Has this woman been tortured already?" Antonio demanded.

"Her hearing was begun yesterday," Frey Ignacio said blandly, "and is being continued today." The Inquisitors frequently evaded the strict laws of the Holy Office that a victim could not be put to the question more than once by discontinuing the question temporarily and resuming it on another day. It was not only the single period of agony, but the repetition of it over and over, which caused the victims to break down, as much from anticipation of further torture as from the agony of the question itself.

With a single movement the torturer ripped from Clarice's body the rough garment worn by the accused during the question, leaving her nude. Antonio felt a surge of fruitless anger at this wanton display of her lovely body to the lascivious gaze of the guards and the members of the tribunal itself. The notary at the end of the table licked his lips nervously; it was obvious that sights such as this were not often afforded the members of the Holy Tribunal. Antonio saw now that Clarice's shoulders were swollen and discolored from the hoist.

At a nod from the torture master, two of his assistants wheeled into the room a strange-looking machine, little more than a short ladder mounted on wheels. Its appearance was deceptive, however, for this was the ladder of the *potro,* the "water torture," so much favored by the Spanish Inquisitors, and one of the most evil machines ever invented.

With rough hands they lay Clarice upon the ladder, face upward, and bound her arms and legs to the wooden frame. To each leg and arm cords were also applied but left loose, encircling the limbs above the knee and elbow. The ladder was then slanted so that her head was lower than her feet, and a leather cuff was applied about her forehead by which her head was lashed to the top crosspiece of the ladder, holding her rigid and unable to move.

"Clarice Strozzi," Frey Ignacio's voice rang out, "are you ready to name your associates?"

"I have confessed all." Her voice was low but clear.

"Proceed, then." His voice was like a whiplash. "Perhaps you would like to see this closer, Doctor," he said graciously. "It has a certain medical interest."

Antonio had no choice but to accede. From the ladder Clarice's eyes stared fixedly at the ceiling, but her face was marble white in its pallor and her lips were bloodless except for a spot of red where her teeth had bitten through the flesh.

Now the torture master took up a peculiarly shaped piece of metal. It had two prongs and a strap with which to fix it in place. Prying open her mouth, he inserted one of the prongs behind her lower teeth and the other inside her upper jaw, distending her mouth just short of dislocating her jaws. With the strap he fixed the instrument to the side of the ladder. Antonio recognized the device from his reading: it was the *bostezo,* or gag. Her nostrils were next securely plugged so that she could breathe only through her mouth. From a small chest containing his accessories the torture master now took a long strip of cloth which he bound across her mouth, covering the gaglike *bostezo*. This was the *toca,* the real device through which this diabolical instrument operated.

"The garrotes," the torture master directed, and his assistants inserted small sticks into the loops about Clarice's legs and arms. Slowly they twisted the sticks, tightening the cords until they compressed the skin.

At a nod from Frey Ignacio, the torture master took up a pitcher of water and began to pour it slowly upon the *toca,* where it lay loosely across the *bostezo* in Clarice's mouth. And now Antonio could see the fiendish ingenuity of this method, for as the loose cloth filled with water, it was carried backward by its own weight, sinking ever deeper into her throat. Inevitably some of the water seeped through the cloth, and in the agony of near strangulation, she tried futilely to swallow and clear her throat for breathing. She could obtain air in no other way, for her nostrils were tightly plugged.

"Tighten the garrotes," the torture master ordered, and his assistants began to twist the sticks that tightened the cords about her limbs. Antonio could see them bite into Clarice's flesh and the skin change from its normal white to an unhealthy bluish tinge as the pressure closed the thin-walled veins, distending the tissues with blood. Torn between the agony of trying to swallow and slow strangulation, Clarice writhed against the lashings that held her body. But she succeeded only in spilling more water from the *toca* and increasing her difficulty in breathing. Slowly her struggles grew weaker and her face took on a bluish tint of near asphyxiation.

"As you can see, Doctor," Frey Ignacio said, "the *potro* is a peculiarly effective instrument."

"It is inhuman," Antonio croaked hoarsely.

"Drastic measures must be used to save souls from eternal damnation. Surely you can see that."

Antonio looked at the Inquisitor. The light that burned in those deep-set eyes was so utterly satanic in its unholy pleasure that the realization came to him with a physical shock. Frey Ignacio was enjoying this spectacle of human agony, enjoying it with that strange perverted sense of pleasure in pain which he had read about but never before seen. Had he but known, it characterized most of the Inquisitors of the day.

Just when it seemed that Clarice must suffocate, the torture master removed the *toca.* Barely conscious, she managed to swallow the water which had accumulated in her throat and drew in her breath with great shuddering gasps. Frey Ignacio bent over her. "Confess, my daughter," he urged. "Name your accomplices and this agony will be spared you."

But Clarice, with a strength of will which Antonio knew he would not have possessed, managed to gasp out, "There is nothing to confess."

"Apply the *toca,*" Frey Ignacio ordered.

Antonio wondered if he could stand it any longer, but knew no way to help Clarice in her agony. Once more the terrible process began, and as he watched her futile struggles to breathe, Antonio remembered how close Lucia had been to this same fate that night at the home of the Marquis of Portalerta when she had barely gotten away before the arrival of the Inquisition guards. What inhuman pleasure the torture of that slender body would have brought to these fiends in black!

The agonizing struggle for breath was repeated again, and once more the garrotes bit into Clarice's limbs. The agony from them alone, Antonio knew, must be almost intolerable. Then suddenly her whole body went limp and there was a strangling sound as water poured unhindered down her throat.

"She has fainted," Antonio cried. "Quick, or she will drown."

But the torture master was on the alert for just such a complication, and he jumped immediately to the *toca* and ripped it from her mouth, lowering the head of the ladder at the same time until her body was almost vertical. Water poured from her throat and lungs, and in a few seconds she coughed and began to breathe again.

"That is enough!" Antonio shouted at Frey Ignacio. "Do you want to kill her?"

"We will discontinue the question," the Inquisitor said blandly, "and resume on the morrow."

"Tomorrow!" Antonio echoed with horror. "Surely you will not do it again."

"We have no choice, my son. The fate of her immortal soul is at stake."

"But canon law forbids the question more than once."

Frey Ignacio said sharply, "We have only discontinued, not finished it. The questioning is not complete until the prisoner confesses to the crime and names those associated in it. Unlash her and remove her to the dungeons," he directed his assistants. Then he turned to Antonio again. "Will you accompany her doctor and see that she recovers from this faint?"

Antonio nodded, too angry to speak. Had words begun to come from his mouth, he knew that they must have been curses upon the inhumanity of the tall figure in the black robe. And that, he realized, would have been playing directly into Frey Ignacio's hands.

The guards placed Clarice on the narrow bench in her cell and departed. Only the turnkey remained, and Antonio said, "I will take care of her. You can return in a short time."

The man hesitated, and Antonio took out a gold coin from his purse. "You can leave us and return in half an hour, can you not?"

The man's eyes gleamed at the sight of the coin. "I understand, señor," he said, pocketing it. It was evident that others had paid occasionally for the privilege of being alone with female prisoners.

Clarice was breathing more quietly now and the color was returning to her limbs, although the cruel marks of the garrotes showed dark red against her white skin. Antonio took a small bottle of hartshorn spirit from his case and held it beneath her nostrils. She coughed from the pungent vapor and opened her eyes.

"Tonio." She started up from the couch, clutching him by the shoulder. "Tonio. Is it over?"

"Yes. You fainted."

"Look out in the corridor," she said urgently. "See if anyone is listening."

Through the barred door he could see that the corridor was empty. "No one is there." He began to rub her limbs to help them recover from the effects of the garrotes.

"It is you he wants, Tonio," Clarice said. "He suspects that I know something from Italy that he can use against you, and he is trying to make me swear that you have engaged in heretical practices before, along with the magnetism."

So he had been right, Antonio realized. And so had Vesalius. This was part of a plan to involve him so deeply that not even the king would dare to interfere in the work of the Holy Office again.

"Tonio." Her eyes were suddenly wide with fear. "You said I fainted. That means they can put me on the ladder again."

He shook his head. "I will not let them. You must not pay for my sins any longer, Clarice."

"No, Tonio," she said. "Nothing can save me now. He has already told me that my sentence is death; by the garrote if I swear to the lies he has written out for me, by fire if I do not."

"At least I can save you the fire, then, by telling him what he wants to know."

"No, Tonio," she pleaded. "I have sinned and I must pay for it. But you have something to give the world." She put her hand upon his. "Promise me that you will do what I am going to ask you."

"What is it?"

"You must promise, Tonio. For me."

He was sure what it was that she wanted of him. But how could he take another person's life upon his conscience? And yet he recognized that it was the merciful, the humane thing to do. He had promised himself that he would take Lucia's life rather than let her suffer the agony through which Clarice was going. Could he do less for Clarice?

"I promise," he said finally. "You want me to help you to take your own life, don't you?"

"Just give me something better than the garroter's noose," she said.

Antonio fumbled in his small case. He carried no poisons, so it would have to be an ordinary drug, taken in an overdose. And the only one effective for such a purpose was the powerful extract of the opium poppy, now being more and more widely used for the relief of pain. From the case he removed a fairly large bottle containing enough of the drug to cause a sleep from which one would never recover. It was certainly a far more pleasant way to die than the garroter's noose. But with the bottle in his hand, he hesitated still. This was murder, in whatever cause committed. Was such an act ever justified? his conscience demanded.

The footsteps of the jailer could be heard returning now, and with a quick movement Clarice snatched the bottle from his hand and hid it under the coverlet. "God bless you, Tonio mio," she whispered.

"The time is up, señor," the turnkey said from the doorway.

Antonio closed his medicine case. "Good-by, Clarice. You are very brave."

"God bless you for your kindness," she whispered.

Outside the building, Antonio looked back at the forbidding gray walls, illuminated by the cold embrace of the moonlight, then turned through the sleeping city toward the house of his patron.

vii

To his surprise, Antonio saw lights burning all over Girolamo Bellarmi's house when he approached, although it was close to midnight.

Could the banker have suffered another heart attack while he had been at the Casa Santa? he wondered, and hurried up the steps, fumbling for his key. But the door was opened before he could unlock it, and he saw Lucia, unnaturally pale, standing there. "Tonio," she cried. "Thank God you have come!"

"What is it?" he asked anxiously. "Your uncle?"

"The Marquis of Grijalva is sick."

"But not here," Antonio said, aghast.

"Yes. He came about an hour ago, looking for you. Oh, Tonio, I am sure he is very ill. And when I couldn't find you——"

"I was at the Casa Santa."

She gasped. "Have you been arrested?"

"No. Frey Ignacio was putting Clarice Strozzi to the question and insisted that I be present."

She understood at once the danger in that situation. "Did she tell about—about the Black Mass?"

"No. Where is Don Pedro?"

"In your bedroom. He collapsed on the steps."

Don Pedro Grijalva lay doubled up in bed, his face ashen pale, his hands clasped tightly over his abdomen as if he were in severe pain. "I have been poisoned, Doctor," he gasped.

Antonio felt his pulse. It was fast and very weak. The rest of the examination fitted the diagnosis of a severe irritation of the stomach such as poison would cause.

"Get hot water," he directed Lucia. "Put mustard in it and have the servants bring in several basins."

"What are you going to do?" the marquis asked weakly.

"Empty your stomach," Antonio said. "How long ago was the poison taken?"

"Several hours. At a dinner given by the Bishop of Toledo. I ate little but a custard at the end of the dinner."

Antonio remembered now that Vesalius had said the Minister of State was giving a dinner at which Don Pedro would be present. But would Don Diego Espinosa dare poison, or have poisoned, the man who had been chosen by the king to replace the notorious Duke of Alba in the Netherlands?

"Surely," he said, "it was an accident. Perhaps something you ate disagreed with you."

"It was no accident," Don Pedro said grimly. "And I ate only the custard." A spasm of pain made him writhe for a moment, then he managed to continue. "What better place to get rid of me? No one would dare voice a suspicion of poisoning at a dinner with the Minister of State."

"You had better be quiet," Antonio admonished him.

"Promise me this, Doctor. If I die, you must perform a post-mortem examination and determine for sure that I was poisoned."

"I am sure nothing will happen," Antonio said soothingly, but in his heart he knew that the signs were already becoming grave.

Don Pedro's eyes closed, and for a moment Antonio thought he had become unconscious, but he opened them again and his lips moved. "I am a soldier, Doctor," he said in a whisper. "I will die when my time comes, but I want my murderer punished. If you find poison, go directly to the king."

The emetic arrived, but by that time Don Pedro had lapsed into a semicoma and it was not possible to use it. Antonio wrote a short note to Vesalius and dispatched it by a servant. At a time like this, with a patient as important as the Marquis of Grijalva dying under strange circumstances, he wanted the older physician's experience and authority behind him.

Andreas Vesalius arrived within a scant half hour, accompanied by his apprentice, De Onis. He examined Don Pedro with Antonio, and when he had finished, his face was grave. "It is unquestionably a case of poisoning," he agreed.

"Can you think of nothing else to do?"

Vesalius tugged at his beard. "A decoction of chinaroot might be effective," he said. "It is our only hope."

"But there is no time to make a decoction," Antonio protested.

"Wait," Vesalius said. "I was treating a mercenary with the French pox this morning. There is an ample amount of the decoction in my cabinet." He turned to De Onis. "You remember where I put it, do you not?"

"On the shelf with the dried roots, I believe, sir," the apprentice said.

"Go quickly to the house and bring it here. And lose no time."

When the apprentice had departed, Antonio said, "Don Pedro is certain that he was poisoned at the dinner given this evening by the Bishop of Toledo."

"Madre de Dios!" Vesalius exclaimed. "They are daring a great deal, but it is just such a plan as might succeed."

"That is what Don Pedro said," Antonio agreed.

"This will undoubtedly alter the king's plan to replace Alba and initiate a better policy in the Netherlands."

"I suppose I am next on the list now," Antonio said thoughtfully.

"What is keeping De Onis?" Vesalius exclaimed angrily a few minutes later. "He should have been back before now." He bent over the sick man and made a brief examination. "We may not even need the chinaroot. His heart is failing."

But it was another half hour before the apprentice arrived, panting, with a bottle clenched in his hand.

"What kept you?" Vesalius snapped, taking the bottle from his grasp.

"I—I had trouble finding it," De Onis gasped.

Vesalius reached for a goblet from the table by the bed and poured the contents of the bottle into it. They would have to take a chance on pouring the decoction down the sick man's throat, hoping that he would swallow it automatically, even in his coma.

"Wait!" Vesalius cried. He held the goblet beneath his nose. "This is not chinaroot."

"It is the flask you requested," De Onis protested, but his swarthy cheeks paled.

"The flask, yes. But not the contents." Vesalius turned savagely upon his apprentice. "What stupidity is this? You have brought mandragora." He handed the goblet to Antonio. "Smell this."

The strong aroma of mandragora assailed Antonio's nostrils. There was enough in the goblet to kill six men, and they had been on the point of pouring it down the throat of the already dying man.

"I took the flask as you instructed me," De Onis babbled. "It is not my fault."

"Not your fault, you worm?" Vesalius shook his fist at his cringing apprentice. "I believe you were deliberately trying to poison the marquis."

Suddenly they realized that something had happened in the room, and for a moment no one knew what it was. Then Antonio cried, "Don Pedro has stopped breathing." Quickly he felt for the pulse. Beneath his fingers it gave a few last faint beats, like the fluttering of a dying bird, then was still.

"He is dead," he said slowly. "We are too late."

Vesalius, too, felt the pulse and confirmed Antonio's diagnosis. "We will never know for sure now whether he was poisoned," he said heavily.

"But we will," Antonio cried in a sudden rise of excitement. "He made me promise to perform a post-mortem examination if he died, to try and prove that he was poisoned by the Bishop of Toledo."

There was a muffled exclamation from the apprentice, but Vesalius paid no attention to him. He was looking at Antonio, his eyes bright with excitement. "*Benissimo!*" he cried, lapsing into Italian. "We will perform the post-mortem examination at once. It should give us the proof we need for the king."

"But the permission," De Onis stammered. "It is illegal to open a body without authority."

"*Bastante!*" Vesalius commanded. "The marquis himself authorized Dr. Servetus before his death. Get your instruments quickly, Antonio."

As Antonio returned from the cabinet with his instruments, Lucia came out of her room. "Don Pedro is dead," he told her soberly.

"Oh," she gasped. "Then he *was* poisoned?"

"Undoubtedly," Antonio agreed.

"But if he is dead, what are you going to do with those?" She pointed to the instruments.

"He asked me to perform an autopsy if he died," Antonio told her.

"But what good will that do now?"

"We may prove that he was poisoned by Don Diego Espinosa, or at least upon his orders."

Her eyes widened with fear and she shivered. "It is dangerous, Tonio," she whispered. "Please don't do it."

"Nothing can go wrong, Lucia," he assured her. "It is merely a dissection. Both Dr. Vesalius and I have done hundreds of them. And we may be able to convict Don Pedro's murderer."

"Be careful, then," she begged. "I—I'm so afraid, Tonio."

"Don't worry," he told her. "Soon we will be in Paris, and safe."

Vesalius had placed a number of candles around the bed upon which Don Pedro's body lay. "Let me do this dissection, please," he begged when Antonio brought the instruments.

"Gladly," Antonio said. "You are more experienced than I am." Neither of them noticed that De Onis was not in the room.

Vesalius removed his shirt. He opened the case of instruments and took out a sharp scalpel. Antonio held a lantern over the body so that the anatomist would have ample light for the dissection, and with a practiced sweep of the scalpel, Vesalius began.

The abdomen was quickly opened; that was where they expected to find the evidence they sought. A reddish-black fluid welled up from the cavity itself. "Is the intestine perforated?" Antonio asked, leaning over the bed.

"I believe so, or at least badly irritated," Vesalius said. "I will examine the stomach." Reaching into the abdominal cavity, he lifted that organ into view. *"Caspita!"* he exclaimed. "Look there!"

All the evidence they needed was plainly visible in the markedly irritated stomach, darkened here and there by patches where the poison had eaten its way into the wall of the organ. "The stomach is almost empty," Vesalius reported.

"He told me he ate nothing but a custard," Antonio said.

"That is why it acted so quickly, then," Vesalius agreed. "Whoever worked out this little plan must have counted on the presence of other food in the stomach to slow the action of the poison and make it less evident what was causing the trouble. But when Don Pedro ate little else, their plan went awry."

"I will look at the heart," he continued, "then we can remove the stomach as evidence for the king."

Among the instruments was a heavy-bladed forcep intending for cutting off teeth. In the hands of the anatomist, it bit through the ribs as if they were twigs. Vesalius worked to cut away enough of the bony cage of the chest to create a window through which the organs could be seen.

Somewhere in the house there was a peculiar sound, as if many feet were moving about. Antonio turned his head to listen, and when it came again, he put down the lantern and moved to the door.

"What is it?" Vesalius asked, tugging at the ribs as he cut through the muscles between them.

"I don't know. A door slammed." For the first time Antonio noticed that the apprentice was not in the room. "Did you send De Onis away?"

"Why, no," Vesalius said. "He was here just before we started the examination." Then he shrugged. "He is a coward. Probably could not stand such a gory sight."

Again Antonio heard the sound, and now it seemed definitely that of many feet tramping heavily. Vesalius lifted the window he was cutting from the dead man's chest with a grunt of satisfaction. "Look there, Antonio," he said. "The heart *in situ* and perfectly normal. Death could have come only from the poison."

Suddenly the door of the room was flung open, pushing Antonio back against the wall. Dazedly he saw armed men pour into the room, the light from the candles shining upon the polished morions and halberds of the Inquisition guards. The tall officer leading them drew up short before the bed, and Vesalius looked up in astonishment. Then a smaller figure pushed to the front and Antonio heard De Onis cry, "Look there! The heart is still beating."

For a second there was absolute stillness in the room, then Vesalius roared like an infuriated bull, "Liar! This man has been dead for almost an hour."

De Onis was babbling excitedly to the tall officer and pointing at the body of Don Pedro Grijalva. The officer hesitated, then, under the urging of the apprentice, cried, *"Madre de Dios!* It is true. You have been cutting open a living man."

Vesalius dropped the scalpel and, with his hands still dripping blood, seized his apprentice by the throat. "You lie! You miserable dog!" he shouted. "This man was dead before you left, and you know it well."

The officer seized Vesalius and pulled him off the trembling De Onis. *"Silencio!"* he snapped. "You are under arrest."

Antonio had recovered his wits now and came from behind the door where he had been driven by its sudden opening. "It is as Dr. Vesalius said, señor," he assured the officer. "The Marquis of Grijalva died almost an hour ago. Both of us will swear it."

"Bastante!" the officer said curtly. "I saw with my own eyes that the heart was beating."

"And so did I," De Onis shrilled.

"Judas!" Vesalius spat at him. "So you were in the pay of the Inquisition all the time, and spying on me."

De Onis drew his slight body proudly erect. "I am a familiar of the Holy Office. And I will see you burn as a heretic."

"Get that blood off your hands and come with us," the officer told Vesalius curtly. "And you too," he added to Antonio.

"But Dr. Servetus was merely observing," Vesalius protested.

With the back of his mailed gauntlet, the officer slapped the anatomist, knocking him to his knees. *"Cállese usted!"* he barked. Vesalius got to his feet slowly, blood trickling from the side of his cheek where the gauntlet had struck him. Now that the anatomist was held by the guards, De Onis stepped closer and spat into his face. Fired by a sudden burning rage, Antonio moved before the guards could detain him, and felt a wild surge of pleasure as his fist smashed into the apprentice's dark face and he saw his eyes suddenly glaze and his body crumple to the floor.

Two of the guards shoved Antonio through the door. As he was stumbling down the stairs between his captors, he saw Lucia staring at them from the doorway of her room, her face white with concern. "Tonio." The words formed on her lips, but he shook his head at her in a warning not to speak and call attention to herself. There was one consolation, he thought, as the little procession marched from the house. They had not included Lucia in the arrest on this trumped-up charge to keep him and Vesalius from making known to the king their indisputable evidence that Don Pedro had been poisoned. But for the unfortunate fact that the traitor, De Onis, had accompanied Vesalius here tonight, their plan would certainly have succeeded.

A few minutes later the portals of the Casa Santa closed behind them. This time, Antonio knew, they would almost certainly never open again for him, except to begin the walk that led to the stake.

viii

The morning after his arrest Antonio was again brought to the audience chamber of the Casa Santa in chains. He was surprised that he had been arraigned so quickly, for the Inquisitors usually left their victims in solitude for some time, counting upon the horror of confinement in the rat- and vermin-infested dungeons and the physical effects of hunger and thirst to further weaken their wills. As he looked around the room he saw with a start of surprise that Clarice was stretched out on the rack. Had she taken the opium he had given her? he wondered. Or had the jailers discovered and destroyed it?

And then he realized that she might have delayed taking the drug until she was certain that they did indeed mean to resume the torture. Having been a prisoner himself, he could understand how she might have waited through the long hours of the night, clinging to the faint hope that something still might save her. But had she been able to swallow it, finally, in time?

"The prisoner, Clarice Strozzi, is in some kind of a stupor," Frey Ignacio told him curtly. "I suspect that it is related to this magnetism in which you are so adept. Bring her out of this stupor."

Antonio went over to the rack upon which Clarice's body was strapped. Leather cuffs about her arms and legs were attached to ratchets by means of which the machine exerted its force. Already they had been tightened until the leather bit into the flesh, but Clarice showed no signs of consciousness.

"She does not speak," the torture master grumbled. "Yet she breathes and her heart beats."

"How long has she been like this?" Antonio asked.

"We found her thus in the dungeon."

The stupor of opium was written in Clarice's slow breathing and the tiny pupils of her eyes when he lifted the lids. She was already beyond any human ability to cause pain, he realized. Fortunately, none of the Inquisition people were likely to recognize the symptoms of opium poisoning, but he knew that he must be very careful not to arouse their suspicions, else the charge against him would be double murder.

"Bring her out of the stupor," Frey Ignacio demanded.

"I can do nothing," Antonio told him.

"You lie! You must have put her into this state when you accompanied her back to the cell last night. The turnkey says you were with her half an hour."

"But I can do nothing for her," Antonio insisted.

"Do you refuse to obey me?"

"It is not that I refuse," Antonio explained. "I cannot do it."

"Put him to the hoist," Frey Ignacio snapped. "We will see if he can be convinced."

A cold fear gripped Antonio. There was nothing he could do for Clarice now, no matter how much they tortured him. "It is against Holy Law to use torture on one who is not charged with a crime," he protested.

Frey Ignacio merely shrugged. "The hoist."

The torture master grinned mirthlessly and, seizing Antonio's wrists, pulled him across the room to where the rope of the hoist hung from its pulley. With deft movements he unlocked the manacles, pulled Antonio's wrists together behind his back and lashed them together with a short length of rope. To this he now attached the end of the long rope of the hoist and pulled down upon the other end until the rope tightened, stretching Antonio's arms up behind him. The pain was severe as overstretched muscles protested against this insult, and Antonio felt the sweat of pain and fear break out on his face.

"Now, Doctor," Frey Ignacio said, "are you still stubborn?"

"But I cannot bring her out of it," Antonio protested.

The torture master swung his weight upon the rope. Slowly, agonizingly, Antonio was lifted from his feet by his backward-extended arms, until the tips of his shoes barely cleared the floor. His body swung there, turning slowly, while pain tore through his shoulders and the muscles of his arms until he cried out with it. For perhaps a minute he swung, while the agony in his shoulders sent waves of nausea through him. Raising his body to try and relieve tortured shoulder joints gave only momentary relief, for his muscles soon tired and the weight of his body sagged against his overextended arms once more.

"Now, Doctor?" There was the same look of unholy pleasure in the Inquisitor's eyes that he had seen there during the torture of Clarice.

"I—I cannot," Antonio gasped. "I swear that I am telling the truth."

The notary had been standing close to Clarice, his eyes fastened gloatingly upon her beauty. Suddenly he cried, "Your Reverence! The woman is dead."

"Dead," Frey Ignacio echoed, his voice suddenly rising. "She cannot be."

The torture master dropped the rope of the hoist and ran to the rack. Frantically he spun the ratchets that were applying pressure to her body. Antonio was left standing beneath the hoist, his wrists still attached to the rope, reeling with pain and nausea. Even in his agony he recognized why they were working so frantically to remove Clarice from the rack. Inquisition law was very strict regarding the death of persons under torture. It was a crime upon the hands of everyone who participated in the questioning. But most guilty of all was the Inquisitor in charge of the hearing. His guilt could be expiated only by a suitable penance, one rigidly insisted upon by the laws of the Holy Office. Inquisitors were therefore very careful not to allow a death to occur under such circumstances, but this time Frey Ignacio had made a grave error. Believing that Clarice's stupor was only another evidence of magnetism, he had put her to the torture again when she was actually near death from opium poisoning.

But if the torture master were able to remove Clarice's body from the rack before she could be pronounced dead, they could still claim that she had not died under the torture, thus freeing Frey Ignacio from blame. The least he could do for Clarice now, Antonio thought, was to insure that the Inquisitor must pay for her death.

In the excitement following the notary's warning Antonio had been ignored, and now he moved to the rack, dragging the long rope attached to his wrists. Quickly he bent over and laid his face against Clarice's breast, knowing that if she were breathing, or her heart beating, he would feel the lift of her chest against his cheek or the pulse of her heartbeat beneath the left breast. With his hands tied behind him as they were, he could not feel for the pulse at the wrist.

Frey Ignacio was the first to divine his intention. "Stop him," he ordered, but before the guards could jerk him away, Antonio raised his head. There had been no movement of Clarice's breast, no flutter of her heart. She had died peacefully, unconscious from the lethal dose of opium she had taken that morning.

"Upon my oath as a physician"—Antonio's solemn pronouncement held all of them, even the Inquisitor, motionless with surprise—"I declare that this woman is dead and that she died upon the rack while under the question."

For an instant the shocked silence in the room was a palpable thing, then Frey Ignacio shrilled like a fishwife, "Heretic murderer! You lie!"

"I am a physician," Antonio said quietly, "a member of the Faculty of Medicine of Madrid. Upon my oath before this notary, I swear that this woman died upon the rack while under torture."

Frey Ignacio was livid with rage, his frail body trembling, his eyes burning like twin coals of hate. For a moment Antonio thought he was going to leap upon him and braced himself for the shock and the pain of those clawlike hands tearing at his face. Then suddenly the Inquisitor's rage was replaced by a crafty look. "You were with her last evening, Doctor," he said. "What did you give her to take her own life?"

"You cannot mitigate your own guilt, Frey Ignacio," Antonio said coldly. "I call upon everyone here to witness that under Holy Law you must expiate the crime of the death of this woman." The very least an Inquisitor could do in expiation, he knew, was to perform a retreat for penance. If he accomplished nothing save to remove Frey Ignacio from Madrid for a while, it would help many a poor devil, if not himself.

"We will search her cell at once," Frey Ignacio said. "There must be some evidence there of whatever drug you gave her. And you will accompany us, Doctor."

At the dungeon block where Clarice had been confined, Frey Ignacio asked the turnkey, "Has anything been removed from the cell of the woman, Clarice Strozzi?"

"But no, Your Reverence," the man said. "Since the doctor, here, left her last night, I have not entered the cell."

"Open it for us."

The narrow bench that served as a bed was the only furniture in the empty cell. Upon it lay the tattered quilt which had served to soften a little the bare surface of the boards. Clarice had placed the bottle of opium under the quilt last night to hide it from the turnkey, and Antonio's heart quickened its beat with apprehension as Frey Ignacio jerked the quilt from the bench. But there was no crash of breaking glass. Somehow Clarice had managed to get rid of the bottle. But how?

And then his eyes spotted the hole in the corner of the cell at the floor level through which water was sluiced occasionally to clear out the refuse and excreta of the occupants. The morning light, falling through the small barred window, struck into this corner, and he saw a gleam, as if something which reflected light had been shoved into the drainage opening. Clarice had pushed the bottle into the drain after taking the medicine, he realized, and at any moment Frey Ignacio's eyes might notice the small drain.

Unobtrusively, while the guards were turning over the debris that littered the floor, Antonio moved along the wall toward the drain. His foot touched it and, moving his toes about, he felt the smooth surface of the bottle against the soft leather of his shoe. With a quick movement he kicked the bottle farther along the drain and seconds later heard the faint tinkle of breaking glass as it dropped into the stone-lined sewer that ran through the walls and carried off the refuse from the Casa Santa.

Frey Ignacio's head jerked up. "What was that?" he snapped.

Nobody else knew, and Antonio volunteered no information, so the search was soon given up as fruitless. The Inquisitor was in a cold rage, certain that Antonio had somehow managed to give Clarice a drug

with which she had taken her life, but he had no proof and must therefore bear the blame himself for her death.

"Take him back to his cell," he said finally and stalked out.

To Antonio, sitting in his own cell, there was small comfort in
having bested Frey Ignacio again. Clarice was dead, Andreas Vesalius
in prison, and who knew when Lucia and Gian would be arrested on
some trumped-up charge? Never had his position been more hopeless
or had there been less chance of escape with his life, when escape had
been so near. A few weeks more would have seen him, Lucia, her uncle,
and Gian out of the reach of the Inquisition. But for the fact that Don
Pedro Grijalva, tortured by the poison which was burning its way
through his body organs, had sought help last night from the man who
once before had saved his life, all would have been well. In all of this
there was one comforting thought: Messer Bellarmi would be sure now
to take Lucia to safety in France as quickly as possible.

ix

Night followed day and week followed week, with nothing to distinguish one day from the next save the change from light to dark and
dark to light. But someone—he suspected the influence of the queen—
was making Antonio's stay in the Casa Santa more comfortable than on
his previous imprisonment. He was in a different block of cells, more
elevated and less patronized by the huge gray rats that prowled the
prison at night. And his diet was considerable better, although still
hardly sufficient to sustain life.

By doling out his meager hoard of money, Antonio managed to obtain from the turnkey regular reports about happenings in the Casa
Santa. It was in this way that he learned about the trial of Andreas
Vesalius before the new Inquisitor who had replaced Frey Ignacio
when he departed on a retreat of penance for the death of Clarice Strozzi.
Vesalius had been tried for heresy and murder in opening the body of
Don Pedro Grijalva when, according to witnesses, the heart was still
beating, and for certain heretical utterances reported by his former apprentice, De Onis. The evidence which would have established the truth
of his claims that the marquis had died of poison had unfortunately
disappeared when Don Raffaele Grijalva, as the next of kin, had claimed
his uncle's body and buried it with indecent haste.

The new Inquisitor, reports ran, had not been nearly so hard upon Vesalius as Frey Ignacio would have been, and his final sentence was one of banishment, rather than death. It was also rumored that the influence of the king had been placed behind his former physician and had played no little part in the final verdict. Hearing all this, Antonio's spirits rose. Without the venom of Frey Ignacio, and before this new and reputedly more lenient Inquisitor, he might have a chance of proving his innocence, or at least of getting off with a lighter sentence. And so, when he was taken to the audience chamber of the Casa Santa one morning, it was with something of a feeling of anticipation that he entered the room.

The chamber itself was, as always, bleak and forbidding, with the macabre engines of the torturer's profession at one end, grim reminders of the power of the Holy Office. But only one man was sitting behind the table, a tall figure in the robe of a Dominican of high station, his head bowed as if in prayer. Something about his shoulders and his spare but powerful frame seemed vaguely familiar to Antonio.

Then the Inquisitor raised his head, and for an instant Antonio's heart ceased to beat. He felt the room sway about him and fought for control of his reeling senses, unable to credit what his eyes clearly perceived.

For it was Fra Felipe Santos who sat behind the table, Santos, his nemesis from Padua. And then the remembered mocking voice broke the silence. *"Buenas dias,* Dr. Servetus," he said. "No doubt you are surprised to find another of your friends from Italy here in Madrid."

"How did you get here?" Antonio croaked.

Fra Felipe leaned his elbows on the table and put his fingertips together. "The Inquisitor of Madrid, Frey Ignacio Molina, and I are very old and dear friends. Naturally when I was informed by Messer Porzia that you had left Italy for Spain and Madrid, I wrote to him about you. Some months ago he notified me that you were here and engaged in certain heretical practices. I came to Madrid as soon as my health permitted, and since Frey Ignacio was absent, I have been selected to serve in his stead as Inquisitor of Madrid until his return."

"You know, then," Antonio said, "that I was cleared of guilt for any heretical practices before the Holy Tribunal."

"By a trick." Fra Felipe shrugged. "But tricks will avail you nothing now. I am not without experience in my position, Dr. Servetus." Antonio remembered now that Santos was reputed to have been an Inquisitor, and that his zeal had resulted in so many deaths under questionable circumstances that he had been moved to another position.

"Unfortunately," the churchman continued, "the painting you stole——"

"It belonged to Madonna Lucia Bellarmi," Antonio corrected.

"So?" The friar's eyebrows lifted. "How poetic! And you recovered it in the service of your lady? That makes my task easier."

"Your task?"

"That of obtaining your confession of guilt for the crimes you have committed and seeing that you are justly punished."

"I have committed no crime," Antonio maintained. "You attacked me and I protected myself from assault."

"If I remember correctly," Santos corrected him, "you attacked me first in Padua to keep me from calling for help. That should be sufficient to insure that you follow in the footsteps of your heretical brother. The laws of Holy Church are very strict regarding crimes against the person of Her servants."

Antonio knew that this was true. But there had been only two of them present at the fight, and it was still the word of the friar against his. "The law requires more than one witness," he pointed out.

"But not when the accused confesses the crime. Here, let me read your confession to you, Doctor. I have taken the liberty of preparing it in advance."

"I will not sign it," Antonio cried. "You have no proof."

"Do not be hasty," Santos said. "At least let me read you the confession. It is very short." He took up a paper lying on the table before him.

"I, Antonio Servetus, physician of Padua in Italy and Madrid in Spain, do confess that on the fifteenth of August, Anno Domini 1563, in the Priory of the Dominican order at Padua, I did, without provocation, attack the person of the Holy Prior of that order, Fra Felipe Santos, with the intention of accomplishing his death. But for the defense of himself by the Holy Prior, I would have succeeded in this design, but, failing in my attack, I did then escape from the priory, leaving him grievously wounded and unattended. For this act I freely confess my guilt, without any use of force against my person and of my own free will, and I request the punishment for my sin prescribed by the laws of our Holy Church."

Santos put down the paper. "You know the punishment prescribed by canon law for such a crime, I believe."

"Yes," Antonio admitted. It was death at the stake, without the mercy of the garrote.

"Are you willing to sign the confession?"

"No," Antonio said firmly. "It is a foul lie."

Santos smiled. "I rather expected you to be stubborn, Doctor," he said. Then he turned to the torture master who was waiting beside his machines. "Bring in the other prisoner."

The door at the far end of the room was opened and a woman was pulled into the room. She wore the rough garment of a prisoner in the Casa Santa, and suddenly Antonio realized why Fra Felipe had seemed so confident that he would have his way. For it was Lucia who stood there, her face pale, her head proudly erect, unutterably lovely even in the rough garb of a prisoner.

"Would you not rather sign the confession, Doctor," Santos asked, "than see this lovely child broken upon the rack?"

Antonio stared at Fra Felipe, even now unable to believe that such cruelty, such a complete disregard of everything that God and His Son stood for, could exist under the guise of a religious order. He saw no mercy or compassion in the eyes of Santos, but rather the same look of unholy delight in human terror and suffering that he had seen in those of Frey Ignacio Molina. He could expect no mercy for himself or Lucia from such fiends under the cassock.

"She is innocent," Antonio said hoarsely. "She has done nothing."

"Perhaps," Fra Felipe said. "We can only know when she has been put to the question." His voice cracked through the room. "Strip her and apply the hoist."

Before Antonio could protest, the squat torture master had seized the rough garment that Lucia wore and torn it from her body. For an instant she stood like a marble statue, frozen with horror and shame, then instinctively one hand moved to cover her breasts, the other to her loins.

Antonio heard the notary at the end of the table draw in his breath in a great shuddering sigh. But it was not the revelation of Lucia's slim, nude loveliness that held his own startled gaze. For, standing thus, shielding her breast and loins from the profane gaze of the men in the room, she was poised in the exact position of the Venus of the Botticelli canvas. And line for line, sweet young curve for curve, even to the symmetry and perfection of her features and the crowning gold of her hair, she was the divine Venus of the painting.

Seeing her thus in the glorious loveliness of flesh and blood, Antonio knew in a moment of blinding revelation that he had been a fool. It was not the Venus of the painting that he had loved all along, but Lucia herself, the girl who had slept in his arms the night Clarice Strozzi had been taken by the Inquisition, the girl who had dared to enter the Casa Santa to help him, the girl who had been steadfastly by his side through all of the adversities which had beset him in Spain.

The artist in him, he recognized now, had fallen in love with the painting before he had ever seen Lucia. For a while, too, he had been unable to separate the artist within him from the man. But it was the man who had loved Lucia since that first day in the priory, and it was the man who cried out now, in the ecstasy of his discovery, "Lucia! It was not the Venus. It was you all the time."

At his words and his tone, the crimson flush of shame began to fade from her face and she lifted her head proudly. Her eyes were luminous as they met his across the room, sharing their love in this tragic moment of its realization.

Fra Felipe Santos leaned forward. "Santa Maria!" he breathed. "She is really the Venus of Botticelli." Then suddenly he began to laugh.

Antonio launched himself across the table at the Inquisitor's throat, knocking over the silver crucifix. But the manacles on his wrists and the leg irons hampered him, and the guard standing close by easily dragged him back short of his goal. "Have you no shame? No humanity?" he raged, struggling still to reach the friar.

Santos wiped his eyes. "Forgive me, Doctor," he said, "but this is something out of a heroic tale. Or perhaps we should say a Greek tragedy. Madonna Lucia *is* the Venus of the Botticelli canvas. I remember now her uncle Mario telling me that Simonetta Vespucci, the sister of Amerigo, was the model for the painting, and that his niece in Florence was the image of it."

"It is really a perfect tragedy," he continued. "You nearly kill me for the painting, then at the end of the story you discover that you love the woman it represents . . . only to lose her in the end."

The words fell upon Antonio's ears like the pronouncement of doom. He had found Lucia only to lose her. But at least in losing her, he thought, he could make sure that she would be safe. Fra Felipe must not be certain that he could convict him upon the same flimsy charges which had served for Vesalius; certainly he could not demand the death penalty when Vesalius had only been banished. So he had devised this confession to insure that he would receive the penalty of death by fire. But in his eagerness to get the confession signed, Fra Felipe might be willing to bargain.

"I will sign the confession," Antonio told him, "if you swear that Madonna Lucia will be allowed to leave the country, free and unmolested."

"That is the chivalrous gesture I would expect from you," Fra Felipe said. "But you are not in a position to bargain."

"I think I am," Antonio told him, hoping his voice sounded cool and certain. "You know you cannot give me the death penalty for the same charge that you used to sentence Vesalius to banishment. But if I sign the confession you can send me to the stake. My price is Madonna Lucia's safety."

"Very well, then," Fra Felipe said. "I agree to your price, as you call it." He reached over to the notary's quill stand—the same crystal ball which Antonio had used to trick Frey Ignacio into magnetizing himself—and took out a quill. Dipping it into the ink, he handed it to Antonio and shoved the paper containing the confession across the table for him to sign.

"No, Tonio! No!" Antonio heard Lucia cry as he bent over to sign the confession that was also his death warrant. But when he lay down the quill, she had already been removed from the room.

x

It was amazing, Antonio thought, how calm one could be in the face of certain death, once all hope had been removed. The calm was compounded partly of relief that there would be no more appearances in the grim audience hall of the Casa Santa where the Holy Tribunal met and partly from the knowledge that Lucia was safe. By now she must certainly be well out of Spain with her uncle, probably already in Paris. His confession had insured their safety, and if his life must be sold for the price of Lucia's, then it was a price he was willing to pay.

But there were darker hours when he thought of what their life to-gether might have been in England, now that he realized how much he loved her and that she loved him. With Lucia beside him to help him with her courage and stimulate him with her spirited intelligence, he could have gone on to new discoveries, new experiments in saving men from disease and suffering. But that was all over now, and he won-dered sometimes why his execution was being postponed. The only rea-son he could think of was that he was being saved for another auto-da-fé, probably for Frey Ignacio's return.

Then, ten days after he had signed the confession, Antonio had a visitor. It was night and the cell was dark when he heard footsteps ap-proaching along the stone-floored corridor. Soon the faint brilliance of a lantern could be seen and a man approached, wearing the robe of a Dominican friar, with the cowl pulled well over his eyes. Only when he faced about and came to the bars of Antonio's cell was his identity apparent.

"Gian!" Antonio exclaimed.

"Careful," the artist warned. "We must whisper."

"But how did you get here?"

"Bribed the guards," Gian said. He leaned closer and dropped his voice to such a low whisper that Antonio could hear him only by press-ing his ear between the bars. "I have been working to arrange your escape."

"It is no use, Gian," Antonio said hopelessly. "You will only get yourself in trouble."

"But they will burn you at the stake, Tonio. It is rumored that you will be executed at an auto-da-fé when Frey Ignacio returns next week."

"I am resigned to it, Gian. Now that Lucia is safe."

"Didn't you know?" Gian asked. "She is still in the Casa Santa."

Antonio gripped the bars. "You must be wrong, Gian. Fra Felipe swore that he would let her leave the country at once if I signed the confession."

"It was a trick," Gian said. "I talked to her here in the prison not more than a few minutes ago."

"But Santos promised——"

"You know that no one connected with the Inquisition can be trusted," Gian said. "Girolamo Bellarmi died the day after Lucia was arrested. . . ."

"God rest his soul," Antonio murmured. The banker had been a good man, but with his weakened heart, the shock of Lucia's arrest could easily have brought on his death.

"Lucia is his heir," Gian continued. "There are large sums to the Bellarmi account still in Madrid, so you would hardly see the Holy Office letting a prize like that escape." The possessions of those convicted of heresy were confiscated by the Holy Office. More than once, Antonio knew, prisoners had been executed because of the riches that their confiscated estates would bring to the Church, and not because of their guilt.

"There is a warrant for my arrest, too," Gian said. "But the queen has been hiding me."

Antonio felt a cold anger against Fra Felipe Santos and all he stood for sweep away all of the calm of resignation he had achieved in the past week. And in that instant he would have cheerfully throttled the lean friar if he could have reached him. There was no place for peace and forbearance in a world where such creatures were given power, he thought. He had tried to help right and truth prevail and faced death for his pains. Now his responsibility was to Lucia; somehow they must help her to escape from the Casa Santa.

"You spoke of escape," he said to Gian. "Do you have any plans?"

"The queen has furnished the money to bribe the guards," Gian said. "If we can get clear of the Casa Santa and Madrid, she will supply us with horses and a safe-conduct that should get us across the border and into France."

"Then our problem is to get clear of here," Antonio said. "But how?"

"It will not be easy," Gian said, "but there are a few things in our favor. A number of new familiars and Dominican friars have recently come to the Casa Santa, and I know the guards outside do not know all of them. The turnkey and several of the inner guards are in my pay, and I am sure that I could get you out of the prison disguised as a friar, but that would not work with Lucia. She is too small."

"We must think of something else, then," Antonio said.

"It is a lot easier to get out dead than alive," Gian said glumly. "Twice I have seen them carrying out coffins when I came in."

"Gian!" Antonio's voice rose with excitement. "We will carry Lucia out in a coffin."

"But how?"

"Can you bring one into the Casa Santa, empty?"

Gian nodded. "Yes. That ought to be easy enough," he said. "They have been carrying them out the rear entrance; that is the way I come in."

"You can do it, then," Antonio urged. "You have to do it, Gian."

"But suppose the outside guard opens the coffin to make sure we have a corpse inside."

"Lucia will look like a corpse," Antonio promised. "I will magnetize her."

"The way Clarice was turned to stone by Lodovici," Gian said, catching Antonio's excitement. "I think it might work, Tonio."

"It has to work," Antonio said soberly. "If it doesn't . . ." Then he said briskly, "You had better get out and make the arrangements. When do you think we should try?"

"Tomorrow night," Gian said promptly. "Frey Ignacio might return earlier than we think. I can have the coffin made in the morning."

xi

As the day passed and the night for the escape grew on, Antonio felt a rising excitement, tinged with apprehension. So many things might go wrong with their daring plan that he could not allow himself to brood upon them, lest he be plunged into despair. But the reward of success! To be clear of these cursed walls and in a free country, with a new life before him and Lucia at his side.

It was two hours before midnight when he heard footsteps and saw the faint glow of a lantern approaching down the corridor. He was waiting at the door when Gian unlocked it with the key he had also obtained through bribery. While Antonio peeled off the verminous garment of the prison and pulled the thick, dark folds of the robe Gian had brought over his head, the artist gave him a quick summary of their progress toward freedom.

"Everything has worked like a charm so far," he reported. "The coffin is in Lucia's cell. My servant is there with her."

"Can we trust him?"

"We have to," Gian said grimly. "But his brother was killed by the Inquisition and he knows he will be a rich man if we win through to France."

"Did you have any trouble getting into the prison with the coffin?"

Antonio asked, pulling the cowl of the dark robe of a familiar over his forehead so that his features were hidden beneath its shadow.

"The guard at the door let me in without question. He will be expecting me out again in a little while."

They moved through the corridors of the darkened prison, seemingly a Dominican friar and a black-robed familiar, frequent enough sights here. It was an effort to hold their eager strides to the measured tread of one bound on priestly duties, but it would not do to betray themselves by their haste.

Lucia was sitting on the bench in her cell, staring at the empty coffin on the floor. Gian's servant, a tall and capable-looking fellow, was dressed like Antonio, save for the hilt of a dagger visible above the cord that encircled his waist.

When Antonio pushed back the cowl of his robe, Lucia threw herself into his arms. "I though you were dead, Tonio," she sobbed.

"It is all right, darling." The term came naturally to his lips as he held her against him and soothed her fears. "Control yourself. Our time is short."

She raised her head and wiped her eyes. "I—I am ready," she said.

"You know what we plan to do?"

"Y-yes." She glanced at the coffin and shivered. "I—I am not afraid," she whispered, "when we are together."

"We will always be together," he promised. "Now lie on the couch and do exactly as I tell you. On no account must you resist."

"I understand." She managed a smile.

Antonio directed the servant to hold the lantern a few feet above Lucia's body, so that she could easily fix her eyes upon the small flame inside it and the glow of light surrounding the flame. There was no time to manufacture any other source of light; the lantern must do.

"Watch the flame, Lucia," he said. "Watch it and think of nothing but what I say."

Obediently her eyes settled upon the burning wick and the pear-shaped brilliance of the flame itself. Never, even in the drama-filled moments when he had tricked Frey Ignacio into becoming magnetized, had Antonio concentrated so hard upon his task. Fixing his eyes upon hers, he began the monotonous chant which he had learned was so effective in bringing on the sleeplike state. Presently Lucia's eyelids drooped and her head rolled to the side until her cheek lay against the dirty pallet that covered the bench.

"Can you hear me, Lucia?" he asked.

"Yes, Tonio," she said drowsily.

"You must do as I say, dear. Your body is growing stiff in every muscle. Do not resist. Soon you will lose all power to move and you will remain rigid until I release you."

"Yes, Tonio," she murmured, and when he touched her arm he saw that it was already stiffening in obedience to his command. Slowly, as he had seen Lodovici Agnolo do, he passed his hands over her body, encompassing each sweet curve through the rough material of her garment, feeling the muscles harden into rigidity under his fingers, until her body was like stone and all color had drained from her face. Lying there, the movement of her breathing so faint that it was hardly perceptible, she did indeed look like a lovely corpse. Antonio repressed an involuntary shiver of dread. Could this be an omen? Then he shook off his indecision and spoke to Gian and the servant.

"We can lift her into the coffin," he said.

Lucia's body did not bend as they put her into the rough board coffin. Setting the top in place, Gian fixed it loosely, leaving large cracks through which she could get air during the short time that she would be in it, if their plans went well. Antonio and the servant were of about the same height, so they lifted the coffin to their shoulders while Gian went ahead with the lantern. "This should get us through the guards all right," he said. "They all know how anxious the Inquisitors are not to have too many people dying in the Casa Santa, or at least not to have it known."

Through the prison they moved silently, seeing no one. Gian's bribes had been large and well placed, backed by the influence of the queen. The whole thing so far had been ridiculously easy, Antonio thought, almost too easy.

Gian stopped and waited for them to come up to him. The corridor here was lit by lamps burning in niches in the wall about a hundred feet apart. "We are nearing the back entrance," he whispered. "Keep your cowls well over your faces and let me do the talking to the guards."

They resumed their progress, and soon the door itself was visible, a few scant yards ahead. Antonio felt his pulse rising with excitement, for they were almost safe beyond the walls of the prison. Suddenly Gian held up his hand and they stopped dead in the shadows between the burning lamps. The outer door was opening, and a murmur of voices came through it. Then two men entered, closing the door behind them. One wore the long robe of a Dominican friar, the other a suit of dark velvet. With a start, Antonio recognized Fra Felipe Santos and Armand de Quadra, the very last pair they could have wished to meet.

The new arrivals were almost upon the little procession when Fra Felipe saw them. "What is this?" he asked sharply.

Gian remained in the shadows. "We are bearing the body of a poor sinner who has died, Your Reverence," he said, holding his lantern low so that the light did not fall on his face beneath the cowl.

"Who are you?" Fra Felipe asked. "I do not remember you."

"Frey Luis Sanchez, Your Reverence. Lately arrived from Barcelona."

That much of the explanation seemed to satisfy Santos, confirming Gian's statement that many of the friars in the Casa Santa were new. But he came closer to the coffin. Antonio kept the board side of it pressed against his face so that his cowl completely hid his features.

"Lower the coffin," Fra Felipe said. "I would see this corpse."

At a nod from Gian they lowered the coffin to the floor.

"Open it," the friar directed Gian curtly. "I can see that the top is loose."

Antonio still stayed well in the shadows while Gian bent over the coffin and inserted his fingers beneath the lid, straining against it as if it were tightly nailed. Slowly he lifted the lid until Lucia's body, covered by the rough garment given the prisoners, was visible inside. But he had begun at the foot of the coffin, so that even with the lid raised, Lucia's face was partly hidden by the partially secured head end of the lid and in the faint light her identity could not be made out. Reaching into the coffin, Gian lifted Lucia by her heels. Her body was as rigid as when they had put her into the coffin. "See," Gian said, "the stiffness of death has already set in."

But as he was lowering her feet into the coffin once more, a fold of the robe dropped away, revealing the perfectly sculptured lines of her calf and lower thigh.

"*Ay Maria!*" Fra Felipe exclaimed. "It is a woman." He reached down and jerked the upper part of the coffin top loose, exposing Lucia's face, marble pale. "The Bellarmi girl. What is this?"

His gaze fixed upon the coffin, Antonio had not noticed that Armand de Quadra had moved closer to him, until the cowl of his robe was suddenly twitched up, exposing his face. "*Cáspita!*" De Quadra cried. "It is Dr. Servetus!" He leaped backward, tugging at his dagger as he did so. "*Socorro!*" The word was forming on his lips as Antonio suddenly leaped upon him, seizing his throat and shutting off the cry. He saw Gian go for Fra Felipe at the same time, but was too busy with De Quadra to pay attention to anything else.

Under the impetus of Antonio's leap, both men crashed to the floor, but Antonio, with the advantage of momentum, landed on top of his opponent. They struggled for a moment, De Quadra to draw the dagger, and Antonio with the double purpose of choking off any outcry by his opponent and preventing him from using the weapon. Then Antonio managed to get his knee on De Quadra's right arm, pinning it to the floor, and was now able to lift the dark man's head and smash it down again and again upon the stones. Only when the body beneath him went limp did he desist from the murderous beating he was giving it.

There was a gurgling cry from beyond the coffin where Gian knelt over Fra Felipe Santos. "Finish up De Quadra, Tonio," Gian called. "I have this son of the devil under control."

But there was nothing to do to De Quadra right now. He was unconscious, and whether fatally wounded or not, Antonio did not know. Drawing the dagger which De Quadra had been trying to reach, Antonio was tempted for a moment to plunge it into De Quadra's breast. Then he remembered that on another occasion, when he had been attacked by the beggars, De Quadra had saved his life, and he began quickly to slit the unconscious man's doublet, tearing strips of cloth from it. The fabric was tough, and with it he bound De Quadra's hands and feet securely. He was fashioning a gag when Gian stood up and said, "What in the devil are you doing, Tonio?"

"He saved my life when the beggars attacked me," Antonio explained. "I am giving it back to him."

"It is more than he deserves," Gian growled. "But hurry about it."

"What about Fra Felipe?"

Gian laughed shortly. "I gave him the mercy he has given many another innocent man—the garrote, with the cord from his own robe."

Through all of this Lucia had slept in the coffin in a magnetic trance. Quickly they replaced the lid, and Antonio and the servant lifted the coffin to their shoulders once more, while Gian dragged the two bodies into an empty cell. The guard outside the door did not question the right of a friar and his assistants to remove a dead sinner from the Casa Santa; it was a frequent enough occurrence not to arouse suspicion. And besides, the Inquisitor himself had just entered the prison and must have passed them in the corridor.

In the dark alley that ran behind the grim stone walls of the Casa Santa, Gian had left a cart and a horse. They shifted the coffin to it now, and, with the servant driving and Antonio and Gian trudging alongside, moved through the deserted streets to the city gate.

"God grant you gagged De Quadra well," Gian said as they walked along. "If he is not found until morning, we will have a head start, and by riding like the devil, we ought to stave off any pursuit."

"Do you have the safe-conduct?" Antonio asked.

"It is with the horses, waiting outside the city."

Gian had chosen to leave by one of the lesser gates, and as they approached it the guard held his lantern aloft and peered at them. "Why do you leave the city at this hour, Holy Friar?" he asked.

"We bear the body of a poor woman, lately dead of the plague, who would be buried in her own village," Gian said.

"The plague!" The guard stepped back quickly, crossing himself. "*Válgame Dios!* Go! Go quickly."

The cart passed through, and Antonio drew a long breath of relief. A half mile beyond the city Gian led the way off the road into a small wooded glen. Five horses waited there, held by a man whose livery was that of the queen's service.

Gian threw back the cowl of his robe. "You have brought the clothing?" he asked.

"*Sí, señor.* There by the tree. Complete costumes for three men and a boy."

"And the safe-conduct?"

"It is here." He handed over a folded paper, sealed with the royal arms.

"Good." Gian handed him a small bag of coins. "You may go, then. And tell Her Majesty that all is well."

The man took one of the horses and bestrode it. "*Qué vaya bien, señores,*" he said, and disappeared toward the road.

"Quick, Tonio," Gian directed as he peeled off his robe. "Get Lucia awake and out of the coffin, while Juan and I change into other clothing. We have no time to lose."

Antonio lifted the lid from the coffin. Lucia lay completely immobile, so apparently lifeless that he knew a moment of terror that she might actually be dead. Then his fingers found her pulse; it was strong and regular in its quiet beating. "Lucia," he said, close to her ear. "Lucia. Can you hear me?"

"Yes, Tonio," she said clearly.

"When I speak your name again, you will awaken. Do you understand?"

"Yes. I understand."

"Lucia!" he cried sharply. "Awaken."

She opened her eyes and sat up in the coffin, looking wonderingly about her. Then she saw Antonio and threw her arms about his neck. "Are we safe, darling?" she begged. "What is this place?"

"We are outside the city gates," he told her and lifted her from the coffin. "Do you remember anything?"

"Not since I went to sleep in the cell."

"You said once that I could not magnetize you. Remember?"

"Yes," she said. "I remember."

"And I have. So there is the question of a forfeit."

"I will gladly pay that forfeit, Tonio," she whispered, drawing his head down until their lips met. His arms closed about her and for a moment they were lost in the ecstasy of their first real kiss. Then Lucia's lips moved beneath his. "I've been wanting to pay it for a long time," she whispered.

"*Per Bacco!*" Gian exclaimed, interrupting their idyll. "There is time enough for that. Hurry and change your clothing. We must ride for France at once."

xii

The carriage whirled around the brow of the hill and halted for a moment so that the driver could let his horses blow before the descent and set the brakes. Antonio had been drowsing on the cushions, tired by the long trip from the channel. He sat up now and looked out of the window.

"Lucia!" He tugged at her elbow. "Look there below us."

Sleepily she stared out the window, then rubbed her eyes, as if she could not believe that what she saw was real. The shining path of the small river and the graceful spires of the buildings upon its farther bank made a picture of quiet beauty in the afternoon sunlight.

"Driver," Antonio called, "what city is that?"

"That there." The driver spat into the dust. "That is Cambridge, sor."

"And the river?"

"They call it the River Cam."

Cambridge University in England. The site of Gonville and Caius College. It was as Antonio had pictured it in his mind, a place of beauty, peace, and freedom.

"Look there at the river, Lucia," Antonio said in sudden excitement. "See how clear it is. That is a good omen."

"An omen, Tonio?" she asked, frowning. "But how?"

"See. It is not like the Bacchiglione. Remember how dark and muddy it was."

"The Bacchiglione in Padua." She shivered. "I remember it now. It was a horrible little stream."

The carriage started again and they lay back against the cushions. Antonio put his arm about Lucia's shoulders and she nestled against him. "Maybe it was not so horrible after all, though," Antonio said with a smile. "The Bacchiglione was a part of Padua, and it was there that I found the painting . . . and you, madonna mia." His arm tightened about her and she gave a little sigh of happiness.

"I went in search of my art, often in danger of my life." The rumble of the carriage wheels set the words of Paracelsus to marching through his brain. *"I have not been ashamed to learn those things which to me have seemed useful—even from vagabonds, barbers, and executioners. . . ."*

Antonio, too, had learned from vagabonds, from barbers, and from executioners, and he knew that he was a better man and physician by virtue of that learning.

"For we know how a lover will go a long way to meet the woman that he loves. . . ."

How long a way he had come! Halfway across Europe. But the woman he loved was in his arms, and who could ask for more?

"How much the more, then, will the lover of wisdom be tempted to go in search of his divine mistress!"

Ahead lay Cambridge, and the new life offered him by Dr. John Caius, another milestone in his search for wisdom. But he understood, with a rising sense of excitement, that this one search would never be ended, that, thrilling though the search might always be, man never quite found wisdom . . . the Divine Mistress.